Other Mystery Novels by
Laurie R. King

Mary Russell Novels
The Beekeeper's Apprentice
A Monstrous Regiment of Women
A Letter of Mary
The Moor
O Jerusalem
Justice Hall
The Game
Locked Rooms

Kate Martinelli Novels
A Grave Talent
To Play the Fool
With Child
Night Work
The Art of Detection

And
A Darker Place
Folly
Keeping Watch

Touchstone

Touchstone

LAURIE R. KING

BANTAM BOOKS

Kin

TOUCHSTONE

A Bantam Book / January 2008

Published by
Bantam Dell
A Division of Random House, Inc.
New York, New York

Book design by Glen Edelstein
Map illustration by Robert Bull

Bantam Books is a registered trademark of Random House, Inc., and the colophon is a trademark of Random House, Inc.

Library of Congress Cataloging-in-Publication Data is on file with the publisher.

978-0-553-80355-6

Printed in the United States of America
Published simultaneously in Canada

www.bantamdell.com

10 9 8 7 6 5 4 3 2 1
BVG

To Michael and Josefa,
with thanks for giving far, far beyond duty's call.

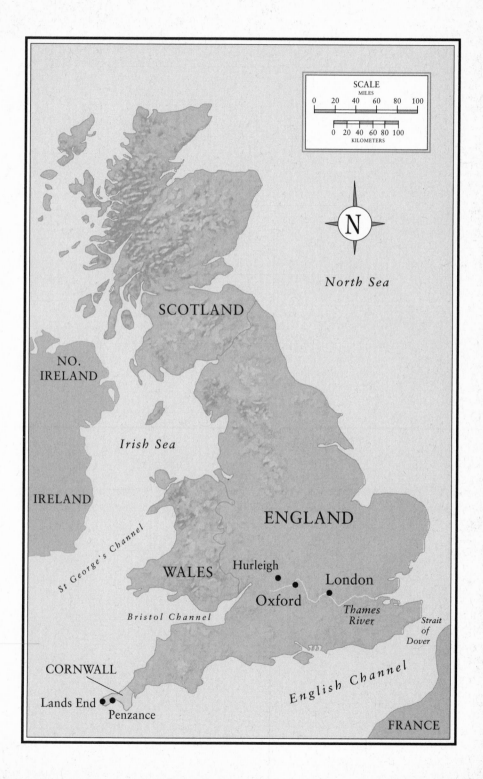

SCALE
MILES
0 20 40 60 80 100

0 20 40 60 80 100
KILOMETERS

N

North Sea

SCOTLAND

NO.
IRELAND

Irish Sea

IRELAND

ENGLAND

Hurleigh

WALES

London

Oxford

Thames
River

Strait
of
Dover

Bristol Channel

CORNWALL

English Channel

Lands End

Penzance

FRANCE

St George's Channel

Prologue

I

March 1921

SMALL THINGS: STRAWS ON CAMELS' BACKS. A spark on a tinder-dry hillside. A whisper of falling snow, settling just below an infinitesimal crack.

For her, it was the scarf.

A small thing, a pure white, light-as-air length of weaver's art, exquisitely rare and unbelievably warm, one of her grandmother's idiosyncratic Christmas whims.

Thirty guineas of screaming luxury, and she tore it from her neck without a thought, to wrap the tiny body going cool in her arms. Make the shroud snug, tuck it around the shriveled limbs, as if it mattered. As if a dead infant could find comfort in swaddling.

Even then, as she thrust the child at its mother and wiped her hands surreptitiously on her coat—even then, the heavy-laden camel staggered on, the snow-pack gave a shudder, but held.

It wasn't until the following day that the hillside of snow began to groan and creak. The following day, when she came with a motorcar to take the Margolins to the cemetery.

She trudged up the ·dark, filthy, stinking stairway to the third floor, knocking on the door to the two tiny, ice-cold rooms that housed the last five Margolins. The family emerged, dressed in its pitiful attempt at funeral finery: Mary first, carrying her bundled two-year-old, then the boys, Tom and Jims. Five-year-old Molly came last, tugging her hat down to hide the shame of lice-cropped hair. She looked down at the little girl, and felt the premonitory tremor, deep within.

Molly was wearing the dead infant's shroud.

Afterwards, the only thing she was grateful for was her own self control, which had stopped the exclamation before it could reach her tongue, kept her hands from snatching her grandmother's gift from the throat of a child the old lady wouldn't have bothered to rein a galloping horse around.

The scarf had been a shroud, yes. But it was also a warm garment, and warmth belonged to the living. The Margolin family simply couldn't afford sentiment.

She made it through the funeral without breaking down. She accompanied the little family back home, she summoned words, she made promises, she sat unseeing as the driver steered her back through the London streets to her flat.

It wasn't until she was alone that the avalanche let go its hold.

The Margolins were one of "her" families. They should have been safe. But everything she was—all the wealth, honor, and authority at her command—had proved just so many delusions of usefulness, inadequate to keep one tiny human being from death. She'd been called and she had come, but before she could summon a doctor, while she'd stood in that dim room with its scrubbed floor and the threadbare, neatly tucked bed-clothes, the wise infant-gray eyes held hers, and the child stopped breathing.

Just stopped.

The death of a badly wounded man was one thing: God knew she'd seen enough of that during the War. This was another matter altogether. She'd looked up in horror at the survivors: bright little Molly pressed against her mother's side, thumb in mouth; Tom and Jims kicking their heels in embarrassment on the bench; their once-pretty mother, Mary, at twenty-five a widow with lank gray hair and rotting teeth, seated dry-eyed on the room's other chair with the toddler.

They'd named the infant Christopher. And because his family could not afford sentiment, he'd gone to the earth without his shroud.

Her teeth chattered against the glass, her fingers refused to carry the silver lighter to the cigarette. She placed her hands on her knees, but the slow, calming breaths refused to come, and sounded more like gasps.

It was exhaustion, as much as anything, that broke her, the bone-deep fatigue that came from too many fourteen-hour days followed by too many sleepless nights. Rage had burned to ash long ago, despair was her daily bread, but the bitter cold and the disgusting surroundings and the glimpse into those newborn eyes, heaped as they were on top of grinding worry and the devastating failure of love, made the world flare and consume itself. In the bleak, scorched hopelessness that followed, she broke.

She bent forward over her knees, her arms curled around the back of her head as if to protect herself from a beating, and she wept.

There was just no end to London's store of graying twenty-five-year-olds; no end to their damaged men, their malnourished children, their dying infants. Huddled before the fireplace, she had a hallucinatory vision of the baby Christopher as a grain of sand, tumbling with ten thousand other grains through an hour-glass. The sheer futility of trying to catch all those grains before they fell overwhelmed her; the sobs came so hard she gagged on them.

But eventually, every avalanche must reach its plateau and settle. The sobs slowed, the choking noises trickled into hiccoughs. She sat upright in the chair, clawed the hair from her swollen eyes, and stretched out a steady hand for her drink. When the cigarette was lit, she stared into the heedless coals, thinking about lives pouring unstopped through an hour-glass.

The poor will be with you always.

Wasn't that the bitter, cold truth? Even if she were given the keys to the Hurleigh coffers, to empty everything—paintings and jewels, houses and land—into the slums of London, it would disappear without a trace. The Hurleigh legacy could be reduced to the bones, and still poor mothers would strip the dead to warm the living.

Yes, money narrowed the neck of the glass, slowing the stream. Money bought medicine, nutrition, warmth, education, giving the poor a chance against the downward pull of the sand.

But it was so *slow,* so terribly, agonizingly slow. What the world needed was a cork to stop the flow completely. Some invention, some idea, some electrifying event that would not only galvanize the working classes, but would stick in the minds of the powerful like a stone in the neck of the hour-glass, to cut off the flow of poor.

Perhaps if she stayed here a while, alone and resting in the quiet, she might think of something.

I I

March 1926

THE SMALL MAN STOOD ON THE HILLTOP, naked beneath the gibbous moon, welcoming the air with his body.

His clothing lay, neatly stacked, in the center of the slab of stone: coat at the bottom, socks tucked into boots at the top. His bright hair stirred with the breeze, catching reflections of pale moonlight. His hands were stretched out at his sides, palms facing the horizon, and he swayed, ever so slightly, to the rhythm of the waves sixty feet below.

Moments like this were rare, when he could let down the barriers and open himself to his surroundings. During daylight hours, even in this remote place, human intrusion was a constant threat. Even on those days when he saw no one, the texture of the outside world was ever on his tongue, the sound of events in far-off London insinuating itself into his mind, like the scuffle of the monster beneath his childhood bed.

In recent weeks, the creature under the bed had begun to stir and swell. It had not yet taken notice of him as he lay frozen beneath the covers of his retreat. There was no real reason to believe it would. It was just as likely to lumber into life, jostling the bed as it emerged, and shamble away to devour some other innocent child.

Of course, if he was already gone from the bed when the monster came looking, that would solve the problem. A slight sway forward, here on the edge of the world, and the salt fingers below would reach for him, embrace him, soothe and welcome and bury his worries forever.

To, and fro. To, and fro. To...

His body would decide. The same body that read the breath of the wind as it flowed off the sea, that drew in the flavor of the land behind him, that noted the passing of an owl a quarter mile inland, that felt the thump of a rabbit going to ground a hundred yards off, that counted the hairs on his forearms stirred by the breeze...

One by one, the barriers slipped away, leaving the man naked and exposed to the night, like some soft and defenseless undersea creature when the waters drew back, and back again as they built into a monstrous swell on the horizon.

The wave was building—even now, he could feel it in the distance. But until it broke over him, or until his body chose to sway forward a fraction too far, he would stand in the moonlight and give himself, body and soul, to the brush of air, the odor of green, the solidity of rock.

To the joy and the terror of pure sensation.

III

April 1926

THE FINGERS PAUSED to warm themselves against the radiator, for the room was very cold. Pressed against the ticking metal, they could feel the vibration of the water within, transferring heat from boiler's flame to inert metal and thence to flesh, making possible the job at hand—which, in a fitting completion of the cycle, entailed the creation of flame.

When circulation was restored, the fingertips rubbed one another into suppleness, then resumed their work. They moved with delicacy and deliberation, sure of themselves and their purpose: switch, wire, detonator, snip, twist, fold; nestle the mechanism against the final purposeful load of explosive, perfect beneath its creator's hand.

Some such objects were raw and ugly, aimed at nothing but immediate effect. The Devices shaped by this pair of hands—this particular builder had never cared for the blunt monosyllable *bomb*—were invariably simple and balanced: elegant. The pleasing irony of a small, perfectly shaped conveyer of brutal mayhem was an essential part of the process—perhaps even the most essential part. Curiously like the radiator, designed to transfer the bright, hot violence of ideas into society's inert status quo: flames into warmth; an infernal machine effecting very human change.

The fingers paused for a moment as the mind considered, then they went on: No, this was not the time for a public speech advocating the transformative aspects of violence.

Still, wasn't that precisely what people did not understand? That death was the very foundation of life; order was built from the raw material of disorder? The Prayer Book had it backwards when it said, *In the midst of life we are in death*—. St. Paul put it more precisely: *That which thou sowest is not quickened, except it die.* A seed had to die before it could come to life. Wasn't that the whole idea behind the Resurrection?

Now, they called it *Anarchy.*

The word had become synonymous with *chaos,* but the true Anarchist community was a place of exquisite balance and stability, a society of equals. True, the path to Anarchy must be carved through the rubble of the status quo, but birth was never an easy business.

Or another analogy: A well placed Device was like a surgeon's blade. It caused pain and shed blood, but it was necessary for healing. A sacrifice for the greater good.

And, truth to tell (shameful truth, never spoken aloud, never acknowledged even to one's self, but somehow, the fingers knew), there was a definite frisson of satisfaction in creating a Device. Not the deaths themselves—one was not an animal, after all, killing for pleasure—but nonetheless, there was an element of gratification about making, literally, an impact on society.

(The hands paused again, with amusement, then finished their task.)

Fingers, slim and deft, tucked the final wire into a more pleasing arrangement. Two meditative hands eased the oversized cover shut, feeling the gentle pressure before the minuscule latch hooked into place.

Simple; elegant.

Order through Anarchy.

Life out of death.

The hands tidied the workbench, patted the Device as if soothing an infant in its cot, then switched off the lights.

On the bench, the gilt letters on the spine of the Device caught the light from the corridor as the door swung open, then shut:

BOOK OF COMMON PRAYER

Chapter One

EIGHT DAYS AFTER stepping off the *Spirit of New Orleans* from New York, Harris Stuyvesant nearly killed a man.

The fact of the near-homicide did not surprise him; that it had taken him eight days to get there, considering the circumstances, was downright astonishing.

Fortunately, his arm drew back from full force at the last instant, so he didn't actually smash the guy's face in. But as he stood over the prostrate figure, watching the woozy eyelids flicker back towards consciousness, the tingle of frustration in his right arm told him what a near thing it had been. He'd been running on rage for so long, driven by fury and failure and the scars on Tim's skull and the vivid memory of bright new blood on a sparkling glass carpet followed by flat black and the sound of the funeral dirges that—well, the guy had got off lucky, that was all.

He couldn't even claim it was self defense. The cops were right there—constables, he should call them, this being England—and they'd already been moving to intercept the red-faced Miners' Union demonstrator who was hammering one meaty forefinger against Stuyvesant's chest to make a point when Stuyvesant's arm came up all on its own and just laid the man out on the paving stones.

A uniformed constable cut Stuyvesant away from the miner's friends as neatly as a sheepdog with a flock and suggested in no uncertain terms that now would be a good time for him to go about his business, sir. Stuyvesant looked into the clean-shaven English face beneath the helmet and felt his fist tighten, but he caught hold of himself before things got out of control.

He nodded to the cop, glanced at the knot of demonstrators forming around the fallen warrior, and bent to pick up the envelope he'd dropped in the scuffle. He turned on his heels and within sixty seconds and two corners found silence, as abrupt and unexpected as the sudden appearance of the Union workers had been five minutes earlier.

He put his back against the dirty London bricks, closed his eyes, and drew in, then let out, one prolonged breath. After a minute, he raised his hand to study the damage: a fresh slice across the already-scarred knuckle, bleeding freely. With his left hand he fished out his handkerchief and wrapped the hand, looking around until he spotted a promising doorway down the street. Inside was a saloon bar. "Whisky," he told the man behind the bar. "Double."

When the glass hit the bar, he dribbled half of it onto the cut—teeth were dirty things—and tossed the rest down his throat. He started to order a repeat, then remembered, and looked at his wristwatch with an oath.

Late already.

Oh, what the hell did it matter? He'd spent the last week chewing the ears of one office-worker after another; what made him think this one would be any different?

But that was just an excuse to stay here and drink.

Stuyvesant slapped some coins on the bar and went out onto the street. It was raining, again. He settled his hat, pulled up his collar, and hurried away.

It had proven a piss-poor time to come to London and talk to men behind desks. He'd known before he left New York that there was a General Strike scheduled at the end of the month, in sympathy for the coal miners. However, this was England, not the States, and he'd figured there would be a lot of big talk followed by a disgruntled, probably last-minute settlement. Instead, the working classes were rumbling, and their talk had gone past coal mining into a confrontation with the ruling class. The polite, Olde Worlde tea-party dispute he'd envisioned, cake-on-a-plate compared to some of the rib-cracking, skull-smashing strikes Stuyvesant had been in, didn't look as if it was going to turn out the way he'd thought, either—not if men like those demonstrators had their way in the matter.

And God, the distraction it had caused in this town! One after another, the desk-bound men he'd come to see had listened to his questions, then given him the same response: Does this have anything to do with the Strike? Then please, I'm busy, there's the door.

Yeah, that miner had been *damned* lucky, considering.

Maybe when this next one showed him the door—Carstairs was his name, Aldous Carstairs, what kind of pansy handle was that?—maybe that would be where his temper broke. Maybe the bureaucrat would get what the demonstrator hadn't.

He couldn't help feeling he had reached the bottom of the barrel when it came to a straightforward investigation. Certainly, he held out little hope that Carstairs would do more than go through motions—he'd heard of the man more or less by accident the previous afternoon, sitting across the desk from a Scotland Yard official he'd met in New York years before. Now an exhausted and harassed-looking official in a day-old shirt who, even before the inevitable tea tray arrived, was sorry he'd let Stuyvesant in.

"No, I've already talked to that man," Stuyvesant told him, in answer to a suggested contact. "Yeah, him, too. *And* him. That idiot? He was one of the first I saw, and frankly, the sooner he retires, the better off your country will be. No, that guy's in France, and his secretary's useless. Now, him I haven't talked to, where—Scotland? Jesus, do I have to go to Scotland to ask about a man who lives in London?"

"I should give you to Carstairs," the Yard official muttered, then immediately regretted the slip and hurried on. "What about—"

"Been there. Who's this Carstairs fellow?" Stuyvesant's instincts had come alert, aware of some overtone in the way the man said the name, but the fellow shook his head.

"Just a name, honestly, he doesn't have anything to do with what you need. I think you should go talk to . . ." Stuyvesant was soon out the door, holding nothing more than three names on a slip of paper.

Outside the office door, a pair of men in bowlers sat waiting. Stuyvesant nodded to them, collected his hat and overcoat, and walked down the hallway and around the corner. There he stopped, staring unseeing at the scrap of paper.

Give you to Carstairs. Not, *Give you Carstairs*, which would have suggested the resolution of a grudge, but a phrase with a touch of fear in the background: *I should feed you to Carstairs*.

Stuyvesant counted to thirty, then doubled back to the Yard man's office. The two men were nowhere in sight when he walked in, and the secretary was just settling back at his desk.

"Sorry," the American said, "I neglected to get a phone number. Just let me pop in—"

"I'm sorry, sir, he has another appointment."

"Oh, I'll just be—wait, maybe I could get it from you instead? The name's Carstairs."

The secretary looked blank for a moment and Stuyvesant resigned himself to a dud, but then the man's eyebrows shot up. "Aldous Carstairs?"

"That's the man. You have a phone number for him?"

The secretary's glance at the closed door was eloquent testimony of the unusual nature of the request, but reluctantly, he went to a book in the bottom drawer of his desk, opened it to a page at the back, and copied out a number.

"Thanks," Stuyvesant told him, and that was how he found himself running ten minutes late on a pouring wet Friday afternoon, a bloody handkerchief around one hand and a sodden scrap of paper in the other, searching for an address that he finally located in an utterly anonymous building a stone's throw from Big Ben.

Chapter Two

THE DOORMAN TOOK one look at the figure that lurched into his tidy foyer and moved to return the straying lunatic to the streets. Stuyvesant pushed down the impulse to deck another Brit and summoned his most charming, lop-sided smile, assuring the man that he did, in fact, have an appointment with Mr. Carstairs, although he'd had a little accident, if he could just phone . . . ?

Without turning his back on the disheveled American, the doorman went to his desk to pick up his telephone. He spoke, listened, grunted, and hung up.

"If you'll just wait a minute."

It was less time than that when a weedy specimen with freckles and twitchy hands came through the connecting door and stopped dead. He looked at Stuyvesant, and at the doorman (who gave him a *What-did-I-say?* shrug), then stood back, holding the door.

"Mr. Carstairs?" Stuyvesant asked.

"His secretary," the man replied. "The Major is expecting you."

He led the sodden visitor through a hallway and up a flight of stairs to a dark, highly polished wooden door. Inside, he took Stuyvesant's hat and coat, hung them over the radiator, and went to the desk, where he pushed a button and said to the air, "Mr.

Stuyvesant." He got the pronunciation right, *Sty* rather than the usual *Stooey*.

The response five seconds later was a click at the inner door; the secretary came back around the desk and opened it. Stuyvesant stepped into the dim office.

The man behind the desk was in his early forties, slightly older than Harris Stuyvesant, and smooth: dark, oiled hair, the sheen of manicured fingernails, a perfectly knotted silk tie, and nary a wrinkle on his spotless shirt. A visitor's gaze might have slid right off him had they not caught on his striking eyes and unlikely mouth.

The eyes were an unrelieved black, with irises so dark they looked like vastly dilated pupils. They reminded Stuyvesant of a wealthy Parisian courtesan he'd known once who attributed her success to belladonna, used to simulate wide-eyed fascination in the gaze she turned upon her clientele. Personally, her eyes had made Stuyvesant uneasy, because they'd robbed him of that subtle and incontrovertible flare of true interest. This man's eyes were the same; they looked like the doorway to an unlit and windowless room, a room from which anyone at all might be looking out.

The man's mouth, on the other hand, was almost obscenely generous, full and red and moist looking. His lips might have made one think of passion, but somehow, a person could not imagine this man lost in a kiss.

When he put down his pen and rose at Stuyvesant's entrance, the American saw the third element to the man's visage: a twisting, long-healed scar down the left side of his face, hairline to collar.

Stuyvesant walked forward, forcing his gaze away from the scar and onto those ungiving eyes. The scar was nothing, after all, compared to some of the damage he'd seen that week, seven and a half years after the war to end wars—although it looked more like the work of a knife than a bayonet. The man held out his hand; in response, Stuyvesant lifted the once-white rag.

"You probably don't want to shake this," he said. "I had a little altercation on the way here with one of your miners. I'll try not to bleed on the carpet."

The dark gaze studied the makeshift dressing, then shifted to Stuyvesant's clothing, and the man's nostrils flared just a touch—why the hell had he stopped for that drink, Stuyvesant asked himself?—before he reached for the telephone on his desk.

"Bring some sticking plasters please, Mr. Lakely," Aldous Carstairs said.

The secretary came in carrying a small box. Carstairs lifted his chin at Stuyvesant's hand, and Lakely efficiently stripped away the handkerchief, wiped away the blood, applied the sticky bandages, and gathered the debris, without a word being exchanged.

"Our guest would probably like a coffee," Carstairs said. Stuyvesant might have hugged him, then and there, had he not noticed that, the entire time the secretary was in the office, he didn't look at his employer once. *I should feed you to Carstairs.*

Not a huggable kind of a guy, Aldous Carstairs.

When the door was shut again, Carstairs held out his hand, starting anew. Stuyvesant took it briefly, grateful the man didn't bear down: his whole hand had begun to throb.

"Aldous Carstairs," the man said.

"Harris Stuyvesant. Thanks for seeing me."

"Do sit down, Mr. Stuyvesant. What can I do for you?"

And for the twelfth—thirteenth? No, fourteenth time—Harris Stuyvesant launched into his tale of woe, which repetition had long since stripped of anything resembling urgency, or even interest: terrorist bombs, Communist plots, ho hum.

He began, as he had thirteen times already, by laying his identification on the man's desk, along with the brief letter from Hoover, which said little more than Harris Stuyvesant was an active agent of the United States Justice Department's Bureau of Investigation, and any assistance would be appreciated. The letter was showing signs of wear.

Carstairs directed his unrevealing regard on the lines of typescript and the signature, then back to Stuyvesant, who gathered away his possessions and began his spiel.

"Like it says, I'm an agent with the Bureau of Investigation. I've come over here, unofficial-like, because we're looking into some possible links between a series of bombs in our country and one of your citizens."

The coffee came then. Both men waited for it to be laid out and the secretary to leave.

"There are, hmm, official channels," Carstairs noted.

"Sure, and sometimes they're fine, but sometimes they're not." Stuyvesant listened to his own voice, and wondered why he was sounding like some small town hick—he'd very nearly said "ain't." *Act like a Bureau agent,* he ordered himself, *not some bloody brawler marching into this fellow's nice office at three in the afternoon stinking of booze.* He took the envelope from his pocket, seeing for the first time the scuff of someone's shoe on its crumpled flap, and removed the contents. One at a time, he unfolded each and laid it in front of the man.

"Last July, there was a fire-bomb at a Communist house in Chicago." He gave Carstairs a minute to look over the outline concerning the fire, then topped it with a newspaper clipping. "In November, a Pennsylvania judge in charge of a sensitive Union case nearly got himself burned to a crisp when his car went up in flames." Another piece of paper: "And in January, five men in a New York hotel room narrowly missed getting blown to pieces. The newspapers haven't put the three together yet, but it's only a matter of time."

He sat back and let the man look at the pages. Three explosions, one gelignite, two incendiaries, all packaged in unexpected but carefully thought out containers. The target of the first one still didn't make much sense, unless there was some rivalry—personal or political—that the Bureau hadn't picked up on, but one confusing motive was the least of his problems.

When he'd reached the end of the pages, Carstairs lifted those dark holes back onto Stuyvesant.

They were approaching the tough part, when thirteen desk-dwellers had showed Stuyvesant the door.

"Took us a while to match up the pieces, but then we noticed that the devices had a couple things in common. One, it seemed they were inside everyday objects—a box of groceries delivered to the Reds in Chicago, a child's doll on the back seat of the judge's car, and a tray full of drinks in the New York hotel. Secondly, witnesses placed an Englishman near two of them."

He put the sketch down first, the one based on the description given by the boy who'd delivered the Reds' groceries. It showed a slim man with dark hair, tinted glasses, and a thin moustache. He could have been any of one in ten men on the sidewalks outside.

On top of the drawing he set a glossy photograph, showing passengers gathered on the deck of a ship, New York's skyline in the background. One figure had a circle around him: a slim man with dark hair and a moustache—and dark glasses.

Suppressing a sigh, he laid down his last piece of evidence: three Photostat copies of passenger manifests, from three sailings, with three black circles.

Invariably, it was this that raised thirteen pairs of eyebrows and had each man behind the desk pushing back to distance himself from absurdity. And Carstairs was no different.

Stuyvesant spoke before the man could drag out the inevitable Scarlet Pimpernel joke. "Yeah, I know how it looks: Richard Bunsen, your Labour Party's fair-haired boy. Crazy, huh? And that's why I'm *not* here officially, because who'd want an official inquiry until we're a little more sure of the facts? Basically, my boss is hoping you can give me something to take Bunsen's name off our list." No need to mention that Stuyvesant himself hoped for evidence in the other direction, like maybe a couple of similar bombs on British soil that tied The Bastard in.

Because Stuyvesant had known in his bones back in January that the three were connected, and knew in his bones now that Bunsen was the one. And Harris Stuyvesant's bones were never wrong.

Well, almost never.

But he hadn't been able to convince John Edgar Hoover, and he hadn't even tried to explain it to the others, any more than he could to Aldous Carstairs. He waited for the man's face to take on the wary expression of someone trapped on a train with a muttering lunatic, and for the man's eyes to slide over to the office door, calculating just how dangerous the American was.

But Carstairs surprised him.

Something shifted in the back of those black eyes, something other than wariness. The Englishman reached down to jerk open a drawer, fumbling through it with unexpected clumsiness before his hand came out with a brown cigarillo. He made much of the business of lighting it, then sat back inside the cloud of smoke. When he raised his gaze again to his visitor, the little crow's feet next to his eyes had gone completely smooth and his face was just a little too open, a little too wide-eyed innocent, to believe.

Stuyvesant had figured Carstairs for some kind of Intelligence man—the uneasiness of the Scotland Yard man and the lack of identifying plaque on the front door of this building told him this wasn't a more open official. And because he'd met several of the domestic Intelligence men already—his equivalents here—he assumed Carstairs inhabited the more clandestine reaches of MI6, Britain's international arm. For a man like that—in other words, a spy—to suddenly twitch with interest, the interest had to be considerable. The man's bland expression showed no more concern than any other Brit across whose desk Stuyvesant had sat in the last week, but that sharp, uncontrolled reaction was like a tug on a fishing line, alerting the American that something had nibbled his hook.

The man's hand dipped into his breast pocket and came out with a leather journal. Cigarillo in one hand, pen in the other, he opened the pages to write half a dozen words. Stuyvesant watched the man's act of nonchalance and thought: *Gotcha!*

Maybe this trip wouldn't be a total wash-out after all.

Then Carstairs put the journal away, rested the smoking cigar in the desk ash-tray, and stood up, holding out his hand.

Baffled, fighting down a surge of angry disappointment, Stuyvesant rose as well.

"I often walk in Hyde Park on Saturday mornings," Carstairs told him. "I should like you to join me there tomorrow, near Speakers' Corner. Shall we say, hmm, eleven o'clock? I might have something for you then."

The form was so familiar, a secret meeting held out in the open, that Stuyvesant responded automatically, with a handshake, a thanks for the coffee, a collecting of his papers, and a retrieval of coat and hat from the pasty-faced secretary. Before he knew it, he was out on the street again, where the rain had turned to sleet, and he wondered what had just happened. He glanced down at his hand, reassured by the sight of the tidy sticking-plasters on his knuckle: Without that, he'd wonder if he had been inside this building at all.

Eight days pounding the London streets, fourteen times trotting out his tale of woe, and here he was, turned out yet again. The hell with it: If he couldn't get at The Bastard Bunsen through the proper channels, he'd take a more direct approach.

Tomorrow.

Tonight he was going to celebrate the close cooperation of American and British law enforcement by getting drunk.

Chapter Three

Stuyvesant's Bayswater hotel walked a narrow line between respectable and seedy, but it was quiet, and had weekly rates. His "luxury room" even had a telephone and a nearly private bath, with a helpful restaurant next door for when he wanted to eat in. The looks of the clientele and staff didn't encourage him to leave his valuables in the desk drawer, but he'd found a bank down the street happy to rent him a safe deposit box. Best of all, the radiators were enthusiastic—a blessing on an evening that had replaced rain with a penetrating cold.

Stuyvesant peeled away the heavy coat, so wet it looked more black than brown, and draped it across the radiator. He put his hat on top, his shoes underneath, and dropped into his chair with the bottle and a glass.

And there he sat, frowning at the amber liquid in his glass.

Harris Stuyvesant was not a person given to introspection. He was a big muscular man who got fidgety when he wasn't moving, and subtlety was not a thing that came naturally.

Still, Stuyvesant had been an agent of the U.S. Bureau of Investigation since 1911, when he was twenty-five years old. Apart from the two years he'd taken off to point his rifle at Germans in northern France, he'd spent the last fifteen years paying attention to unexpected details, noting them, returning to them until he understood what they meant. He'd also spent so many years undercover—play-acting around the clock, asleep or awake, with his life on the line—that he'd long since learned that when his body made one of its snap decisions, he'd better go along with it.

So he had to wonder why, when he'd been faced with yet another law enforcement bureaucrat, that little switch in the undercover part of Stuyvesant's mind had flipped and started him play-acting. Because it definitely had: Before his trousers' seat hit the chair in Aldous Carstairs' office, he'd been acting a role.

He didn't think it was just the business of feeling like an utter oaf off the streets in the presence of a man who exuded authority and competence: He'd held his own in conversations with railway barons and U.S. Presidents, and whatever authority Carstairs had, it couldn't be anywhere near that level.

No, some aspect of Carstairs had set Stuyvesant's inner alarm to jangling, kicking him into a near-instantaneous assumption of the role of bumpkin, both disarming and concealing. He hadn't even been aware of his visceral mistrust of the man until he heard his own stretched vowels, found he was slumped like an idiot in the chair, felt his fingers go up to rumple his hair: Gee, golly.

Gee, golly, indeed, he now said to himself with interest: That guy with the knife scar and the belladonna eyes just alarmed the crap out of little Harris Stuyvesant.

He took a first swallow from his glass, and felt the satisfying burn down his gullet.

If he'd shown Carstairs his usual, more or less competent face, Stuyvesant wondered, would the man have given himself away with that sharp reaction? Would his guard have been up, as it had not been for the galoot in the chair?

And more to the point, had the man merely found a novel way to ease the departure of an unwanted visitor, or did he honestly intend to meet Stuyvesant at Hyde Park in the morning?

Maybe, Stuyvesant decided, he wouldn't finish off the whole bottle tonight. Just in case.

He woke the next morning with a hell of a head and no inclination whatsoever to be made a fool of. Still, the narrow slice of sky he could see out of his grimy window was actually blue for a change, and he decided that he couldn't very well not show up at all. So he shaved and dressed and forced down breakfast, then walked through the spring-greened streets towards Hyde Park. He came out from the back roads directly across from the corner that Carstairs had specified, and looked across the streaming traffic at a riot.

This corner of Hyde Park, an area dedicated to the spirit of free and open debate, was always a hive of activity, but the scene over there now was several steps up from any Speakers' Corner tumult he'd seen yet. A sea of hats seethed in motion, hedged in between road and park by half a dozen mounted policemen. Stuyvesant hesitated, but it appeared that the crowd's anger was still at the verbal stage, and the police had it in hand.

Nothing like a man on a horse for intimidating a crowd, Stuyvesant always said.

The restless mass was, inevitably, a group of Miners' Union supporters trading vehement insults with anti-Union forces. It was the same unrest that festered and fevered throughout the city, come to a head here like a boil. Had it been a hot summer's day, the boil might have burst and spilled its furious contents into a window-smashing spree down Oxford Street, but this was April, and even if the bitter wind felt more like snow than spring, the English sun was nonetheless shining, and the night's frost had melted on all but the north-facing lawns. On a morning like this, a man would have to be furious indeed not to succumb to some degree of bonhomie.

Still, not wanting another split knuckle, he gave the yelling debaters wide berth, retreating down the Bayswater road a distance before crossing over to the park. When he came back towards the Corner, he found Aldous Carstairs sitting on a bench, his beautifully gloved hands gathered primly atop a slim dispatch case.

"Morning," Stuyvesant said when he was near enough for his voice to reach over the nearby commotion. He stuck out his hand, and again received the soft grasp.

"Your man Bunsen moves in some interesting circles," was Carstairs' greeting.

Right down to business, then. Stuyvesant lowered himself to the bench beside the Englishman.

"Is that so?"

"One might say that the fellow is a, hmm, veritable Scarlet Pimpernel of the working classes, if your suspicions about him are justified. An open and relatively respectable life here, a mad bomber on the other side of the Atlantic."

The American sighed, perversely disappointed that Carstairs hadn't come up with a more original criticism. Didn't bureaucrats have anything better to do than read that romantic claptrap? British aristocrat-spies in the French Revolution—that Orczy woman should have been strangled. "I really don't—"

"Do not mind me, Mr. Stuyvesant, I am only pulling your leg. Although the merry conceit of an aristocrat-turned-secret-agent is not a great deal more unlikely than a man of Richard Bunsen's background being chosen by the Labour Party. It is true that his mentor, Matthew Ruddle, is one of the more left-wing Members of Parliament, but I wouldn't have thought him an out-and-out radical. The Trades Union tends to be suspicious of extreme politics."

"I don't know if Bunsen's respectability means that the Labour Party has decided it doesn't mind Red agitators, or if he's just good at putting on a respectable face. He's giving a speech down in Battersea on Thursday night—I thought I'd go listen to it, see if I can figure out which is the case."

"That should prove educational for you. In any event, it's not un-heard of, is it, for a man to live two lives? Sometimes, the one life seems to, hmm, fill in the gaps in the other. Actually, I was referring to a less publicized aspect of Mr. Bunsen's life. Do you know who I mean by the Hurleigh family?"

"As in the Duke of Hurleigh? Sure. Our papers love them, and not just the scandal rags—if your country ever wants to try taking

back their colonies, that'd be the family to send over to convince us."
But the name conjured some other, more specific stir in the recesses of
Stuyvesant's mind. What?

"As you say, the Hurleighs are of interest to a broad spectrum of
the public. And similarly broad is their spectrum of influence:
Members of the Hurleigh clan determine policy in everything from a
lady's choice of frock to a government's choice of ambassador."

"Okay. What about them?"

"Captain Bunsen may be having an affair with the eldest child,
Laura."

"Jesus." Stuyvesant's eyes absently tracked two girls in drab winter coats topped by bright spring cloche hats, whose progress was being thwarted by the turmoil on the corner, but behind his eyes, his
mind was in nearly as much turmoil as the crowd. Could his
"demmed, elusive Pimpernel" be literally hand in hand with the
bluest blood in the realm?

But yes, that's what the name Hurleigh had stirred up in his mind:
a Lady Laura Hurleigh on the passenger manifest of two of the ships
Bunsen had traveled on. Stuyvesant would have to retrieve his full
folder of case notes from the bank to be sure, but he thought it was
the July and January crossings. And if he remembered correctly, both
times her cabin had been just down the corridor from his.

Well, well: Richard Bunsen, lover to a Hurleigh. Could The
Bastard have used such a woman to camouflage his ties to American
radicals?

Or could it be that Stuyvesant was wrong about the man?

He shook himself mentally: Of course he could be wrong about
Bunsen, for Christ sake—he wasn't so utterly fixed on the man's guilt
that he walked around with his eyes shut. But his bones had brought
him here, and after spending a week's spare hours in reading rooms,
hunting down the man's speeches and articles in back issues of the
newspapers, he still didn't think his bones were wrong.

However, this information changed things, no doubt about that.
If nothing else, it raised the question of how in hell he was supposed
to infiltrate a circle as heady as that one. Quite a different matter
from his usual working-men-and-students set.

"You're pretty sure?"

"It is common knowledge among a certain coterie of, so to speak, political bohemians."

"Artistic types," Stuyvesant said. He'd met girls like Laura Hurleigh—Lady Laura, he supposed: rich, spoiled, eager to grab any fruit that society said was forbidden. Girls who played at politics, with no particular conviction except that if their elders disapproved, it must be worthy. Tiresome girls.

"Quite."

Well, he thought, staring at the two young women without seeing either of them, I suppose I could try that approach. He couldn't very well clothe himself in the personality of a member of the leisured classes—he was ten years too old, twenty pounds of muscle too heavy, and a whole lot of dollars short of what it called for—but if he didn't find a way in through Bunsen's Union connections, he'd try being a starving artist. A Modernistic sculptor, maybe, since he had the build for a man who spent his life bashing stone.

"You need an 'in,' " Carstairs noted; he might have been reading Stuyvesant's thoughts.

"You got one?" Stuyvesant asked, not expecting much.

"I may."

That caught Stuyvesant's attention.

"I need to come at this obliquely," Carstairs began. When Stuyvesant nodded his understanding, the man sat back and took out his cigar case. The girls came along the path, and one of them caught Stuyvesant's eye. Another day, he'd have risen to the occasion; this time he merely gave a polite touch to the brim of his hat. Disappointed, they went on; when Carstairs had his cigarillo alight, he continued.

"During the War," the Englishman said, "I was with Intelligence. I spent time in a number of different divisions, but I ended up in the, hmm, research wing. Things cooled off considerably, of course, when the War ended, but there were certain programs that maintained their funding, and mine was one of those.

"I cannot go into any detail, you'll understand, but I will tell you that from time to time we investigated reports of individuals with particular . . . gifts. Most of them turned out to be either delusions or outright fakes, but every so often, a man or woman would come along with, hmm, knacks we couldn't quite explain. And when that happened, we tended to keep an eye on that person. Still do, for that matter, although I personally have almost nothing to do with research these days."

"Okay," Stuyvesant said.

"There is one man, currently living in Cornwall, who came to my attention shortly after Armistice. He'd been wounded and was convalescing near London. I interviewed him, supervised a series of tests, and found that, indeed, some of his abilities were verifiable. Unfortunately, his wartime experiences had left him, shall we say, vulnerable to stress, and he proved...unsuitable for our purposes. Still, every so often I take a look at him, to see how he is, and to see if his skills remain. When last I had word, he appeared to be, hmm, recovering nicely."

"Shell shock?"

"Of the worst kind."

"I've seen a few." Felt it himself, too, although thanks to the ox-like Stuyvesant constitution and a job to get back to, he'd pulled out of it entirely. Almost entirely: Back-firing engines occasionally found him diving for cover. "What do you mean by 'abilities'? Mind-reading? Talking to spirits?"

Carstairs bristled. "Mr. Stuyvesant, do I seem to you like a gullible person?"

"No," the American admitted.

"Then please rest assured that our, hmm, tests of his abilities were thought out with care. This man is not a mind-reader. It is not parlor tricks. He is, as they say, the real thing."

As they were talking, the crowd on the corner had continued to grow. Now, one of the speakers, who was either seven feet tall or standing on a soap-box, launched himself into the sea of hats—working-men's cloth caps, office-workers' bowlers, and fashionable soft felt—heading in the direction of his rival, thirty feet away. A roar rose up, whistles pierced the air, and the policemen urged their enormous mounts forward. Carstairs stood impatiently.

"Let us leave this entertainment for the quieter reaches of the park. It's a pity to waste a fine spring day."

It was hardly spring, not going by the thermometer anyway, but Stuyvesant had grown up in New York and he wasn't going to be intimidated by anything less than knee-deep snow. Carstairs led him into the park, away from the riot, while Stuyvesant's mind chewed on the possibility that this shady Englishman wasn't just feeding him a heap of horse crap, for some unguessable reason of his own.

"What's this guy's name? And what is it he can do?"

"His name is Grey. Captain Bennett Grey." Carstairs' oddly sensuous mouth seemed to linger over the name. "As for his abilities, I think the details shall have to wait for a time. Let us say merely that Captain Grey knows things he should not be able to, as if he sees into people. He can, as it were, tell gold from gilt at a touch." This phrase seemed to please its speaker; one corner of his mouth curled a fraction.

Jesus, these Brits, Stuyvesant thought—you ask them a simple question and they give you Shakespeare, or hints to a maze. Were they always as convoluted as he'd found them, or was all this wool-pulling a way of hiding their Strike jitters? Every bureaucrat he'd talked to acted as if he felt solely responsible for holding the working class at bay with a stack of forms.

"Okay, so Captain Grey has some funny skills. Why should I be interested in him?"

Carstairs' cigar had gone out, so he slowed his steps to concentrate on restoring it to a clean, burning end, then resumed. "I needed to tell you about Captain Grey so you would know why Richard Bunsen's name caught my attention when you brought it up. In fact, I had to go back into the files to refresh my memory, but it turns out that we have been, hmm, aware of Mr. Bunsen as early as 1919, when he was arrested for inciting mutiny.

"He's an interesting fellow, quite bright, by all accounts very good looking, although I haven't met him myself. Comes from what you might call mixed stock. His maternal grandfather was knighted, but turned out to have something of a weakness for the horses, so there wasn't much to pass on. After he died, the daughter took a position in a boys' school near Leeds to support herself and her mother. There she married a retired accountant, the son of a stone mason, who himself had been born to a family of coal miners. A heritage, you understand, that Bunsen flaunts when he wishes to claim working-class origins.

"The accountant died when young Richard was ten. The mother worked herself into an early grave to get the boy to a good school, where he shed his accent and learned to fit in—to a certain extent. He was invited to leave that school at fifteen when he threw his first rock through a window—seemed the headmaster had instructed his pretty daughter to have nothing to do with young Bunsen, and the boy resented it. Threatened to burn the school down, in fact."

"A temper, then?"

"Quite. He kept himself under control through his remaining years at a lesser school, did well enough to get into university in London, and joined the Army in 1914, at the age of twenty. He served until Armistice, most of the time in France. Injured twice, once seriously enough for home leave, when I'd say he had too much time to sit and think about things. As I said, he was arrested in the spring of 1919 for inciting soldiers awaiting demobilization to take things into their own hands. To mutiny.

"Charges were dismissed, eventually, but after that, one began to see Bunsen's name regularly in the *Workers' Weekly*, articles or reports of speeches given at Communist rallies. He made a trip to Moscow in 1920, although he quieted down a little afterwards. I'd have said he was becoming a little disillusioned with the Workers' Party, although he was arrested again in 1921, during our last unrest among the coal miners. He got banged around a bit and spent a few weeks in prison. That may have effected a change of heart in the man, because he drew back from the more extreme policies he'd been promoting, and within a year began to cultivate friends in key places. Such as Matthew Ruddle, Labour Party Member of Parliament."

Bunsen was thirty-two years old, Stuyvesant reflected, and firebrands often cooled with age, as the anger and energy of their radical youth diminished. However, sometimes the bright ones simply learned to hide their fire under a basket.

And if Bunsen was saving his most radical tendencies for export, it might make it easier to put on a mask of calm and reason at home. He wouldn't be the first revolutionary to lead a double life.

"And this, finally—" Carstairs began, but Stuyvesant interrupted.

"Sorry, I knew some of what you've told me, his age and his rank and some of his history, but one thing I've never heard was what he did during the War, whether he was frontline or rear echelon. I don't suppose you know?"

Carstairs raised his face and gave Stuyvesant a smile that was startlingly full and warm, a smile that even touched those cold obsidian eyes.

"I wondered when you would ask me that. Halfway through the War, while he was recovering from his wound, Captain Richard Bunsen entered a training course that his maternal forefathers might have understood, one that kept him underground, there to be a leader among a tightly knit group of workers.

"Bunsen was, hmm, a sapper. He crawled through tunnels dug by his men, to lay explosive charges beneath enemy lines."

Chapter Four

CARSTAIRS' WIDE MOUTH CURLED slightly at Stuyvesant's reaction, but Stuyvesant could not begrudge him his gloat—the man deserved it, even if he'd forced Stuyvesant to tease it out of him like a big fish on a light line. This one piece of knowledge alone made his trip across the ocean worth-while.

"Demolitions, huh? Thank you, Major Carstairs."

"It adds a certain pleasing, hmm, completeness to the picture, does it not? And this brings us around to your particular need. As I was saying, Bunsen appears to have been distancing himself from the radical fringe. He is working his way up in the more mainstream political world, in part by immersing himself in Union work, but also through his establishment of a politically orientated organization with the, shall we say, rather optimistic name of Look Forward, which sponsors speakers, free legal representation, and educational opportunities to the working classes.

"As a part of this transformation, Bunsen takes care to make regular appearances in the vicinity of Good Works. In recent years, many of those stem from his attachment to Lady Laura Hurleigh. She is a founding member of a group of health care clinics called Women's Help, which operate in the poorest areas of London. An as-

sociation with these clinics bestows on Bunsen a distinct cachet of respectability and responsibility."

"Like they say, you can't buy that kind of press."

"Er, quite. In any case, Lady Laura has a number of staff who
oversee the day-to-day running of the clinics, but her overall assistant, her right-hand woman, if you will, who appears recently to
have taken on a number of functions in the Bunsen organization as
well"—(if he dragged this out any longer, Stuyvesant was going to
throttle it out of him)—"is a sweet but naïve young lady by the name
of Sarah Grey."

Ha! Stuyvesant thought—at last. "Grey. Related to your mind-
reader?"

"His sister. But please don't call him—"

"Yeah, I know, he's just another shell-shocked officer."

Carstairs frowned again at the end of his cigar, although it was
burning just fine. "You know, Agent Stuyvesant, I am grateful to you
for bringing me your question regarding Bunsen yesterday. Not only
have you caused me to focus on a potential troublemaker, but in reviewing his file, I remembered Captain Grey, and realized that I
hadn't been in touch with him in some time. Honestly, I'd nearly forgotten about him, but I'd be neglecting my duty if I didn't check on
him."

When someone like Aldous Carstairs used the word *honestly*—
and in a speech devoid of *hmm*s, *shall we says,* or *so to speak*s—it
might have been a neon arrow flashing at the opposite.

"Glad to be of service. So, how does your man Grey come into
this?"

"Almost not at all, considering how much of a hermit the man
has become. I gather that he and his sister—whom I met briefly, long
ago—see each other rarely, although they no doubt exchange letters.
However, they are in some contact, which is what brought him to
mind as a potential link in your chain. What if Captain Grey were to
provide you with an introduction to his sister? Would that give you
enough of a foot in Bunsen's door?"

To this point, all they'd traded was information; now, Carstairs
was proposing action, a thing that could put Stuyvesant in his debt.
"It would save me days of footwork," Stuyvesant admitted slowly.

Weeks, even. "But why would Grey do that? He doesn't know me from Adam."

The smile returned, but the earlier flower of warmth had been replaced by something very cold indeed. "He would do it if *I* asked him."

"Doesn't sound to me like your Captain Grey would be that enthusiastic about it."

"Mr. Stuyvesant, I assume that America's enemies are like our own, serious and without qualms. If you're going to go all polite and ethical on me, perhaps you ought to return to New York."

Stuyvesant replied lightly, "Oh, it's not being a bastard that worries me. It's just that forcing someone to help has a way of back-firing in your face."

"Perhaps, Mr. Stuyvesant, you haven't tried the correct kind of force." Carstairs dropped the stub of cigarillo to the ground and stepped on it. "So, would you care to come to Cornwall with me and ask him?"

Stuyvesant turned away to survey a not terribly inspiring vista, pretending to consider the offer while in fact he was composing his face. He was badly taken aback by the first honest emotion he'd seen in the man—frankly, he wished he hadn't seen it.

What Carstairs had shown Stuyvesant, either inadvertently or on purpose, was clear, raw *pleasure*. The black eyes had sparkled, his heel had nearly danced as it came down on the smoldering tobacco; suddenly, Stuyvesant was as physically aware of the man as he would have been of a dog with bared teeth; he found that he had instinctively half turned to face him rather than have Carstairs at his back.

"You need me to be there?"

"If you're going to pretend to be Captain Grey's friend when you meet his sister, you ought at least know what he looks like and how he lives. And I can see no reason, once you have met him, why I should not give you further information on him. Some of it may prove useful when you are in conversation with his sister."

"You could just tell me now."

"Actually," Carstairs said, sounding very final, "I'd prefer that you meet Captain Grey without, as it were, preconceptions. Afterwards, I will tell you all about him."

Stuyvesant couldn't imagine why Carstairs was so almighty eager to take him to see this Grey. Did the man, unlike everyone else in the city, have nothing better to do than hare off to Cornwall? There was something going on here he wasn't too sure about, some invisible trip wire in front of his toes.

Still, it wasn't like he had a whole lot of other choices on his plate.

"Okay, if you think we need to go to Cornwall, I'll go with you. When do we leave?"

"Ten o'clock tomorrow evening."

The instructions that followed made it clear that Carstairs had the trip planned out before they met. Before they parted, Carstairs handed him the case, telling him that it contained a few items about the players in their little drama.

"One last thing," he said, his hands still locked on the handle.

"What's that?" Stuyvesant asked, fighting the urge to rip the thing out of the man's hand.

"His sister. I would request that you make it clear to Captain Grey that his sister is in considerable danger of finding herself enmeshed in a kind of political action that has, hmm, profound consequences. If he cares for her, he must intervene."

"I'll do what I can."

Carstairs relinquished his hold on the case, and strolled away into the park.

Stuyvesant was so eager to see the papers that he walked over to the nearest bench and took out his reading glasses, then and there. He found, however, that *a few items* was distressingly accurate. And those were, for the most part, about Lady Laura Hurleigh and Sarah Grey, with almost nothing about Richard Bunsen. And nothing at all concerning Bennett Grey.

He folded away his glasses and tucked Carstairs' case under his arm, making his way back to the library he'd been using that week, wrestling with his thoughts.

Richard Bunsen, his suspect, was a Red trained in the use of explosives. And beyond the mere fact that he possessed the requisite skills, this was a man who had occupied a distinct niche in the military hierarchy: the tightly knit world of the sappers, who labored out of sight of their compatriots, burrowing in silence through the terrible wet earth, raising their thin props against the suffocating weight overhead. Once their secret tunnel reached enemy lines, the miners themselves would draw back, leaving the field to the demolitions man, to lay his charges and breach the enemy's defenses from the hidden depths. The demo man worked with the miners, but not only was he an officer, he was also subtly apart, slightly above those of his own rank, in the aristocracy of the trenches. He had proved himself, time and again, as a man with icy resolve, unwavering focus, and the steadiest hands on the Front.

Richard Bunsen had been that man. And not only had he survived, he appeared to be one of those rare men who'd had *a good war:* Despite injury and long service, he'd come through with his wits, his nerves, his body, and, most particularly, his reputation intact.

And now, eight years after the war ended, thirty-two-year-old Richard Bunsen, decorated officer and passionate advocate of the working man, had managed to snare the daughter of one of the highest families in the land as his mistress. On the surface, an admirable sort of fellow, as was this enigmatic Captain Grey whom Stuyvesant would cross the country to see. Stuyvesant could only pray he didn't actually come to like either man. It had happened before, that he liked his enemy, but it always made things tough.

And in the other corner of the ring, he thought, Aldous Carstairs: behind-the-lines Intelligence major, whose mouth suggested debauchery and whose handshake spoke of distaste. A man Scotland Yard didn't care to acknowledge. A man who for some inexplicable reason relished the idea of using force on Captain Bennett Grey. And the man who was, apparently, to be Stuyvesant's confederate on these shores.

He'd met men like Carstairs before, men who came to the world of Intelligence for the power. And occasionally, for the pleasure: During the War, Intelligence meant interrogations. In the years since, Stuyvesant had done his share of questioning, hard interrogations with weighty consequences. Enemies, as Carstairs had said, who were serious and without qualms. He'd used his fists when he had to—hard men required hard treatment, and sometimes the only way to get their respect was to beat it into them. But he'd never permitted one of his interrogations to descend into outright torture.

And he'd never taken any pleasure from the process. He'd never enjoyed seeing a man broken. He'd never felt bigger or happier or fulfilled when his opponent gave way.

However, he'd seen men who did. Law enforcement, especially Intelligence, could provide a haven for such men.

Men like Aldous Carstairs.

In a lifetime of having to overlook the means in the interest of the end, he couldn't remember ever having less enthusiasm about a colleague.

BOOK TWO

Cornwall

MONDAY, APRIL 12, 1926

Chapter Five

THE INVADER CAME UP THE HILLSIDE TRACK, contemptuous of the mud clinging to its flanks and the fresh crumple in its left fender, souvenir of an encounter with the close-laid rock wall. Wheels that had begun the morning pristine from a garage-hand's cloth wallowed through muck-filled ruts; a crack was spreading from the lower edge of the driver's side wind-screen.

The walls grew higher, the track narrower, every minute. An onlooker—say, someone standing before the lonely white building where the track came to its end—might think the motorcar headed for a final resting place, like a cork down the neck of its bottle: primitive green Cornwall tightening around this incongruous black manifestation of the Jazz Age.

As though confirming the suspicion of its fate, the car vanished behind some trees. For a time, the only signs of life on the ancient green patchwork of fields were three ambling cows and a two-legged figure in red, moving rapidly down a slope half a mile away. The fitful sea breeze dropped; the eternal grumble of the nearest tin-mine workings emerged from the hush, punctuated by a snatch of sweet-voiced birdsong and the bawl of a calf.

The verdant countryside into whose maw the car had apparently dropped was just about the end of the world as far as England was concerned—maps showed Land's End proper a few miles to the south, but the track's goal would meet the description for anyone but a surveyor: a small whitewashed stone cottage and its outbuildings, nestled into the breast of the last hill before the Atlantic.

The whitewashed cottage was a very long way from anywhere.

After a moment, the breeze picked up and the motorcar reemerged, shaking itself free of the copse. The carnivore growl of its engine noise deepened as the driver faced a steep bit, and smoothed out as the rise was breasted.

Then came a particularly tight corner, following boundaries laid two thousand years before, which seemed a likely candidate for the rustic bottleneck to claim this shiny cork. The intruder spent a long time there, inching ahead and falling back, tires spinning, engine revving in futility. Finally, the passenger door opened with a crack against the stone wall and a tall figure in brown forced itself out, clambering over fender and stone to take up a position of guidance in front. Arms were waved, shouted instructions dispersed on the gentle breeze, as the motor inched first forward, then back, then forward again. Finally, with a roar of the engine and a screech of metal audible a mile away, the car muscled itself through the angle. As it crept alongside the brown figure, the passenger yanked open the door, paused to scrape one foot against the grassy verge, and folded himself back inside. The car started up again, closing on the cottage.

Not until sixty feet from its goal did the rock walls finally drop away. The machine leaped ahead, eager as a lover, then slowed with an air of satisfaction at the lane's end. A panicked chicken darted across the open yard. The motorcar braked, settling back on its wheels. Its engine shut off.

All was still.

The passenger flung open his door and climbed out, looking relieved. He walked over to survey the countryside, which the stone walls had hidden as they climbed the hill, and gave an admiring whistle at the long sweep of green on which civilization was thinly spread. "Damn. I never get tired of the views this country has to offer."

Three hundred miles from London, but it might have been three thousand—Cornwall was a different world. Harris Stuyvesant was a city boy by birth and by nature, Bowery-born and Manhattan-centered, but frankly, he was just as glad to be away from the English capital. He'd remembered liking it just fine on his way home from the Front back in '19, but at present, London was little more than a drab, smoke-stained warren of angry, frightened people. The pedestrians were all grim and edgy, the men eyeing each other, the women's laughter high and brittle. Even before Friday's brawl with the demonstrator, the back of Stuyvesant's neck had tingled with the expectation of sudden violence.

On the other hand, this patch of countryside at the far edge of England, which under normal circumstances he'd have dismissed as empty space in need of a soda fountain and a good movie house, had a certain something. Even that penny-ante town of Penzance, walking along the sea-front while his companion had a shave (and calmed down—Jesus, the man's tongue, verbally peeling flesh from the garage man when he found there was a car but no driver!), had seemed a genial human place of cobblestones, fishing masts, and grubby, grinning infants, as if it had never heard the word *strike*, never seen a coal miner, never been introduced to the idea of a union. He'd breathed in the clean reek of fish and seaweed, and felt his bunched muscles subside for the first time in weeks.

Until he'd had to climb into that car with Aldous Carstairs.

Now Carstairs got out, too, studying the farmyard until he was satisfied that his quarry was not there before he went to join the American.

It was one of those bright spring days when the green of the new grass almost hurts the eyes, and the darker green of tree and hedgerow comes as a welcome relief. In the nearest field, each brown blade of the winter weeds stood out in sharp detail; the wind-blown daffodils blossoming in the protected lee of the stone wall might have been spatters of yellow paint.

Stuyvesant traveled a slow circle, replacing the oppressive air of the motorcar with the fragrant, fresh stuff that flowed merrily into his lungs. Freed from the uneasy atmosphere of the car, he completed his circuit and was again facing the farm buildings: small, square stone house with fresh white surface and moss-heavy slate roof; a larger shed or small barn, bare of paint; and between them a clothes-line with two dish-cloths, a wood pile with a well-used chopping block, and a wired chicken-run. In the background, strips of freshly turned earth marked the beginnings of this year's vegetable garden.

The American lifted his sights past the walls to the middle view, studying a series of low rollicking shapes in the nearby field, half buried under grass and winter-dead brambles. "Looks like once upon a time there was a hell of a house over there," he said, in the bumptious American manner he'd worn since Friday. "Although that must've been a while and a half ago, to leave only those foundations."

He never knew what the other man might have responded with, because the answer came from nowhere, and everywhere:

"It is a city of the dead."

Chapter Six

As THE MOTORCAR CAME UP the rough track, the small man stood motionless in the shadow of the barn. He'd been uneasy all morning, aware of the world around him trembling like a soap bubble, about to wink out of existence; now he knew why. His nostrils flared as the chemical stink of the machine cut through the thick fragrance of spring, the sharp smell of chicken droppings from the bottom of his right shoe, and the warm animal odor trickling out of the little window overhead, ghostly reminder of the cow housed there ten years earlier.

His ears told him the motor had been well maintained, although one of the pistons was firing a fraction late, and a part of the car's fender was scraping a tire in the right-hand turns. He could also hear the distant distress of Jenks' cow, which had encountered a motorcar on the road three years back and been nervous about them ever since. His own three chickens were scratching and clucking unconcernedly around the chopping block, not having yet noticed the intruder, but he'd heard the feral cat abandon the saucer of drippings at the back door to creep through the gap in the garden wall, where it could spy on the farmyard without being seen.

His eyes told him nothing, since the motor was not yet in sight— but he did not require vision to know who was coming. He'd felt the pressure building for weeks now, and had known it was only a matter of time. If he'd been truly psychic, as the man coming for him wished, he'd have known the day before and quietly slipped away. Now, with the danger so close, flight seemed an outright declaration of cowardice.

His grip tightened on the handle of the axe he had been using when the sound of the motor reached his ears, his fingertips reminding him of the growing weakness in the wood, straining fibers where a crack would eventually develop. He must replace it soon.

If . . .

He stayed in the shadow of the building until the sleek motorcar with the Penzance number plate oozed into the yard like honey laced with poison. The moment it appeared in the lane, the small man's eyes went to the passenger, lumpish in appearance but betraying a very sensible, and commendable, mistrust of the man behind the wheel.

The passenger, dressed in brown, was the first to emerge, his door flung open, a loud voice ringing through the small yard between white cottage and moss-covered shed. "Jesus H. Christ!" it exclaimed, in an accent as unmistakably American as its sentiments. "Haven't these people ever heard of the automobile?"

The man might have been chosen to illustrate the word *Colonial*. In his prime at about forty, he stood well over six feet tall, with shoulders to match his height. His movements were quick for a large man, suggesting restlessness beneath the surface. He looked at the world through a pair of cheerfully cynical blue eyes set in a face that was more interesting than handsome, with hastily assembled features—big nose, broad forehead, a pugnacious jaw offsetting his responsive mouth. Little dark dots along the left side of his face testified to an experience with shrapnel, and the line of his nose took one or two more turns than Nature had designed. His coarse light brown hair, untamed by oil and uncovered by hat, showed no trace of gray or of thinning. He hadn't shaved that morning, although the stubble was pale; most eyes would have had to be close to see it.

The American thrust his bare hands into the pockets of his tweed overcoat and walked off to look at the view, letting fly a sharp whistle. "Damn," he said. "I never get tired of the views this country has to offer."

The other door clicked open and the driver eased out onto the farm yard surface, a fastidious greyhound to the American's bull terrier. The man was an unlikely chauffeur, as polished as the motorcar had been before its recent abuse, freshly shaved and dressed in an unrelieved black that might have been appropriate in a City meeting, or a funeral.

Perhaps it was the American's presence that made him seem a shade smaller and a great deal more self-contained than he had five years ago. Some things had not changed: the unnerving sensuality of his lips and the blackness of his eyes, those invisible pupils that gave away nothing of the man within. One feature, however, was new: the thin, pink scar that traveled down the side of his face.

Looking at it, the small man found himself smiling.

The driver raised a gloved hand to his perfect black hair, a gesture that seemed designed to smooth from his mind the effects of the arduous journey; with his other hand, he set his felt hat into place.

The impenetrable eyes swept the farmyard and found it empty of life. The driver went to stand near the American, the set of his head indicating that he was more there to judge the view than to admire it. The men gave an appearance of cooperation, even friendliness, but to the watching figure, they were as stiff-legged as a pair of bristling dogs.

"Looks like once upon a time there was a hell of a house over there," the American said. His voice was a shade too loud, his shoulders seemed to want to ease themselves against the manner he wore, a manner that fit him as poorly as another man's coat. "Although that must've been a while and a half ago, to leave only those foundations."

The dark man's lips curled and parted, perhaps to offer a sardonic comment on the American fascination for anything old enough to grow moss, but his pronouncement was interrupted by a voice that bounced off the stones and became directionless.

"It is a city of the dead."

The startled American yanked his hands from his pockets and sent the skirts of his greatcoat dancing, but his companion, either less surprised or more practiced at concealment, swiveled deliberately on one glossy heel as he searched out the source of the words. His attention had traveled past the figure, whose garments were the precise shade of the lichen-draped stones behind him, when a gleam of sunlight played off the freshly honed edge of the axe on the man's shoulder. The black gaze snapped back to the man; in a moment, the wide mouth curled up, lazy and relaxed.

The woodcutter was not a tall man, perhaps a shade over five and a half feet, with thick white-blond hair in need of a trim. He was clean-shaven, his body muscular beneath once-brown corduroy trousers and a once-good herringbone jacket, both garments tidy and well mended—unlike his cloth cap, which looked like something dredged from the bottom of a cow stall. His eyes were a startling green in a weathered face, his eyelashes darker than his hair and long. Despite the weathering, his boyish build made him seem young.

Black eyes met green without quailing; if anything, they grew more openly amused. Finally, the American broke the silence. "What do you mean, 'a city of the dead'? Is this how you people build cemeteries around here?"

"I have, in fact, come across bones," the man answered. (His light voice lacked the catches and burrs of the local dialect—not a native Cornishman, then, the American automatically noted. Or if so, he'd shed the accent. In fact, when it came to that ineffable English air of Authority and Right, this rustic figure sounded closer to the real thing than Carstairs in his beautifully tailored clothing.) "But no, it is a village of a people long gone. Phoenicians, according to local mythology. Major, I distinctly remember saying that if I saw you again, I would kill you."

Major Aldous Carstairs' lazy smile deepened, and his voice when he spoke was low, almost intimate. "Captain Grey, it is so very good to see you again. May I present Mr. Harris Stuyvesant from America? Mr. Stuyvesant, Captain Bennett Grey."

Stuyvesant looked from the sharpened steel on the man's shoulder to the expression on his face, and decided not to offer his hand. "Hi," he said, his fingers sketching a wave.

Grey still hadn't taken his eyes from the Englishman. "Major."

It wasn't that Carstairs didn't hear that raw threat, Stuyvesant thought: The man's face might be arranged into the fond expression of a parent indulging a child's whim, but Stuyvesant was close enough to feel his tension—the muscles beneath that fancy coat were just waiting for the command to dive for the car. Anyone less cold-blooded than Aldous Carstairs would have been sweating into his well-ironed white shirt.

But give the icy bastard credit: His voice gave away no trace of fear as he said, "I believe, Captain Grey, that your precise words were, 'If I lay eyes on you again, be prepared to die.' However, before you come after me with that archaic weapon, I should hope you might listen to a request. It concerns . . . your sister."

Stuyvesant had plenty of time to consider those last two words, words that clicked like a queen on a chess-board, words with a whole lot of history in them. He had time to speculate about the axe on Grey's shoulder, if it was why Carstairs had wanted him along. And to wonder if, should the woodcutter come at them, he maybe shouldn't just stand back and let him swing: God knew, anyone who said those words to Harris Stuyvesant in that way wouldn't walk away in one piece.

But the man Grey just stood, motionless.

The American was beginning to think Carstairs' words had set off some peculiar mental process, turning the fellow into one of those standing stones they'd passed in the fields that morning, when Cornwall itself broke the tension by dropping into the tableau a wild-eyed countryman in a bright red fisherman's jersey.

Almost literally dropping: The unlikely figure tumbled over the wall into the farmyard as if thrown there, picking himself up and trotting across the yard in an oddly crablike gait. He scuttled over to Bennett Grey and seized the small man's free hand, edging around in back of him to glare over Grey's head at the others with a pair of blue eyes so pale they seemed white. His large body was draped in much-patched trousers held up by twine, and the red jersey looked as if it had been rolling in gorse bushes. He was probably near to Grey in age, but Stuyvesant half expected him to poke his thumb into his mouth to complete the picture of childishness.

Grey finally moved, to crane his neck and look at the person behind him.

"Naouw, Robbie, shudden tha be at oam helpin' tha Mutherr?"

The Cornishman answered in the same peculiar tongue. "Ah 'eard the motorr. Ah diddun loik its looks. Ah knawed you wud wan' ma help."

Behind the impenetrable accent, it was clear that the man was simple as a six-year-old. He clutched Grey's hand and scowled from Carstairs to Stuyvesant; if he'd been a dog he'd have been growling.

But Grey gave a laugh that sounded only the slightest bit forced, and reached down to lean his long axe against the side of the building. "Robbie, tha's a good lad, but thee mun go back to tha Mutherr naow. Ahm foin. These twa gennelmun come all the way from London town to talk t'me, so Ah mun keep them, naow, must Ah?"

Robbie's shoulders relaxed, and he turned and eyed the motor for a moment before tilting his head and whispering loudly into Grey's ear, "Ah wanna zit een 'un."

"Na, Robbie, you wudden loik the smell. Motorrs like tha' are not fit for thee. Off tha go, me 'andsum. Say good day to Mr. Stuyvesant and Major Carstairs."

With great reluctance, either at abandoning Grey or leaving the shiny motor unexperienced, the Cornish lad tugged at his cap and withdrew. Grey had to urge him twice more before Robbie threw his leg over the wall and dropped away on the other side.

The instant he was gone, that green gaze snapped back onto Carstairs.

"Does your American friend here know the details of what you're about?"

"Some of them. Not all."

"Of course not. No matter. Major, I want you out of my sight until four o'clock. That gives your Mr. Stuyvesant four and a half hours to tell me everything he knows. You'd better hope he's convincing."

Carstairs' look of amusement faded. "Grey, really, I—"

"You're giving me a headache, Major. Four o'clock."

The Englishman studied Grey as though committing his face to memory. He glanced at Stuyvesant, then, to the American's astonishment, walked off. No argument, no protest at the cold or the lack of transport, just tugged at his gloves and walked away down the track they'd come up.

In moments the walls had swallowed Carstairs, but Grey waited, long after the sound of footsteps on gravel faded. Stuyvesant shifted, took his cigarette case from his left breast pocket, turned it over in his hand once or twice before putting it away again, then cleared his throat, preparing to speak. Grey held up a finger to stop him, his eyes on the end of the adjoining field: a brief flicker of dark, glimpsed through a narrow break in the wall, and Carstairs was gone.

Grey blew out a long breath and leaned back against the shed's stone wall, eyes shut, both hands coming up to press their heels against his eye sockets, fingers in his hair. Stuyvesant had thought he meant a figurative headache, but apparently not: The man did not look boyish now.

"Do you work for him?" Grey's voice sounded strained.

"No. I only met him three days ago."

"He's planning something. What is he planning?"

"Planning...? I'm sorry, I honestly don't know."

After a few seconds, the hands came away from the face. The man raised his head to drill Stuyvesant with that emerald stare. He seemed to be listening intently, not only to Stuyvesant's denial, echoing off the stone walls, but to his own inner voice.

Stuyvesant found himself opening his mouth to speak, to explain his statement, to swear that honestly, he wasn't—

Harris Stuyvesant, as cool under pressure as any man in the Bureau, ready to blather and vow and declare his innocence like a two-bit criminal feeling the handcuffs.

Abruptly, Grey nodded his head, as if resigned to a decision handed down by some internal court, then bent to retrieve the axe. Stuyvesant's protest died unspoken.

The small man strode across the yard towards the house. As he passed the chopping block, his arm came up and he sank the heavy tool, single-handed, two inches deep in the hard surface. He climbed the concave stone steps and went inside, leaving the door standing open.

Harris Stuyvesant ran a hand over his hair, not quite sure what had just happened.

All the same, he figured an open door was an invitation. Or at least, as much invitation as he was likely to get.

Chapter Seven

Two steps up and a duck of the head brought the big American inside the stone cottage. He paused to let his eyes adjust to the light, and found he was in the hallway of a building even smaller than it had appeared from the outside. To his left was a closed door. To his right was a room with a pair of easy chairs before a time-blackened fireplace; a clock ticked on the mantelpiece. One entire wall was solid with books, its shelves beginning to make inroads on a second wall. A small table beside one chair held a stack of books, an unlit paraffin lamp, and a ceramic ash-tray with a pipe. On a larger table beneath the window stood a small crystal-wireless set.

The room's only sign of disorder was a drift of newspapers beside the chair. One of them was the Friday *Times*, with a determinedly low-key headline tut-tutting over the Strike as if it were little more than a college prank. On top of the *Times* was a paper whose font he didn't recognize, folded to an article—he took a step in, just to see— about the Organisation for the Maintenance of Supplies. It was a name he'd come across once or twice during the last week, some semi-official group that sounded like a cross between old boy's club and reactionary militia. The sort of group that might make him question his stand against Communism, were it to raise its head on the other side of the Atlantic.

A clink of glass pulled Stuyvesant's mind from the building hysteria of faraway London and drew him deeper into the house, to another doorway, where he ducked his head again, so as not to be brained on the lintel. Here lay a bright and obsessively tidy kitchen: wooden table with patterned red-and-yellow oil-cloth pinned to its top, three wooden chairs, a scrubbed stone sink and single tap, and open shelves, lined with more of the oil-cloth, that held plates, cups, glasses, and a variety of canisters and packages. The windows were spotless, no easy task this near the sea; the room was cozy with the sun and the heat from the black iron stove.

Bennett Grey was standing next to the sink, his back to the room as he drank thirstily. He swallowed—two, three gulps—then set the glass down hard. His right arm came up with a clatter of glass against glass as he poured from a bottle, then he carried the fresh drink around the table, to drop heavily into one of the chairs. He set his elbows on the oil-cloth and cradled his temples in both hands; Stuyvesant might not have been in the room.

The American eyed the bottle sitting in a patch of sunlight. Its shoulders held a light coating of dust, now showing clear marks from Grey's fingers: not a daily comfort, then.

He ran his eyes over the room, taking in the bachelor's neatness, the precise borders of the paint and the solidity of the windows. Seven eggs, a spectrum from white to brown, rested on the back of the counter in a lop-sided basket; four elegant wine-glasses with gold trim sat next to three eggshell porcelain teacups on one rough shelf, over a drying-rack filled with dinner plates Stuyvesant's mother would have crooned over. He'd have laid money that the utensils in the drawer would be solid silver, and that thought made him suddenly, unreasonably, angry.

He felt like taking that carefully preserved medicinal bottle of hooch and smashing it into that spotless stone sink. Or maybe he could just pick up the little man and shake him, headache or no, until Grey told him what the hell was going on and why Aldous goddamn Carstairs had brought him here.

But impatience was rarely a helpful tool—one piece of wisdom he'd gained at high cost over the years. And face it: If he wasn't here, in this pretty piece of countryside, he'd be chewing at the carpets in London with nothing to do but walk the streets and keep from beating up Union sympathizers until the Bastard's Battersea speech on Thursday.

Considering the blanket of anger draped over London at the moment, much better to be here, frustration or no. He gave a mental shrug, then pulled one of the cut-glass tumblers off the shelf, pouring himself a scant two fingers of the clear liquid. He took off his overcoat, sat down in the chair across from Captain Bennett Grey, and felt the bumptious American act slide away at last.

Grey peered out at the glass from beneath his hands. "Sorry, I didn't take you for an early drinker."

"I'm not, any more than you are. But I've been in London for the last week and a half, which is about as restful as strolling through a pack of rabid dogs, followed by twenty-four hours in the company of your friend in the black coat. I think just this once my sainted mother would permit a belt before lunch."

Despite his brave words, Stuyvesant raised his glass with caution, warned by the powerful fumes. He took a sip. The liquid seared a path from lips to stomach lining, and he coughed, blinking against the astounded tears in his eyes. "Jesus, what is this?"

"I try not to ask," Grey told him. "One of my neighbors distills it. It makes an excellent fire-starter, if you're ever caught with wet wood."

Stuyvesant gently set the glass down far across the table, half expecting its contents to crawl out and come across the bright oil-cloth at him. He'd drunk his share of bathtub gin since the Volstead Act had passed, but this was one for the books. In self defense, he pulled out his case and placed a cigarette between his lips, then hesitated, lighter in hand. Surely if the vapors from the glass were as explosive as they smelled, the coals in the stove would have blown out the kitchen windows already? Still, he brought the flame gingerly towards his face, and was relieved when his exhaled breath did not turn into a flame-thrower.

He snapped the lighter out, then looked around until his eyes hit on a tin saucer with dark stains in the bottom, and got up to retrieve it. Before sitting again, he shed his jacket, both for the comfort and to set an informal, just-us-boys note to the upcoming conversation.

Grey finished his second drink more slowly than his first, but in all, Stuyvesant figured, the man had just downed eight or ten ounces of raw liquor—extremely raw liquor—with no reaction. Or rather, with one reaction: The man was no longer squeezing his head to keep it in place.

"You find this stuff cures headaches?" the American asked.

"It's about the only thing that does."

Stuyvesant flicked the ash from his cigarette over the tin saucer. "I take it Major Carstairs gives you a headache?"

"Like a spike through the brain. It sounds as though he gave you one, as well."

"Not like that."

"I hope to God not, for your sake."

"However, I don't. Seem to give you one, that is."

"The day is young," Grey said grimly.

Stuyvesant sat back against the chair to study the man on the other side of the table. The information he'd managed to drag from Carstairs about Grey had struck him as a closely calibrated doling out of facts, more tantalizing than informative. Still, the bare outline of Grey's life had led him to expect a typical shell-shock victim: jumpy, pale, and pitiful. Instead he was faced with this sturdy brown-skinned farmer with the high-class accent, whose gaze was even and hands without tremor. Who, moreover, had just managed to squeeze out a little humor despite a pounding fury inside his skull. He'd set out from London anticipating the need to conceal a healthy man's distaste for a weakling like Grey, yet what he felt now was something very like sympathy.

"Why?" he asked.

"Why does the Major give me one, or why should you keep trying to?"

"Why don't you have a headache from me? Yet."

"Because you're not hiding things."

Hiding things: Well, that was Carstairs, all right. "You sound pretty sure about it. That I'm not hiding things." Grey shot him a glance, and went back to massaging his temples. "I mean, doesn't everybody?"

"The things most people conceal are small and private embarrassments. People like the Major hide themselves; they hide *from* themselves; and it's an agony to me." Grey dropped his hands, studying his visitor with the same disturbing intensity that he'd shown when listening to Stuyvesant earlier—the American felt as if Grey was counting the pores on his face. "You haven't the faintest idea what I'm talking about, have you?"

"Not really, no."

"The Major brought you here without telling you about me?"

"Basically, Carstairs told me just enough to get me on the train. He said you'd been injured, left with some, what he called 'peculiar abilities,' and came here to get away from things. He seemed to think you might be able to help me with a, er, problem I'm having. Oh— and he said you weren't a mind-reader."

After a moment, Grey's mouth twitched, and the ghost of a handsome man flitted briefly through the worn features. "Must have cost him something to admit that," he said. "Tell me, does he still pull out that damnable note-book of his? I know he still smokes those bloody awful cigars, I could smell them from across the yard."

"Yeah, he writes notes sometimes in a little book. Why? What's in it?"

"God knows. It used to make me shudder, that book. Look, would you like some tea, or there's coffee?"

"Coffee'd be great," Stuyvesant agreed, thinking that it might be good to get some into Grey, as well; if he had a little more than four hours to figure out how the man was to help him, he didn't want to waste it watching the blond head snoring face-down on the table. Grey pushed back from the table and stood—or tried to, but his balance failed and his leg gave out on him, tipping him back into the chair and nearly upending it. Stuyvesant's big hand shot out and seized one flailing wrist, snapping Grey back against the table. This time when Grey's head went into his hands, it was from dizziness, not pain.

Stuyvesant got up instead and went to hunt through the cupboards for a packet of coffee grounds and a pot. He filled the kettle and stirred up the fire, talking all the while: Keep Grey focused, keep him awake, and, most of all, keep him from going for a refill on the rotgut. And if it took chattering like a cleaning lady, that's what he'd do.

"Look. Carstairs told you I know what he's got in mind, or some of it anyway, but like I said, I really don't have anything more than an educated guess. Maybe I ought to begin with me—how I got here, what I'm after—and we can go from there. That sound good to you?"

"Fine."

"Okay. Harris John Stuyvesant, at your service. I'm an agent for the U.S. Bureau of Investigation. You don't see a lot of Bureau agents outside the States, but for the last five or six years, my job's been agitators. Anarchists, Reds, Unions, the lot. Same as you have here, for the most part, although our strikes tend to be more violent than yours, and a lot of the chief agitators were born outside the country. Then again," he mused, "most of our workers were born outside the country as well, so maybe it doesn't signify. Anyway, until recently the Bureau's main goal, outside of bank jobs, has been to keep the agitators under control. Now, what with Prohibition and all, things are shifting to straight crime, but I'm still mainly—"

"Anarchists." Grey seemed to be addressing the oil-cloth. "Did you have anything to do with the arrests of Sacco and Vanzetti?"

Yeah, Stuyvesant thought: Grey might live at the end of the world, but he kept up with the London papers, and apparently some kind of wireless broadcasts penetrated this remote toe of England. He might know as much about the two Italians as any man on the streets of New York. "I worked on the case for a while, but I got myself reassigned when I flat out told my boss he had the wrong guys. Those two aren't lily-white innocents by a long shot, but they're not guilty of *that* murder."

"Will they be executed?"

Stuyvesant shifted the kettle to a hotter spot, then raised his eyes to the window, tracing the lines of Grey's Phoenician city. What had those ancient residents done by way of law enforcement? "I hope to Christ not. They're on appeal now. I'd say they have a good chance of getting off, or at least getting reduced sentences. Hell, they've got half-decent alibis and there's even another man's confession floating around, they're sure to get—"

"Stop!" Grey's cry broke into the American's monologue. He was cradling his head again, nursing its pain. "For God's sake, man, if you don't believe it, don't say you do!"

Stuyvesant stared at the other man in bewilderment, which slowly edged into understanding. *He knows things,* Carstairs had said Saturday in Hyde Park. *He sees into people.* Well, Grey had just seen through the threadbare argument that Stuyvesant had held a thousand times over the past months, never quite managing to convince himself of its truth. The blunt fact was, Niccola Sacco and Bartolomeo Vanzetti were scapegoats who'd been loaded up with the country's nightmares and driven in the direction of the execution chamber.

But if Bennett Grey could see through the determined self deception of a perfect stranger like Harris Stuyvesant, how could he possibly carry on everyday relations with his fellows? Was that why he lived ten miles from Nowhere? How could the poor bastard so much as go into town and buy a loaf of bread, if everyday guile hammered a tenpenny nail into his skull? "Sorry," Stuyvesant said. "Yeah, you're right. The truth is, I don't know if those two'll escape the electric chair. There's a lot of people hot to make an example of them." *My boss, for one.* "You know how it works—if you can't find the real villains, find a couple of convenient ones and push them in people's faces. I keep trying to convince myself that they're going to win their appeal. I...I don't much like feeling ashamed of my country."

Grey relaxed a fraction. "Thank you. Now, you were telling me about your work."

"Right." Stuyvesant tipped back the lid of the kettle, decided the contents were close enough to boiling, poured water over the grounds in the pot, and was transported to another time and place.

Perhaps it happened because his mind was occupied with the matter of winning over this man, or because he felt momentarily safe from both the overt madness of London and the shadowy menace that seemed to accompany Aldous Carstairs. Or maybe there was something about his companion that evoked the memory, but at the crisp sound of water meeting coffee grounds and the rich uprush of aroma, Stuyvesant was abruptly standing in a place of eternal clamminess and muck, the weight of a helmet pushed back on his head, the awareness of lice in his armpits and groin, the ache of trench-foot on his toes. The rumble of guns was far away, not enough to bury the sound of Kowalsky reading aloud the latest drivel from his girlfriend in Sioux Falls, or the sound of the men up the trench playing poker, or the scraps of conversation Tim was having with Sergeant Jimmy DiCicco (nick-named The Padre because of his clean mouth), who was Stuyvesant's partner in the business of Keeping Tim Safe.

Kowalsky was blown to pieces and The Padre took a bullet through the helmet when he poked his head over the parapet, and Tim...

The memory-moment held him, and his men were there, all of them whole and safe and immortal, while he brewed up coffee, in a calm moment, in the trenches.

Chapter Eight

STUYVESANT BLINKED. The sandbagged walls vanished, replaced by a clean, dry, old-fashioned kitchen in the south of England. Boy, he thought, haven't had a visitation of the past that strong in a long time. He pushed away the inevitable creeping sensation down the back of his neck and glanced at his companion, but Grey hadn't noticed that his visitor was briefly out of the room. Where had the conversation got to? Oh yeah—work.

"Like I say, most of my cases have to do with Unions. This last year, I've been trying to run to earth rumors of what you might call outside consultation among the agitators. I mean, radicals are always a pain in the ass, but lately it's more than that. You get to know your enemy, don't you? How they think, what they can and can't do. But recently our home-grown troublemakers have been coming up with things they've never thought of before, clever and politically savvy and ruthless—terrorism, planned and targeted, not just their usual outburst, hitting out at authority."

"For example?"

"Okay, for example. Two months ago last week we just happened to foil a bomb plot. Absolute blind luck, checking a hotel room that'd already been gone over when the lead guy happened to notice one of the bottles on the drink stand was in a different place from the night before. And very fortunately, he used his eyes before he used his hands, and saw a tiny stub of freshly cut copper wire sticking out from under the edge of that bottle. If he'd picked it up, several ounces of gelignite—you know what that is? Nice, stable, simple-to-use form of nitroglycerine?—anyway, quite a wad of it, packed inside a couple pounds of roofing nails that might've gone off at knee level. If he hadn't spotted it, the bottle would have been picked up about an hour later, when a Senator offered a drink to a couple of bank presidents, three Congressmen, two other Senators, and the Bureau Director."

No need to mention that when the bomb squad had gotten there, they'd found the device was a dud, that with the last push of the wires into their housing, one small connection had come awry. The bomb was real, the gelignite active: so what if later it was anticlimactic?

"They were there to discuss ways to infiltrate Bolshevik groups in factories. The meeting had been written about in the papers, but the hotel they were meeting in was only announced three days before. That's damned fast work."

"Lucky man, to spot the bomb."

"Boy, you're right there."

"That was you, wasn't it?"

Stuyvesant's jaw dropped. "How'd you guess that?"

"Did you find who put it there?"

"The Bureau is hunting for one of the hotel maids who didn't show up for work the next day and—" Stuyvesant broke off, realizing that, chatter or not, he had gotten enormously sidetracked here. "You don't really want to know all this, do you?"

"Not particularly. Although I think you want to tell me."

It was such an odd thing to say, Stuyvesant could only stare at him. But damn it, the man was right. It was dead stupid to dump the whole story on a perfect stranger, but yes, he did want to talk. He'd always found it easier to see the details of a case when he'd hashed it over with someone. But the nearest thing to a partner was on the other side of a lot of ocean, and who was this guy going to blab to, anyway, the pigs? Simpleton Robbie?

Not that he was here because of anything resembling a case. This trip Carstairs pushed him into was going to be a complete waste of time anyway, he knew it. Hell, the whole English venture was nuts; he'd have been better off setting a match to so many dollar bills and waiting for The Bastard to return to New York, when he could just plant some evidence on him like any sane man would. But instead he'd done it right and he'd played along, and now he was stuck with four hours to kill until Carstairs came back. Why not throw up his hands and talk about it? It might help him think, and it was better than sitting here staring at the walls.

"Okay. Well, like I said, the maid had vamoosed—packed her bags and left her apartment, and the Bureau has a call out for her across the country."

"They think she did it?"

"No—for one thing, she'd worked there over a year, too long just to set this up. It looked like the girl was only a maid, with nothing about her to suggest she could build a thing like that—the device was a real work of art: well thought out as to the timing, enough gelignite to make sure nobody in that room walked away. But the girl had been seen at one or two Communist meetings, and we figured some-one had to open the door for the bomber.

"One witness said she'd been talking with a man, earlier that day. The description the witness gave was pretty useless—slim, slicked-down hair, smoky glasses, thin moustache—but one of the girl's neighbors had seen her a day or two earlier with a man who fit the same description, guy with an English accent. We figured she'd let him in to set the bomb, then either ran away with him, or heard what he'd done and got scared and took off on her own. She was foreign—Mexico, maybe Central America.

"Now, in and of itself, an English accent doesn't tell us much—half the men in New York have an accent of some kind—but it was a thing I'd heard before, an Englishman in the vicinity of a clever de-vice. So I took the description and I—"

"What were the other devices?" Grey interrupted to ask.

Again Stuyvesant hesitated; again he shrugged, and told him about the fire that had started it all.

"Last summer, a number of us Bureau agents were in Chicago, helping the local force with some agitators, when somebody had the bright idea of holding a raid. And not just a raid, but they thought it would be good to give the Reds warning, to give them time to clear out. Make 'em look like cowards, you know?

"Of course, Reds are more likely to want martyrdom than to save their skin, and what the warning gave them was time to summon a mob. However, the cops had said they were going to do a raid, so they did the raid, broke down the door and started hauling people away. And it would have been okay, since there were plenty of cops on hand to keep the mob under control, but before they got the house cleared, a fire broke out in the kitchen, on the middle floor. And unfortuantely, one young woman had gone back upstairs to get her coat, and when the whole center floor went up in flames, she had no place to go but up, and finally off the roof. Margery Anne Wallingford was her name. She died. The mob watched it happen, blamed the cops, a riot started up, half the city began to beat on each other's heads."

Stuyvesant kept his voice even, but it took some effort. He took a steadying breath, and went on.

"When the riot was over and the coals were cool, we went sifting through them for evidence that they'd been assembling bombs and set one off, on purpose or by accident, but we didn't find any other equipment. Which may have meant they'd just had the one that they'd intended to set elsewhere, but when I talked to the Reds they'd arrested, one of them happened to mention a box of groceries that had been delivered earlier that day. He'd just carried it up and left it on the kitchen table, because who had time for groceries when a raid was coming?

"Tell you the truth, the whole thing was damn confusing. I might've thought there was some rival group, except that this bunch had so many internal disputes they were beginning to break into factions, anyway. I spent a long time digging around to see if this particular crew had stepped on the toes of some Comrades, but I couldn't find anything. But if not rivals, why would the Reds burn down their own house? It couldn't have been an accident—if the bomb was intended for elsewhere, they had all the time in the world to get rid of the thing before the raid. And if they'd meant it as a trap to kill cops, the timing and the location were both rotten."

"You don't entertain the thought that the girl chose deliberately to go into the fire?"

"Martyrdom to rally the cause? If there'd been more noise around it, I'd have wondered, but there wasn't, not even a letter.

"My nasty suspicious mind even began to wonder if it had started as a fake, designed to play on public sympathy—you know, evil cops setting fire to honest Communists' headquarters. In that case, only the leaders would have been in on it, and once they were in the paddy wagon there was no one to stop the girl from going up for her coat.

"The one thing I did find was the kid who'd delivered the box of groceries. He'd been stopped on the street and given a quarter to take it to an address, that was all he knew. By an Englishman with a moustache.

"Okay, that was last July. Then in November, a hard-guy judge in Cranston was about to present a key ruling on a Union dispute, and he got in his car to drive to work one morning—driving himself that day, as his driver had called in sick—and half a mile down the road, the car burst into flames. He was quicker than you'd guess, looking at him, and scrambled out with nothing worse than blisters all up his back, but it was a close thing. We figured that one was in a china doll sitting on the back seat—he had a granddaughter, no doubt thought it was hers until *whoosh,* up it went.

"We had no reason to think it had anything to do with the July bomb, you understand, except they were two incendiary devices, which may have been placed inside everyday objects.

"And in January, my bottle bomb, as nice a piece of death-dealing as you could ask for. Three *booms,* three innocuous settings, two Englishmen, nothing to tie them together but one agent's suspicious mind."

"What aren't you telling me?"

Stuyvesant glanced over his shoulder. "Sorry?"

"Mr. Stuyvesant, your voice drips with the memory of blood. Why is that?"

"Bombs are bloody things."

"There is a personal element in your intonation."

Stuyvesant went to the cupboard for two cups, came back to the sink, and set them beside the coffee. "I don't talk about my personal life."

"If you want my help, you had better change that policy."

"It's nothing to do with the investigation." Not really.

"Nonetheless."

Son of a bitch. Damn Carstairs, anyway. Stuyvesant leaned both hands on the tiled surface and spoke to the window.

"That riot, last July? My kid brother got caught up in it. Tim's fourteen years younger than me and our dad died when he was five, so I've always been more like a father than a brother. He's followed on my heels since he could crawl, enlisted when he was still just sixteen—lied about his age—and showed up on the Front six months after I did. I didn't even try to get him sent home, just tucked him under my wing and kept him from doing anything too stupid. After the War, I made him go to college. And when he graduated and wanted to follow me into the Bureau, I kept an eye on him there, too. Just . . . not close enough.

"He was off duty when the riot started up, but he knew I was out of town so he went to help out and got caught up in it. Nearest doctors could figure, he got knocked down and someone kicked him in the head. He lived, sort of. He can sometimes remember his wife's name."

Stuyvesant turned around to look at the other man.

"So yeah. I'd say there's a personal element in my goddamned intonation."

Chapter Nine

THE SILENCE HELD for a minute, then Grey said, "I'm sorry."

Sorry about Tim or sorry to have asked? "Yeah, well, these things happen."

"And you say you feel that bomb was linked to the others."

"I did." Stuyvesant shook off the guilt and grief that rode his days, and gave the coffee a stir. "Where was I? Oh yeah, the Englishman. I took the description we had and compared it to passenger manifests, to and from England, at the dates involved. And eventually I narrowed it down to one man."

"Sounds like a lot of work."

"Understatement of the year."

It had been a ridiculous amount of work, and of the kind Stuyvesant was least suited for—his forte was fists, not files. The worst of it was, because his boss thought he had a bee in his bonnet, most of it needed to be done in his off hours. First combing through what seemed like a thousand manifests covering the periods before and after the three incidents, poring over fine print by his desk lamp, looking for men with British passports traveling alone.

And he'd found them—a lot of them, but he'd gradually eliminated the possibilities down to a small handful of names, and then one, who had traveled in a first class cabin in July and January, and by second class in November. It took him another two weeks to track down the pursers for all three voyages, but when he did, the July employee gave Stuyvesant his first slim break: a group photo from the passage in July that included a man who more or less matched the description.

When he'd taken that photo to the January ship's purser, the man had said yes, it looked like the same man. The November purser disagreed; however, it turned out that crossing had been rough, and the man in the second class cabin had stayed in bed most of the time, groaning and ill. The hotel maid's friend said maybe, could be, hard to tell. The boy who'd carried the groceries in Chicago had been positive.

The passenger's name was Richard Bunsen. A few phone calls, and he'd decided it was The Bastard's real name.

The Director needed more than that to set an international investigation under way. But when Stuyvesant gave him more, when he described just who Bunsen was, Hoover had practically laughed him out of the office. And J. Edgar had a point: Why would an Englishman cross the ocean to bomb Americans, anyway? Were they talking about some international mastermind?

Stuyvesant had to admit it was unlikely. But he was haunted by that easy, self-satisfied face in the shipboard photo, and he'd been an agent long enough to know that motive was often the last piece of an investigation that fell into place. Hoover wasn't convinced, but in the end he'd given way, and the Bureau had shelled out fifty bucks for the ticket, though nothing more. So here was Harris Stuyvesant, at the end of the world, listening to the sound of his savings going up in smoke.

"I couldn't find much about him, but enough to suggest that one of the names he'd traveled under had been his own, and he was indeed English. So, long story short, some of us talked it over and decided it was high time for our two countries to pool our knowledge, and I drew the short straw to—"

"Mr. Stuyvesant," Grey broke in, the cold edge back in his voice. "If you can't give this to me straight, leave. Now."

Stuyvesant felt a surge of anger, but the look in those green eyes had him turning his back to stir the coffee again. Okay, fine, more white lies, but what was he supposed to say? That he'd set himself on Bunsen's trail because his pretty young sister-in-law had cried all over his shirt-front until he'd sworn to find the man responsible? That he'd come because he couldn't close his eyes without seeing Tim's slack features? That every time he looked at the scars zig-zagging over the kid's head, he saw Helen's features beneath them?

That it should have been him, there in that riot, not Tim?

"Okay, yeah. Carstairs doesn't know this, but it's true, my presence here is not a hundred percent official. You see, the Bureau's Director and I, we had a little falling out about where the investigation was going. He's got what you might call a personal interest, since it was him who would've got blown up in that room.

"I know what you're thinking—that he ought to be kissing my feet that I saw the wire. And he is, or he'd have fired me flat instead of buying me a ticket for a little vacation. He thinks I'm going the wrong way with it. That I'm following...chance coincidences."

Grey raised his head, distracted from the headache by that tiny pause. He listened to the echoes and saw the sudden rigidity in the man's neck: The American was hiding something.

"Tell me about those chance coincidences."

"There aren't any."

"Stuyvesant—"

"No."

Grey sat slowly back, trying to ignore the throb of his pulse inside his skull. With that one flat word, the tension had gone clear out of the big man. *Kick me out if you must,* the American might as well have said aloud, *but I'm simply not giving you that.*

It would do Grey no good to press, that he could see. The line was drawn in the other man's mind, and he would not cross it, not if Grey offered to serve his enemy up on a platter.

Open refusal was a thing Grey could live with.

"So, you and your Director had a falling out."

Stuyvesant blinked. A clear lie, and Grey hadn't caught it. After a moment, his stirring arm began to move again. "Yeah, we agreed to disagree. Of course, the Bureau's got exactly no authority overseas anyways, so even if I *was* here officially, it wouldn't be worth a plugged nickel. But over the years I've made low friends in high places, and one of them arranged for me to be attached to the ambassador's office here as a kind of advisor, for when I need some kind of official status. I've still got no weight to throw around, but at this point I'm after information, not an arrest."

"The coffee sieve's in the drawer."

Stuyvesant found the sieve he hadn't realized he was looking for, and set it over the first cup. "I arrived in London on April 1—which turned out to be appropriate, considering the fool's game I've been playing—and spent last week working my way through one office after another, but nobody'd heard of any bombs set in clever containers, and nobody wanted to listen to my ideas. Of course, I didn't exactly choose the best time for it, considering how every pencil pusher in the country has his eye on the Strike and nothing but the Strike." He hesitated with the coffee pot suspended over the cup to glance at Grey. "I assume you do know about the Strike?"

" 'Not a penny off the pay, not a second on the day.' The coal subsidy expires on the thirtieth, and the mine owners swear they will lock the workers out. Churchill's ministry want revenge for being forced to give way last summer, the miners demand a living wage at their present hours, the Bolsheviks threaten blood running in the streets, and the right-wing are maneuvering to outlaw the Left entirely. Both sides are dug in and obstinate, both sides hate the other. If all the Trades Unions go out as they're promising, there will be no trains; no buses; no coal dug, moved, or delivered; no newspapers; limited electricity; and only the most basic of foodstuffs. Do I have the gist of it?"

"That's the picture that I have," Stuyvesant agreed.

"The newspapers have tried to appear sanguine, but reading between the lines, and listening to the voices on the wireless, there is already considerable disruption."

The understatement startled a laugh out of Stuyvesant. "You ain't kidding, Jack. London feels like some fire-and-brimstone preacher's End of the World, like there's a volcano building under the city and everyone's tip-toeing around on the crust. Half the people think the Army will shove the miners back into their box at bayonet-point; the other half expect to see children starving on the streets and politicians dangling by their neckties from Westminster Bridge."

"It's been coming for years," Grey said. "When the government agreed to extend the coal subsidies in August, the press heaped fury on their heads. At this point, the two sides are implacable enemies: The working class wants to topple the governing class to its knees, while the ruling class wants nothing short of utter defeat and demoralization of the worker. The middle classes could go either way—one compelling act, or one repellent outrage, and the battle is won."

Stuyvesant shook his head. "And two weeks ago on the boat over I was thinking this Strike would be a tempest in a teacup, that I'd be in and out before the deadline came anywhere near. Instead, I've had to fight to see the assistants to the assistants, and even then they gave me distracted hums and haws and a cup of tea and here's your hat— I've drunk more tea in the last ten days than in the forty years before. When I stumbled across Carstairs on Friday and told my story for what seemed like the hundredth time, I'd begun to think maybe this idea of some international conspiracy was just a brain-wave and everyone was too damned polite to tell me I'd gone crackers."

He laid the sieve in the sink and looked around for an ice-box, finding instead a zinc-lined box with a jug of milk in it, which he took out, smelled for freshness, and put on the table.

"Now, I don't know what agency Carstairs is with, since he didn't exactly have a brass plate on his door, but it doesn't much matter because nobody in law enforcement or Intelligence ever wants to share information—and for sure with someone from another country. What, admit we got problems? No, sir, everything's just hunky-dory on *this* side of the Atlantic, thank you very much, and if you've got troubles, you can't blame us, now please go away.

"So with Carstairs, I went through my speech, like I said, for the umpteenth time and waited to be shown the door with that English politeness that's like a stiletto in a bouquet of roses, but he just looked at me with those black eyes of his, and then he said, 'I might know what you are looking for.' I nearly fell over backwards." The big man carried the two cups to the table, along with the sugar pot and a couple of (yes, silver) spoons. He sat down, spooned in the sugar, stirred, and sipped: almost cold, what with all the gabbing.

"'Course, even then nothing happened too fast. He sent me away, told me to meet him in Hyde Park the next morning, and seems to've spent the hours in between checking my *bona fides*. And the next day, instead of telling me what I'd asked about, he said he wanted me to meet a man who could tell gold from gilt at a touch. His words. Which was just about all he'd say, except that you might be a link in the chain, and he'd give me more details after I'd met you. Oh, and like I said, that you weren't a mind-reader."

Grey stirred milk into his cup and said thoughtfully, "Gold from gilt."

"Yeah. Frankly, I don't know what that's got to do with anything, although I imagine it would be a handy skill."

"Not a mind-reader," Grey said, still stuck on Carstairs' words. Stuyvesant couldn't tell if Grey was surprised because he would not have expected the judgment from Carstairs, or because he couldn't believe he was discussing the subject at all. Whichever it was, it seemed to help him make up his mind. "On the other hand..." he said, and stretched his arm across the table, palm up. "Let me have your cigarette case."

Obediently, the American took the slim silver object from his breast pocket and placed it on the callused palm. Fingers stained and rough with labor closed over it.

Not that hard use had made the hands clumsy. The fingers turned the object over and over twice, like a bar of wet soap, then worked the fastening at the bottom. The lid popped open, revealing the cigarettes, all but one of which were from a packet Stuyvesant had bought at the train station in London the day before. Grey ran the contents under his nose, then closed the cover. He flipped the case over and his work-thickened thumb-nail sought out the invisible, hair's-breadth seam along the back. Stuyvesant raised an eyebrow as the back of the case came open. Grey glanced at the folded white paper tucked within, then pinched the cover shut without touching the contents and laid the case on the table.

"A woman gave this to you, ten or twelve years ago. A short, blonde, intelligent young woman with a quirky sense of humor. You loved her. She died. The hidden compartment holds her photograph, although she didn't give it to you. You took the case to war with you, carrying it over your heart then as you do now. When you left New York you were in a hurry, and did not think to bring a supply of your favorite cigarettes. You have just a few left. You bought these others in London, probably at the train station.

"Shall I go on?"

Chapter Ten

STUYVESANT STARED at Grey, then picked up the glass he'd left in the middle of the table and took a swallow. This time he wheezed in reaction, a spasm that reached to his diaphragm, but did not cough. "How?"

"How do I know these things? I don't know how I know. I never do, although sometimes I can follow—" Grey stopped and tilted his head, listening to something Stuyvesant had not heard. He raised his voice, slipping into the dialect he had used earlier. "Robbie, pard, tha may's well come in, tha'll get a crick in thy neck listenin' loik that."

After a moment, a cloth cap appeared in the door's polished glass, followed by the tousled head, pale eyes, downy face of adolescence, and finally the red wool shoulders. The latch lifted and the simple lad came in, sidling up to Grey, picking at the loose threads of his jersey in a show of embarrassment.

"This is my neighbor, Robbie Trevalian," Grey told the American. "He likes to keep me safe. Robbie, say 'ello t' Mr. Stuyvesant."

The Cornishman kept his head lowered, but slid his eyes sideways to examine the guest. "Thet nahm's tew long," he complained.

"My other name's Harris," Stuyvesant told him. "How about using that?"

"Robbie, me 'ansum, Ah godda jawb fur thee," Grey told him.

The head came up, the translucent eyes gleamed with joy. "Wass tha'?"

Grey pulled out his pocket-watch and laid it on the table, opening the cover. "Thee sawr that other gennlemun, went off daun the lane?"

"Th' man in black?" Robbie's voice contained an oddly fastidious note of distaste.

"That's right. Ah told 'un ee cudden come back 'til four o'clock. Can thee show me where four o'clock is?"

Robbie bent over the instrument, face screwed in concentration. "Long 'and here, short 'and there."

"Tha's a beauty at clocks, all right. Naow, if ee starts to come up the lane afore that, you tell him Mr. Grey's not home to him until four. Can you do that?"

"Mr. Grey's not oam t'im unnil four," he parroted, hitting Grey's precise intonation.

Grey snapped shut the watch and held it out by the chain. The watch-dog carefully gathered it up and poured it into his capacious pocket, then tugged his cap brim at Stuyvesant and shot out the door, leaving it open to the chilly air. Grey rose to shut it, his balance only slightly compromised now.

"I take it that the kid doesn't give you a headache?" Stuyvesant asked in amusement.

"No. Or at least, not the same kind of headache. Simple people, small children, the very old, they're restful. I met a holy man once whose presence was so comforting I wanted to weep."

Stuyvesant retrieved his cigarette case, opened the lid, and offered Grey one. Grey shook his head, so Stuyvesant closed the lid and turned the silver object over in his own, considerably less hardened hands. "You were telling me how you know those things."

"I was telling you that I don't know how I know them," Grey corrected him.

Stuyvesant thought that was all he was going to get from Grey, but after a minute, the man seemed to come to a decision. He sat back and raised his chin as if meeting a challenge, and watched the impact his words had on his guest.

"I was injured during the War, in a way that stripped me of all barriers. Let's imagine you and I are walking down a city street. You hear noise, but only as a background to the conversation we're having; I walk beside you and hear what you're saying, but only as one element in a flood of sounds and sights and smells: the precise beat of a hundred shoes hitting the pavement, the rub of each moving part of the five combustion engines going past, the sourness of the milk on a doorstep that wasn't collected that morning, the tug of the breeze on a flag, a palimpsest of fifty conversations. I can tell you which shoe is loose on the rag-and-bone man's horse, whether the bricklayer on the next street is left- or right-handed, and which of the door-frames we are passing have wood rot."

He paused, studying the American's face. Whatever he saw there satisfied him, because he went on.

"You ask how I know these things. How would you explain to a race of blind people that there was a horse on a hillside half a mile away? How would you begin to describe your perception of the shape and color of the animal, the motion the legs make, its progress against the landscape? They would only know the horse if they could hear its hoof beats, smell its skin, touch its body.

"I see a man handling a delicate silver cigarette case whose engraving has been worn down by years of rubbing one thumb across it in a gesture of affection and loss. I see his initials engraved on the front, in a highly original and overly elaborate font, which could only be a visual joke. I see the signs of long, hard service, and a furrow carved along the back, where the shrapnel that hit the man's left face and shoulder cut into the silver. I see a faint, hidden seam in the back with a polished spot where it has been opened regularly. Inside I see a much-handled photograph, folded to fit the space, where a woman would have provided one trimmed to fit. I see a blonde hair pinned to the photograph. And I see a tough man with one vein of vulnerability running through his hard competence, a weakness for weakness. You're the kind of man who would without a thought risk his life to rescue a kitten from a drain, and as instantly and without second thought, thrash half to death the man who threw it there. When you were young, you could only have fallen in love with a small, blonde woman."

Stuyvesant's face was without expression, then he gave a little grimace and said, "You're wrong there, I've always been a man for leggy redheads. But you're right about the cigarettes. How'd you know I didn't bring them from home?"

Grey gave him a curious look, amusement and outrage. "Only one in that case is American, and you finger it longingly before settling for the local brand. The others are permeated with the stink of London, not the salt air of Cornwall. And she was blonde."

"She was not." But Stuyvesant was beginning to see why an Intelligence man like Carstairs might be interested in a Cornish hermit.

"And before you begin to wonder how you might train someone to perceive things as I do, I should tell you that the continual scraping of the world against raw nerve is a fine means of driving a man mad. One need only look at the scar on the Major's face as proof."

"That was your doing?" Stuyvesant was surprised to hear a trace of admiration in his voice, and jerked at his own leash: Carstairs was the ally he needed, not this man.

"You might call it my letter of resignation from his little project."

"What project was that?" Grey gave no sign of having heard the question, but Stuyvesant persisted. "Is that what Carstairs is after, a program to teach people your . . . skills?"

The green eyes flashed in a sudden pulse of irritation. "Who the hell knows what Major bloody Carstairs has in that devious mind of his? Ah, Jesus," he said, standing up so fast the chair crashed over. "This place just stinks of the bastard. I can't hear myself think. I must have some air before the rain starts."

Weaving slightly, Grey stumbled out of the kitchen, leaving the door open to a spring day with not a cloud in sight.

Stuyvesant downed the last of his cold coffee, and picked up his silver case from the table. His broad thumb soothed the letters of his name, letters Helen had designed herself for the purpose (her giggle, as she told him of the engraver's disapproval), then moved around to pop open the hidden back of the case. He looked down at the folded photograph, but he did not take it out, just snapped the cover shut again and slid it back into the breast pocket of his shirt, over his heart.

He shrugged into his jacket and went after his host.

Chapter Eleven

ON THE PENZANCE ROAD, nearly a mile away, Aldous Carstairs leaned into a gap in the hedgerow, aiming a set of small but powerful field-glasses at the white cottage. This was the only spot on the entire road where the building could be seen; he had known of it long before his hired car had left Penzance that morning.

Five years ago, Grey had gone to ground in that cottage, leaving Carstairs with his plans shredded, his future bleak, and his body shaken. But Grey's betrayal had taught Carstairs an invaluable lesson: Beware eagerness.

Five years ago, Carstairs had been forced into a rapid re-evaluation and drastic change of plans; Captain Bennett Grey had receded into a persistent but distant presence on the horizon.

Not that Carstairs had ever taken his eyes entirely off Grey. He had all but memorized the Ordnance Survey maps for this part of Cornwall, knew the names and susceptibilities of every local official, constable to postmistress. Every two months, one of Carstairs' men passed through, selling pots and pans and making gossipy conversation about, among other topics, the blond hermit on the hill: Carstairs studied his agent's reports and photographs with care. He knew Grey's contacts, had known of Grey's first, tentative ventures into the nearby towns, and had agonized over the balance between surveillance and discretion: It was damned difficult to watch a man in open countryside like this—no doubt the reason Grey chose it. And it had proved even harder to lay hands on a local farmer willing to sell information on his likable, boyish, war hero of a neighbor.

For five years, Bennett Grey had rusticated down here while in London, Aldous Carstairs worked to shape a new vision—one that could incorporate Grey at some future time, but was not dependent on him. He discovered that, with Grey set to the side, he was free to focus without distraction on his renewed vision, striving to build a thing that would hold through the storms of uncontrollable events. He laboriously cemented relationships, created rock-solid foundations, and sought out others who could share his idea of the future.

With each passing year, his creation became clearer, more attainable, more necessary. Inevitable, even—Carstairs had begun to feel as if the nation's every event and decision was feeding directly into his needs. All was balanced, perfect, necessary. And all was scheduled to reach its pinnacle inside the next three weeks.

Then came Friday afternoon, when an unkempt, ill-mannered American lout dropped out of the heavens to offer Carstairs, not only his first real access to Grey in all those years, but an expansion of what he had envisioned as an afterthought into something considerably closer to the center of things.

It was like a light going on in a room one hadn't realized was dim, or rain on one of those mythic desert creatures that fold up through years of drought.

However, Carstairs had learned his lesson well. So he had said nothing, although he'd wanted to shout aloud in astonishment. He had sent the lout away, had spent the night exploring the implications and sending out his feelers. Only at the end of that had he decided to trust his original impulse, and come to Cornwall.

In the two days since, he had seen nothing to make him doubt his decision. He still was far from understanding where this development would lead him, but the tantalizing awareness that things had changed because of the American's request, that wheels were grinding into motion in unexpected ways, filled him with a mix of equal parts exhilaration and terror.

Exhilaration because he could suddenly see that, with Grey, so much became possible—one glance at those green eyes today and he'd shivered with the thrill of knowing that time had not cured Grey of his singular talents. Terror because he knew that what he was building was at the moment agonizingly precarious. At a certain point in its construction, even the grandest cathedral was vulnerable to a minor tremor: One clumsy nudge could send the future tumbling. And if the American threatened to provide that nudge, well, Carstairs needed to be on hand, to remove him before he could do any damage.

Nineteen days from now the coal mines would slam shut; the last thing he'd needed was to break off for a diversion into the reeking, pig-clotted reaches of the Empire. Plus, the other message in those green eyes—that Bennett Grey loathed him as much as ever—told him that even with this opening, winning Grey's cooperation was going to be delicate work indeed. True, the conquest would be all the more satisfying for its difficulty: He'd always found the challenge of Grey . . . invigorating.

If *only* that American idiot had bumbled in a few weeks earlier!

Ah well, mustn't be greedy. The nearness of the deadlines might necessitate a touch more brutality, might mean treading a larger number of people into the dust—for one thing, that American might need putting in place—but as always, one had to keep the end in mind, not the process.

As they said, birth was a messy business.

Or as the great Niccolò put it: *Non è cosa più difficile a trattare che farsi capo introdurre nuovi ordini.* There is nothing more difficult to bring about than introducing a new order.

And really, adding Grey's talents to the wave of momentum he could feel building beneath him, could bring Carstairs in serious danger of being carried through the very doors of Downing Street.

Which would never do.

He would set the delicate mechanism of this country back on the right path—he, Aldous Carstairs, would do so—but he'd be damned if he would do it in the glare of public life. Leave that to the Medicis of the world.

At last, a figure appeared in his lenses: Bennett Grey came out from the back of the rustic structure to limp furiously up the hill.

That leg was still bothering him, it seemed: He should have let the Project surgeons have another go at it.

The leg, the stomach wound, the chunk knocked out of the shoulder, the stubborn infection on the side of his head—after all these years, Carstairs could still list the precise details of Grey's scars, outward signs of the man's inner transformation. I wonder if the last pieces of grit ever worked their way out of Grey's scalp? he mused. That scalp, now hidden beneath thick blond hair, had been freshly shaved when Carstairs first laid eyes on Grey; the naked, pale skin had given Grey a childlike look that contrasted deliciously with the sullenness in his green eyes.

Carstairs followed the small blond man's progress around those ridiculous antiquarian hillocks. No doubt he was making for the hilltop where the reports said he was wont to sit by the hour, staring off to sea, invisible from this patch of—

Suddenly Grey's foot slipped and nearly brought him to grief; Carstairs caught his breath, but Grey's hand shot out in time, and he pulled himself upright.

Idiotic boy, Carstairs thought in exasperation. What if he'd fallen and cracked his head, what would become of all that precious potential then? I ought to have him taken into custody for his own protection.

And here came the yokel, plodding along in the rear, too far from Grey to be of any help, planting his great Yankee clodhopper boots deep into Grey's Cornish soil. Carstairs shifted the glasses in time to see Grey disappear over the rise, then lowered them again to follow Stuyvesant. The American stopped from time to time, gawping like a tourist in Trafalgar Square; once he turned around and appeared to look straight at Carstairs, but the watcher did not move, and the gap was narrow, the lenses shaded; after a moment, the man turned and continued on his way.

When Stuyvesant, too, had gone over the rise into invisibility, Carstairs pulled away from the bushes, making a face when a hawthorn caught at his sleeve and snagged a thread loose. He extricated his sleeve, then slid the binoculars into his overcoat pocket and took out his note-book, to write a few words. He capped his pen with a flourish and put the leather journal away, satisfied that all had gone more or less as anticipated.

Although, he reflected, he hadn't anticipated being banished by Grey into this primitive wasteland, given over to the slender mercies of the Celtic peasant. He scowled at the standing stone in the field before him. Enormous effort had gone into bringing that rock here, time and sweat and danger to prop it upright, and for what? Here it stood, covered with multicolored blotches of lichen that looked like a skin disease, tipped like a drunk in the direction of the sea, girdled by a black ring where it had served as scratching-post for three millennia of scrofulous cattle.

But as he tugged on his gloves, he studied the standing stone, and wondered if it might not be a parable. The message of the stone standing in the field was not the absurdity of the labor, but the fact that once the props, ropes, and sweat were cleared away and forgotten, what remained seemed magical.

As once the props, the chaos, and the behind-the-scenes manipulation were cleared away, the British people would look at their new world, and see merely the magic of its rightness.

Aldous Carstairs glanced at his wrist-watch, his expression rueful. How on earth was the Machiavelli of the new age expected to pass four hours in this place without being driven to murder?

Chapter Twelve

STUYVESANT TRAILED Grey at a distance, letting the man work off the alcohol-fueled anger, watching the small figure stump through the lumpy pasture that he had called a Phoenician village. It was the knee that caused Grey's uneven gait, Stuyvesant saw—that and the drink: He used his right leg to climb, drawing the left up behind it. Probably the same war injury that had blown him to pieces and—if Carstairs wasn't just feeding him a line of crap, if Grey's business with the cigarette case hadn't been some kind of stunt—had left the officer some pretty strange talents.

Grey wove a path among the hummocks and walls that lay half hidden beneath centuries of grass and ivy, ferns and bramble, hawthorn and gorse. Twice he clambered over waist-high remains of walls, where the grass showed evidence of regular passage; once he nearly fell; another time he paused to shed his jacket. The buried village ended, but Grey kept on, over a rickety stile and along a sheep-worn path to the top of the hill, where an enormous stone slab protruded from the turf. He climbed onto it and turned his back to Cornwall while he rolled up his shirt-sleeves, then abruptly vanished; Stuyvesant hoped that merely meant that he had sat down.

Stuyvesant took his time, pausing to examine the exposed

stonework, turning occasionally to admire the view. Twice he found himself kneading the back of his neck, as if the hairs there felt some distant marksman settling his sights on an out-of-place Bureau agent, but he could see nothing, and told himself that it was just a memory spilling over from that earlier trench sensation. Much as he had disliked having Carstairs so close, he was finding it equally uncomfortable not knowing where the man was.

But he told himself not to be childish: If Carstairs wanted him dead, he wouldn't have had to travel to Cornwall to do it.

Still, the back of his neck was not much interested in logic, and subsided only when he cleared the ridge and the countryside was temporarily out of sight.

The stone slab was on the very crest of the hill, surrounded by a nest of brambles and gorse. Between the thickness of the thing and the rise it sat on, he could not see Grey at all. It had to have been put here, Stuyvesant supposed—one of those massive and mystifying prehistoric structures, Stonehenge's little cousins, that he'd seen standing, singly or in groups, across the face of Cornwall. Tombs or temples or something. Sacrificial altars for the local druids.

In any case, this was not just a piece of bedrock from which the soil had eroded; its presence was artificial, although it must have weighed tons: There was room for three or four men to stretch out on top.

As Grey was stretched out, sprawled with the abandon of a sleeping boy, head resting on his folded jacket, face raised to the sun. Feeling oddly middle-aged, forced to use the rough footholds as a ladder where Grey had gone up them as a stairway, Stuyvesant scrambled onto the high surface. Once there, he brushed off his hands and stepped to the end of the rock—only to shy suddenly back, startled by the precipitous drop at his feet. The brambles had hidden how close the rock was to the cliff's edge: One kick from Grey's boot and he'd have been airborne.

He glanced involuntarily down at the small man. Despite his shut eyes, Grey's mouth now had a distinct curve, as if he'd felt his companion's abrupt movement, known the reason, and found it amusing. Disconcerted, Stuyvesant retreated to the far side of the deliciously warm stone and settled with his feet pointing towards the mainland: No Bureau agent worth his salt would sit with his back exposed, but the nerve-endings along his spine reassured him that the drop to the sea was as good as a wall. He laid his coat to one side and thumbed open the buttons to his waistcoat, leaning back on braced arms and crossing his outstretched legs at the ankles. His upper foot beat a rhythm in the air until he noticed it, and stopped.

At first, his mind circled furiously around the problem of Bennett Grey: Who was he, why had Stuyvesant been brought to him, how could he use the man to get at The Bastard? But after a few minutes, a bird passing high overhead distracted him from purposeful thoughts, and he couldn't help noticing how sweet the air was, and how the sky was an endless arc of blue with a smatter of decorative clouds out to the west. When he glanced over his shoulder, he saw that the outstretched water, far from being huge and empty, supported a surprising number of boats, both near the shore and out to the horizon.

Harris Stuyvesant filled his lungs, and eased the breath out. No offices here, no bureaucrats shoving cups of tea at him, no muscular toughs in cloth caps jamming their leaflets in his face, demanding that he admit the iniquities of mine owners. No knots of tension, no sudden wariness on seeing a handful of men coming down the sidewalk at him. No sidewalks, for that matter. No parcels or carts that could hide a bomb—that sudden flash: shattering glass, torn bodies.

He took another slow breath, and felt peace slip over him like a glove. He wanted to lie down next to Grey and take a nap.

Instead, he sat upright and patted his pockets for the cigarette case, keeping his eyes on the countryside. He could now see that the ruined foundations of the field below formed three clusters of rough joined circles, marks from a prehistoric giant's bubble pipe.

"Nice view."

"The Beacon, they call it."

Stuyvesant glanced over his shoulder at the cliff's edge, but could see no indication of a structure. "An early light-house that fell into the water?"

"More like an enormous pile of firewood. In 1588."

"Fifteen...? Ah, the Armada."

"Possibly the first beacon lit, on July 19. And very probably by an inhabitant of my cottage."

"You'd think they'd at least have carved the date over the door. I mean, there's history and there's *History*."

"Just another day, fending off the Spanish threat."

"And is that really a Phoenician village?"

"The men from the land of purple," Grey said, his voice going dreamy. "A nation of sailors who plied the seas from Alexandria to the gates of Gibraltar and beyond, their ships mighty with sail and oar, who traveled at night by the pole star. A trading people, the Phoenicians, peace-loving for the most part, who nonetheless held off a siege of Nebuchadnezzar for thirteen years. All in all, not a bad paradigm for a sea-going people.

"However, no," he added, his voice coming down to earth. "I shouldn't think that is a Phoenician village. Although it was no doubt some kind of settlement, round houses with a wide rampart either to keep in cattle or for defense, take your pick. This is the land of the Celt, Mr. Stuyvesant, who brought their Trevethy and their Tregonning, their Penwith and Penhallam, their stone circles and standing rows, their barrows and cairns.

"But I enjoy the idea of Phoenicians trading along the English coastline, carrying alluvial tin from Cornwall to far-off Tyre and Sidon and Rome. Certainly their ships traveled the coasts of Spain and France, and the Channel is narrow; what would be more natural than to venture across on a summer's day and find the Celts of Brittany here, too, raising their standing stones, worshipping their mid-winter gods, speaking their melodious tongue that survived Rome and the Anglo Saxons and is only now dying out? When I sit up here on the Beacon in the moonlight, out of the corner of my eye I can see their sails rising through the mist, hear the creak and splash of their ranked oars, watch their swarthy faces greeting Robbie's forefathers, smell the cook-fires as they set up on the shore."

It was hypnotic, Grey's vision unfolding behind Stuyvesant's eyes, until he, too, could picture the sails that had rotted into dust twenty centuries before, hear the voices speaking a tongue dead nearly as long. "There was an archaeologist from Cambridge," Grey went on, "two or three summers ago, who was digging up a site a bit like it on the other side of St. Just. He showed up here one day and wanted to poke about—you can see, if you look carefully, the lines of a hill fort atop that last rise. But the Celts were an odd people, at home with the Other World, and it does not seem right to throw the cold light of science onto their magical constructions. So I told him he could argue with the next owner about it after I was dead."

Silence fell, natural as breath. Stuyvesant blinked, and realized that he still had the silver case in his hand, his thumb traveling back and forth over the engraving on the front, his fingers aware of the shrapnel gouge on the back. He clicked it open and allowed his fingers to meditate over the cigarettes, automatically bypassing the solitary American citizen; then he caught himself, and pulled that one out and placed it between his lips. He turned to extend the case to Grey, and was struck by the man's face: skin gone rosy with warmth, with a faint sheen of sweat, head back and mouth half open to suck in the sea air. The man's every pore was slack with pleasure as he reveled in the sensation of lying on a warm rock in the sun on a cool spring day.

Then Stuyvesant's perception shifted, and he realized it was not just pleasure he was seeing, but something close to ecstasy. Grey looked like a man having sex.

Startled, the American turned away sharply to dig around for his lighter. As the breeze cleared the smoke from his face, he noticed a spot of red far below: Robbie, perched like a gargoyle atop the wall, guarding the way to his hero's abode.

He glanced sideways again at the rapturous expression of his companion, and said, "You must feel like God, up here on a day like this."

"There aren't all that many days like this," Grey murmured.

"Is the view the reason you moved to Cornwall? Your voice doesn't sound like you were born and raised here."

"Cornwall is a refuge for me, not a birthplace. I came here because I started walking, and here was where I ran out of ground. I stayed because I can see the enemy coming, with enough warning for me to take a running leap into the sea if I want." Grey's voice was light, but Stuyvesant did not think he was altogether joking. Then again, Grey had seen Carstairs coming: Did he have other enemies? Or had he simply not wanted to take his running leap?

"Tell me, Captain Grey, if you sometimes find people physically unbearable, do you find Nature as powerful a sensation in the opposite direction?"

Grey let his head flop sideways towards his interrogator; one eyelid opened to reveal a slit of green. "Now, there is one question that would never even occur to the Major. Or, I venture to say, to most of the agents in your Bureau of Investigation. Which I suppose is why I agreed to talk to you." It also appeared to be a question Grey did not intend to answer. He spotted the silver case and the lighter sitting on top of the American's folded tweed coat, and to Stuyvesant's relief, half raised himself out of his sprawl to reach for the case.

"Do you know—" Stuyvesant stopped, then gave a brief, embarrassed laugh and continued. "This is going to sound pretty stupid, but do *you* know just who Aldous Carstairs is? In the government, I mean. I came across him in a sort of roundabout way and like I said, I never got around to asking his position."

"I doubt that he'd have told you if you asked. The Major I knew envisioned himself as a secular *éminence grise*. He taught himself to read Italian so he could quote Machiavelli, with an atrocious accent I might add. I shouldn't be surprised if his position doesn't actually exist. I should think all governments have people like him—the man behind the scenes, the man who takes care of things when prominent people can't afford to dirty their hands. The man no one acknowledges, and everyone uses. If you're fortunate, he's happy to live in his dark hole, like a cockroach beneath the floorboards. If you're not, he takes you over."

"He's not with Intelligence, then?"

"He was, but by now he could be anything. You'd probably find the Major is his own show, no matter what the paperwork says." Grey got his cigarette going and lay back, one ankle propped across the other upraised knee.

"He called it the Truth Project," he told Stuyvesant without preface. "A civilian project intended to explore quick, humane alternatives to traditional slow, ineffective, and often brutal interrogation techniques, although I always got the impression that the Project itself was just one part of some larger intent." Before Stuyvesant could decide how to respond, Grey went on. "You may as well tell me about my sister."

"I don't know your sister."

"You will, if the Major has anything to say in the matter. You'll like her."

"Why, is she blonde and needing protection?"

Grey laughed, a surprisingly free and unencumbered sound. "Blonde, yes, although she's grown out of her kitten phase. Come to think of it, you're probably finding kittens a bit tiresome yourself. Ten years ago, you'd have groveled at Sarah's feet. What is she involved in, that she's attracted the Major's attention?"

Stuyvesant squinted at the crazy quilt of fields below, trying to rein in his irritation. Back at the house, Grey had called him tough, and he was—but he knew his toughness was also a mask, in daily life as much as in working undercover. Not many would have guessed that Harris Stuyvesant, big, hard, humorless Fed, could easily lose half a day in an art museum, or that about one time in ten, a night at the opera brought tears to his eyes. It was extremely disconcerting to think that this man could so readily trace the softness in him.

"Yeah, well," he said, "I'll do my best not to ravage the girl. I don't know exactly what she's involved with—like I said, Aldous Carstairs isn't the most generous font of information. But when I gave him the name of the man I'm after, Carstairs happened to know that your sister has been seen in his company recently. And before Big Brother Grey asks: no, it doesn't look like your sister and my man are linked directly. It's more that they have a friend in common, a young woman by the name of Laura Hurleigh."

Chapter Thirteen

GREY'S RIGHT HAND, carrying the cigarette to his mouth, hesitated for an instant before completing its arc. "Laura Hurleigh. Yes, I know that my sister works with her. I knew the Hurleighs myself, a long time ago."

"The whole world knows the Hurleighs." Even in the States it was a rare month that didn't see some exploit of one Hurleigh or another written up for the amusement of the masses. After Carstairs told him the young woman's name on Saturday, Stuyvesant had gone to the reading room to bone up on *Debrett's* and *Burke's* guides to the peers, and to leaf through back issues of the *Times* and the *Illustrated London News*. But even before that research, he'd known of the Hurleighs: blood bluer than that of the current residents of Buckingham Palace; a history stretching back to the Magna Carta; related to half the titles in the realm; with a country house in Gloucestershire, a much-photographed house in London, a Scottish hunting lodge, and an innate knack for quirky and occasionally bizarre behavior.

Debrett's history of the family began with 1215, when a Hurleigh ancestor had been among the barons forcing concessions from a king at Runnymede, and went on to recount a story concerning a seventeenth-century Hurleigh, a chicken, and the Queen. *Burke's* more laconically recited battles won by Hurleighs over three centuries—Stuyvesant got the impression that the Hurleigh decorations would fill the back of a good-sized delivery van—culminating with the heroic death in France of this generation's eldest son, Thomas, and a minor *coup de guerre* in the 1916 Palestine campaign by the current Hurleigh heir, Daniel, shortly after his twenty-second birthday.

On the non-military fields of battle, the current generation looked to live up to the iconoclastic strain in the family line: One Hurleigh sister wrote a wildly successful gossip column for one of the afternoon newspapers, breathless and daring and regularly skirting the edge of actionable; another was an outspoken advocate of nudism, with a preference for conducting interviews in her chosen state. The current, eleventh, Duke, whose given names were Godlake Reginald Gryffin Herbert Noah, held a string of titles (some of which were so obscure their origins had cobwebs, such as Holder of the Pen to the Prince of Wales). He had been a close personal friend and informal advisor to three monarchs and seven of the last ten prime ministers, and was known for his extensive collection of Staffordshire porcelain dogs, his expertise in Roman Britain, and his picturesque habit of running intruders off his land with a pack of hounds—rumor had it there was an annual cup for pranksters from nearby Oxford, given to the first team to plant their college flag on the Hurleigh doorstep during something called Eights Week. The family did have a few quiet and hard-working members, some of whom went so far as to generate income, but those dull and responsible Hurleighs were for the most part overlooked by the press.

"That is true. But I mean to say, I knew them to stay with—they're distant cousins through our mothers—our grandmothers used to ride with the same hunts. I used to meet Thomas and Laura at children's parties and such, and I spent two or three long vacs at Hurleigh House, beginning when I was maybe twelve. I was between Thomas and Daniel in age."

That Bennett Grey had grown up alongside the Hurleighs confirmed Stuyvesant's suspicions of the man's class. Even in the relatively egalitarian U.S. of A., the rich tended to live in each other's pockets; in England, he thought, it was unlikely that children of the aristocracy would be permitted to mingle with those too far below them in rank. Grey might be chopping his own firewood now, but Stuyvesant would lay money that he'd started out in a house considerably grander than the stone cottage below.

"What is Laura doing with your agitator?" Grey asked.

"Didn't you know? All the best upper-class girls have to collect a few revolutionaries before they settle down to a good marriage and good works."

Grey sat up, tucking his heels under him. "Is this confirmed, or a tabloid rumor?"

"Twice in the past year, Lady Laura traveled to the States on the same ship as my agitator."

There was a moment of silence, as Grey thought about this. "A commoner?"

"One grandfather was knighted, the other was a stone mason, son of a coal miner."

"I can imagine what the Duchess had to say about the liaison."

"I don't suppose Lady Laura's parents care for it any more than an untitled family would. But apparently she has an independent income from a granny who died, which gives her a fair bit of leeway when it comes to thumbing her nose at Daddy." This tidbit of gossip was thanks to one of the scandal sheets, disapproving of Lady Laura's unseemly dedication to the great unwashed of the East End through her free medical clinics.

"The Laura I knew would never thumb her nose at her father unless there was a purpose for doing so. Laura has always been a brilliant natural strategist—she'd be far more likely to pat the Duke's graying head, sit down with him, and in five minutes flat have him believing the whole thing was his idea. And I've seen Laura get around the Duchess, as well, a claim few can make. So, which of Laura's crazes had got my sister into trouble? The clinics or the politics?"

"I'd say the politics." It would seem that Grey kept up with his sister's interests, despite Carstairs' claim that the siblings saw each other sporadically. "Although I don't know that she's in any trouble, exactly."

"The Major thinks she is. How do you tie in?"

"Okay, it's like this. Because the man I'm after has been very good at covering his trail, as far as my bosses are concerned he's no

more than a suspect. I came here for two reasons: One, to see if he's
been doing the same things here that nobody's been talking about,
and two, to find out about him. He doesn't have a record here, other
than small stuff, so I plan to work my way into his circle and take a
look from the inside. It's what I do best—in my job, we call it going
undercover. Basically I follow my nose and see what I can unearth."

"And in the course of your information-gathering, you met the
Major, and he suggested you might use me to make contact with
Sarah, and from her to your man?"

This was no turnip-head farmer, that was for sure. "In my experience, the only sure way into any radical group is by personal introduction. If I were just to walk in off the street, it would take me
months to earn as much trust as I could get if someone on the inside
vouched for me."

"My sister being the one you want to vouch for you." Grey's
voice had gone cool.

"I'd be undercover—he'll probably never know who I am,"
Stuyvesant protested, but it sounded weak even to his own ears.

"Unless you arrest him in America, and have to testify in court."

"Well, I wouldn't—"

"Stuyvesant, for God's sake!"

Stuyvesant scratched at the bristle on his chin, casting around for
some way out of this, but in the end, he had to shake his head. "Yeah,
damn it, you're right, it's a lousy idea." And it was—Stuyvesant wouldn't
have put up with trying to use one of his sisters like this, either. God damn
Carstairs. "And I don't know how much good it would do, anyway—
sounds to me like your sister spends most of her time at the clinics, and I
don't imagine she has a lot of time to spare for my man's kind of politics.
No, it's a pretty thin connection altogether, I'd say.

"Tell you the truth," he muttered in disgust, "I haven't a clue why
Carstairs bothered dragging me out here."

"He brought you here in order to follow in your shadow—you
offered him an opportunity, however thin, to approach me." Grey
saw Stuyvesant's puzzled expression, and his mouth curled in what
might have been a smile, or a grimace of pain. "The Major's been circling around me like a jilted lover for five years, since I left his precious research project in shambles and came to Cornwall."

"Five years?" Stuyvesant said, trying not to sound too dubious. "The man must have the patience of a tick. You have ticks in this country?"

"Waiting for the approach of warm blood. They watch me, you know—his men do; they question my neighbors. Twice they've broken in and gone through my possessions."

Stuyvesant smoked for a minute, considering. On the one hand, Grey's suspicions sounded like what the head-shrinkers would call *paranoia,* where enemies lurk in every corner. On the other hand, there'd been Carstairs' odd jolt of reaction.

"You know," he said finally, "when I met Carstairs on Friday and brought up Bunsen's name, I thought at the time it was funny how fast he made the jump from Bunsen to Laura Hurleigh to your sister. Almost like he'd been waiting, like you say, for some kind of opportunity. I'm truly sorry, Captain Grey. My questions seem to have dropped you in the soup."

Grey seemed interested neither in the declaration of guilt, nor the apology. "Bunsen?"

"Like the burner."

"This is the Bunsen who—"

"Yeah," Stuyvesant interrupted, "it's *that* Richard Bunsen: decorated soldier, Labour Party golden boy, working-man's friend. And you can just leave out the Scarlet Pimpernel remarks, I've heard 'em all."

"I can imagine you have." He sounded bemused, as if his thoughts had gone somewhere else.

"My sister has mentioned Richard Bunsen, in her letters. She says I met him when we were children, although I don't remember doing so. I know the family remotely—there was a Bunsen a year behind me at Oxford. A brother, maybe? No, more like a cousin." He still sounded distracted.

Stuyvesant had been right to think they were living in each other's pockets—although Bunsen's foothold as far up as Grey's social class might be a little shaky. Stuyvesant wondered if Aldous Carstairs might not actually have had a point in bringing him here: If in the U.S. it made sense to work the personal contacts in getting close to someone, here in Britain the network of relationships was probably ten times as strong. And what if Carstairs did have a—what did they call it?—a fixation on Grey? It didn't necessarily mean that all his suggestions should be rejected out of hand. Sure, only some pretty strong personal interest would explain why Carstairs was willing to spend two days coming to see Grey, but that didn't mean that what he wanted didn't go hand in hand with Stuyvesant's needs.

And conversely, assuming Carstairs was being genuinely helpful, maybe Stuyvesant should in turn try to smooth Carstairs' way with Grey a little, as he'd sort of agreed to do.

"In any case, I have to tell you, there's a real possibility that, Scarlet Pimpernel or no, Richard Bunsen is headed for a world of trouble. And if your sister's in the vicinity when the wall falls on him, she could end up getting caught up in it. If you don't want to see your sister in prison—"

"Don't," Grey said sharply.

"It's true, I'm afraid," Stuyvesant told him. "That sort of arrest— up-and-coming politician, ancient family—the smaller fish like your sister will—"

"Stop it!" The American looked over at his companion, and was surprised to see his face twisted with pain. "If you cannot bring your-self to talk straight, I'm going to walk away, and my sister will just have to take her chances."

Talk straight? After a minute, Stuyvesant shook his head. He'd been so set on selling the Bunsen connection he hadn't realized that he was constructing a straw man around Sarah Grey for her brother to follow. Stuyvesant prided himself on his ability to manipulate, and sometimes found himself doing it even when there was no need to bully or cajole. Here, clearly, that approach would not work. "Okay. But seriously? If Richard Bunsen is who I think he is, he constitutes a grave threat, to the United States, and to Britain."

"Fine, he's a dangerous man. But you don't need my assistance to line him up in your sights and kill him."

Chapter Fourteen

"WHOA," SAID STUYVESANT, "back up there a minute. I'm not looking to kill anyone."

"Mr. Stuyvesant, who do you think you're talking to—Robbie? Of course you intend to kill him. I can see it in the set of your shoulders, the edge in your voice when you say his name, the twitch in your fingers. Lie to the Major, lie to yourself if you want, but you can't lie to me, not about a thing like that."

"Look, that's frustration you're seeing, not some kind of plan. Okay, I'm not saying that the possibility of . . . taking a short-cut to justice hasn't crossed my mind, but that's just a story I tell myself to keep me going. What I want is to see The Bastard in an American jail."

"Not hanged?"

"I wouldn't mind that. But I'm not going to act as executioner." Not unless I have to.

"If you say so."

Stuyvesant wasn't sure the man believed him, but he'd said his piece. "Er, can I ask you something?"

"Go ahead."

"Am I right in thinking that the idea wouldn't bother you all that much?"

"Mr. Stuyvesant, I enlisted the week I came down from Oxford, in July 1915. I spent the next three years on the Western Front, pushing one man after another over the parapets to his death. If I'd ever had Ludendorff sitting in front of me, I'd have happily sliced his throat in cold blood on the chance it would shorten the war by a single day. So no: If you prove Bunsen's been committing acts of terror, your killing him wouldn't disturb my sleep."

The trench sensation that had touched Stuyvesant earlier returned: The open country seemed to shimmer behind sandbag walls, the sea air bore a whiff of rotting meat, and he could feel his face muscles sag with chronic exhaustion and shell shock. Looking into Grey's eyes, he saw the same awareness.

Grey blinked first, and the trenches retreated, then flickered out. Stuyvesant turned away, and noticed that the hand lifting the cigarette to his face had a tremble in it. In annoyance, he flicked the remains into the air, remembering too late the two good draws left on one of his prized American imports.

"In any case," Grey said, "I don't know the man myself, and I do not care to set up my sister like that. And if you imagine that the fact I went to university with his cousin qualifies me to write a letter of introduction to Bunsen, you are sadly out of date."

Grey's scorn grated against Stuyvesant's irritation. "Oh, for Christ sake. Okay, so Carstairs has you on his brain and dragged me here to chase a wild goose, but I couldn't very well know that before I left London, could I? When he comes back, I'll help him get that poor abused car down your godforsaken road so you can go back to chopping your kindling. There's other ways to get at Bunsen without bringing your sister into it."

Stuyvesant frowned at the red smudge in the distance, but after a minute, he couldn't help sneaking a glance at his companion. Grey had stretched out again and was propped back on his elbows, looking at the endless sea. He'd come away without his hat; in the warmth, his unruly blond hair had begun to curl, and the hair on his tanned forearms glistened like gold. Despite Stuyvesant's words, the man's brow remained unfurrowed, the hands relaxed. Then again, Stuyvesant had meant what he said, at least in part.

He began to see why Carstairs might want Grey so badly: A man could get used to having that barometer of truth close at hand.

If he could overlook the fact that the barometer's needle moved to a stimulus of pain.

"So how does it work, this . . . ability of yours?" he asked. "You just pick up small giveaways?" Like a poker player, or any of a hundred varieties of con man.

He thought Grey was not going to answer, but after a while the Englishman sat up and crossed his legs. "I suppose it comes down to that, but in fact there's really no vocabulary for talking about it."

"Explaining sight to a blind man?"

"Or music to the deaf. Analogies are the closest way to describe it—some behaviors give off color. Seeing someone's agitation makes my skin crawl."

"Or Aldous Carstairs makes your yard stink so badly you can't hear yourself think."

"Mixed metaphors of perception," Grey admitted. "It makes no sense, except to me it contains perfect logic. When Robbie's mother gets angry it makes my teeth ache. Possibly because she doesn't let her anger out, just chews on it? I don't know."

"So it's, what, the turmoil that you feel?"

"*Dissonance* might be a closer description. I came across a fake Rembrandt portrait a while ago; standing in front of it was like being assaulted by the clamor of a dozen mismatched bells, out of tune and very disturbing. Dissonance seems . . . well, call it the vehicle on which other sensations ride." He sounded unsure of his words, almost tentative; Stuyvesant wondered if he had ever talked about this before, apart from whatever the people of Carstairs' "Project" had got out of him.

"And if Robbie's mother just got mad and swore and slammed the pans around? Is that 'dissonance'?"

"Mr. Stuyvesant, this is precisely what the Major could never understand—either that or refused to accept. The answer is no: If she got honestly angry, I'd feel the anger, but my teeth wouldn't ache. It's like . . . how to put this? A con artist makes my skin crawl because he's torn between what he wants and what he thinks I want. He's afraid of missing some clue in my behavior that will tell him how to clinch the deal, he's charming on the surface and greedy underneath, and that dichotomy is...dissonant. Physically disturbing. Like a rolling barrage, you know?" Stuyvesant knew: a long stretch of standing under firing guns left a man with liquid bones and severe twitches in every muscle. "But if he's a monomaniac, with what they call an *idée fixe,* if he is deluded down to his bones and has sincerely convinced himself of the truth of every lie that comes out of his mouth, all I feel is a sort of queasy mistrust."

"So you couldn't, say, walk through a crowd and know which man in it is contemplating murder?"

"If the intent was tied up in rage and fear and hesitation and uncertainty, then yes, the man's turmoil would shout at me. Just as I would know the man who was, quietly and in the back of his mind, nurturing the real intent of murder and had not yet acknowledged it to himself. Or am I wrong about that, too?" he asked.

Stuyvesant held his face completely still, to give nothing away, but Grey looked amused by the attempt.

"She wasn't a redhead, was she?"

"You can't be right all the time."

"I wish you could convince the Major of that. But to get back to killing. I think that if a man were to hold a coming murder in the front of his mind as a given fact, absolute and unquestioning; if the intent and the sense of necessity and inevitability reached all the way down to his deepest sense of himself, then no, there would be nothing to tear at him and make his body react. The most evil creature on earth, the devil incarnate, would probably slip right past me, assuming he truly believed that what he was doing was the right thing. His body and his mind would be easy with his acts, so he'd ring with the same note, as it were, down to his bones."

Stuyvesant had a vivid image of a madman he'd helped arrest once, an ordinary, balding bank teller who had butchered six people, efficiently hidden their bodies, scrubbed his hands, and taken the train home. They'd caught him more or less by accident, three weeks later, and when the handcuffs went on, the man had patted the hand of his appalled secretary and told her to cancel his appointments for the next few days. He'd calmly admitted the murders, and never offered any explanation, even as he was being led to the electric chair. All he'd ever said in his defense was, "It was necessary."

"And Carstairs—"

"Couldn't understand why I wouldn't march through Whitechapel and point out the sinners. Or through Whitehall, for that matter."

And if Grey actually went through the corridors of Whitehall pointing out the villains, Stuyvesant wondered how long it would take before someone in power arranged for a knife in the back one dark night? Some gift: curse was more like it.

"So you have a blind spot." More than one—Stuyvesant suspected that the man could be distracted from the truth, especially in the presence of pain and alcohol: He hadn't picked up on the flaw that had rendered the January bomb inert; perhaps because Stuyvesant's remembered terror was all too real?

"Absolute conviction is the same as absolute innocence, when it comes to my being able to read a person."

"Funny, but I'd have thought Major Carstairs would come under that heading."

Grey's thumb came up to brush against his temple, a response to the name. "I reacted badly to the Major's sudden appearance today. The first couple of years I came here, I couldn't bear anyone but Robbie, but the past months I've had little trouble controlling it. I can manage Penzance on market days without undue problems. I thought my skin was finally growing thicker. Looks like I was wrong."

"Don't know about that. Sounds to me like Aldous Carstairs is connected with a lot of your past you'd rather not think about. It might have been simply memory, not...the other thing, that put your hackles up."

"You may be right," he said, sounding relieved at the idea.

"But still," Stuyvesant persisted, "it surprises me that you read Carstairs as being pulled in two directions. The man strikes me as being single-minded as a rattlesnake."

"He does give one the impression of absolute conviction, does he not? But it isn't at all true. He grew up in shabby gentility, and ended up detesting wealth and poverty alike. He hates himself most of all for emulating the leisured classes: his accent never slips, but his vocabulary sometimes does. His mother was a Chapel foundation-stone, his father a violent drunk, so gentle forgiveness infuriates him and tyranny both revolts and attracts him.

"He's ambitious but hides it, and commits acts of brutality by telling himself the end result requires it of him. In fact, he takes considerable pleasure out of causing pain—I understand he was a highly effective interrogator during the War—but at the same time, he deeply loathes himself for that pleasure. I have no doubt that he sees his pursuit of me as an honest attempt to serve King and country, yet at the same time, his temptation to make me squirm is almost more than he can bear. It's a sexual quirk, of course, at least in part—another thing to hate me for. But he's also afraid of me, that I might tell others what's inside him. No, the Major would be far easier to cope with if he were simply evil. Can I trouble you for another smoke?"

Speechless, Stuyvesant held out the silver case and lighter with hands that looked as steady and capable as ever. Which was kind of surprising since Grey's little speech shook him nearly as badly as that out-of-the-blue shoot-out with the bootleggers, three years before. *An almost sexual pleasure. His temptation to make me squirm...* Said so matter-of-factly. Stuyvesant had caught a glimpse of something of the sort in Carstairs, very briefly, during that first meeting in London, but... Jesus H. Christ.

"It's a wonder you didn't come after him with that axe, the minute you laid eyes on him." Or turned and run—which was what Stuyvesant would have done if he'd seen Carstairs get out of a car accompanied by a six-foot-two, wide-shouldered thug like him.

"It was tempting. And if you're thinking that it's dangerous to possess knowledge about the Major, I'm probably one of the few people in the world who is absolutely safe from him, so long as he believes there's a faint chance I might return to his beloved Project. You, however—that's another matter."

"Me? I don't even know the man, much less his secrets." Other than what Grey had just told him.

"Nonetheless, I've seen how he looks at you. He loathes you—everything you stand for, from your size to your country to the morality that stiffens your spine. You think I'm the only one he's tried to ruin over the years? I should take care, if I were you. Things happen to people whom the Major hates."

He can try, Stuyvesant said to himself. The idea of being permitted to defend himself against Aldous Carstairs was oddly attractive. "What about you? What did Carstairs do to make you attack him?"

"Me? His scar, you mean? No one thing; more a matter of final straws. The last months I was at his clinic—that's what he called it, though it was more a laboratory than anything else—his people had been working on a machine to read the truth. I was the means by which results were checked and readings calibrated."

"A lie-detector? We've got a bunch of guys working on that—sweat, pulse, blood pressure. Problem is, what those machines seem to read is nervousness, and even innocent people can get a little jumpy talking to cops." The most promising design was called a polygraph, and law enforcement agencies around the country had their eyes on Berkeley, California, whose police department had begun to use one in their interrogations. So far, however, the courts hadn't been convinced.

"I heard something about that, but this is considerably more sophisticated."

"Wonder what it is? Never mind—go on."

"One of the nurses he'd tested had come up with some wrong readings on his machine, and he wanted to know what she was hiding. So the three of us were in a room, him keeping at her and keeping at me and pressing to know what I was feeling about her, and was it worse after this question or the last, and finally the poor bloody girl just broke and started sobbing and it turned out she'd been assaulted by her brother five years earlier—sexually, you understand—and when I looked at the Major he wore this . . . gloating expression. That was just more than I could take, so I picked up her water glass and smashed it into his face. It's possible I may have been about to turn it on my own throat next, but the guards came through the door before I could and that was an end to it."

Stuyvesant would not have believed a man could refer to his own thwarted suicide in such academic tones, as if the only thing left unsettled was a mild curiosity. He hugged his knees to his chest.

The decorative clouds that had graced the western sky were beginning to move in; one of them, scudding high above, sent a shadow racing across the land. The waiting figure atop the wall far below vanished for a moment, then the darkness cleared and the red shone out again.

"Well, that might explain why Carstairs broke into a sweat when he saw you standing there with that hulking great weapon on your shoulder."

After a moment, Grey made a peculiar choking noise. Stuyvesant jerked around and saw the man's contorted face, but to his astonishment, Grey was laughing, baring his teeth to the sky while his hand slapped the rock in pleasure. "Yes, oh yes, that was worth the price of admission, wasn't it?"

Stuyvesant gave a chuckle, but a moment later the dark shadow reached them and the day went abruptly cold. He picked up his coat and put it on, but as he'd hoped (for Stuyvesant was, in his own way, very good at interrogations) Grey couldn't leave matters unfinished.

"If you can't reach your man Bunsen through my sister and Laura Hurleigh, how do you propose to do so?"

"Haven't a clue, yet. But don't worry, I'll manage."

"Stuyvesant," Grey shouted, "will you for Christ sake stop trying to manipulate me!"

Stuyvesant threw up his hands. "Jesus, you don't make it easy on a poor Bureau agent, do you? Okay, look: Carstairs' original idea was that we could talk you into writing your sister to say that you and I were great pals and I was interested in her work. I'd go meet her, take a look at the clinics, and eventually she'd introduce me to her friend Richard Bunsen. Like I said, I've done a lot of undercover work, Grey; I'm good at getting close to people. Very good. And that's all I need to do—to get close to Bunsen and get a sense of whether he could be our man, to see, among other things, if he has an alibi for the times our agitator was in the States. Clearly, having you make an introduction through your sister would have saved me some time. But I can see why you wouldn't want to do anything that brings you within arm's reach of Aldous Carstairs."

To Stuyvesant's interest, and gratitude, Grey did not storm off as he had threatened. Then again, Stuyvesant supposed that what he had told Grey wasn't really a lie: He might still be nurturing faint hopes that Grey would write that letter, but really, he was more or less resigned to writing this Cornish trip off as a bust.

However, Grey did not climb to his feet and accuse him of deceit, which was a good sign, and the silence that fell was more thoughtful than uncomfortable. After a while, Grey seemed to come to a decision. He said, "I actually had a letter from my sister not very long ago."

"That's good." Carstairs was right: The two were still in communication.

"She happened to mention that there's a Friday-to-Monday at Hurleigh House coming up." Stuyvesant grunted, and forbore to comment that Fridays and Mondays tended to take place in that order everywhere. "She'll be going, and a number of the other Hurleighs will be there. It starts the sixteenth. What's the date today, the thirteenth?"

"Today's Monday, so it's the twelfth. Are you talking about a week-end party?"

"Yes. Although I shouldn't use the word *week-end* in the Duchess's hearing: She may be unconventional, but she's a tyrant when it comes to language. Are you sure that today is Monday?"

"Unless Cornwall operates on a different calendar from London."

"If you say so. I heard the church-bells two days ago, so I thought . . . well, it must have been a Saturday wedding. Doesn't matter—the point is, Sarah ended her letter as she usually does, by saying that she'd love to see me, if ever I got the urge to come out of my hermitage."

"Does this roundabout tale have anything to do with me?"

Grey's face was transformed when he grinned, an expression that clutched Stuyvesant's heart with its familiar mix of insouciance and dread, the devil-take-all look his kid brother Tim's face had worn on the edge of battle. "Mr. Stuyvesant, how would you like to be my companion to a week-end with the mad Hurleighs?"

Chapter Fifteen

THE RAIN WAS FALLING STEADILY as Harris Stuyvesant followed
Aldous Carstairs onto the train, huffing its readiness in the Penzance
station. The carriage closed in around them as the attendant led the
way down the corridor, pointing out the common sitting compartment, two of its six chairs occupied by men with glasses in their
hands, as he took them to their private sleeping compartments.
Carstairs permitted Stuyvesant the first one, and said, "If you join me
next door, we can speak in private."

Reluctantly, retaining his hat and coat to make it clear he wasn't
staying, Stuyvesant followed Carstairs into the second cubicle, which
would have been simply snug without three men inside. Even when
the attendant had left, having satisfied Carstairs' demands for greater
heat and a wooden coat-hanger for his overcoat, the space was
crowded, its air oppressive after a day spent in the out of doors.

Stuyvesant slouched into the compartment's tiny seat, hands
stuffed into the pockets of his mud-smeared overcoat, for which the
garage's clothes-brush had proved inadequate. The rain that had begun shortly after he and Grey returned to the cottage was now pouring down the dark window, twisting the figures moving across the
platform's lights. As Carstairs fussed with his own coat, damp but

unsullied, whistles sounded, doors slammed, and the train shuddered, reluctantly letting go of the platform and turning its face towards London. Five minutes longer over the flat tire, and they'd have been stuck here overnight.

Which, Stuyvesant reflected, wouldn't have been altogether bad, to be parked in this quiet fishing village instead of being thrust back into the furious hive of workers and oppressors that was London. It made his teeth grind in anticipation. However, staying here would also mean prolonging his acquaintance with Carstairs, and the sooner he was rid of "the Major," the better.

The two men had spoken little since Carstairs trudged back up the lane to Grey's cottage, rain dripping from his hat brim, Robbie dogging his heels. Pressing time and the deteriorating weather had Carstairs hunched over the steering wheel all the way to Penzance, his attention focused on the slick road. Their only exchange, other than trading curses over the car's inadequate tire-repair kit, had been while they were barely out of Grey's yard: Carstairs asked whether Stuyvesant had any success, and Stuyvesant could only manage a brusque reply, that he'd been asked to accompany Grey and his sister to Hurleigh House in four days. Carstairs had grunted, then addressed himself to the treacherous lane.

The grunt had sounded more like satisfaction than surprise, Stuyvesant thought: Had he honestly not been surprised? Was it possible the man knew Grey so well he could second-guess him? Then again, if Carstairs' people were indeed keeping an eye on Grey, as Grey claimed, they could also be opening his mail. In which case Carstairs had known of Sarah Grey's invitation, there for the taking.

All in all, he thought it more likely that it had just been an involuntary reaction, instantly quashed, to the way Stuyvesant had managed to get Grey's cooperation where Carstairs could not. Either way, Stuyvesant was happy enough for the ensuing silence. Now, if he could only prolong it until they reached Paddington. He let his hat come to rest against the window, narrowing his eyes, feigning the approach of sleep.

The other man took no notice. He brushed off the spotless bed, laid a newspaper down to protect it from his shoes, and perched atop the bed-clothes, easing the gloves from his hands. He took out one of the thin brown cigars he affected, and when he had found an ash-tray for the spent match, said "Tell me, what did you think of our Captain Grey?"

At the sardonic voice, coupled with the insinuations behind the "our," a mighty urge welled up in Harris Stuyvesant, an almost over-whelming impulse to rise up and smash the man's face in, cigarillo and all. *You don't own me, you bastard, and I'm not going to do your shit work for you.*

He stifled the impulse instantly, unclenching his fists in his pock-ets and wondering why the hell Carstairs got his goat like this (... *a considerable pleasure out of causing pain* ...). Of course, that dirty stunt Carstairs had pulled as they were leaving Grey's compound made it hard to look the man in the face—but wasn't that part of the job, working with people you'd travel across town to avoid? Stuyvesant would use him, then move on. Like he did in any job, even those where he had to do things that made him feel like a scab and a toady and the lowest of the low-lifes. God knew he'd had enough ex-perience with that, over the years.

Honestly, Bennett Grey wasn't his problem. Was. Not. His. Problem. Grey was a step along the way—a small step, little more than the promise of an introduction, but that was better than any-thing he'd got in London.

Even if Grey had been Stuyvesant's concern, didn't it all boil down to a straightforward question? The man had a skill; his coun-try needed it; why not allow Carstairs to haul him in by the scruff of his neck and make him help out?

And if he'd fallen into antipathy with Carstairs, it was the same in reverse with Grey. A few hours in the man's company, and he felt more for him than he'd felt for some of the women he'd slept with over the years. The—what else to call it?—intimacy of the conversa-tion on that rock above the sea had just turned him all to mush, af-fected him like all the leggy redheads and blonde kitten-women of the world rolled into one. Without the sex, he hastened to add—what-ever it was he felt about Bennett Grey, it had nothing to do with sex. But the fact was, if the rain-clouds hadn't interrupted their little tête-à-tête and sent them down to the cottage, he'd probably still be there, perched with Robbie atop the wall, mismatched gargoyles guarding the good captain from intruders.

It was enough to make you believe in chemistry. Or the stars.

But whatever the reason—chemistry, astrology, or just that Carstairs reminded him of all the parts of his job that he didn't like—having to sit in a compartment with Major Aldous Carstairs and his *hmm*s and his impenetrable eyes and his fucking brown cigar made him want to slug the bastard unconscious.

Maybe Grey's raw nerves were contagious.

Yeah, and maybe he ought to pull himself together and act like a professional.

Which was a laugh, considering that he didn't know if he'd have a job when he got home. Ah, the hell with it.

"I don't really know what to make of him," he replied. "I'll have to think about it. Right now, I need a drink. I'll be in the seating compartment." He slammed out before Carstairs could offer to join him.

Eyes half shut, legs outstretched, Aldous Carstairs mouthed the slim cigar, drawing a comforting lungful of the fragrant smoke. He opened his lips to let the smoke spill slowly out, and reached into his breast pocket for the slim leather note-book he carried always. He did not open it right away, just laid it on his knee and sat, smoking and looking in the glass at his face superimposed on the last of the town's lights, contemplating how his will might be superimposed on the life of Captain Bennett Grey.

Rain on a dead land. The brush of an old lover's perfume on the nostrils. The rebirth of opportunity to a man who'd all but given up.

Wheels turning.

Grey—*Grey!*—after all this time: threat in one hand, temptation in the other had done the job. And surely the weight of Grey's presence, even if only in the back of Carstairs' own mind, would be enough to tip the balance of coming events?

Since the previous summer, Carstairs had spent every waking moment working to convince those that mattered that a General Strike would be, not a catastrophe, but an unparalleled opportunity. At this very hour, a brief document—future generations would know it as the Carstairs Proposal, although for the present, it went nameless—was circulating among certain chosen individuals. A small document, philosophical in tone, with implications that could reach into all aspects of British life.

What its thesis boiled down to was that in the next month, Britain would have the chance to silence, once and for all, those who would turn the country on its end, those who would make the country a place where the able served the ignorant, the experienced waited upon the raw and untutored. Britain would have the opportunity, under the impetus of the Strike, to reshape itself and redefine what its very constitution intended. Nothing extreme, nothing radical, merely a shift in attitudes.

He had chosen the time to circulate the Proposal with care. During the next three weeks, Britannia would be rudely awakened to the extremity of its danger. She would feel rough hands around her throat, and would scrabble wildly for a weapon with which to defend herself.

And Aldous Carstairs would be there to provide it.

Then when the Strike was smashed and rule of law returned to the land? With the danger fresh in their minds, their hearts still pounding with how close it had been, Britain's leaders—from Baldwin and Churchill all the way down to the most infant M.P.—would listen to reason, and consider the Proposal, and in the end, acknowledge that a law was worth nothing without the means of enforcing it.

Again, Aldous Carstairs would be there with the answer.

Not that the great British public would see his hand in the matter, not in this generation, at any rate. But the men of importance, they would know, and they would finally give Carstairs what he needed to do his job.

It might surprise some of them to find that he did not want power, certainly not beyond his own interests. Once the Proposal was implemented, he would step down, and return to his long-time pet, the Project.

Five years ago, Carstairs had been shocked to find that he simply lacked the authority to demand the continuance of the Project. Five years ago, truth to tell, he'd had to play every card in his hand just to keep it from being shut down entirely—a hard lesson, *Intra le alter cagioni che ti areca de male, lo essere disarmato ti fa contennendo:* Among the other evils which being disarmed brings is that you are despised. Since then, he had kept his head down, made a policy out of being useful to each generation of officials, and kept the Project alive by hiding it beneath larger concerns.

But now he had Grey.

He corrected himself: He did not have the man yet. But he would.

The authority he needed had not yet solidified. But it would.

He blew smoke at the window, watching how it rolled along the cold glass without seeming to touch it. That was where Aldous Carstairs lay, he thought: as the invisible barrier between two forces.

He had no wish to be noticed by the masses. Niccolò Machiavelli— a cliché to those who had never read the man's work—was a brilliant analyst whose primary mistake had been to accept visible authority, which both compromised his decisions and gave his enemies a target. Carstairs preferred the shadows, not because they were safe, but because it meant others were overly exposed by comparison.

It made them nervous.

It made them afraid.

His work often involved making people afraid of him, and he was good at it because it didn't bother him. If ever he made a family crest, its motto would be *È molto più sicuro essere temuto che amato:* It is safer to be feared than to be loved. In fact, sometimes fear in the eyes of others brought him not just the satisfaction of a job well done, but a truer, more visceral gratification. Something near to happiness.

Such as today. He really shouldn't tease the boy so, but a cat is designed to toy with its mouse, and Aldous Carstairs was designed to play with the likes of Bennett Grey: earnest, upstanding, passionate, readily wounded. It was a serious game—a bit like chess, in its way— but it was also an amusement.

Every so often, a move in one of these chess-like games took him by surprise. Five years ago, he had been in a state of distraction, caught up in the last paroxysm of the Miners' Union, and hadn't anticipated Grey's sudden and violent rebellion. Grey had squirted from his grasp like a wet melon seed, triggering calamity in all directions. Not only had it brought Carstairs' professional life to the edge of an abyss, but half an inch farther and that drinking glass would have sliced his artery. At the memory, his bare fingers caressed the ridge along his jaw and neck, and he shivered at the sensation: Thought of the blood and the choking, the shouting and pain, still had the power to make him queasy.

Yes, the lesson concerning the dangers of over-eagerness had been hard won. He had made a firm policy out of double-checking himself at every turn, at pausing before decisions, at analyzing all possible effects of a move. And it had paid off.

Harder to learn had been the lesson of when to suspend careful thought.

Take this afternoon's action. Carstairs' act as they were leaving could be interpreted as the petulant impulse of a hard-pressed man, petty revenge for having been forced to wander around in the rain, ruining a pair of shoes he'd rather liked, and taking refuge in the reeking kitchen of some nearby peasants: a statement amounting to, You piss on me, I'll piss back at you. Certainly the outraged American took it that way.

On the other hand, if one began with the assumption that Aldous Carstairs was never impetuous, that he took no unconsidered action, then his act became, not personal spitefulness, but the smooth, seemingly automatic move of a highly experienced operative. He had appeared to submit instantly to Grey's commands at every turn, acquiescing to the man's every whim; but just as Grey was thinking he'd got away with it, by his act, Carstairs had shown him who was actually in control.

Yes, he thought with satisfaction; it had, in fact, been the act of a born interrogator. Never let them settle; never let them know what you were really after.

And never, never let them go, even when they thought you had done so.

Especially when they thought you had done so.

Slow; inexorable: That was the way to win.

He opened his small note-book then, settling the cigar in the inadequate ash container while he recorded his thoughts concerning the day's events: He could still feel the wheels turning, and was beginning to catch a glimpse of how. As always, the dangerous act of committing his ideas to paper helped make them clear.

Not that he worried that his plans would ever be uncovered, not really—his enemies might break the language code, but the key references were known only to him. And he needed the note-books. Some day, when his labors in the public interest were ended, he would retire to a sun-drenched villa and write his book on political life—preferably, *sans* his predecessor Niccolò's preliminary arrest and torture.

No, it would not do at all, to open his note-books' secrets to other eyes—even Machiavelli set prudence alongside force in governing men. Still, some notes would be necessary when it came time to set down his memoirs, to illustrate the great arc of ambition he had laid out for himself.

Take, for example, the three brief notations on the previous page. The first concerned a memorandum to the Prime Minister that he and Kell of Section Five had discussed, with suggestions for the deployment of the Organisation for the Maintenance of Supplies. Baldwin was, as always, hesitant about using the authority he had been given, but together, Kell and Carstairs had taken a firm hand, with satisfactory results. The second note concerned last week's meeting with Steel-Maitland, the outcome of which was not yet certain. And the third, in the precise writing his secretary would have recognized with dismay as a sign of anger, the words read, in their code, *Why was I not informed of the American's presence?*

He had done nothing yet to follow that up, since after writing it he had found a memorandum concerning the man and his questions, buried deep in his in-box. He couldn't decide yet if heads were to roll. However, he should have known about the American's interests before the man walked into his office.

Three notes, two illustrating authority, the other a reminder of the hazards of distraction. Now, on the next page, he wrote six lines concerning his day: three of summary, three of future action. He capped his pen and slipped the small book away.

He did not yet write about the changes set in motion by the

restoration of Grey to consideration, because those changes were still but a tantalizing glimmer in his mind. He must make time to think at leisure, during the upcoming days, to let his mind work out a stratagem.

It would make a gem of a chapter in his memoirs, beginning with that fatuous ninny, that gift from the heavens, Mr. Harris Stuyvesant, heaving his bulk through the office door and dropping it into Carstairs' guest chair, genial as a dog and ignorant as a brick.

It took an experienced man to spot a gem in a muck. When the American had opened his mouth to bray the name of his quarry, not one man in fifty would have seen that the man Bunsen—himself not worth a fart in the wind—had connections with the most enormous potential. And not one man in a thousand would have known that the American was exactly what Captain Bennett Grey would respond to: Grey was a born leader of men, the role assigned him by his person and his class, and after all these years with no one but pigs and peasants for social intercourse, he had to be positively *lusting* for someone to command. Carstairs had seen it happen: nurses, patients, even doctors with an intractable problem would find themselves gravitating in the direction of Bennett Grey; in response, Grey's spine would straighten and he would summon the reserves to provide the leadership they craved.

Wheels within wheels.

The machine had begun to turn a fraction faster on Friday night, when Director Hoover's voice came down the tinny telephone receiver. He had met Hoover some years before, and recognized him as a kindred spirit, a man who knew how to get things done. Hoover had remembered Carstairs, too, and had been open concerning his problems with Agent Stuyvesant: how close to the edge Stuyvesant had been pushed by the near-death of his brother, how unreasonable the man had been after Hoover's recent promotion. How frustrating Hoover found it to have his agent so comprehensively fixed on Bunsen as a villain.

On Saturday, while not knowing precisely where the path would take him, Carstairs had laid the scent for Stuyvesant to follow. And on Monday, when Stuyvesant appeared at Grey's cottage door, doggy and innocent and cut off by an ocean from his own organization, the good captain had been unable to resist the call. Add the dual impulses of carrot and stick, and it was a wonder the captain hadn't insisted on packing a bag and coming to London with them.

If Aldous Carstairs had been another man, he'd have pulled down the compartment's shades and done a giddy dance: Finally, *finally* he'd found a tool to prise Grey out of Cornwall.

The rest of the plan would take shape, he had no doubt.

He rewarded himself with a few minutes over the newspaper, reading the amusing account of Captain Amundsen's polar airship, then crushed out his cigar. He glanced at his reflection in the window once more, then stood up with a sigh. Perhaps he should go past Monica's on his way home. That was one of the advantages of the place, there were always girls up and around, and after a day like he'd had, a man needed some of the tension taken out.

But first, it was time to get back to work on the thick-headed American.

He'd given the man plenty of time to drown his sulks.

Chapter Sixteen

DOWN IN THE SEATING COMPARTMENT, halfway through his second double whisky, the tension in Stuyvesant's shoulders began to subside. Thank God for booze, he thought—although the ready availability in this country had taken a few days to get used to, and his impulse on seeing a bottle placed on the table was still to reach out and tuck it someplace discreet. The Eighteenth Amendment was the most half baked, harebrained, dunderhead of a law anyone could be asked to enforce, like legislating mother love or the number of sunny days in May. Invariably, it hadn't diminished the amount of liquor available by one drop, just cut the quality. And of course shifted the profits firmly into the hands of the criminals. Didn't lawmakers ever think about the laws a bunch of old women asked them to pass?

Once upon a time, his job had thrown him at enemies who mattered. When he started at the Bureau, he'd worked to bring down bank robbers; after Helen, he'd gone after political subversives. Now, however, the Bureau had this damned Volstead bee in its bonnet, so that every year, a bigger and bigger slice of its budget went to hunting rumrunners, and every year, fewer and fewer agents were assigned to political crimes.

Stuyvesant sometimes thought that when a bomb went off in

the White House, there'd be nobody left who knew how to investigate it.

He should've quit in July, after Hoover refused to pour the entire Bureau into the fire-bomb and riot that left Tim sitting in the parlor, grinning amiably at the dog. Or in January, when his boss had brushed away Stuyvesant's theory of a single terrorist who had set three bombs and slipped away each time, undetected.

Slipped away to England, if Stuyvesant's hunch had any validity at all, where he had a life in the open, a future in front of him, and nothing to connect him to crimes across the Atlantic.

Or he had, until Harris Stuyvesant got fed up with the crap, cashed in half his savings account, and sailed from New York, leaving behind a director on the edge of firing him and a will leaving what he had in the bank to his sister-in-law, Doris.

But he had to stop this. Every time his mind dwelled on poor Tim, he ended up maudlin drunk, and that would never do, to be drunk while Aldous Carstairs was near.

Did Carstairs ever get drunk? He couldn't picture it. Couldn't picture the man with a wife at home or a dog at his heels, couldn't even imagine him doing anything as mundane as sitting in front of the fire with a book.

He was a cold bastard, there was no doubt. No doubt, either, that he was superb at his job, whatever that job's precise details might be: Stuyvesant sure wouldn't want Carstairs on his tail.

Grey, strangely enough—damaged, remote, and vulnerable Captain Grey—had seemed equal to the task. Not in a direct confrontation, maybe—one look at Carstairs and he'd been crippled by headache. And his face had gone stark white at the end, when Carstairs had kicked his apparent defeat upside down and marked the day his own like a dog at a lamp-post. Still, he couldn't help feeling that under that soft and easily wounded flesh, Grey was pure steel.

If there weren't so much riding on this, he'd almost be tempted to stand back and watch the upcoming battle. Right now, he wouldn't be able to say who he'd lay his money on, the Captain or the Major.

And what about this idea of Grey being able to see into people's minds, anyway? Sitting beside him on that rock, it all made a lot of sense, but the farther he got from the man's voice, the more dubious it seemed. Could it happen that a man's protective gear could be stripped from him like that, and leave him able to see—what was the saying?—the skull beneath the skin?

Stuyvesant ran the day over in his mind, beginning with the act with the cigarette case. That hadn't just been the act of a five-and-dime Madame Zola. Which meant that the rest of it might be true, as well.

There sure had to be *some* reason Carstairs was so hot for the man; his not-a-mind-reader abilities would explain that, no question.

He looked up, registering a presence at his side. The attendant was there, asking if he wished another drink. The other two men had finished theirs, and left him alone in the compartment.

"Yeah, I'll have one more. One. And if I ask for anything after that, you're not going to give it to me, agreed?" He peeled off a Treasury bill and held it out over the man's little tray.

"Very good, sir," the man said, and Stuyvesant let the bill drop.

He knew that if he had to deal with Carstairs any more tonight, he'd want a whole string of drinks, but with that hefty a tip, it would take some doing to get it out of the attendant. He nursed his glass, watching the occasional light dance past the rain-washed window.

After a while, Stuyvesant became aware of a small, grim trickle of amusement. How do you play a witness without playing him? How do you get a thing that you're not permitted to want? Fifteen years of questioning wary men and women, and today was one for the books—how do you trick a man who can see your lies even when you hardly see them yourself? Answer: First you trick yourself. He couldn't get Grey to help him by convincing him he should, so he distracted Grey by convincing himself that Grey shouldn't help him.

God, he was good at his job, even when the person he was trying to outsmart was Harris Stuyvesant.

He wished he had Tim to share that joke with. Of all his big Catholic family, he and Tim had been the ones to talk the same language, and even thinking about the lad made his heart ache. Or he'd settle for Tony, whom he hadn't seen since the Tangetti case. Or even Ethel, that singer he'd recruited back in '22 to fill an enormous gap in the Bureau's resources: the wives and girlfriends of criminals, who knew all kinds of stuff it was a pity to miss. With Ethel on the job, he didn't have to. Ethel was sure great at listening, to criminals or Bureau agents.

But all he had at the moment was Aldous Carstairs, slippery-tongued, black-eyed, smooth-haired Major Aldous Carstairs who excelled at the kinds of interrogations that called for pain. He might be an ally, but he would never be a friend, and Stuyvesant would have given a lot just now for a friend.

Instead, speak of the devil, and up he pops: Aldous Carstairs himself was standing where the attendant had stood, and Stuyvesant instantly regretted the large tip that had ensured a lack of further alcohol.

"Mr. Stuyvesant, I thought I might ask the gentleman if he could arrange some sandwiches for us, since we had no time for dinner. Is that acceptable to you? And it appears this room will be private enough for a conversation."

"I ate with Grey," Stuyvesant told him, although if it had been anyone but Carstairs, he would have welcomed sandwiches.

It would be a long time until Paddington.

Chapter Seventeen

AFTER CARSTAIRS AND THE ATTENDANT HAD DISCUSSED, in tiresome detail, the possibilities of sandwiches and wine, he dismissed the employee and came into the compartment, settling into the chair opposite Stuyvesant. The wine arrived swiftly. The attendant poured a glass for Carstairs, then hesitated until Stuyvesant nodded at him: Wine wasn't booze, not really.

Carstairs took a swallow, gave it grudging approval, then said, "So tell me, Mr. Stuyvesant, what did you and Captain Grey talk about?"

"The War, mostly." Stuyvesant had anticipated the question, and chosen his answer deliberately—any man with a history of interrogations was unlikely to have served on the front line.

As he'd expected, Carstairs veered around the touchy question of What did you do in the War, Daddy? "But he actually proposed coming out to see his sister, at Hurleigh House?"

"He'll wire his sister tomorrow, to make sure she's still going, but we left it that I'd meet him at Paddington Friday morning."

"Will you need a motor?"

"I'll take care of it, thanks."

"I'm not altogether certain I shouldn't be there."

"If you're there, he won't get off the train."

"You could be right. In that case, I shall have to ask that you report in regularly. That's not an option, it's going to be a necessity."

"I'll see what I can do. Now look," Stuyvesant said, before the man could come up with one more interruption. "You said that after I'd met Grey, you'd give me his story."

"Yes," Carstairs said. "I did tell you that. But first, please, one more diversion: May I ask if while you were with Captain Grey, you saw any evidence of his, hmm, special talent?"

"Sure. He told me all about it."

"He *did*?" Carstairs' voice nearly squeaked in surprise, and he leaned back in his chair, not taking those dark eyes off Stuyvesant.

"Yes."

Carstairs' right hand dipped into his inner pocket and came out with the slim note-book, which he placed on the chair-side table, resting his hand on its cover. The naked fingertips described small circles on the leather, under their own impulse. "Mr. Stuy—"

"You're telling me he doesn't usually talk about it."

"Towards the end of his time with us, it was difficult to persuade him even to admit to any unusual talents."

"Well, he was perfectly willing to talk to me. And yeah, he told me he can pick up deceptions in the way people behave. Usually things to do with, what did he call it? 'Dissonance,' I think it was."

The dark eyes across from him seemed about to swallow him up; the fingers tightened on the leather book. "Fascinating," Carstairs breathed. "Tell me, Mr.—"

"No, it's your turn. What happened to the poor bastard?"

Reluctantly, Carstairs withdrew his hungry gaze, let go of the note-book, and at long last, gave Stuyvesant the information he had promised three days before.

"Bennett Grey was born in Hampshire, in 1894, eldest of three children—his younger brother and sister are still alive, his drunk of a father broke his neck going over a fence in 1912. Eton and Balliol. Oxford, that is. He was twenty when War broke out, but he bowed to his mother's wishes and stayed on until he'd got his degree in June, then enlisted. Sandhurst, then France. In May 1918, he was in the front line preparing for a raid when a shell—possibly German, although the report said it was one of ours—landed at his feet and went off."

"Jesus. Why wasn't he killed?"

"Some flaw in the shell or the terrain directed the blast just enough to one side that it flung him into the air instead of blowing him apart. Although he insisted later that he had, in fact, been blown to pieces."

"I'd guess that being blown *up* and being blown *apart* would feel pretty much the same."

"Granted, except that his words were, 'I was taken apart and put back together again, in a moment.' In any case, his injuries were severe, and it wasn't until a year later that I began to hear rumors of a sanitarium patient with peculiar abilities."

" 'Peculiar abilities' being the ability to read a person like a book?"

Carstairs shot Stuyvesant a speculative look. "We're venturing into the realm of official secrets here."

"Yeah, I'm pretty good with those."

"So I am told. I had a trans-Atlantic telephone conversation with your director after you left my office Friday evening," he explained. "I was assured that, although you were often insubordinate to the brink of being fired, you could be trusted with the highest secrets in the land."

"Nice to know he likes me." Hoover was, to Stuyvesant's mind, a self-righteous prig.

"In that regard, what I have to say is not to reach any ears lower than that of your Director himself."

"Look, I don't know what I'll need to do with it, but if you want me to say I'm not going to blab about your official secrets to anyone below me on the totem-pole, then sure, I promise not to blab." Carstairs' lips twitched at the slang, as Stuyvesant had expected. Since coming here, it seemed that the more irritated he got, the more strongly he acted the Greater American Booby. But hell, why rein it in? The Brits were turning out to be more tight-assed about official secrets than anyone but the Germans. And we were supposed to be their bestest allies! "But now I've met the man, I don't know what you think you've got in Grey. If you're imagining he can see through walls or read minds or something, well, I got a bridge in New York I'd like you to invest in."

"I've told you he's not a bloody mind-reader," Carstairs snapped, a brief slip of control that gave Stuyvesant considerable satisfaction.

"However, I am saying that he knows things he shouldn't be able to, and that he, hmm, sees into people in a remarkable way. Objects, as well—if one gives him a genuine antique and a very good fake, he will know without question which is right, even if the questioner does not. In the same way, if one has him listen in on an interrogation, he can put his finger on precisely those places where the prisoner lies."

"Have you ever heard the phrase 'a painful awareness,' Mr. Stuyvesant?"

"Sure."

"Think of it as that. Because of what happened to him, Captain Grey is painfully aware of the tiniest details around him, as if he lacks, hmm, a normal man's skin. His code name in the project he was helping us with was Touchstone. For the metal, not the Shakespearean fool."

Well, thought Stuyvesant, at least both men were agreed as to the nature of Grey's "gift." "I'm not much of a man for Shakespeare. Then again, I'm no metallurgist, either. What's *touchstone*?"

"It's a soft stone used to prove the purity of gold or silver. But the alchemists used quicksilver, or mercury, because when one touches gold to mercury, the liquid is drawn up to cover the solid, making it look like lead. The inestimable value of touchstone is in the way it reveals the true nature of gold. In the same way, Captain Grey is drawn to the true nature of the person or thing he encounters: He cannot help himself, he reacts and reveals the nature of the person. True or false? Gold or pyrite?"

"Sounds like a useful sort of skill to have around," Stuyvesant commented. God knew, Grey had been getting truth out of Stuyvesant within minutes of their meeting. Still, he couldn't put out of his mind a picture of Grey's fingertips, digging into his shaggy blond skull.

"Indeed. Unfortunately, that's where the reality of 'a painful awareness' comes in. He cannot separate out what we'd like him to judge from everything else. That inability made him, as I mentioned the other day, a bit...unstable."

"Unstable how?" Grey would have heard the false ring of the question, Stuyvesant reflected; Carstairs did not.

"He began to respond with violence, and we had to let him go.

My medical team thought it likely that, given a chance to live on his own, he might toughen up enough to try again. That was, as I told you, nearly five years ago. Frankly, I'd nearly forgotten about him."

Stuyvesant kept his face straight—straight enough for Carstairs. Any man who heard the name Bunsen and came up with Grey had to be listening awfully hard. In fact, Stuyvesant suspected that if he said the name Richard Bunsen now—Bunsen being, after all, the supposed point of this whole expedition—Carstairs would look blank for just that one revealing instant.

But Carstairs was one step ahead of him. "So there you have Captain Grey's story. Tell me again, Mr. Stuyvesant: What led you to believe that our countries have a, hmm, shared interest in this agitator?"

As the bottle went down, Stuyvesant gave him a longer version of the story he'd told Friday, although less detailed than what he'd said to Grey. The attendant finally reappeared, bearing a plate of dry-looking sandwiches. When he was out of earshot, Stuyvesant concluded, "It's one thing to cope with home-grown radicals who make up their terrorism as they go. It's another thing altogether when they send for an expert to show them how it's done."

"You suggest that tutor to be Richard Bunsen."

"There's a lot pointing to him."

"And you would like him dealt with before your country finds itself threatened by a General Strike of its own."

"Well, we've got a ways to go before we reach that point, but yeah, the bud is the place to nip these things."

"Here, it has gone far past the bud stage. One might even say the flower threatens to bear fruit. Forgive me if this is traveling familiar ground, Mr. Stuyvesant, but you know this country had a little, hmm, flirtation with Communism two years ago?"

"You mean your Labour government? Sure, I read the papers—our papers, anyway. You went Socialist for most of 1924—Red anthems in Parliament, rumors that you were changing from the pound sterling to the ruble, doing away with the royal family and the institution of marriage, all the rest. It didn't last long."

"No, it did not. The British voter came to his senses."

"So, what, you think maybe Labour's going to be voted back in?"

After a week of being lectured at by one bureaucrat after another, Stuyvesant thought he might vote Red himself, if they'd promise to trim some of the damned governmental deadwood.

"Actually," Carstairs said, "they may not bother with an election this time."

The American glanced sharply across at his companion. Carstairs' face was deadly serious.

"What, you honestly believe this talk about an actual . . . *revolution?*" In *England?*" He laughed in disbelief, but Carstairs just held his eyes until Stuyvesant's laughter faded, then he picked up a second sandwich.

"If the possibility surprises you, Mr. Stuyvesant, I can only say you have no idea of the state this country is in. Since the War ended, pressures have been mounting. Our government have been, to put it bluntly, preparing for war. A class war. On the one side are the ruling and middle classes, the backbone of Britain, who look to the eastern horizon and see the nightmare of Russia, slaughtering their aristocracy, handing over all property to the worker, swallowing up their neighbors, stretching out greedy fingers for Britain. On the other side stand the workers, who have received generous privileges and subsidies during the War years and insist that, despite the current tight economy, those privileges are rights. The economy is coming off its artificial wartime boost and settling down. We're going back onto the gold standard, which will narrow the profits on exports. The bottom line is, we all must tighten our belts."

This was a phrase Stuyvesant had heard dozens of times over the years, and frankly, although his job required him to back the owners, with him it only went so far. He knew from experience which belts got tightened in the end.

But if Carstairs wasn't just talking through his hat about the threat of revolution, it was no wonder London was in such a state. He'd feel a little tetchy, himself.

"You've heard of the Zinoviev letter?" Carstairs mused.

"Wasn't that—" Stuyvesant began, but the man seemed to be thinking aloud and did not wait for his response.

"Two years ago, in October 1924, Labour lost the vote of confidence and an election was called. It was clear to everyone that the fate of the country hung in the balance, that the Socialists absolutely had to be evicted from Downing Street. A second vote in their favor, or even in the favor of their partners, the Liberal Party, might well have tipped this country into the arms of the Bolsheviks. You may doubt it, but those in Britain who mattered knew that it could happen, that in the blink of an eye, the entire continent of Europe would turn Bolshevist.

"A day or two after the vote of no-confidence, a letter arrived at the Foreign Office, intercepted by a government agency. It had come from Grigori Zinoviev. You know the name?"

"Zinoviev is president of the International Communist Party." He was remembering this letter now.

"Precisely. The letter amounted to a set of instructions from Moscow, with Zinoviev urging his British comrades to push for the proposed treaty with Russia—a treaty that, among other gestures of support, would include a substantial 'loan' to the new Bolshevist state. The letter went on to address the possibility of armed insurrection. It spoke for the establishment of Communist cells among British working men—particularly munitions workers—and among British troops, especially those stationed near cities. The words *class war* figured prominently in the letter, standing against the military preparations of the 'bourgeoisie.' Two weeks after it was received, four days before the general election, this letter appeared in the *Daily Mail*."

The U.S. of A. doesn't have the corner on the dirty politics market, Stuyvesant thought. The current Teapot Dome scandal was only money, after all, not an entire country's political fate.

"Which led the 'bourgeoisie' to vote Labour out. By a landslide, as I recall."

Carstairs nodded. "The Tories would have won in any case, but with the looming threat of a Communist takeover, the vote was overwhelming. The proposed treaties with Russia were abandoned, loans were canceled, and the British government could return to the business of putting the country together."

"I also remember," Stuyvesant interrupted, reaching for the wine bottle, "that questions were raised concerning the letter's authenticity."

"That is true. Certainly the Communists themselves denied it."

"Because it was all pretty convenient, wasn't it? The timing and all. And such an unlikely thing to land in the lap of the people it did."

"Also true. And that has led to a part of the current, hmm, problem."

"Your nice middle-class bourgeoisie voter is beginning to wonder if he's been had?"

"Shall we say, rather, that certain elements of society are playing up the letter's more dubious interpretation."

"In other words, your Reds are pointing out to people that they were manipulated into voting Conservative."

"It is an underlying theme, in the Communist propaganda efforts."

"Well you know, when you fake evidence, especially inflammatory evidence, it has a way of coming back and biting you on the ass."

"Few would claim that anyone in the Conservative Party faked it."

"But they sure jumped on it in a big way."

"It was heaven sent," Carstairs admitted.

"If none of the Tories faked it, who did?"

"It hasn't been proved that anyone faked it. Only that it was leaked at a convenient moment."

"The letter came through your Intelligence people, didn't it? MI6?"

"I believe so."

"Is that who you're with?" Stuyvesant asked bluntly.

"Me? Heavens no, nothing nearly so flamboyant. Although I have worked with them in the past."

The American fiddled with his glass and decided not to bother asking point blank if Aldous Carstairs had been responsible for the Zinoviev letter. He would only deny it. In any case, as far as the government was concerned, someone had to do it, so it was done. "Is the letter about to blow up again?"

"I shouldn't think so. The uncertainty of its provenance has caused certain, hmm, problems, but those are generally both small and localized, and found among those who would mistrust anything the government had to say, no matter the evidence."

"So why the hell are we talking about it? What's it got to do with Richard Bunsen?"

"I am, in fact, coming around to that. The Zinoviev letter has, inadvertently, taught the agitators an invaluable, if painful, lesson: That a powerful, last-minute blow is nearly impossible to counteract."

"Are your people thinking about some last-minute effort to take the wind out of the General Strike? Another Zinoviev letter?"

"Oh no," Carstairs said, sounding surprised. "As I said, the government have been preparing for the Strike ever since 'Red Friday' last August, when Mr. Churchill extended the coal subsidy. And not just the government, but private citizenry have banded together in an organized resistance to any attempt at overthrowing the legally constituted order."

What had the papers called it, Stuyvesant asked himself—the Organisation for the Continuation of Order?

"In that time, we have ensured the security of essential supplies"—(*supplies,* thought Stuyvesant—not *order:* Maintenance of Supplies, a name of such unadorned simplicity that a cynic begins to suspect some large, dark entity stirring below the surface)—"medical care, communications, peace-keeping forces—no, the government are fully prepared to outlast any strike. What concerns me is that, to all appearances, the Unions have made no preparations whatsoever. They appear to be blithely convinced that the government will back down again.

"Now, this may be simply that they are confident that God is on their side, that the manifest rightness of their cause will win the day. However, there are some good minds in the Unions, and one cannot but wonder if they know something we do not. If perhaps the Union leadership might have a card up their collective sleeves, to be pulled out in a decisive, last-minute *coup de guerre.*"

"A sort of reverse Zinoviev affair," Stuyvesant said.

"As you say, some last-minute revelation that would tip public sympathy towards the miners. Sympathy is building; a push in their favor could have a, hmm, disastrous effect. There is a tide in the affairs of men, the Bard says, and in this case, the tide is an industrial action that could be fashioned into the point of a wedge. A wedge aimed at a complete overthrow of the government."

"Your revolution," Stuyvesant said flatly. How had Grey put it? *The middle classes are teetering, waiting to be convinced.* "You honestly believe the British people are so fed up with their system of government that they'd sweep it into the sea and follow the Bolsheviks?"

"If you put it to them in those words, certainly not. But there is a pervasive and growing mistrust for authority in this country, which among some has reached open contempt for the entire parliamentary system. I believe," Carstairs said, then corrected himself. "I *fear*, it would just take one powerful and carefully judged blow and, without intending outright revolution, the country would nonetheless find itself tumbling in that direction. The next three weeks could determine the well-being of the British state for the next hundred years."

Stuyvesant looked into the man's black eyes, and for once did not doubt Carstairs' sincerity: The man believed that his nation was in peril.

If that was the case, and given the clear and fast-approaching deadline, why was he messing around with a trip to Cornwall?

Unless he thought Grey might somehow help with the coming threat.

Or . . . did his interest include Bunsen?

"Mr. Carstairs, do I get the feeling that you're taking Richard Bunsen more seriously than you did on Friday?"

"Mr. Stuyvesant, I don't think I need to tell you that in our business, one is forever watching for the unexpected. On the face of it, Richard Bunsen seems an unlikely candidate for the man to spark open class warfare on British soil. But now that my attention has been drawn to him, I will admit, he interests me. I find the possibility that he has been practicing his bomb-making skills at a safe distance from his own back garden distinctly troubling. Had I a plenitude of men at my command, I would insert someone into his organization, but my men are currently stretched in a number of directions that remain, to my mind, as likely a threat as this one.

"However, if you like, I will assist you. Given, that is, the clear understanding that you will pass on to me anything of interest regarding Richard Bunsen."

"Sure. And what do you want in exchange?" One Cornish mind-reader, perhaps?

"Merely that you keep me *au fait* with Captain Grey's . . . situation."

"With an eye towards helping you get him back?"

" 'Get him back'?"

"For your Truth Project, I think it's called." Calibrating the machines that would take the place of torture.

Carstairs' inky eyes might have been holes in the night sky, bottomless and unreadable. After a long moment, his eyelids blinked slowly over them, and he looked to one side for the attendant. He said nothing at all to Stuyvesant, just glanced over the slip of paper and peeled money from his billfold.

When the man had left, the Englishman laid his table napkin on the empty plate and braced his hands on his chair.

"Mr. Stuyvesant, let me simply say this. I am impressed with how far you got Captain Grey to open up. He would not do that for many, and that you arrived with me did not assist your cause any, as no doubt you have seen. However, it is clear that you have joined the Friends of Captain Grey camp. It's completely understandable. He is quite a, hmm, likable fellow. Let me warn you. Do not let Grey's charisma and your shared experience of trench warfare blind you to the evidence before your eyes."

And with that, he drained his glass and left.

Chapter Eighteen

STUYVESANT WATCHED Aldous Carstairs disappear into the corridor, and wondered what the hell had just happened.

That last little exchange had felt like a gauntlet thrown down, a declaration of war, which really, *really* wasn't what he'd had in mind. Use the man, keep your distance, but do not make him an enemy.

Jesus Christ, he thought, I must never drink in the vicinity of a man who pulls all my triggers like that man does.

He walked down the corridor to his compartment and closed the door behind him. The hat and coat that he had tossed onto the bed earlier had been tidied away, the bed-clothes pulled down, but the space was so stuffy and cramped, the thought of climbing into bed was intolerable. He dropped his jacket on the foot of the blankets and kicked off his shoes before sidling around to wrestle the window open.

That was better. Wet and noisy, but with his upper body outside, his head cleared. When he drew back inside he could feel the rain dripping from his hair, and there were smuts on his once-white shirt. He took it off, and sat in his undershirt with a cigarette, the squeals and rattles and wet air washing around him.

Think, man.

Okay, first thing was, Carstairs had a point. Normally—professionally—Harris Stuyvesant kept an amiable face over a watchful attitude: Only when he felt fairly certain about which way the wind was blowing—friend or foe—would he let down his internal fences and stick his hand over. With Grey, he somehow hadn't bothered with the fences: From the moment he saw the man standing by the farm shed, it had been liking at first sight. By the time he left, he'd felt so close to the man, he'd even been considering how to keep Carstairs away from him.

If Agent Harris Stuyvesant had played a witness the way Grey played *him,* he'd be proud of his skills.

He didn't *think* it had been a deliberate effort on Grey's part. He didn't *feel* he'd been manipulated; he was just responding to the force of Grey's personality.

Then again, it didn't have to be deliberate. Grey could simply have perceived what it was this American would respond to, and—if his nerves were indeed "rubbed raw" by conflict—automatically shaped himself to fit. Come to think of it, wasn't that more or less what Stuyvesant did every time he went undercover? See what his quarry wanted, and become it?

A small town grew and faded outside the windows, most of its houses dark. A few minutes later, a set of head-lamps waited at a crossing, and a sudden flare of light behind the wind-screen revealed two people, heads together over the match.

Aldous Carstairs, he thought: What was he after?

Human beings assume that others share their preoccupations. Show a photograph of a family in a sitting room to a new mother, she will notice the children; show the same photo to a career criminal, he will point out the exits and where any valuables might be hidden; give it to a middle-aged salesman, and he'll tell you all you need to know about the family's income and interests.

Show a suspected bomb-maker to Aldous Carstairs, and he sees Bennett Grey. Ask about mind-reading and he talks about interrogation. Remind him that you wish to lay hands on the bomb-maker, and he describes a convoluted path winding from a two-year-old piece of political chicanery to a would-be revolution, following it up with the danger of a "last-minute *coup de guerre.*" Ask him about a strike, he talks revolution.

We have ensured the security of essential supplies, Carstairs had said. *There is a mistrust for authority in this country.*

Sounded to Stuyvesant as if Carstairs intended to do something about the current state of affairs.

Something that had to do with Bennett Grey?

Or were the two matters on separate, although equally important, tracks?

And why was it that the extreme opponents of Communist doctrine were every bit as bad as the Reds, as if politics was not a straight left-and-right but a line that looped around to blend at the fringes? That a fight against Bolsheviks might be a battle against those at the other end of the spectrum as well?

Towns and stations came and went; telegraph lines rose and fell. Midnight came, then one o'clock, leaving Stuyvesant alone with the rain on the window and Carstairs' words in his head.

Long hours after pulling out of Penzance, the train left open countryside. The distances between the farms and hamlets shortened, then the villages grew, and soon were piling up on each other. Looking ahead at a curve in the tracks, Stuyvesant could see the glow in the sky that presaged London.

He lit a cigarette and studied his silver case. He played with the clasp, invisible to anyone but a Bennett Grey, then popped the lid and took out the hidden photograph and its pinned-on lock of hair, unfolding it and laying it on the un-slept-in bed.

It was an ordinary, unposed snapshot of the woman he loved. Or, rather, had loved, six years ago. He had taken it on the deck of a ferry, in August 1920, the day he first knew that he was going to marry her. The wind tumbled her curly hair, unfashionably long by today's standards but considered short then. The same could be said of her dress, its hem pressed up against her leg to show more than she had intended.

Helen had given him the snippet of hair, to wear close to his heart, but she had never seen the photograph. No one but Stuyvesant had ever seen it, since the film was in his camera when she died, and he had developed and printed it on his own in the Bureau darkroom. He wondered what he would have done, if Bennett Grey had moved to take it from its hiding place. He was glad Grey hadn't tried.

Carstairs was right. Oh, he was slimy and political and no doubt as dangerous as a puddle of gas, but he was also right: Stuyvesant would have to watch himself, to mistrust and second-guess his every reaction to Captain Bennett Grey.

Chapter Nineteen

BACK IN HIS COMPARTMENT, gazing out the glass of his own tightly shut window, Aldous Carstairs wondered if that last exchange had been sufficient to obscure what had gone before. He thought it would, considering the lack of subtlety in the American's mind, but he wished he could be certain.

He'd said too much. The second glass of wine had been a mistake. But at the time, he couldn't help thinking aloud, as the sense of rushing events drew him forward.

What he wanted to do was to seize the collar of every passer-by and demand, *Do you not see the moment, fast approaching?*

But the man in the streets did not think of it. That was left to men such as Aldous Carstairs, men willing to take on themselves the responsibility of reshaping an empire's future.

One thing Carstairs knew, without doubt: If Britain was to be put onto a proper footing in this century, if she was to stand firm before the ravenous monster on the other side of Europe and to stamp out the monster's spawn hatching within her shores, she needed authority over her own people. Unfortunate but true: The enemy lay not across the Channel, but here in the very heart of England.

Which meant that bringing the unwashed and angry to heel in the coming weeks was crucial. It was vital. It was everything. He sympathized with the working class themselves, truly he did, but the parasites who rode on their backs, those who saw the valid frustrations of the coal miner as a means of reducing the country to shambles—it was those men who were the true enemy.

Thus, the importance of the Carstairs Proposal. If it was done correctly, the distracted British public would scarcely know it had taken place. Things would simply begin to run smoothly. The change would be polite and for the most part law-abiding, the bloodshed minimal, and what commotion it entailed could easily be hidden beneath the dust cloud and shouting of the Strike itself.

He lit another cigar, and watched his reflection watching him.

History might even define the Carstairs Proposal, he thought, as a very English *coup d'etat*.

Chapter Twenty

BENNETT GREY STOOD IN THE DOORWAY of his whitewashed cottage. When the motorcar's black roof-top had disappeared behind the walls, when the engine noise started to fade, the shakes began. His bones felt oddly liquid. He wanted to scream, to weep, to pound his fist against the wall until it left bloodstains, to swallow the entire bottle waiting on the kitchen table and poison himself into a coma. He wanted to grab his shotgun and gallop across the two fields to the lane's dog-leg and, when the bugger slowed for the sharp turn, to vault the stone wall and ram the shotgun barrel through the window and pull both triggers, taking the driver's smooth head right off his shoulders.

And if that American got in the way, well, too bad. Too *fucking* bad.

Or, he could put his own head in front of the gun's double barrels. Ah, death, constant companion and seductress, the faithful whore, singing her Siren song, that endless melody that lay beneath every hour of his life here.

Not today, my love, you sweet-tongued bitch. Or not yet today.

When the Major had come up the drive shortly after four o'clock, Robbie close behind with the silver watch in his hand, Grey and

Stuyvesant were already outside. Grey had put up a hand to stop the intruder.

"Mr. Stuyvesant and I have settled things," he'd called across the yard. "I'm willing to work with him on this: Not you, him. If that is not acceptable, just say the word, and I'll write my sister a letter warning her off her friends."

The Major did not like it, not one bit. However, having brought the American into it, he couldn't very well pull him away. In the end, he nodded and tossed his hat into the motor, followed by the black overcoat.

But instead of getting in behind the wheel, the son of a bitch had stood and looked at him over the roof of the car, peeling off his black leather gloves as he did so. He had then walked around the car's bonnet, into full view of the householder, and opened his flies to piss, long and hard, across the rain-damp stones of the wall.

Precisely where Grey's eyes were guaranteed to hit, every time he came out of his front door.

A place he couldn't help walking past a dozen times a day.

Utterly childish, to piss on another man's wall. And yet calculated to be absolutely enraging. Even Robbie knew it was wrong; although it was raining by then, he'd indignantly hauled a bucket of water to slosh across the spot as soon as the sounds of the engine faded.

Water wouldn't erase that stain; it might as well have been acid-etched into the stones. Grey's impulse was to hitch his neighbor's horse to the wall and drag it to the sea.

"Bennett, art a ailish?"

"I'm fine, Robbie. I need you to go home now."

"Thee duzzen look foin. Ah'll go fetch Motherr. Her'll bring ee med'cin—"

"Robbie," he said, his voice wavering with the effort of control, "I have to be alone. If you don't go home, I shall have to shout at you. Go home. I'll see you tomorrow."

Shouting was the ultimate threat to the simple lad, since it reduced him to quivering tears and made him wet his trousers. Grey peeled his taut fingers off the creaking wood of the door-frame and shut the door, firmly but without violence. Inside and alone, he stood with his eyes closed, body swaying with the effort it took not to pound his fist—or his skull—against the wallpaper.

Aldous Carstairs. Jesus Christ, the Major was back in his life. One sight of those eyes and Grey's entire carefully constructed world had tumbled to ruin like a child's block tower.

You're five years older and a hell of a lot more settled in yourself, he berated himself; he has no control over you.

But Jesus, the Major with his gloves and his wires and sliding out his note-book and his *questions,* Christ, the questions that just wouldn't stop—

Have a drink, one drink, make yourself move, you don't have to see the Major, just that Stuyvesant fellow, you can get along well enough with him.

Yes but the *questions...*

And the Major had a plan, some dark scheme taking shape in the back of that twisted mind, he could see it in the flash of the man's eyes, hear it in the play of his voice: The man might as well have spoken it aloud: *Don't worry, Captain Grey, I will be back for you.*

Oh, Sarah, my dearest sister, what has your impetuous nature got us into? Don't you know what this means?

A thousand pinpricks of sensation plucked at his skin: the drift of air and the sound of the neighbor's rooster and Robbie's dejected footsteps, in retreat across the gravel. The growl of the Major's motor, the lingering traces of his smell on Grey's clothing, the disturbance the American left in the house, plucking and worrying at him until he felt a shriek rise in his throat like vomit.

In the end, Grey gave in and limped through the cottage to the bedroom. He banged the shutters closed (*the creak of the hinges, the smell of the dust that rose from them*) and went to the room's back corner (*hair/a mouse dropping/ a tiny stone from the drive/a curl of dry leaf with the smell of verbena*) and for the first time in months, forced his bad leg to kneel onto the cool stone floor (*grit and the cutter's blade and the eternal smell of stone*). He folded himself up, inching forward until his skull was jammed into the meeting point of walls and floor. It made him feel like a damned ostrich, or an infant in a cold and unyielding womb, but when the world around him went overly bright and threatened to break over his head, the only thing that helped was to put himself into this pathetic, vulnerable, useless position. It was dark, it was solid, he was alone. It was the embodiment of abject surrender, a complete relinquishing of the iron control that kept him alive.

Being trapped allowed his ragged breath to slow. Gradually, the sweat dried; eventually, the frantic *lubdub lubdub* of his heart grew quieter. Sensation retreated; thoughts became ordered; the ritual of memory began.

The whistle against his lips tasted of brass, cold and raw. His dry tongue tried to moisten it and settle it into place. Lungs filled, lips pursed, then breath, pushing out against the sour metal taste: one blow against the mouthpiece to bring the company to readiness; the second breath to send the ladders slapping up against the sandbags; the third would trigger motion, all his men, his trusting and responsive brothers, summoning their muscles against the gut-clenching, balls-withering knowledge that once they had climbed the rungs and cleared the parapet, run and dived to earth and settled their guns to their shoulders, there they would be, out in the open, with nothing but the air to shield them from German bullets.

The whistle against his lips tasted of brass.

He licked the whistle and wrapped his mouth around it. The men jostled at the base of the ladders—a last furtive drag on a cigarette, hands reaching to check on chinstraps, shoulders shifting, one of Hamilton's crude tension-jokes, some coughing. He drew breath deep into his lungs, and then suddenly, strangely, the earth shifted. He staggered, the whistle jerking loose on the lanyard around his neck. Belatedly, the sound reached him: incoming shell, followed by the compressive noise of a small building hitting the ground. His men shouted silently, all those beloved faces twisting in fear as they scrambled away, slow and urgent—down the trench, over the top, anywhere that was not *there*. Bullets began to *zip* overhead, where the sky was, and then Bennett Grey's world screamed.

That was what it felt like, then and ever afterwards: like standing before the mouth of the world when it came open to shriek out its agony and outrage and bewilderment. The nerve-shattering noise drove straight through him, permeating muscle and bone in a wave too enormous to begin to comprehend. He only knew it by its opening blast and by the fact that it changed every cell in his body, twisting each and every one of those millions of tiny blocks of life, reversing the flow of blood through his veins and making his very bones momentarily soft and malleable; when the scream ended, every drop of him—from the hairs on his forearms to the whorls on his fingers to the building-block tower of vertebrae up his spinal column—had . . . *altered,* in some slight but unmistakable way. As though the essence of Bennett Grey had been decanted and then poured back into someone else's subtly different form.

It was an artillery shell, they told him later. It had plowed deep into the near-liquid floor of the rain-soaked trench, paused a moment, and exploded. Had it gone off two seconds earlier, the shell would have scattered pieces of him over a wide patch of no-man's-land, hammering bits of bloody flesh into the trench walls, twisting his rifle into uselessness, launching his helmet in the direction of Paris.

Instead, it erupted at his very feet, flipping him right out of the trench like some circus act and burying him in the muck.

When Bennett began to trickle into his new body, his first slow awareness was the absence of sound. Such a blessing, silence, after that incredible shudder of a scream that had lasted for the snap of a finger, or for a fortnight. But when the mouth of the world finally closed, in the wake of thundering cacophony came peace and the sweet tranquillity of innocence. The body that he was slowly coming to fill seemed a place of comfort and quiet; the surface on which it rested was soft as a feather bed; the sky above was a calm, unassuming, undemanding canopy of pale gray, like the breast of a nesting dove.

He lay, nestled like a baby into the pitted ground, watching the sky out of his left eye. A crow flew across the canopy, and some time later, another. Thoughts flitted across the expanse of his mind in much the same manner. He was a child atop a grass-covered hill on a summer's day; in a few minutes, he would let it all go. He would tip and roll and launch himself down the fragrant close-cropped greenness, a laughing, dizzy-making tumble down the long hill of summer to the cool, clear, sweet stream that lay at the bottom. The world was a good place, with no rough edges—not even any stones protruding from the turf—just warm and comforting and delicious and always new.

Except that he had to breathe. Truly, if he'd had a choice he would just have lay there, motionless until the night fell and darkness took him. But his new body grew uncomfortable, then insistent, and when the final measure of his spirit had dribbled into this borrowed flesh, the impulse for air was triggered. His lungs began to work, and in an instant, like an infant ripped from snug warmth and slapped into autonomy, the world slapped Bennett from his dream: The summer's afternoon exploded into a cold, stinking, terrifying maelstrom.

He still couldn't hear a thing, but he knew where he was, and it wasn't any summer's hillside. He was hurt—the body he was in wouldn't tell him just how badly, but it was bad—and he was both exposed and hidden, somewhere behind the British wire. His ears were filled with a thick nothingness. Maybe they were just clotted with mud? He could try to clear them, but that would mean he'd have to move: Lying still, he'd look like a dead body, which meant Jerry wouldn't bother shooting at him. It would also mean that his own men wouldn't make an effort to retrieve him until dark.

By which time it would be too late for Bennett Grey.

He eased his head an inch to one side, tiny, jerky, unfamiliar motions, muscles he'd never worked before. Dark mud came into view at the corner of his vision; he could feel it oozing up his cheek as his face settled into the muck. He could see no movement, feel only the thud of guns through the fragile gauze that was his skin—not too close, those guns: down the line a little.

He began to raise his head to look around him, but stopped when some inner voice warned him it would hurt. Instead, he began to wriggle his right side and elbow more deeply into the soupy ground, easing his left side up into view.

He was buried.

A little bit more, and the mud would have closed over him before he'd regained consciousness, allowing him to drift away into that summer's afternoon. Instead, he lay locked in a tormented body under the clammy entombing soil, his face staring out of a pit that was visibly growing narrower as the muck settled.

Would it be so bad, he wondered? Just close your eyes for a minute and it'll be over, and you can have the roll down the turf to the stream, forever and ever, amen. No more orders, received or—worse—given. No taste of brass whistles on the lips. No more letters to a dead soldier's parents. Twenty-nine months of horror, filth, and disgust is enough. Let go.

But to his exasperation, this unfamiliar body did not want to give itself over to the mud. With the unthinking instincts of a new-born colt, his head twisted, his shoulders rotated, weak struggles against the weight of France. Both arms worked to reach the air, fingernails clawed up the buttons of his uniform, scrabbling against this *thing* that wanted, gentle and patient, to pull him into the earth. Finally, his left hand was at his chin and pushing, then his right joined it, and they thrust in unison.

A soft boulder lay half across him. The thing was soft like the mud but with marginally more substance; pushing an elbow against it only shoved Bennett more firmly into the welcoming embrace of the soil.

Then his elbow broke into the boulder's spongy wetness, and the smell (so *that* was where Walters had gone) of the trenches washed into his lungs.

Bennett himself was well familiar with corpses buried without benefit of clergy, soldiers and parts of soldiers long tidied away by explosions and collapsing trenches, unceremoniously brought to light by later shells, newer trenches. The stink of them coated the throat and, even after months of familiarity, brought a gag in the guts, but once they had been cleared away or re-buried, the proximity of a rotting foot or half-exposed skull had long since ceased to disturb his meals.

However, this new body of his had never met such a thing before, and at such close quarters, it panicked. With little half-screams of horror it pushed at the *thing,* which only made matters worse. He squirmed madly, desperately, to one side, deeper into the mud, he didn't care, just so it took him out from under it. He was aware that one of his legs violently protested any movement at all, and that his gut muscles threatened to spill out the same way this poor bastard's rotted guts were spilling all over Bennett's face and arms, but he couldn't help it, he only wanted to be away, *away,* God get me away from this.

He didn't hear the voices behind him, English voices reacting to his unexpected emergence from the carnage. He couldn't have said in which direction his own trench lay, nor did his mind pay any attention to the possibility of German snipers.

But his skin listened. That new-born skin, raw and soft as a fledgling from its shell, wrapped itself around the flailing muscles and bones and held them close and calm. His eyes tracked the spatter of bullets in the mud, then watched them shift away as they were attracted by the motions of a nearby victim. The other man's arm jerked and went limp, while Bennett lay unmoving within his skin, waiting for the spatters to seek him out again.

He was dimly aware of men moving in the nearby trench. The skin of his exposed left cheek felt a string of bullets passing overhead as the Vickers gun came into play (and why had he never noticed before how distinctive their gun's voice was, as personal and identifiable as any that issued from a human larynx?). The part of him that was against the ground felt the slap of ladder against sandbags followed by the pounding of feet as four men—no, five—wallowed through the muck towards him. He could even have put names on the men, if he'd turned his mind to it. His shoulder felt the approach of hands an instant before the fingers seized him, turned him, dragged him moaning and alive across the intervening terrain. He was dimly aware that he should be grateful for their attentions, but the rough treatment against his wounds made his new-born body retreat into itself, and the world went dim, and then he left it for a long, long time.

The explosion deafened his ears, shattered his left leg, planted shrapnel in his belly and scalp, and rattled his brain in its casing. It also scoured him miraculously clean of infection. His left leg was a mass of scar tissue from knee to thigh, but it healed without problem, as did the stitches up his belly. His scalp gradually expelled the tiny fragments of debris. His hearing crept back in stages, although the doctors told him he would always have a ringing in the left one. They could find nothing to explain the continued sensitivity of his skin, so intense he would gasp at the mere brush of a nurse's fingers. In the end they assured him that it, too, would fade, although he could tell that they thought his problem was mental, yet another variation on shell shock.

The explosion had scoured him clean in other ways, as well. He stopped talking about it when he realized how nervous he was making the padre, who clearly didn't care to be informed that one of his flock had been cleansed of sin, but that was what it felt like to Bennett. He was like a new-born, with no toughness yet to protect him from harm.

A year after the war ended, Bennett was walking again, albeit with a cane. When they wheeled him outside to the hospital's covered verandah, he could hear the caretaker's canary down at the lodge-house and the breathing of the man upstairs, in spite of the ringing in his ears. The headaches came less often, the last shrapnel fragments had been picked from his scalp, and maybe one night a week he would go as much as four hours without waking to the sensation of rotten flesh squelching through his fingers.

But the normal filtering mechanism on his mind had been stripped away. The tiniest of sights, sounds, smells competed with the big ones for his attention. It felt like looking at ten million blades of grass and being unable to see a lawn. And in reaction to this endless bombardment of impressions, his skin only grew worse. It crawled, it itched, it trembled, it went into spasms of horror. Mostly it did this around other people, and the more abrasive the person, the worse it was. Other acts and relationships were intense, even earth-shattering (and why did he think that fellow Stuyvesant had known, how sex for Grey was like being struck by God's own lightning?) but everyday social intercourse could be unbearable, the daily lies and misdemeanors people committed without thought grating against him like a hasp.

Then Aldous Carstairs found him, and brought him to the clinic, and there he lived through nineteen months of growing hell, a nightmare he could not wake from—and oh, the bitter irony of that name, the Truth Project, that sent a hard twinge of toothache through his jaw every time he heard it. Only a fluke—when the Major couldn't speak to countermand Grey's departure orders—had made escape possible.

He fled home for a few days, desperately attempting normality, but his mother's glances tore at him, the presence of others filled him with dread. He'd got as far as setting up an interview with a prospective employer, but riding the trolley to the appointment found him sweating and grinding his teeth, so overwhelmed he ended up hunched over with his hands clamped to his ears: The other passengers had edged away in concern, and he had been taken off before he reached his appointment.

Normal life was clearly not an option.

And so one morning, when Sarah went to see why Bennett had not come down for breakfast, the family found him gone. He left notes, asking that no one try to find him. Bennett Grey put his rucksack on his back and disappeared, permitting the earth to swallow him up at last.

They had either respected his wishes, or else his disappearing act was remarkably efficient, because he had heard from no one until he wrote his bank to arrange for the purchase of the Cornwall land half a year later. Within the week, his sister appeared at the cottage door, but to his relief, she turned out to be one person whose presence he could bear. To his mixed relief and disappointment, Sarah was the only one who came.

He saw her once or twice a year. To the rest of the family he wrote dutiful letters. He gradually ventured into the nearby villages and towns. And every so often, he was driven into a hard corner like a baby seeking a demon's womb.

He lay in the comforting cold hardness with the flavor of brass on his lips, until eventually he slept. He woke with the dawn, abominably stiff and thinking about his sister, and about Laura Hurleigh, but mostly about the American, strangely hard and soft at the same time.

Snap judgments were in Grey's very nature, now: no more second thoughts. Every relationship established since the War had its character set hard in the first few seconds. The Major: terror and loathing; Robbie Trevalian: relaxed amusement; Robbie's mother: interest with a generous dose of reserve. The American: fear and absolute trust. The moment Harris Stuyvesant emerged from the Major's car, Grey had felt as if he was meeting the man assigned to guide him through hell.

Stuyvesant had lied to him. He'd tried to manipulate him, would try again in the future, but Grey couldn't help it: He was drawn to this stranger like a magnet to its mate.

Attraction was dangerous: *Stuyvesant* was dangerous. He arrived with the Major, a bad enough beginning, then followed it up with lies and manipulations and a flat refusal to talk about some key event in his past. And despite these warnings, the man's pull had drawn from Grey revelations that he'd given to few, not even to Sarah.

Yes, the American rang solid and true. Did that make him all the more of a threat?

BOOK THREE

Hurleigh House

FRIDAY, APRIL 16, 1926
TO
SUNDAY, APRIL 18, 1926

Chapter Twenty-One

FOUR DAYS LATER, on a cool, damp Friday morning, Harris Stuyvesant found a parking place two streets away from Paddington Station. He maneuvered the spanking-new Model T to the curb, happy that he'd gone to the extra effort of finagling the London Ford dealer out of his newest one—hard to say if the man had been more impressed by the personal appearance of the American ambassador, or the telegram from Henry Ford himself.

Because it was not exactly a permitted spot he pulled into, he scribbled a note saying "Police Business" and laid it on the dashboard before trotting through the drizzle to the station.

The train from Penzance had pulled in some time before, but the letter from Grey had specified not to come until eight o'clock, when the passengers in the sleeping cars were roused and sent about their business. Stuyvesant reached the train about five minutes before the hour, and bought a paper to occupy himself with. As passengers made their way down the platform, he pawed past the notices to the news, and looked over the whistling-in-the-dark headlines—although even in the *Times*, the daily "Coal Report" headline had recently changed to "Coal Crisis." He glanced up occasionally, but caught no sight of Bennett Grey; after eight, the thin stream of passengers showed signs of drying up altogether.

At ten after, Stuyvesant began to mutter under his breath, cursing the man who hadn't the nerve to wire or phone ahead and say he'd backed out of the plan, but before he could turn away, the door to one of the carriages filled, and Grey was there.

He was a man transformed from the Cornish woodcutter: Travelworn and rumpled, yes, but he'd had his hair trimmed and oiled before leaving Penzance, and was wearing an ordinary if out-of-date brown suit, polished shoes, and overcoat. Not much could be done about his working-man's hands, but the nails were clean and neat.

Beneath the surface shine, however, Grey had the look of the haggard, front-line soldier about him, as if he hadn't slept since Stuyvesant drove out of the farm yard on Monday afternoon. Maybe he was just hung over. However, he seemed calm enough, resigned to the noise and the press of people, and only flinched at the scream of a whistle from the next platform over.

The enormous space beat its cacophony down at them, and Stuyvesant had to resist the impulse to push Grey back onto the train and return him to Cornwall. Instead, he reached out to shake Grey's hand, but the hand the small man held out in return had a valise in it, so Stuyvesant took its handles instead.

"My car's this way," he said. Once outside, he turned to speak and found Grey lagging far behind: The man was limping again, more than he had climbing over rough ground in Cornwall. He lurched his way up to Stuyvesant, then stopped, raising his face to the gray sky.

"You sure you want to do this?" Stuyvesant asked. The man really didn't look at all well.

"Yes. I am just stiff, after all that sitting."

"Weren't there any sleepers?"

"Yes. So I sat on the bed."

"Yeah, me too. Well, I'm parked a couple streets away. Do you want to stop somewhere for breakfast? Or we could go by my hotel and get you a bath and a shave."

"I'd rather get out of the city first, if you don't mind," Grey said. "There used to be a little hotel in Henley that did a good breakfast."

"Fine," Stuyvesant told him, and led the way more slowly. At the car, he opened the back door and added Grey's valise to his, tossed his hat and overcoat on top, and climbed in behind the wheel. Once inside, he could smell the alcohol on his passenger, and was not surprised when Grey fell asleep before they'd shaken off London, curled against the car window. Harris Stuyvesant was alone with his thoughts, thoughts that centered around Richard Bunsen and the speech the man had given the previous evening in a rented hall in Battersea.

When Stuyvesant had arrived at the venue Thursday evening, he found it packed to the walls with Union supporters. Big as he was, dressed as he was, no one questioned his presence or his beliefs as he pushed through the doors and found a seat. He was one working man among three hundred others, and if he kept his mouth shut, no one would look at him twice.

And he would indeed keep his mouth shut. Not only did he have no wish to catch Richard Bunsen's eye, but he could feel the waves of frustration rolling off those around him; he'd been in enough crowded, angry halls to know that these were men just aching for a dust-up.

The first speaker did little to soothe their tensions. He was a Labour M.P. who must have been elected for his excellent works rather than his speaking ability, since he was dull and earnest and dropped his notes twice, ending up nearly inaudible above the rising murmur of the crowd.

Not that Stuyvesant would have paid him much mind even if he'd been golden of tongue and leather of lung. Stuyvesant's attention was entirely on the man sitting in one of the four chairs arranged behind the present speaker; the man listening closely, nodding occasionally, once tipping his ear to a comment from the large sweating figure beside him, smiling his response. The man waiting his turn at the podium with no more sign of nerves than if he were sitting on a train platform waiting for the 8:14. The man whose moustached face had looked out of a shipboard photograph, smiling and care-free. Stuyvesant couldn't tell what color his eyes were, and he wasn't wearing tinted glasses, but it was him.

Richard Bunsen did not look like a terrorist.

Then again, Stuyvesant hadn't expected he would.

But Stuyvesant had left his revolver back at the hotel, just in case his feelings got the better of him.

After what seemed a very long time, the man at the podium stopped moving his mouth and began to gather his papers, broad hints that his speech was finished. A smatter of people began to clap, but before he could scuttle back to the empty chair a voice rang out, clear above the thin applause.

"What's Baldwin doing about the Samuel Report?"

The M.P., caught halfway to his chair, looked at the man who had introduced him, then returned to the podium. He couldn't say if the Prime Minister was re-considering an acceptance of the Samuel Commission's report. No, he did not believe—

"Notices have gone up in the pits!"

The noise from the audience that followed this announcement brought the hair up on the back of Stuyvesant's neck. It was the voice of the mob, the gut-deep sound of men backed into a corner and about to come out swinging. He'd heard the noise before, about two minutes before a mob moved from talk to action, and he gathered his coat around him and looked for the exit.

At least one of the men on the stage had also heard that sound before. The heavyset man who had introduced the current speaker stood up fast and came forward to plant himself on the very edge of the stage, his voice battering the entire hall to silence. No one noticed the M.P. going back to his chair.

"You *want* the rest of the country to think of us as dangerous louts? You *want* Sam and Sally Schoolmarm to agree with the government that Labour has to be put down like a mad dog? Then just go ahead with your growling and see how long before they bring out the Army—and don't you tell me you don't care, because it's your families the Army will be aiming their rifles at." The mutter that had begun to rise up at the word *Army* went dead still. He held their eyes, and after a minute the anger came off the boiling point, and he was talking to three hundred workers again, not a mob.

"As I speak, the Industrial Committee is meeting with the Prime Minister. This week-end, our brothers Arthur Cook and Herbert Smith travel to Brussels to meet with the Miners' International. Our job is to stand firm. Our job is to show we're reasonable men and women with reasonable demands. We are in the right and they are in the wrong. Our job is to keep saying so until the rest of the country agrees."

He stood there, hands in his pockets, and let his audience think about it for a minute. Then he said, "Now, you want to listen to what Mr. Bunsen has to say? Or you want to go out and bust some heads?"

The answer being, of course, that they wanted to go out and bust heads, but the deft touch of humor brought them back to earth. Three hundred backsides settled into their seats. The heavyset man nodded to Bunsen, made a brief introduction, and turned over the stage to the young politician.

Stuyvesant had anticipated Bunsen's charisma. He'd felt the pull of personality often enough among politicians, crooks, and radical leaders that he'd have been surprised not to find it here—especially since the man's working-class qualifications alone were not sufficient to put him onto that stage. Bunsen could not have done the thick-set man's task of settling the audience back into their seats after their stir of anger: too young, too educated, too slim and clean-handed.

But once the true worker had reminded his fellows of the larger goal (and Stuyvesant began to suspect that the whole evening had been stage-handled very cleverly indeed), he turned the meeting over to Bunsen, as if to say, This is the man we need to talk to the men in the silk hats: One of us, gone through their public school, graduated from their university.

And Bunsen hit precisely the right note: He made no obvious pretense to be working class, for they'd have jeered him off the stage. Nor did he stand on his education and accent and speak down to them. His attitude seemed to be, You are as you are; I am as I was made; by bringing our strengths together we can make this work. The emotions he sought to rouse were not just anger and outrage, but righteousness and determination.

It was compelling. *He* was compelling, even for Stuyvesant, who looked at the stage and saw demonstrated all the vitality young Tim had lost, who sat in the hall of English laborers and remembered a young woman whose life had come down to the terrible choice of paving stones over flames.

Bunsen spoke for nearly an hour, using no notes, his voice at all times reaching the hall's farthest corners. Phrases of inspiration and confidence flowed like warm honey, explaining his popularity among Union and Labour alike (to say nothing of certain elements among the blue blood). But again, Stuyvesant had expected eloquence.

What he hadn't expected was how damned *reasonable* the man would sound. Richard Bunsen made his ideas seem the simplest, most obvious solutions to the nation's problems, common sense at its most common. He balanced grim figures with moments of humor, he spoke clearly but without oversimplifying, and he talked of the right to dignity alongside the right to a living wage. His criticisms of the oppressor used hard words ("The very Parliament building in which men vote to take bread from the miner's child was built by the hands of working men; it is heated by the toil of working men; it must speak with the voice of the working man.") but a more-in-sorrow attitude that was extremely effective for conveying conviction and determination. "Capitalism is theft," he declared, then followed the statement not by a show of outrage, but by saying, "It cannot help itself, that is its nature. It is up to us to refuse to be victims any more. They will not steal from us, from our wives, from the mouths of our children, for one more day. They will not."

His gestures and the attitude of his body were wide, but natural, as if he was standing comfortably among friends. Before long, Stuyvesant found himself nodding more than his role called for.

Bunsen ended on the same note of putting steel in the spines of his audience: "A popular movement always entails great personal sacrifice. And my friends, we have already made that sacrifice. Now it is time for our just reward."

By the end of his speech, the entire crowd, including a certain American infiltrator, were hanging on Bunsen's every word. The applause was prolonged, and Bunsen capped the speech itself by a disarming show of surprise—from a distance, Stuyvesant could have sworn the man was blushing.

Stuyvesant slapped his hands together, for a bravura performance.

The audience quieted reluctantly for the third speaker, Battersea's own Member of Parliament. He was a curious individual, a Communist whose name came with difficulty from the tongue of the stocky, working-class master of ceremonies. Shapurji Saklatvala looked and spoke like a Hindu aristocrat, but the words he uttered were inflammatory, so much so that, had he spoken earlier in the evening, the mob might well have risen and spilled out onto the streets in a bloody fury.

But the hour was late, and here and there, a man would rise and slip away—not, Stuyvesant thought, for an act of violence, but for jobs on the night shifts, since most carried laden dinner-pails. When one rose near him, the American followed in his wake.

Outside, it had begun to drizzle. The police constables assigned to the meeting were getting wet, he noticed, and they watched with envy as Stuyvesant paused in the hall's dry entrance to light a cigarette. He stood there in the shelter for a minute, wondering how the hell a bomb-making terrorist could put on such a seamless act that an experienced Bureau agent couldn't find a flaw.

Unless Bunsen wasn't a bomb-making terrorist. Unless Richard Bunsen was a well-meaning radical who honestly was as reasonable as he sounded.

Stuyvesant wondered if he'd just heard so many of those speeches in his life, they set off alarms even when there was nothing alarming. Like the idea of "great personal sacrifice." Why was it always the poor working stiffs who ended up making the sacrifice, and not the man egging them on?

With the cigarette only half smoked down, Stuyvesant dropped it to the ground and crushed it under his heel, making an effort to do the same with his doubts. Charisma was not reason; one can smile and be a villain.

He settled his hat, pulled up his collar, and walked off into the dark city.

Despite the rain, he ended up walking all the way from the far reaches of Battersea to his Bayswater hotel. The river encouraged thought, and the quiet streets made for a pleasant change from the daytime hostilities.

He had to knock for the night manager to open up for him. In his room, he poured some Scotch into a glass and stood in the dark, looking out at the empty street.

When the glass was empty, he took off his overcoat and draped it over the radiator, unlaced his shoes and tucked them underneath, and got a towel to dry his hat and face.

He put the hat on top of the wardrobe and hung his suit coat inside. Loosing his neck-tie and beginning to undo the buttons of his shirt, he moved over to the desk, shifting the desk lamp so a bar of light shone down the back of the desk. He glanced downwards, frowned, and squatted to look more closely.

It was routine, by now: Before leaving the room, he stuck a sliver of match-wood in the back of the top drawer, every time. It was not much bigger than an eye-lash, far too small for anyone but him to notice, but substantial enough that it could only be dislodged by opening the drawer.

Tonight it lay, half an inch of wood fiber, against the base of the wall. Tonight, when the maids were long finished work.

Stuyvesant sat back on his heels. Well, well. Someone's searched my room.

But the thought was followed by another, one that had him upright and backing rapidly to the door. He stood there for a long time, caught in the same icy sensation he'd felt in January when he glanced down and noticed a tiny dot of freshly cut copper wire at the base of the bottle his hand was half an inch from picking up.

There's a bomb in the desk.

Chapter Twenty-Two

IT TOOK HIM AN HOUR to be satisfied that he had bombs on the brain, not in his room—not in the desk, nor under the mattress, nor under the lid of the toilet cistern in the bath-room next door. But it was a nerve-wracking sixty minutes, and it left him lying tense in bed trying to second-guess the thoroughness of his hunt.

No, the room had been searched, not booby-trapped, and with an admirable professionalism. Had it not been for that one small sliver of pale wood, he might never have noticed the slight displacement of his possessions.

In fact, there had been nothing much to find, apart from the gun. His case notes and Bureau identification lay in a bank vault half a mile away. His passport was in the hotel safe, but even if the searcher had been willing to expose himself to the manager by offering a bribe, the passport would tell him nothing he didn't already know.

Still, between the late hour and the residual tension, he hadn't had a whole lot of sleep Thursday night.

And now, Friday morning, as workers and lorries funneled through the highways into the great city, Harris Stuyvesant drove his borrowed Ford against the tide, following the Thames River valley and the Automobile Club instructions he'd been given, his mind going over and over the previous evening's events. Now he'd had time to get used to the idea, he had to admit, it wasn't really out of line for Aldous Carstairs to have ordered a search. Stuyvesant had practically invited it, telling him he'd be out Thursday night.

No, the search of his room was aggravating, but understandable. Much better to return his attention to Richard Bunsen. Looking back, hadn't the man been just a little too polished, too open and honest to be real?

And really, the speech had about zero substance, once you thought about it. No call for action, no rousing of rabbles, no specific complaints or threats. It was almost as if Bunsen thought the actions of the audience were peripheral to the real action.

He began to see what Carstairs had been talking about—that the Unions, unlike the government, appeared to be doing little to prepare for the Strike.

His thoughts and the RAC map took him out of London and through towns and villages with names from the unfortunate—Slough—to the curious: Maidenhead, Hurley Bottom, and Nettlebed. Henley-on-Thames tempted him with a drifting aroma of frying bacon from an inn, but at his side Bennett Grey slept on, with restless twitches and murmurs, and only fully woke when the motorcar slowed entering Oxford.

Grey stretched like a cat, dry-scrubbed his face, and peered out of the window to catch sight of the distinctive spires of Magdalen College. "Good Lord, Oxford already? You certainly are a restful sort of fellow, Stuyvesant." He circled the kinks out of his neck and examined the sky, which had been clear blue since London.

"Going to be a pretty day," Stuyvesant offered.

"Rain tomorrow, though," Grey opined. "So tell me, what clever tale did you and the Major come up with to explain your presence in my life? What do they call it—a cover story?"

"Actually, Carstairs doesn't have much to do with our little week-end, although he's hoping I'll report in. I'm more or less flying solo, from here on out. Yeah, I didn't want to wake you up, but we probably ought to stop somewhere and talk it over. You know any place to eat?"

"Turn up here, we can leave the motor and walk down to Queen Street."

Stuyvesant followed his passenger's directions and found parking to the north of the high street. Instead of lunch, however, Grey led him through twisty lanes and past ancient colleges, dodging trams, cars, cyclists, and lorries across the congested high street, then down a dim alleyway to end up inside the doors of a Turkish baths.

Spending time with another man in a bath-house, moving from bath to steam-room to massage table, leaves a person with little to hide. By the end of it, Stuyvesant had seen most of Grey's scars, and knew which of them required the lightest of touches from the masseuse. He listened to Grey's family history, both the surface facts and the information that lay between the lines. He heard as well those parts of his biography that Grey omitted: He said nothing of lovers, nothing of his father apart from the mere fact of his death in 1912, and nothing of his time with Aldous Carstairs.

Sensitive scars, requiring the lightest of touches.

In return, Stuyvesant displayed his own scars and his own story: big Catholic family; a university education cut short by his father's death at a factory; a job at a bank, followed by the Bureau, where bank crimes were investigated. Time out for the Army, then back to the Bureau, moving two years later to political crime.

Neither of them talked about the War.

Two hours later, cleansed, pummeled, smooth of cheek, and famished, they walked up the high street in search of food. The sidewalks were crowded with busy shoppers and lounging students and they found a restaurant Grey remembered, ordered their meal, and sat, staring down at their glasses with that discomfort that follows revelation. To break it, both men spoke at once.

"I thought perhaps—" Stuyvesant began.

"Why do they do it?" asked Grey.

They looked at each other, and relaxed.

"You first," Stuyvesant said. "Why does who do what?"

"Your terrorists. I'd have thought men resorted to random violence only when they felt utterly oppressed and excluded from power. When one feels there is no alternative, I imagine that terror might seem a viable means of striking back. But surely one cannot say that of a man like Bunsen? He's halfway to being a Member of Parliament."

"Bunsen doesn't fit the mold, that's true. Terrorists—whether they're Anarchists, Communists, or any other flavor of ist—are usually young, romantic idealists who believe body and soul in a cause, convinced that a shove in the right direction can change the world in a day. They are rarely the actual members of the oppressed classes— for one thing, they have enough free time and energy to think about something other than just putting bread on the table. They're often educated, either formally or by their own reading, and attach themselves to what they see as their true family, be that a class, a religion, or an ethnic group. They have little interest and no empathy outside their circle—as far as they're concerned, unbelievers do not really exist. It's massive egotism, of course, to feel you know better than anyone out there, but then, don't you find that sort of egotism in most people who change the world? Religious leaders, great generals, inventors, thinkers. Even Members of Parliament."

"You sound remarkably sympathetic, considering it's your job to arrest them."

"They can be enormously attractive—energetic and bright, passionate about their cause. They don't often have a great sense of humor, since they take themselves pretty seriously, but sure, I'd rather spend time with a political agitator than your average bank president. But they're wrong in what they do, wrong and dangerous, and I have no problem keeping my likes separate from my job."

"However, Bunsen's more than a job."

"Yeah." No point in denying it with this man.

"And what were you about to say?" Grey asked.

"Oh, nothing so profound and philosophical. I was just going to say that maybe we should get our stories straight, how we met and what my job is and all."

A cover story is best when it sticks close to the truth, so one doesn't need to think about it. By the end of the meal they were in agreement; and replete, restored, and ready with a complete if somewhat fictional history, they walked back to the motorcar.

Steering the car through Oxford's Medieval streets, Stuyvesant settled himself into his identity, that of a Ford Motor sales representative whose work brought him to England every year or so. He was here with a man whose farm he had stumbled across, while on a hiking holiday in Cornwall two summers before.

They left the town and entered the Oxfordshire countryside, and he asked Grey a few questions about his family, to fill in the gaps. Grey's mother, who sounded as if she used her robust ill health to keep her family under control, rattled around in the all but empty family home eighty miles to the east. His brother had emigrated to Canada, his sister, Sarah, lived in London; the last three years she'd come down in the late spring for a week in Cornwall.

"She's not married?" Stuyvesant asked.

"She was engaged briefly, to a nice boy who died of a bullet to the head his first month on the Front. That was the official story; in fact, he died raving of sepsis ten days after taking a round in the belly."

"Yeah. Our boys tended to get shot cleanly in the head, too, in letters home."

"Since then Sarah's devoted herself to good works—first the Vote, then literacy, now health care for the poor."

"Carstairs told me a little about the medical clinics."

"I think there's five now, four in London and one in Manchester."

"Does your sister work at one of them in particular?"

"She and Laura Hurleigh run the whole show. Laura's in charge of the big picture, raising funds and gaining support, while Sarah actually runs the operation. Which may be why she's more or less taken over Bunsen's group as well. She's a funny girl, is Sarah—a great one for getting things organized and running smoothly, and then she'll drop everything in favor of a snap decision that changes everything. Usually for the better, I admit. She says it's because her mind works faster than her brain. In any case, it's not just brotherly pride to say the place wouldn't survive without her."

"Tell me about Lady Laura Hurleigh."

"Anyone who reads the papers probably knows as much about her as I do now. When I was young, I spent a certain amount of time with the family, but I haven't seen most of them since before the War."

Stuyvesant shot him a glance, hearing a lack of conviction in

Grey's voice, but his passenger was gazing intently out of the side window at a pair of children galloping bareback across a field, and he couldn't be sure if it was deception he was hearing, or distraction.

"You know her well enough to put in a good word for me?"

"Yes."

"Tell me about the family."

"The Duchess of Hurleigh is a distant relation on my mother's side—my mother's brother's wife's cousin. I spent a couple of summers with them when I was growing up—Mother was very ill for a while, and I suppose the idea was the Hurleighs had enough children that they wouldn't notice one more. I dare say my father was pleased to have me out of the way during the holidays, and I was very happy in the uproar at Hurleigh House. I was in the same year at school as the oldest boy, Thomas, and one year above the current heir, Daniel."

"There are five or six children, aren't there?"

"There were seven: Laura, Thomas, Daniel, Constance, Pamela, Patrick, and Evelyn, in that order. Thomas was killed in the spring of '15, just a few days after his son was born. The child died in the influenza epidemic of 1919. That was the only grandchild, so far."

"Still, it's a respectable size of family, for non-Catholics."

"Hurleighs have been remarkably consistent over the ages in having large families with many boys. Up to now."

"What, there's two sons left, aren't there?"

"Probably the least in any generation for three hundred years."

"Okay, but they must be young."

"Patrick is, certainly. And my sister tells me Daniel is now engaged. He wasn't yet twenty when the War started, and it shook him badly. Went through a wild patch but he seems to be settling down. He'd have gone far if the War had dragged on another year or two—but then, the Hurleighs have always been brilliant strategists on a battlefield."

"The other brother—Patrick—he was too young to enlist?"

"He must be twenty now—no, I remember reading about his twenty-first birthday last autumn. It made the newspapers when half the party came up before the magistrate the next morning. Must have been October—everyone but Evie has a birthday in September or October. Evie didn't come along until January. The Duchess was incensed, which may explain why they stopped at seven. And of course, without the War, three sons would have been seen as sufficient to preserve even the Hurleigh name," he added somewhat enigmatically.

But Stuyvesant had gotten well tangled up in this string of non sequiturs, and finally had to ask for help. "Sorry, I'm not following you."

"What, the name? Oh, well, with ancient titles like Hurleigh, there's invariably a title and then a family name, since even if they started out one and the same, sooner or later the direct line runs out of males and everything shifts sideways to a cousin or what have you. But with the Hurleighs, the surname and title are one. I don't know if there are any other titled families in the country like that."

"So the original Duke was named Hurleigh, and he took Hurleigh as his title as well?"

"Exactly. Ralph de Hurleigh, that would have been, Marquess of Pontforth, made duke in the late sixteenth century."

"I see. And why does the timing come into their stopping at seven children?"

"Timing? Oh—the hunting season. That pregnancy cut the Duchess out of an entire season. I don't know if she's forgiven her husband yet."

"Ah," Stuyvesant said wisely. "Fox hunting."

"I should have asked: Do you ride?"

"I know which end of the horse to face."

"Well, with any luck, the season will be over here. If it's not, I'd suggest you develop piles or rheumatism or something, unless you want to spend tomorrow hiking ten miles cross-country back from the ditch some diabolical gelding tips you into."

"Painful experience?"

"Memorable, certainly," Grey said with feeling. "The Duchess is absolutely mad about hunting. Not as comprehensively mad as her husband, but when it comes to horseflesh and hedges, they are the center of her universe."

"But the Duke hunts, too, doesn't he? Seems to me I heard some story about him running students off his land with a pack of hounds."

"I'd doubt it, more like he sets the house dogs on them. If

students come during hunting season when the dogs are expected to be fresh, he brings out the shotgun instead."

Stuyvesant glanced at him; Grey appeared serious.

"Honestly?"

"Oh yes. Sarah and I used to call him Uncle God—his name is Godlake, but God seemed more appropriate. He's an interesting mixture of twelfth and twentieth centuries. Feudal to his bones but with a peculiar fascination for modern mores. There was a huge uproar two years ago when the Duke gave a speech in the House of Lords supporting the Labour Socialists. The Duke of Hurleigh, of all people! The King was shocked, and called him on the carpet to explain that he hadn't meant to suggest that the Communists had any justification for murdering the King's cousin the Tsar, just that shaking things up a little might stimulate the blood of England. He's big on the blood of England, the Duke is."

"Even if he's shedding it with a shotgun."

"He's a terrible shot, hasn't hit an undergraduate yet. Although rumor had it that, during that same year, he invited MacDonald and his daughter out for a weekend and young Ishbel winged a prowling Christchurch man."

"MacDonald the Prime Minister?"

"And his daughter."

"You've got to be kidding."

"Have I?"

"The papers would have been full of it, a Prime Minister's daughter shooting an Oxford student on Hurleigh land? There'd have been an enormous stink."

"You think so? You could be right, perhaps it was merely a rumor. However, my dear Stuyvesant, you need to remember that our newspaper barons belong to the same clubs as our aristocracy. Not everything juicy makes it to ink."

That, come to think of it, was true. The newspapers might well have splashed the event all over their front pages had it merely involved the MacDonalds, but enter the Duke of Hurleigh, and English heritage stepped in. Hurleighs had won major battles for a dozen monarchs in a score of countries; Hurleighs had played billiards with kings since the game was invented; Hurleighs had advised prime ministers since the days of Cromwell.

Yes, without question, a house guest of the Duke of Hurleigh would be permitted to plant the odd piece of lead shot in an importunate Oxford undergraduate.

And what of a stray American motorcar salesman? Stuyvesant was aware of a touch of something like heartburn, or anxiety. "I wonder if he'll set the dogs on me, or just reach for the gun."

"Neither, if you can convince him you're a poor benighted Colonial who is filled with humiliation at not having had an Englishman's opportunities in life, such as learning to ride properly. Of course, then you'll have to expect a series of pitying lectures."

"Couldn't I just be a lost cause?"

"You could try that approach, if you didn't object to being invisible the rest of the week-end. Just for pity's sake don't suggest that foxes should be dispatched with a gun: You'll have both of them on your neck. Daniel brought a school friend home who had the temerity to suggest such a thing: The police had to be called to rescue him from the tree the dogs had run him up."

"Thanks for the warning."

"And another thing I should mention," Grey said. "The Duke has a knack of blurting out the most appalling *bons mots* and Spoonerisms when he's upset. When the children were young and we used to race about, wild as a tribe of red Indians, he'd come storming out of his library and bellow at us to 'cease and desist from all this damnable hurly-burly.' It always reduced us to helpless giggles, which only made matters worse, as his rages could be honestly terrifying. One summer Thomas and I started a newspaper called the *Hurleigh Burleigh,* but we had to stop because even talking about it made us dissolve in tears of laughter."

"So: no talk of shooting foxes, no reacting to accidental word play, come up with an excuse for not riding, and never use the word *week-end* in front of the Duchess."

"That should see you nicely started."

"I think I'd rather infiltrate a ring of rum-smugglers. The most I'd have to worry about then would be handguns and brass knuckles."

"You'll be fine. As I said, the Duke likes Americans, when they're humble enough. If they're not, he curses them for 'spongers'—he hates to feel people are sponging off him—and vanishes until they've all left."

Stuyvesant drove in silence for a while, holding to himself the un- likely image of this deeply wounded man beside him caught up in a fit of boyish giggles. Six miles farther, and Grey directed him to turn off.

They had left the relatively flat farming country around Oxford and entered a landscape of small hills and many trees, set with houses made of a honey-tinted stone. Sheep decorated the hillsides, many of them trailing lambs.

"Are these what they call the Cotswolds?" Stuyvesant asked.

"You haven't been here before?"

"I spent two weeks in England in 1919, on my way home from France, working my way from London up to the Lakes District. It was February. All I can remember is how damned cold it was, and how little food I could find."

"I can imagine. Take a right up there past the church."

They were negotiating the narrow road—in a city he'd have called it an alleyway—through Hurleigh village, which comprised a bank of houses whose doors opened directly onto the road, some shops with window boxes of spring flowers, a hall of some kind, and a church. The village green, where the weekly market would be held, had a war memorial at one end, a stone pillar with names of the dead. Every village they'd been through had a memorial, large or small, grand or simple, all of them just beginning to shed the raw look of fresh-cut stone.

The road left the village just past the church-yard, passing be- tween stone walls topped with clipped hedgerows that bristled with spring nettles. After a mile, the ground dropped away and the hedges lowered, and Stuyvesant saw they were traveling up a wooded valley at whose bottom ran a tidy reed-grown stream. Nestled into the op- posite hillside was a cluster of buildings with a square bell tower ris- ing above the trees, a miniature village. It could have illustrated the perfect, timeless beauty of England: quiet, unassuming, precisely the right proportions for their setting, the very arrangement of buildings God had in mind to adorn that patch of landscape.

After passing three small but prosperous-looking farms, the track veered and dove across the stream by way of a ford. Just upstream was a narrow bridge for foot traffic and livestock, a series of graceful stone arches connecting the banks. Stuyvesant geared down and aimed the car's nose into the rock-laid dip beside it, splashing through six inches of smooth brownish water before slithering up the slope on the other side. Here the road divided, and Grey pointed him towards the left; only then did Stuyvesant realize that the cluster of buildings he'd been admiring was their destination.

Hurleigh House was not what Stuyvesant had expected.

Chapter Twenty-Three

"COUNTRY HOUSE" WAS THE STANDARD British understatement used to describe what Americans would call a mansion, if not a palace: Enormous, ornate, and self contained, the British country house could be an entire village under one roof, designed primarily to impress the hell out of everyone in sight.

Hurleigh House was small, as country houses went—and that by itself spoke of the profound eccentricities of generation after generation of Hurleighs. In any other family, some eighteenth-century modernizer would have razed its Tudor bones to bare ground, carved away the hills behind it, and lifted up in its place a piece of generic Baroque glory. Instead, here was simply a house in the country. Only a part of the structure had the tiny windows and small stones of great age, but the changes and additions had been sympathetic, as though subsequent generations had merely consulted an original master plan whenever they needed to add space.

It was a place like its family, both influential and apart. As if a pope had set up house in a cave, taking with him the authority of the papacy, but leaving behind all the trappings.

The drive came out from under the trees near the stream and through a stand of Brobdingnagian rhododendrons. They passed a

stables with open doors, then a stables with closed doors, followed
by a long stretch of walled orchard with old, nicely pruned trees and
a gate with a glimpse of white chickens scratching in the grass. The
orchard gave way to a kitchen garden with neat rows of staked peas
and lettuces, followed by a lodge-house, narrow but deep. This building was kept at a demure distance from the main house by the beginnings of a seventy-five-foot-long curve of greenery that wrapped
around the circle formed by the end of the drive: assorted shrubs at
either end, bracketing a stretch of high, closely trimmed hedge.

It was an oddly anticlimactic arrival to the house, designed more
to speed the departure of visitors than to welcome them in. Even the
house itself turned a shoulder to the drive, presenting a noncommit-
tal façade of stone, roof-lines, and small windows that looked like af-
terthoughts. The wall of green was interrupted by three gates: a low,
wooden one leading to the lodge-house, a slightly wider iron one set
just to the right of the house itself, and downhill from the house, half-
concealed by an ancient tumble of rose vine with enormous white
blossoms just coming into bloom, another wooden one.

Next to the iron gate at the drive's end-point there was a gas
street-lamp on a tall post. The house had no *porte cochere,* no broad
steps up to wide carved doors, and the drive's circle surrounded not a
fountain or sculpture of brazen lions, but a small, thoughtful moun-
tain of deliberately arranged boulders and rocks, planted with alpine
miniatures. Stuyvesant wondered if they had come to the servants'
entrance.

Near the street-lamp stood a man of perhaps sixty, wearing a
dark suit, and a young woman in a plain blue dress. The man's suit
seemed a touch formal for a family member in his own house in the
country, and the girl's woolen dress was as plain as her face and hair.
Stuyvesant tried to think which of the family these might be.

Whoever they were, the man was beaming with pleasure at the
sight of Bennett Grey. "Good afternoon, Captain Grey," he said;
there were traces of Scotland in his voice.

"Hello, Gallagher, good to see you again. This is Mr. Stuyvesant,
from America."

"Good day, sir," the man said, at which point his deferential attitude
and Grey's lack of an honorific arranged themselves in Stuyvesant's

mind, and he caught his hand before it was fully extended: These were servants. Gallagher appeared not to notice the truncated gesture. "I fear I've been forced to put you and your guest into the barn. We shall have quite a full house by tomorrow."

"We'll be very comfortable there, I have no doubt. Is my sister here yet?"

"I believe her train should be in Oxford within the hour. Shall I tell her that you have arrived?"

"If you would, thanks—I didn't know when she was coming, or I'd have picked her up as we came through. I think I'll take my friend for a walk up the Peak. Drinks at the usual time?"

"Six o'clock in the solar, although if you care for tea beforehand, you need only ring. Shall I come and show you to your rooms?"

"Have there been any changes, since I was here last?"

"Nothing has changed in the barn in thirty years, sir."

"If that's the case, why don't we just help ourselves to any free rooms?"

"As you like, sir. Your bags will be over directly."

"You left the keys in the motor, didn't you, Stuyvesant?"

"They're in the ignition."

"Come along, then. Thank you, Gallagher."

"Sir," the butler said.

Somewhat bemused, Stuyvesant trotted after Grey. "We're sleeping in a barn? I spotted a nice-looking inn, back at that last village."

Grey laughed, a sound so care-free, it might have issued from the boy who had known Hurleigh House during that unimaginable idyll before the guns of France. "Don't worry, there won't be a hay-stack in sight."

A shady path followed the north side of the house, through a miniature woodland of fern, primrose, and tiny white flowers. To the left were a couple of narrow doors with over-hangs, both of them tucked behind shrubs. To the right, where the sun cleared the roof-lines, was a strip of rose garden, the leaves glossy with spring growth and showing the first tentative flowers. An unruly stand of dark ever-green shrubs forced the path into a dog-leg, then the barn came into view.

It had, indeed, once been an agricultural out-building—had functioned as such for centuries, by the look of the bulging walls and the various shapes of stones used in repairs—but its purpose had changed before the century's turn. Generous windows had been hacked out of the ancient Cotswold stone; when they stepped through the door into the barn's wide entrance, it was startlingly cozy within.

Stuyvesant did not know much about English houses, but of one thing he was sure: Heat was not a priority.

Even without the unaccustomed warmth, the barn's entrance was a singular space: The walls were teeming with frescoes: Near the door was painted a twining grape arbor through which could be seen men and women in togas with odd instruments; down the hallway the vista opened onto a landscape of olive trees and ancient buildings. Underfoot, the floor was mosaic, tiny tiles in colorful geometric patterns. And, Stuyvesant noticed, no radiators. He squatted down to lay a hand on the stone tapestry. "The floor is warm," he said in surprise.

"That's the hypocaust. Grandfather Hurleigh—the present Duke's father," Grey explained, "had a passion for the Romans. Ancient Rome, that is. One of his plows dug up some bricks that turned out to be from a Roman villa, and he had the whole thing meticulously excavated by a team from Oxford. There used to be a scale model of it in the library, and when Grandmamma Hurleigh asked for a place to put the family—they had nine children, and each of them had at least four children—he jumped at the chance to build an hypocaust. Roman under-floor heating. Although this one is fed by pipes, else he'd have had to tear down the barn and build from the ground up. While he was at it, he brought in a crew of Italian mosaicists to do the floor, and hired young art students for the frescoes. Those musicians are his children."

"Which explains the English-looking faces on top of the Roman robes," Stuyvesant commented.

"That countryside is odd as well, neither Italian nor English. Which I suppose is not altogether inappropriate for Roman Britain. Let us see, is anyone in here? No—how is this?"

They had climbed the stairs, following a painted valley of small farms in summer browns along their right. In the upper corridor,

Grey turned left and crossed the hallway to the farthest door down, where he stuck his head inside, checking for signs of occupation, before standing back to let Stuyvesant enter.

The room was awash with light. It was not large, about fourteen feet on a side, but both external walls had a broad mullioned window topped by a half-circle of painted glass depicting a hill with a tree. After a moment, Stuyvesant saw that they were the same hill and tree, flipped to make a mirror image, although the tree on the east wall bore bright springtime leaves, while its mate to the right dazzled the floor with the oranges and maroons of autumn.

The arboreal theme extended to the bed itself, a mahogany object with four tall posts carved to resemble bark and drapes woven with a pattern of leaves.

"I'm going to feel like I'm sleeping in a tree-house," he told Grey, and was surprised to hear the pleasure in his voice—this was like some childhood hideaway, and it appealed to a boyish urge he'd have thought well buried. He was smiling as he studied the room, which fortunately was papered not in leaves, but an off-white and light green stripe. The south window showed the long view down the valley, the one on the left overlooked the house and the shady garden they had come through.

"More comfortable than hay and a stable-blanket?"

"You Brits have some interesting ideas about barns."

"I shouldn't expect to find anything like this outside the Hurleigh sphere. The family has been noted for its eccentricities for centuries. Ah, here come your things."

The maid in the blue dress and a young man in corduroy trousers and a pull-over—a footman, Stuyvesant supposed—appeared up the stairs, cases in hand. "Mr. Stuyvesant will be in here," Grey told them, "and you can put my kit down at the end."

"The coach room or the secret room?" she asked.

"The secret room will do fine—er, what is your name?"

"Deedee, sir," she told him, sketching a brief approximation of a curtsey. "And this is Alex."

"You're both new here since the War, I think?"

"We are, sir, although Alex's mother was in service here when she was young."

Grey turned to study the young man's face. "Emily? Something, started with a P."

"Porter, sir."

"You have her eyes. She used to sneak us bread and dripping, when we came begging at the kitchen door. Remember me to her, would you?"

"Will do, sir."

Alex laid Stuyvesant's battered leather case on the holder beside the wardrobe and carried the other case down the hallway. Stuyvesant turned an eye on Grey. " 'The secret room'?"

Grey gave him a grin that made the man look a decade younger than the headache-ridden wretch of Cornwall. "Come and see when you're settled in."

Turning back into his room, Stuyvesant nearly ran down the young maid, who lingered just inside the door. "Sir, if I might have the key to your valise, I could put your clothing away."

"Oh, no, honey—er, Deedee. That's fine. I'll do it myself. Thanks."

The young woman turned pink and slipped out, closing the door gently behind her. Stuyvesant, making a mental note not to call the staff "honey," slid the bolt and carried his valise over to the bed. He pulled a small key from his watch-pocket, unlocked the case, and up-ended shirts, linen, evening dress, and shaving kit onto the bed. He then righted the case and reached inside, peeling the bottom back with his fingernails until he touched cold steel.

The Colt was smaller than his revolver of choice, sacrificing power and accuracy for ease of concealment. He couldn't see himself swaggering into an English drawing room with a six-shooter strapped to his side, but no way was he going on a job unarmed— and sure, he had a lock-blade knife and the well-worn brass knuckles he'd had made to fit his hand, but those didn't really count as "armed." At the reminder, he burrowed back into the valise's false bottom and came up with the knuckles as well; the knife was already in his pocket.

The question was, where to put the weapons? Not that anyone was going to search his room here, but he had a feeling that his valise was going to be tidied away as soon as his back was turned, so he looked around for a place where servants might not go, or curious snoops poke their noses. It took him five minutes of prying to discover a loose board on the floor of the wardrobe. He settled the gun and the knuckles in there and pushed the board back into place.

He thrust his clothes onto hangers and stuck them in the wardrobe, shoveled his other garments into the drawers, and arranged his shiny evening shoes and his worn walking boots atop the loose board. When he had splashed water on his face in the corner sink, he crossed the hall-way to use the toilet, then followed the voices to the other end of the barn.

Grey's chosen room was the last on the same side of the corridor, with one door between it and Stuyvesant's. It was simple room, stark even, compared with the one Stuyvesant had been given, but more serene than secretive: unadorned bed-posts, a plain blue bed-cover wound about with rows of stitching, a subtle geometric design on the floor's throw-rug. It might have been a monk's dwelling, except for the quality of each object.

Grey was still talking with the two servants when Stuyvesant tapped at the open door and put his head in. Alex instantly took his leave, looking abashed at having been caught chatting with a guest. The maid, Deedee, scurried out after him, some of Grey's garments draped over her arm.

" 'Secret room,' huh?" Stuyvesant asked. Grey did not answer, merely raised his eyebrows and waited for the American to figure it out.

The woven rug on the floor caught Stuyvesant's eye first: The geometric design wound around and around and back and forth, some lines coming to a halt, others connecting: a maze, in blue and brown wool. And the stitching on the bed-cover? Another labyrinth, intricate and tightly detailed; it would take hours to unlock the puzzle.

His eyes traveled across the walls, then to the bed itself. Its corner-posts were capped with flattened pyramids; one of them was at a slight angle to the others. He examined it, running his fingers up and down the post to search for the controls, but he had to go all the way to the bottom before he found the button that freed the post cap.

The shallow space beneath the cap was empty. He replaced it, pressed down until he heard a click, then investigated the other three posts. All were empty but for a sweet-wrapper in the bottom of one.

He returned his attention to the walls. The wallpaper here was blue and brown, in stripes similar to those in his room. He left the room and went through the corridor into the middle room, which had been converted to storage and was stacked high with chests, trunks, and folded bedding. He measured its width with his eyes, then went back into Grey's bedroom, walking directly over to the joining wall to explore the wallpaper stripes with his finger-tips. How many walls had he searched in this fashion, he wondered, in the seven years since the Volstead Act went through?

"The way most hidden doors get discovered is," he said in the tone of a lecturer, "that the top cuts across the wall where there shouldn't be a seam. But if the entire wall is made up of a series of doors, floor to picture-rail—ah." Leaning against the wall freed the latch, revealing a built-in cupboard, two sheets of wallpaper wide. Behind this section of false wall was a chest of drawers; the next had the room's clothes-rail. When Stuyvesant was finished, six doors, each some thirty inches wide and eight feet tall, stood ajar.

Grey picked up his valise and put it onto a shelf in the wall, and walked down the row of doors, pressing them shut.

"Did I find all the secrets?" Stuyvesant asked him.

"Not quite. But I'd like some fresh air before the others arrive. Shall we go?"

"What's in the other rooms?"

"The barn has seven bedrooms, no two alike. The most interesting is the one directly underneath yours, which is made up to look like a crypt, complete with a *trompe l'oeil* wall of skulls. Oddly popular with certain kinds of Hurleigh guests, although I didn't take you for someone whose taste runs in that direction. Also, the room across from yours is said to have one of the country's more impressive collections of taxidermy. Somewhat macabre, but again, a surprising number of guests like to stay there. Here, this room's rather fun."

He opened the door directly across from his, and gestured the American inside.

Stuyvesant came to a halt in the doorway. "How the hell did they get that in here?" *That* was a full-sized, open-topped, gilt-encrusted ceremonial coach the size of a small barge. The wheels had been removed and permanent steps added on either side, and where the seats had been, surrounded by the carvings and the gilt, was now a feather bed laid with shiny gold satin bed-clothes.

"I believe they hoisted it into the barn and the work went on around it. You want to see the other rooms?"

Stuyvesant raised a hand in protest and said, "I think that's enough for right now. That fresh air you were talking about sounds good."

"Fine, but do not let me neglect to show you the chapel during the week-end. You've never seen anything like it."

Stuyvesant had never seen anything like the entire Hurleigh getup: Roman architecture; servants dressed like family; guest rooms with trees and skulls and gilt coaches; a passion for foxhounds; regular grist for the gossip rags; and, it would appear, some kind of radical political doctrine.

It wasn't just Hurleigh House: the Hurleighs themselves were not exactly what he'd expected of an ancient titled English family.

Chapter Twenty-Four

THEY LEFT THE BARN through a narrow door set into the western wall. Grey launched himself fearlessly down the rather shaky external stairway, but Stuyvesant took the steps more cautiously, lingering a moment at the top to survey the view. While they'd been inside, the bright spring sun of their arrival had slipped into an afternoon that held a lingering taste of winter. The sun preserved some of the winter's low angle, which meant that portions of the opposite slope of the valley were in shade, while Hurleigh House and the river below it were dazzled in light.

Considering the dampness that came with having running water two hundred yards from the front door, Hurleigh House's site was surprisingly comfortable. The valley floor might be an absolute swamp after a heavy rain and that tidy little ford rendered impassible, but the ridge behind Stuyvesant rose well above the chimney-pots, sheltering the house's back from wind while its face collected all the winter sunlight in the world.

Whoever had chosen this place for his house had paid attention to detail.

(Although Stuyvesant wasn't too sure what that long-dead

Hurleigh would have made of his descendant's whimsical conversion of the barn.)

He trotted down the stairs, catching up with Grey on the footpath that ran through the open trees.

"Parts of the place look pretty old."

"The barn is Medieval, as are the Hall and parts of the kitchen. Fair bits of the east wing are Tudor. We'll have drinks in the solar, which hasn't changed since it was built in 1577—the date's on the fireplace. I say, will those shoes do for hillside scrambling, or are they only good for pavements?"

"One way to find out," Stuyvesant answered. Fortunately, when they left the woods and entered the open grasslands, the vegetation was dry enough that he did not slither too much, and he did not drop too far behind Grey as they left the path and climbed towards the ridge top. It took concentration, though, and Stuyvesant had no opportunity to look around him until they reached what Grey had called the Peak, a knob of rock resembling a construction of wet sand dribbled from a giant child's beach shovel.

The Peak overlooked the stream, and was high enough that the countryside beyond stretched out, with the spires of the distant Hurleigh village church rising beyond the trees and hedgerows.

Grey was looking, not at the valley, but at the grass hillside that dropped away on the other side; his face wore an odd, bittersweet expression. There was nothing particularly compelling about the hillside, just a long sweep of grass stretching almost to the stream below—although if Stuyvesant had been eight years old, he might have found the slope irresistible.

Grey finally turned away and continued across the uneven surface, arms outstretched for balance, to drop with an experienced twist of the hips onto a flattish lump. Stuyvesant followed, choosing a lower but somewhat smoother rock for the seat of his own trousers.

He sat, and he looked.

There really wasn't a lot to say about what he saw. How can a man comment on perfection? The house, the valley, the width of the stream, the cows grazing on the opposite hillside: simple, ancient, and unmistakably English.

Grey heard his faint sigh, and nodded. "I used to spend hours up here. Life at home went through some difficult patches, but up here I could be free. I would sit up here, belittling my problems against three thousand years of history."

"We Americans usually go for the night sky when we need to feel small. With us, a thing is old when our grandfather saw it."

"Nearest anyone can figure, the name Hurleigh is a corruption of the Old English *hohley*, with *hoh* meaning heel or ridge, and *ley* a clearing in a wood." He stretched his left hand in the direction of the house, then moved it to encompass the higher ground behind them. "The ridge behind us is a foot-path that's been used since before Stonehenge." The hand moved again, back in the direction of the house; Stuyvesant noticed that Grey's fingers seemed to feel the contour of the countryside they moved over, reading the texture of its history like a blind man reading Braille. "When the stables were built, workmen uncovered a cache of Saxon coins. And between them—you see the uneven bit of ground to the right of those three flowering trees?"

"The boulder pushing up the grass?"

"I think if you dug down, you'd find that boulder was a bit of Roman Britain. Some rich man's villa, a general's escape from the battlefield, perhaps, or a merchant who decided not to go home again."

"Is that what Grandpa Hurleigh dug up?"

"No. I'm not sure anyone knows it's there—I've just noticed it myself, although I must have sat and stared at that hillside for a hundred hours, over the years."

After a while, Stuyvesant took out his cigarette case, thumbing it meditatively before he opened it and offered one to his companion. Grey shook his head; Stuyvesant took one out and lit it. The line of the shadow crept into the middle of the stream now, the water all but hidden by the reeds.

Stuyvesant glanced sideways. "You going to be okay, here?"

By way of response, perhaps, Grey reached into his coat and drew out a decorative silver flask. He unscrewed the top and took a swallow, then held it out for Stuyvesant. The American hesitated; he could smell that booze with the explosive effect. But he accepted the flask and ventured a sip. The stuff still brought tears to his eyes.

However, once the immediate vapors had dispersed, the odor of the drink did not linger. You'd hardly know Grey had been drinking.

"So what is that made of?"

"Mostly potatoes, I believe. The flavor comes either from a dash of petrol or a dose of rotting plums, perhaps both. As I said, I do not enquire too closely. And to answer your question, I do not know if I shall be all right. At the moment I am. With luck, I shall remain so." He took another swig, then screwed on the top.

"You don't have to stay," Stuyvesant told him. "If you don't feel up to it, all you have to do is introduce me to your sister and we'll turn around and get back on the train. I can take it from there, in London."

Grey turned the flask over and over in his hands. After a minute, he spoke in a meditative voice. "I have grown very tired of my limitations. Even before you showed up in my yard, the thought of being forever condemned to a few square miles of deserted countryside was becoming intolerable. There are times when I stand on the Beacon and the call of the sea below is nearly irresistible. If Cornwall is a home from which I can come and go, I can live there with ease; if it is a prison, I cannot."

"So, this is a test, coming here?"

"An experiment, perhaps. To see precisely where my boundaries lie."

And, Stuyvesant thought, to see precisely what it cost to nudge them out a little. "Just so you're not letting Carstairs get you into a corner."

Grey's mouth twitched with bitter humor. "My only corner," he said, "is the one I get into myself."

Stuyvesant glanced sharply at his companion, then looked away and drawled, "Well, personally, I'd have thought conversation with your neighbor Robbie would offer about as much intellectual stimulation as a fellow could take. But then I'm not an Oxford man."

The easy grin slid back into place. "Aow, the Robbie leaves me lampered, ee do."

"Well, I'll tell you right now, thank you for doing this to help me out. I do honestly think it's important. And if there's anything I can do to make things easier for you, just let—"

Grey jumped to his feet and Stuyvesant broke off, thinking for a wild moment that the man was about to enact his threatened dive off the nearest high rock. But once upright, Grey stood frozen, his eyes fixed on the other side of the valley: A car was coming down the road that led to the house.

Without a word, Grey scrambled off the rocks and limped swiftly down the path. Before Stuyvesant reached the foot-path, Grey had disappeared into the first stand of trees. The man's urgency was baffling, but contagious, and Stuyvesant paused only to shut the snicket latch on the gate Grey had left open, lest wandering livestock invade the gardens. He found the second gate standing open as well, closed it, and walked along the north side of Hurleigh House to the drive.

Grey was standing forward on his toes, hands clenched in his pockets. The butler, Gallagher, came out of the house, followed by Deedee; the four of them waited.

The clatter of a laboring engine badly in need of adjusting echoed down the valley as the motorcar climbed the road from the ford. A minute later, it came into sight, a seven-year-old Morris trailing a black haze. It cleared the hill, entering a patch of sunlight: Grey settled back on his heels and his shoulders lost their tension; a moment later, Stuyvesant realized simultaneously that this unlikely rattletrap was the Hurleigh estate's transportation, and that the passenger briefly illuminated by a flash of sunlight was not the passenger Grey had been expecting.

But not a stranger, either: Grey's hands came out of his pockets, the fingers relaxed, and he glanced at Stuyvesant with a twinkle.

"My sister," he said.

Whom had he been expecting?

Chapter Twenty-Five

THE CAR HAD NOT COME TO A FULL STOP when its back door flew open and a diminutive blonde figure launched herself at Grey, nearly sending him head over heels into the hedge.

For an instant, England stood still for Harris Stuyvesant, as his mind shouted, *Helen!* But the message came up against a wall of self control, because of course this was not Helen, it was a stranger, with the wrong hair and green eyes where they should have been blue. He shoved the escaping remnants of memory into their box and nailed down the top.

He watched Grey swing the blonde creature around and felt as if he'd had a sharp kick in the gut. The girl laughed into her brother's beaming face, and Stuyvesant found himself grinning at her exuberance. Even Gallagher and Deedee looked on with fondness until they remembered themselves and bent to the task of the luggage.

Grey set his sister down and, his arm draped across her shoulders, turned to Stuyvesant. "Stuy—" He broke off. "What is it?"

The American just raised a pair of innocent eyebrows. Grey frowned, but got the message, and went on. "Stuyvesant, this is my sister, Sarah. Sal, this is Harris Stuyvesant."

"Ma'am," he said, raising his hat.

She planted a hand on her own absurdly tiny headgear and tipped her head to look up at him: pale yellow hair, wind-blown from the motorcar's open window; dancing green eyes, the exact color of her brother's, with the first crinkles of laugh-lines at their corners; a delicious spray of freckles decorating her slightly upturned nose and the V of skin left exposed by her frock. Nothing like Helen, he was relieved to see.

"An American!" she declared.

Stuyvesant wasn't sure what had given him away, his dress, manner, or the one syllable he had spoken, but he nodded, feeling remarkably large and clumsy. "That's right."

"I adore Americans. They always make me want to run out and buy a pair of cowboy boots."

"You'd look charming in them, I'm sure, Miss Grey." It was hard going to keep his eyes away from the freckles in the hollow of her throat, which had to be just about the sexiest thing he'd ever seen.

"Oh, Bennett, this is just too clever of you, to bring me an American to make me laugh. Where on earth did you find him?"

"He found me. I was minding my own business one day a couple of summers ago, digging my potatoes and thinking my thoughts, when this figure appeared up the lane with a rucksack, stick, and walking boots. Frankly, I think he'd taken a wrong turn on the way to Land's End, but being an immensely competent sort of chap generally, he'd never admit to being lost. He works for the Ford company—although I'm sorry to have to tell you that he's sold out from his working-class beginnings and wears a white collar now. When I heard he was going to be over here, teaching the natives how to sell the American product, I thought I'd bring him to you."

"Like a dog bringing a dug-up bone," Stuyvesant added, reaching out to wrap his oversized mitt around the small hand Sarah Grey was offering.

She laughed—a surprisingly deep, rich laugh, not the giggle her appearance led one to expect—and let her cool fingers rest in his for a moment before turning to her brother. "I say, Bennett, I know it's far too early to expect drinks *chez* Hurleigh, but really, your little sister is feeling a little moldy after that pig of a journey, and she could use just a tiny bit of a jolt. Can you possibly summon a G and T?"

Grey raised his eyes to consult the butler. "I shall bring ice straightaway, sir. Miss Grey, Lady Laura suggested that you be given the Blue Room, if that is acceptable?"

"No, I'll have a room in the barn, and leave the house for the family."

Gallagher's face kept its control at this suggestion, but only just. "Miss, there is a sufficiency of rooms in the house for all, I should think—"

"My dear Mr. Gallagher, I've been coming here since I was in pigtails. At that time, I stayed in the house because it wouldn't have been proper not to. But this is 1926 and I'm grown up enough to choose for myself. I'll be perfectly all right in the barn. My brother will act as chaperone." The authority in her voice was unexpected but nicely judged, and it silenced the butler. Before Gallagher could come up with a decisive counter-argument, she asked, "Has anyone claimed the wave room yet?"

The butler cast a pleading look at the rebel's brother, who shook his head to say that Gallagher was on his own. The man sighed. "The wave room is free, Miss. The wave room," he commanded the other two, and they split up, Deedee and the driver heading towards the barn with Sarah's bags, Gallagher to the house, disapproval in every thread of his black coat.

"You mustn't torment Gallagher, Sal," Grey said.

"I refuse to be cosseted like a Victorian maiden," she said. "Besides, the house smells of dog."

The Greys wandered after the luggage, Sarah's arm through that of her brother, Stuyvesant walking behind as the two blond siblings chattered about the health of their mother, a business venture of their Canadian brother, and the expected birth of his second child. They might have been twins, he thought: Her hair was a shade lighter than his, now that his barber had trimmed the sun-bleached ends, and despite heeled shoes she was an inch shorter, but their eyes were identical, and the profiles they turned to each other shared the same nose. Even the tilt of their heads were mirror images, tipped towards the other as they walked, her shoulder tucked into his biceps.

So this was the wedge Aldous Carstairs had used to detach Grey from his Cornish stronghold, Stuyvesant mused—or maybe the bait on the hook of Carstairs' Project. In either case, very attractive bait she was, with the first cloche hat he'd seen that didn't resemble an overturned bucket, a silk frock that failed to conceal the unfashionable curves of her body, and a set of calves that made him appreciate the recent rise in hems.

Inside the barn door, Grey's sister turned left and made a bee-line for the last room on the right.

When he looked inside, Stuyvesant saw that the décor here was, indeed, a wave, with the bed its boat, riding a building swell of gray-blue water that rose unevenly up two of the walls. The furniture seemed about to pitch and toss on the blue-green rug. Sarah looked up at Stuyvesant's face and let fly with that rich laugh again.

"A mite disorientating, isn't it?"

"You don't wake up sea-sick?"

"Never. Although I dreamt once that I was swimming with dolphins."

He blinked at the picture conjured by his mind's eye, this young woman rising and dodging through the waves among those sleek creatures that had played alongside the *Spirit of New Orleans* three weeks before. Fortunately, whatever he might have blurted out was interrupted by the clearing of a throat, and they turned to see Gallagher, carrying a tray with a sweating silver ice-bucket.

"Shall I place this in the general room, sir?" he asked Grey.

"Oh, bless you," Sarah answered, and they moved across the hallway, leaving Deedee to the unpacking.

With only the room's name to go by, Stuyvesant was braced for anything: a life-sized statue of Napoleon, perhaps, or frescoed groupings of high-ranking military personnel throughout the ages, but in fact it was just a comfortable room with a fireplace and a number of sofas and overstuffed chairs: general-purpose, rather than military general. The furniture was upholstered in maroon and dark blue leather, but the paintings on the walls were unexpectedly *avant-garde*—Stuyvesant recognized a Picasso and a Matisse, and there were several more by artists whose work he had never seen before. It was an enormously attractive and comfortable room, the afternoon sun through the west windows making the colors glow like stained glass. The fire was welcome, although it made it almost too warm.

Gallagher placed the tray on the well-laden drinks cupboard in one corner and asked Grey, "Would you care for—"

"Thank you, Gallagher, we can take it from here. I'm sure you have a hundred things waiting for you."

"Very well, sir."

"I—sorry," Grey said, as his word interrupted the butler's progress out the door. "I just wondered if you'd heard when the Family are expected back."

"Her Grace generally returns near dark; His Grace is in his study; Lady Pamela is expected back from Gloucester at any time; Lady Constance and Lady Evelyn are dressing for dinner; Lord Daniel and Lady Laura indicated that they would return in time for cocktails. Lord Patrick is in the library with a friend."

"Heavens, the full complement of Hurleighs will assemble. Thank you, Gallagher. We'll change and be over in half an hour or so."

"Thank you, sir." With a brief dip of the head, he left.

The moment the door shut, Grey wheeled on his sister. "What happened to you?"

"How on earth—?"

"You didn't want Gallagher to know, but something happened. You're hurt."

"Oh just—it's nothing. A little bang, just shook me up a little. I'll tell you about it, but please, Bennett, you mustn't mother-hen me."

He kept his eyes on her with that listening attitude Stuyvesant had seen before, and then the tension left him and he straightened, knuckling his temple as if to soothe a residue of ache.

"Stuyvesant, would you pour my sister a drink? She puts on a wild front, but in fact she prefers it heavy on the tonic water."

Stuyvesant splashed gin over ice and filled the glass with fizz for Sarah Grey. He scooped some ice in another glass, poured a generous measure of gin over it, and raised a questioning eyebrow at Grey, who made a keep-going gesture with a finger. Stuyvesant tipped the bottle again until Grey nodded; maybe five ounces of gin. He poured a dash of water on top, gave him the drink, and made a considerably weaker one for himself.

Grey held his up, and said, "To friends and family."

"Friends and family," they echoed. Sarah took a thirsty swallow, kicked off her shoes, and pulled her stockinged feet up into the large chair with a sigh of contentment. She had watched the amount of gin going into her brother's glass without comment, but Stuyvesant thought that some of her cheerfulness had faded.

"So, Sal my gal," Grey said as he dropped into the chair beside hers. "Give over."

"Honestly, Bennett, it was nothing. A fight broke out on the train, just short of Oxford Station, and I got a bit jostled. It was more unpleasant than frightening."

"A fight, actually on the train?"

"There were some boys who'd been down in London playing at constables—practicing for the Strike, you know? And they'd stopped in for a couple of drinks before they got on the train, plus they'd brought flasks with them, and as the spires came into view they picked an argument with an elderly man who'd been harrumphing his way through the newspaper. One of the boys said—well, it hardly matters what he said, it was deucedly rude, and the man got up and threatened to thrash him for his impertinence—I think that's what he said, his accent was rather thick—and that brought the rest of the carriage into it—"

"—including you," her brother interjected.

"Well, yes, I could hardly let them abuse the poor fellow, and they were such self-righteous prigs, you can't imagine."

"I can, you know."

"Yes, I suppose. But it actually looked as though they might take out their play-constable truncheons and use them on the fellow, and I stood up and went over, so that he wouldn't be all on his lonesome, don't you know? And one of the boys fell over, actually tripped over his own great feet, and bumped into me. I banged my head against the wall and my hat fell off, but it served to sober them up so it was in a good cause."

The two men stared at her. Stuyvesant wanted to get out the car and drive into Oxford to hunt down a pack of drunk students, but Grey kept himself well under control.

"Sarah, sister dear, you really mustn't get into brawls with drunken undergraduates. Your impetuosity will get you into hot water one of these days."

"It was just an accident, they were terribly apologetic, but if I hadn't intervened they might have hit the old man."

"What newspaper was the old gent reading?"

"Well..."

"The *Workers' Weekly?*"

"Oh, it might have been, but so what? A man has the right to read his paper, hasn't he?"

"What I'd like to know is what a group of undergraduates were doing in the third class compartment. Yes," Grey said, although he hadn't been looking in Stuyvesant's direction to see the surprise on his face, "my sister considers it an obligation to travel with the horny-handed sons of toil rather than splurge on comfort."

"I shouldn't be surprised if the ticket-seller in London had seen their state and refused to place them in first class."

"Thus getting them off to an irritable start."

"If I'd been a man, I'd have pushed one or two of them out of the window," she declared.

"I have no doubt that you would make a top-rank bare-knuckle fighter, Sal."

"But you, dear brother," she said with an air of transferring the spotlight. "What on earth brought you out of Cornwall?"

"As I told you in my letter, I wanted to see you."

"You could have come to London. Or home. I'm there quite a lot, and you could've said hello to Mother in the bargain."

"I didn't want to see Mother, I wanted to see you. And Stuyvesant happened to be in the country, so when you wrote to tell me you were going to be here, I thought it a once-in-a-lifetime chance to show the old man one of the more interesting institutions of the English social world. I did send the Duchess a wire asking if it would be too rude to invite myself and a friend. She wrote back one word: *Pleased.*"

"You came to Hurleigh House to show your friend the sights?" Sarah sounded frankly disbelieving.

Grey downed an inch of almost pure liquid courage, then said, "I've been feeling better. Stronger. I wanted to see if I could handle it."

Sarah softened instantly, and stretched across to squeeze his hand. "I'm glad, Bennett. Really so glad."

Which response made the gin go sour in Stuyvesant's mouth. Still, in a manner of speaking, Grey's explanation might be almost true.

"But, dear boy," she continued, "do try to play down the Mother's Ruin. It takes the edge off things, I know, but in the long run it can make life difficult." The bright gaze shifted to her brother's friend. "And you, Mr. Stuyvesant; I expect you to keep an eye on him. If he shows signs of falling too far into a bottle, take him for a long walk up the Peak, or down to Batty's Tump."

"I shall do my best, Miss Grey."

Grey balanced the glass on the arm of his chair and stretched his feet towards the fire. "And you, young thing. When you're not brawling with the strike-breakers, what's the pash these days?"

"Really, Bennett, you are so out of touch. We're all deeply serious now, nobody has 'pashes' any more; we have 'causes.' And as you well know, when I'm not at home listening to Mother complain that I'm never there, I divide my time between Women's Help in the East End— that's the free clinic—and Look Forward—that's the political group." Her words were light, even dismissive, but Stuyvesant could see that she took both groups seriously. "I don't think I've told you about Laura's latest conquest—" She paused for an aside to Stuyvesant. "Laura Hurleigh, that is, who doesn't like to be called 'Lady.' She started the first clinic, and helps run them. Laura's latest conquest for Look Forward is Cora Burton-Styles. You remember her?"

"God. Cora Burton-Styles is seared into my memory." Grey said it with feeling.

Sarah laughed and turned again to Stuyvesant. "When my brother was fourteen, he fell head over heels in love with a neighbor, Cora Burton-Styles, probably because she was nearly a foot taller and could beat up any boy her brothers brought home. Unfortunately, Bennett's very best friend had fallen for her at the same time. So the two boys decided that the only way to handle the problem was to set a quest— terribly King Arthur, you see? The first one to climb to her window and give her a red rose without getting caught would win the rights to her affections. Only the problem was, *la belle dame sans merci* was indeed *sans merci,* and when Bennett's lovelorn face appeared in Cora's first-floor window late one night, a rose clenched between his teeth, she screamed, flung open the window, and bashed at him with her silver hair-brush. He fell fifteen feet and landed on some prize peonies, and Cora's father swore that if Bennett ever set foot on the place again, he'd take a shotgun to him."

"Nearly broke my neck," Grey remembered. "I've loathed peonies ever since."

"Lucky they weren't rose bushes," Stuyvesant commented.

"And after all that," Sarah concluded, "in the end it turned out that Cora doesn't like boys much anyway, so it was all for naught."

"But she's lending a hand with this political group—what did you call it, March Forward?" Stuyvesant asked, steering the conversation in a direction that might do some good.

"*Look* Forward. Yes, donating money, mostly. Some of us feel it's the only hope. Bennett doesn't take me seriously, 'cause I'm only his little sister, but honest, this country is in such awful shape, even I have become aware of it. A person has to be pretty blind not to see how terrible the inequality is—I have school friends whose sole interests in life are Paris fashion and getting invited to the smart parties, when a five-mile circle drawn around their houses will find children who go to bed hungry, men working for less than they made in 1905, and women who have one baby after another with no medical attention at all. And Laura and I thought, if people like us don't stand up and make a fuss about it, who will?"

"So Look Forward advocates political change?" Stuyvesant asked.

"Among other things. Basically, it's a meeting-place of minds," she told him, eyes shining, feet coming to the ground so she could lean forward in emphasis. "Look Forward draws from all the levels of society, rich and poor, right and left, in an attempt to overcome the traditional boundaries and distinctions. We've brought together Union leaders and Members of Parliament, miners' wives and lady office-workers, dock-workers and undergraduates. One of the projects we're working on now is a children's play camp in the summer, with children from all backgrounds coming together for two weeks to play together and learn from each other."

If her speech sounded like words composed by another, there was no doubting the sincerity of her belief. Stuyvesant found himself smiling at her enthusiasm. He caught himself up short, and turned his mind to business. "I haven't heard about the group. Are there many members?"

"Hundreds," she said, sounding proud.

"Do you have a leader?"

"Leadership is archaic," she said promptly. "Most of the world's problems stem from hierarchies—laws that support the status quo, leaders whose main interest is keeping the under-classes in line. We all do what is required according to our strengths."

"So if you need someone to talk to a Member of Parliament, you'd send a miner's wife with a child on her hip?"

She shook a finger at him. "Mr. Stuyvesant, you're teasing me. But yes, wouldn't that be ideal, to see a coal miner's wife sitting down in conversation with the Prime Minister? However, we're young, we are forced into compromise."

"So there's no particular leadership. Who makes the decisions about projects and directions?"

"A group of us talk everything over. Laura Hurleigh is probably the most active member at the moment. Richard—Richard Bunsen—is the one who started it, but of late he's been rather wrapped up in matters to do with the Miners' Union."

"Along with the rest of the country," Grey remarked.

"I've heard that name, Bunsen," Stuyvesant said, sounding uncertain.

"Richard is beginning to make a name for himself in politics," she said. "That's probably where you heard of him. He's a fine public speaker, with a real sense for what the nation needs—some of his projects have just taken off like wildfire. You'd like him. So would you, Bennett. Now, don't scowl at me, Richard's an interesting man. He may drop by here during the weekend, but even if he doesn't, now that you're coming out of your hibernation, I'll make certain you meet him. You'd have a lot to say to each other."

"We shall see," Grey said. "Another drink, Sis?"

She tipped the glass so the ice rattled against her teeth, and said, "No, that'll do me nicely. All shakes, gone, see?" She held out her hand, and it was indeed quite steady. "I must go dress, I feel as though I'd been dragged through the shrubbery behind one of Her Grace's hunters."

"You don't look it," her brother said, before Stuyvesant could. Both men got to their feet as she rose to go.

"My brother, the honey-tongued devil. Shout me up when you're going over," she told him. "I won't be long."

"Funny thing is," Grey confided to Stuyvesant as they walked up the stairs, "she actually won't be long. One of the most ungirlish girls I know."

"Still, that's a nasty thing to have happened."

"Yes. Except that if I know her, she'll make it into a joke and dine off the adventure for a month."

In his room, Stuyvesant found his evening wear laid out on the bed, wrinkles banished; similarly, the clothing he had hung in the wardrobe had been meticulously re-arranged, the shirts pressed, the suits brushed to perfection. Even his hair-brushes and shaving implements had been cleaned and laid in neat order. The shoes he had left on the floor of the wardrobe had been polished and replaced, but to his relief, the loose board had been overlooked.

The valise was nowhere to be seen. However, he thought as he gazed at his reflection in the toes of his evening shoes, if he'd left the gun out, the maid would probably have oiled it punctiliously, polished each of the bullets to a shine, and put it back precisely where she'd found it.

He crossed the hall to the bath-room and washed off the day's grime, then came back and, standing in his under-shorts at the room's small mirrored sink—hot water piped in here, too—he shaved with care. He checked himself for stray tufts, eyed what he could see of his chest critically, deciding it wasn't all that bad for a man of forty. He brushed his hair with his favorite (unscented) hair oil, cleaned his nails, and set about the painstaking task of clothing himself in evening wear. As he was threading the studs through the stiff fabric and cursing under his breath, he heard the footsteps and voices of arriving guests, two young men by the sound of it. They took the two rooms on the other side of the hallway—carriage and taxidermy—banging and calling out to each other. Doors shut and the sound of quiet butlerian footsteps was broken when a door rattled open and a voice asked Gallagher if the drinks tray was downstairs.

He reassured the guest that he would check the ice and the tonic. The young man said, "Right-ho." The door banged shut; Gallagher's footsteps retreated down the stairs; Stuyvesant moved to another stud, musing on the fact that the young guest had not expected Gallagher actually to fetch him a drink.

Stuyvesant had limited experience with the ways of the English, but over the years, he had spent a certain amount of time among the American rich. The rigidity of pre-war households had relaxed a great deal, mostly because few could still afford the number of servants they had once employed. Still, he'd have thought that servants, when available, might generally be expected to wait on guests.

He was on the last stud when he heard a door open and close and footsteps approaching down the hallway. Stuyvesant stretched out an arm to pull open his door, then stepped back to the mirror.

"I'll just be a second," he told Grey when the blond man appeared. "Whoever staged a lightning raid on my wardrobe and plastered my shirt-front with starch did not account for large and clumsy fingers."

"Large, perhaps." Grey leaned against the door and watched as Stuyvesant adjusted the neck-tie around his collar and began shaping the knot.

"Tell me, the role of the servants here seems a little unusual. I mean, I've been in houses where you practically have to lock the bath-room door to keep the maid from scrubbing your back for you. Here you're left to fetch your own drinks, but then they go and iron your clothes and polish your shoes when you're not looking." He scowled at the bow and tugged it loose to start over.

Grey chuckled. "The Duke's interpretation of aristocracy takes some getting used to. You see, when he was a young man, he went through a radical phase. He decided feudalism was A Bad Thing, so he changed the way his servants lived—decent housing, education for their children, no demeaning labor, fair pay, the lot."

"Sounds positively Bohemian—I'm surprised they didn't hang him for high treason."

"The House of Lords cherishes its eccentrics. Then during the War, Laura had another bash at his hibernating radicalism. She badgered him into banning all the trappings—which among other things meant the livery."

Stuyvesant just grunted in response, having reached a tricky part with the tie.

"Push down with your middle finger," Grey suggested, which did, indeed, help. He waited until the tie was past danger, then continued. "Unfortunately, the servants rather liked some of the trappings, and as for the rest, well, they had their own very definite way of running things. Basically, for the past forty years it's been a tug-of-war. No livery, but the clothing they wear might as well be a uniform. And guests mustn't be overly coddled, both because it's one of the Duke's pet rants and, more rationally, since it loads on the work too much—this house has less than half the number of servants it had twenty years ago. On the other hand, the maids can't bear to see a guest poorly turned out—it reflects badly on their professional standards.

"What it boils down to is if an able-bodied guest can do a thing without stepping on the house's toes, he's expected to do it. Fetching his own drinks from the general room comes under that category; fetching a bucket of ice from the pantry does not, since that would require his intrusion onto the servants' territory. A guest is expected to dress and to draw his own bath—or have his man do it for him, if he's brought one—but a guest cannot be expected to carry a shirt to the laundry, heat up a flatiron, and produce a freshly pressed garment, as that would be another intrusion on Gallagher's realm."

While Grey was talking, Stuyvesant had tweaked the tie to his satisfaction. He pulled a handkerchief from the drawer, shook his head at its remarkable crispness, and tucked it into his pocket, looking at the result in the mirror. He'd been right, last year, to spring for the more expensive suit, which he could wear with pride, no matter the surroundings.

He smoothed his hair a last time, and followed Grey into the hallway. "So if I go shooting I wait to be given a gun, but once I have it, I carry and load it myself."

"You've got the flavor of the thing."

"And if I ride, I rub down the horse afterwards myself."

"That might be one of the gray areas. I'd say, you start the process and, if no one comes to take the job over, you've been judged competent enough to be trusted with the animal's welfare."

Stuyvesant grinned. "Sounds about what I'd expect of a titled family that tools around in a decrepit old Morris instead of a Rolls or a Daimler."

"That's the Hurleighs for you."

At the bottom of the stairway, Stuyvesant hesitated. "Didn't your sister want us to let her know when we were going over?"

"She's already gone. Nearly ten minutes ago."

Ten minutes ago, Grey had been in his own room, behind closed doors, at the far end of the building from the main door, yet he had heard his sister go out. Stuyvesant nodded, and stepped outside.

Instead of following the path towards the drive, this time they circled the house, and Stuyvesant entered Hurleigh's formal garden for the first time.

It was nearing dusk, a clear April evening. The air was rich with scents: fresh-turned soil, mown grass, the musk of a rose, some spicy herb, and a number of unidentifiable teasing traces of growing pleasures. The sky's arc described the full spectrum of blue, from near-white to throbbing violet; lamps had been hung from branches and in the small building at the center of the rectangle, lamps so delicate they seemed less to push back the gathering darkness than to pull it in and play with it. The sounds of merriment spilled into the garden from above, voices and music, punctuated by the occasional clink of glass.

Suddenly, the anticlimactic arrival made sense: Hurleigh House was intended to be entered by its front door, which could only be reached through this garden. Slightly longer, slightly deeper than the house, terraced on a gentle slope towards the river below, the entire garden—the shape of its paths, the arrangement of benches and pools, the very plantings—demanded that the visitor pause before entering the house, to reflect on the nature of Garden as Paradise.

The big manor houses, the Blenheims and the Chatsworths, illustrated a family hammering its name across a vast stretch of landscape. Their approach was that of the gods: a sweep of the arm here, and acres of parkland rolled out like a carpet; an outstretched finger described a circle there, and behold, a lake was born, to reflect the house and provide the ladies with their afternoon stroll.

Hurleigh showed an entirely different approach to the horticultural arts. Here was retreat and shelter, not the steam-roller of transformation. Within these ancient garden walls, poised between moving water and wooded hills, was a world in miniature: ordered, inward-looking, everything in its place—Nature improved upon, not dominated. It reminded Stuyvesant of tapestries he'd seen in France, spangled with flowers and long-skirted women, peopled with unlikely looking lap-dogs and birds.

He would not have been astonished to find a unicorn, legs tucked demurely to its chest, studying him from beneath the wall's long tangle of fragrant white roses.

Reluctantly, he moved to join Grey, who was waiting on the steps, apparently unmoved by the magic. When Stuyvesant paused on the step below him for a final glance, he noticed that the first lights had come on across the valley, underscoring the oncoming darkness.

Grey's hand slipped into his breast pocket, and came out with a flat shiny object.

The silver flask glittered in the lamp-light as Grey uncapped it and raised it to his lips. Two large swallows followed by the familiar reek of the Cornish liquor, and he capped the flask and turned to the house.

Without a word, Stuyvesant followed.

Chapter Twenty-Six

THE YOUNG FOOTMAN WHO HAD CARRIED their bags to their rooms that afternoon was posted at the door, his pull-over and corduroy trousers replaced by a magnificent uniform coat studded with gold buttons and draped with gold fringe, gold thread, and gold braid. It must have weighed twenty pounds. Closer inspection showed the preposterous garment to be at least a hundred years old, but it didn't take a man of Grey's sensitivity to perceive the lad's enormous pleasure in it—he seemed two inches taller than he had in mufti. The uniform was actually just the coat, since the trousers beneath it were modern and black rather than the knee-breeches that would have been more appropriate, but with the hem coming past his knees even in the front, the anachronism was hardly noticeable.

Stuyvesant half expected to have the young man bawl their names into the hallway, maybe with a blast of trumpets for good measure.

Instead, he just yanked the door open and tried hard to present a face of dignity.

"You look splendid, Alex," Grey told him.

"It's not too much?" he asked, sounding less like a manservant than one schoolboy to another.

"Not in the least."

"We found it in one of the dressing-up trunks in the attic—the Hurleighs used to put on plays during the holidays, worthy of the West End, they were. Deedee was going through the trunks for the moth and said it was the same as in one of the paintings in the gallery. We thought the guests would enjoy it."

"It might have been cut to fit you," Grey assured him.

"Had a couple of moth-holes in it," Alex confided. "But Mrs. Bleaks got out her needle and set them right in an instant."

"Busby Berkeley couldn't have chosen better," Stuyvesant said.

Alex beamed, taking the remark as a compliment, and swept them inside with a wave suited to a courtier with a feathered hat. If the Duke had wanted to bury the feudal elements at Hurleigh House, he'd certainly succeeded with this footman, whose film-star panache overcame the costume's Gilbert-and-Sullivan absurdity.

Grey started up the stairs that rose up across from the entrance, then glanced upwards. Despite the pull of distant voices, he came back to Stuyvesant's level. "Let's just pop in and show you the Great Hall—one of the family can take you on a proper tour later, but you should see the Hall without distraction."

The Great Hall was a sizable cube that was clearly more of a room to impress than a room to sit around in. It was designed for a style of living that had died out so long ago Stuyvesant found it surprising that no Hurleigh had stuck his head in one day and thought, "Surely we can use this space for something better." A bowling alley, say, or an indoor tennis court. Then again, a grand family might have need for a grand room, for the occasional hunt ball if nothing else. And what if the King and all his retainers dropped in for dinner?

The two men moved into the center of the Hall. The walls and ceiling had changed little since the carpenters had taken down their scaffolding, centuries before: plaster had been repaired, not replaced with new-fangled designs. Tapestries covered one wall although, lacking light from the two massive chandeliers, the room was too dim for the faded designs to be more than vague shapes: a tree rising along one side, a group of heads down below. The fireplace could take logs the size of a man; the antlers decorating the wall above it might have belonged to some prehistoric forefather of a deer.

"When was this built?" Stuyvesant's voice was small in the quiet expanse.

"Parts of it are Norman. But in its present form, family documents have it completed in 1455."

Fourteen fifty-five. For four hundred and seventy-one years, Stuyvesant reflected, Hurleighs have walked into this room and lifted their eyes to those beams. The Renaissance rose, London burned, Elizabeth reigned and died, thirteen Colonies fought their way free of the King. Pestilence raged, industry and an empire rose up. Sons went forth to fight and die in sun-baked lands, bombs rained on London, and all the while, Hurleighs walked into this room and looked up at those beams.

Perhaps it wasn't so astonishing, after all, that this room hadn't fallen to another purpose.

Stuyvesant shook his head. "Can't you just hear the man saying to his builder, 'My family's going to be needing this room four centuries from now; let's make sure they don't have to fix anything because we cut a few corners here and there'?"

"It is true. It breathes an unquestioning belief in its time and place."

They stood for another few seconds, and Grey asked, "You want a drink?"

"God, yes," Stuyvesant said, and followed Grey out of the past.

The stairway was wide and dark and felt nearly as old as the Great Hall. In fact, Stuyvesant thought, the whole place felt ancient—clean and polished and comfortably lived in, yes, but the very air seemed heavy with centuries. Grey started briskly up the stairs, but Stuyvesant took his time, feeling the solid wood of the stairway flex infinitesimally under his weight like a living thing, its myriad joins loosed by tens of thousands of similar weights.

The stairs formed a sort of tower, with a landing halfway up and walls on all four sides. A faded stained-glass window in the north wall depicted an elaborate family tree, its details all but invisible with the growing darkness outside. As he rounded the landing, Stuyvesant glanced up.

On the wall facing the window hung a painting larger than most of the walls in Stuyvesant's New York apartment, showing a family dressed in sixteenth-century ruffs and pearls. The stocky, fair-haired father wore the sword on his hip as a tool rather than a decoration; his slim, Spanish-looking wife—dark, faintly almondine eyes, black hair, and a nose that on a less dramatic face would have been unfortunate—was sitting with a cloud of lace in her lap; between husband and wife were two girls and a boy, all three with their mother's dark coloring. The woman's left arm was gathered around the lace-draped infant, but the artist, whose name Stuyvesant did not recognize but who might have been a student of Titian, had placed her other arm across the back of the chaise, arranging its curve to mirror that of her husband's sword. At first glance, she seemed merely to be gesturing the children to her, but an attentive viewer could not miss the resemblance between woman and weapon: thin, taut, and razor-sharp. Another artist—one who permitted his artistic frustrations to come out on the canvas—might have depicted the Englishman as a buffoon. It wouldn't have been difficult to do so, given a woman like that at his side, but this artist had shown only the pride and affection, and maybe even a trace of amusement, in both of his subjects' stances and the set of their heads. A formidable pair.

On the walls separating the family portrait from the window, two Reynolds portraits, a man and a woman, gazed at each other across the stairs. Had it not been for his dress, which was two hundred years more recent, the man might have been the Spanish woman's brother—dark, slim, haughty, and with that unmistakable nose—a descendant, without a doubt, but one who showed no trace of his blond ancestor's coloring. The man stood with one hand resting on a desk, whose arrangement of objects no doubt conveyed allegorical meaning to the initiated. The woman across the stairway from him was seated, her full hair a glossy brown, the ornate white folds at her bodice hinting at the breasts beneath. A baby, little more than a swirl of white with a face, lay in a rocking bed at her side.

Bemused, Stuyvesant ordered his feet to continue upwards. When the stairs came to an end, passing beneath the Elizabethan couple, he found behind it not a room, but a hallway. The wall across from him was pierced by two doors, both open, between which stood an ancient, roughly carved wooden trunk with iron straps and a clasp so enormous it would require a padlock the size of his fist. The trunk looked as if it might have floated ashore after the sinking of the Armada, filled with maps and doubloons and letters of marque. On the wall above it were three small framed pieces of needlework mounted behind glass, faded to invisibility.

The rest of the hallway was lined with six—no, seven glass cases containing porcelain figurines, most of them canine: King Charles spaniels, Dalmatians, Alsatians, and brace after brace of bull terriers.

The Duke's collection was indeed extensive.

With an effort, Stuyvesant pulled himself away from porcelain Canidae and continued in the direction of the voices.

Behind both open doorways stretched a long gallery nearly the entire length of the house. Facing south, it was warm from the day's sunlight, but the expanse of mullioned windows must have made the two wide fireplaces a necessity in winter. The floorboards clicked slightly as Stuyvesant moved inside, as they would have clicked with the daily passing of family and friends, the long-skirted women and the men with lace at their throats. Here was where generations of Hurleigh women paced up and down, up and down during the dreary English winters, listening to musicians, reading aloud, gazing at the garden and the river beyond, yearning after spring. Here was where generations of Hurleigh men had gathered, away from the walls that might conceal listening servants, to speak in low voices about the doings of kings and of kingmakers, plotting business and politics, reviewing rivalries and partnerships.

It was nearly the undoing of Harris Stuyvesant. The walls were linenfold woodwork, lovingly polished by generations of servants; a worn, faded carpet ran the length of the room; he took three steps onto it before museum treasures on the walls brought him to a standstill. He stopped and frankly gaped at the scintillating Venice of Canaletto, and next to that, Gainsborough's summer England. Another step brought him to Matthias Grünewald, then Claude Lorrain; on the opposite wall rested a Hogarth; down at the other end he spotted a Constable.

He could no more have left that room unexplored than if he'd been chained to a wall. He made a slow, stunned circuit, all by himself with a collection that would have been the pride of a good-sized city in the States. When he eventually made it back to the Canaletto, he glanced down the room to his right to where the sound of conversation entered, and for the first time noticed Gallagher, posted at the door to what must be the solar. With reluctance, Stuyvesant made his way back up the length of the gallery, a series of Hurleighs looking down their long, Spanish noses at him from the walls. Near the end, he spotted the one wearing Alex's coat; on him, it did not look in the least preposterous.

Where the gallery had been mostly space with a few seats along the walls, the solar was a snug, well-furnished room, a jumble of dark carpets and heavy furniture. When Stuyvesant came in, Bennett Grey broke off his conversation with an iron-haired lady, who wore her dress and jewels as if impatiently trying them on in a shop. He gestured for the American to approach. "Duchess, may I present my friend Harris Stuyvesant? Stuyvesant, Her Grace, the Duchess of Hurleigh."

Stuyvesant wasn't sure if he was supposed to bow over her hand or not, so he compromised with a sort of dip of the upper body as he took her fingers—strong fingers, accustomed to getting their way with a lifetime of horses.

"Mr. Stuyvesant, Bennett tells me you are a sales representative for the Ford motorcar people?"

"Yes, Your Grace, that's what I'm doing now, but I—"

"You must speak with my husband. He is contemplating the purchase of another motorcar, and has been told that the French are building excellent machines."

"I suppose, although next year Ford is introducing the new Model—" Stuyvesant began.

"Personally, I do not believe the French can be trusted with anything that does not come from a vine or the teats of an animal, far less a complex mechanism such as a motorcar. My husband, however, believes otherwise. You shall have your work cut out for you to convince him to the contrary."

"Ma'am, I wouldn't dream of inflicting my sales pitch on anyone so good as to invite me to their house for a social visit. However," he added, seeing the slight frown between her gray eyes, "if the topic comes around in the course of conversation, you may rest assured that I'll do all I can to uphold the reputation of my employers."

One aristocratically arched eyebrow rose as she considered the possibility that he had just made a joke, and then she granted him a small upturn of the mouth. "You do that, Mr. Stuyvesant."

Grey touched Stuyvesant on the elbow to steer him on, murmuring into his ear, "That Yankee charm."

"Nice old bat," Stuyvesant murmured back.

"Let's get ourselves a real drink," Grey said, tossing back the champagne in his glass and depositing the empty on a table.

A slim boy with a weak chin and slick black hair stood behind an armoire that should have been in a museum, but was currently laid with a white linen cloth and an arrangement of bottles resembling the New York skyline. His evening suit looked too expensive for a servant, and indeed, when he spoke, Stuyvesant recognized the voice of one of the late arrivals. He was at least a decade younger than Grey and clearly did not know him, but amiably picked up a bottle from the makeshift cocktail bar and dumped gin and tonic into a glass, then with somewhat more enthusiasm concocted a martini for Stuyvesant. He was pouring it from his silver shaker when a hand snaked from behind to rest on Grey's sleeve. Grey jerked at the touch, sloshing gin onto two centuries of polish. The hand withdrew, to be replaced by the person of a buxom young woman with a tight cap of perfectly arranged and perfectly artificial blonde curls.

This creature leaned forward, her bandeau feather threatening to insert itself into Stuyvesant's left nostril, to peer in a myopic fashion into Grey's face. While she was occupied with his companion, the American ran his eyes over her eccentric costume, which consisted of: bead-and-feather bandeau; a brief silk dress that had been designed for a person with fewer curves; a voluminous and brightly colored silk overcoat that threatened to slip to the floor with every motion; at least six strings of what looked like brightly colored pebbles and broken glass beads; bare legs with rather more hair than one was accustomed to seeing; and a pair of brown leather sandals that the lady might well have cobbled herself. She was holding a glass of what looked suspiciously like fruit juice.

Stuyvesant was hard put to keep his mouth straight.

"Oh, Bennett," the young woman was gushing, "how *shame-making* of me to forget. But, sweet boy, it's utterly *divine* to see you,

I couldn't *believe* it when I heard you were coming. How are you? Perhaps I shouldn't ask."

"Hello, Constance, you're looking as lovely as ever. This is my friend Harris Stuyvesant, come to inspect the behavior of the natives. Stuyvesant, the Lady Constance Hurleigh."

"Pleased to meet you, Lady Constance," he said, drawing back again from the swing of the feather.

"Ah, yes, the American! Where are you from, Mr. Stuyvesant?"

"I was born in New York, although recent—"

"Oh, I *adore* New York, it just gives me a shiver down my spine every time Lady Liberty comes into view. The last time I was in New York, a friend took me in a circle around the statue in his aeroplane. Such a *thrill*—have you ridden in an aeroplane, Mr. Stuyvesant?"

"Once or tw—"

"I'll never fly again. My naturopath swears that flying is just *ruinous* on the body's internal timing mechanism and that one's skin never recovers from the upset. And of course the skin is the largest organ in the body, did you know that?"

"I've heard that, yes." By speaking firmly and quickly, he managed to slip in an entire four-syllable sentence. Lady Constance clearly took after her mother in the realm of conversation.

"This nation *so* neglects its skin. It's shameful, we never allow the sun to fall on us without hats and clothing, which robs us of precious vitamins and causes the underlying muscles to tighten and twist."

The repetition of the word *skin* brought enlightenment: This was the nude Hurleigh. He shot Grey a glance, found the man's eyes laughing at him, and pulled his attention back to this voluptuous blonde armful. "You don't say?" Perhaps if he showed enough interest, she would offer a demonstration: That should enliven the evening considerably.

But after a few minutes of increasingly technical monologue concerning gymnosophy, natural healing, and the chemical reactions of the body to the sun's rays, Grey cut in. "Constance, dear heart, I must present Stuyvesant to your father. You'll have all week-end to tell him everything you know about nudity."

"It's not nudity, you naughty man, it's *naturism*. And I shall expect to see you again, Mr. Stuyvesant."

Stuyvesant paused for a refill from the boy's silver shaker, then allowed Grey to haul him off.

This time, they bypassed the others and made straight for the fire and the figure seated with his back to the rest of the room, drink in one hand and half-smoked cigar in the other. The keystone of the fireplace arch before him read:

ANNO
1577
RdeH

Stuyvesant wondered how it would feel, to run your fingers over a stone your ancestors had installed ten generations before.

Grey inserted himself between chair and stones and stood at attention, saying, "Your Grace, it's very good to see you again. May I present my American friend Mr. Harris Stuyvesant?"

The man whose attention was reluctantly pulled from a contemplation of the flames—eleventh Duke of Hurleigh, descendant of Magna Carta signers, consulting tactician to generals, collector of porcelain animals, scourge of Oxford pranksters, Boer War hero, son and begetter of heroes, the man on whose shoulders one of the noblest families in the Empire was entering the modern age—resembled an aging bloodhound. He fixed Grey with a look, grunted by way of greeting, then tipped his head to survey Stuyvesant, head to foot. He did not appear impressed.

"Stuyvesant, eh? Any relation?"

"To the governor? Distant, Your Grace."

"Money?"

"The other side got it."

"Pity."

"Sometimes. Other times it's a burden I'm just as happy not to have."

The dark eyes came to a focus with that remark. Stuyvesant stood easily under the scrutiny, his thoughts entirely hidden. He'd been looked at by harder men than this in his time. Not a whole lot of them, true, but a few.

"So what d'you do?"

"Sell cars. Fix them, too. You've got a problem with your Morris, by the way. Probably just the magneto timing off a bit. I thought I might look at it, if you don't mind?"

The jowls went still, the cigar and drink dangled, forgotten. "Got a man for that."

"It's a tricky job, he may not have had time."

"Been out," the Duke admitted. "Broken leg. Not going to pay."

"Oh, I wouldn't think of asking payment of a man whose liquor I'm drinking," Stuyvesant said in a shocked voice. Grey made a stifled noise and half-turned towards the fire. "I just like to see machines run sweetly."

"As you wish," Hurleigh said. But as Grey was bowing them away from his presence, he grumbled, "Come talk to me sometime, before you go. Like to meet an American with a bit of sense."

"I'll look forward to it," Stuyvesant said, and followed Grey away, leaving the Duke to his contemplation of the flames.

"How on earth did you know that approach?" Grey demanded.

"What, to offer a rich man something for nothing? Or to make him think one of his guests might be paying for his keep? You told me yourself he hates spongers."

The man and two young women standing in earshot listened to the exchange in frank interest. "What have you been doing to Daddy, Bennett?" asked the girl whose coloring proclaimed her a Hurleigh.

"Hello, Evie, good to see you." Introductions were made: Lady Evelyn Hurleigh, fourth and youngest daughter, polished and perfect and just turned nineteen, who was giving up a week-end in London's prime husband-hunting season to report in to the country. She'd brought with her a girlfriend from London who might have been a twin: bare, sun-tanned arms, shingle-bobbed hair whose lower edges could etch glass, and expensive silk frocks that left no doubt concerning the girls' matching boyish figures. Both wore face-paint—eyebrows plucked to an arch of astonishment, kohl exaggerating the eyes, and a red bow of mouth—atop bored expressions borrowed from a fifty-year-old roué. With them was the elder of the two surviving Hurleigh brothers, thirty-one-year-old Daniel, Marquess of Pontforth.

At first glance, the Hurleigh heir gave off the same nonchalant, too-young-for-the-War air as the chinless wonder who had mixed the martini. But this man was past thirty, and the childhood freedom of growing up the spare (as the saying went) to his brother's heir had long worn away: The Marquess's spine was ramrod-straight, his mouth wary, and his eyes twitched in continuous surveillance of the room. Stuyvesant had seen enough wounded officers to know this was one whose injuries went deeper than the physical; he would have bet that the glass the man gripped so hard was not his first of the evening.

Introductions were made; Stuyvesant shook hands, but Bennett saluted them with his drink. The thought occurred to Stuyvesant that he'd yet to see Grey shake hands with anyone.

"Honestly, Bennett, what *did* you say?" Evie persisted. "I've never seen Daddy meet someone and not end up roaring at them at least once."

Grey explained what had happened; halfway through, Evie's eyes started to sparkle and Daniel seemed to relax a bit.

"Well done, old man," Daniel told Stuyvesant. "The Pater's a tightwad until you get to know him, but you bowled right down his pitch."

"He's a tightwad even when you do know him," his sister protested, and said to the others, "When Daddy heard about someone putting a pay telephone booth in his house, nothing would do but that we had one installed as well."

"Oh, Evie, come now, the Pa's not just tight. When it suits him, he'll shell out like there's no tomorrow. Remember the elephant? That must have cost him a packet."

His sister laughed gaily, showing off an excellent set of very white teeth. "Oh, the elephant! I couldn't have been more than three or four."

Daniel explained. "One day—it was in August, so I was home for the long vac—we were sitting down to breakfast when the most ungodly row broke out from outside. When we went down the drive to see, there was a circus elephant and its handler marching across the ford."

Evie broke in, unable to preserve her air of professional boredom in the face of the tale. "You see, Patrick and Pamma had been arguing about that story of the blind men and the elephant, and Daddy overheard them. So when he happened to find out the circus was coming to Oxford, he decided to give us all an illustration, and arranged to have the elephant brought here 'specially, just for us."

"Mama had a fit because the dogs went bananas and her favorite hunter spooked and pulled a tendon, but it was one of the high points of our childhood, owning an elephant for an entire day."

"It was absolute magic," his sister agreed, her eyes wide at the memory.

Stuyvesant found himself rather looking forward to conversing with this patriarch of the Hurleighs.

The final leg of their circumnavigation of the room brought them to a quartet who might have been chosen as an illustration of Young Society. Grey's sister was there, Sarah's fair waves a perfect counterpoint to the glossy dark cap of her female companion and the darkly Brillantined heads of two men. All were laughing at a story the pudgy younger man was telling, and Sarah hooked her arm through her brother's without breaking into the tale—one touch Grey seemed willing to tolerate.

"—just too divine," the boy finished up. "It might have been Zuleika Dobson's admirers tumbling into the Isis!"

Stuyvesant wondered if the laughter wasn't just a little forced; certainly, Sarah wasted no time in turning to her brother and making introductions. The remarkably handsome man with the aristocratic nose was the younger Hurleigh son, Patrick; he ran an unimpressed eye down Stuyvesant's evening dress and offered a limp hand.

In a flash, Grey's enigmatic remark back in the car came back to Stuyvesant: that before the War, three sons would have been sufficient to preserve the Hurleigh name. He'd overlooked the remark at the time, because there were, after all, two sons left, but if one was so badly shaken by the War that eight years later his eyes were still jumpy, and the other, by all indications, lacked an interest in procreation, what of the Hurleigh heritage now?

He showed none of this, merely shaking the boy's hand and going on to the others. The girl was Hurleigh sister number three, Pamela, the society gossip columnist, a more mature version of débutante Evelyn—Pamela's face held no trace of baby fat, and the eyes beneath the kohl had a glint of hardness. She gave Grey a brief twitch of the lips, but studied this big American with a gleam of speculation that he feared had nothing to do with newspaper columns. Without taking her eyes off him, she introduced the rotund young storyteller as Gilbert Dubuque, owner of what Pamela called a "darling" antiques shop in Henley-on-Thames, a phrase that made Dubuque preen with pleasure. Dubuque's evening shirt had ruffles down the front; he, too, studied Stuyvesant with a gleam in his eyes. Stuyvesant wasn't surprised when the man found an excuse to reach out a manicured hand and give him a playful slap on the arm.

Stuyvesant gave him a bland smile, retreated a fraction, and glanced at Grey, anticipating a twinkle of mischief. Instead, he saw a face taut with the onset of pain; Grey's free hand came up to massage his temple. The American waited until Grey looked his way, then gave the Englishman a brief jerk of his head. Relief flared in Grey's eyes, and in a minute he found excuse to move away—unfortunately, taking Sarah with him. Doubly unfortunately, Gilbert Dubuque had seen Stuyvesant's gesture of dismissal and read into it a very different meaning: He looked delighted, and sidled closer to Stuyvesant's elbow.

Stuyvesant gritted his teeth and submitted to the flirtations of two people in whom he had less than no interest, making shallow and dutiful conversation, doing his best to appear both broke (for the shopkeeper's sake) and dull (he really didn't want his name in Lady Pamela's widely read gossip column). It was hard going, and he wondered when the hell the dinner gong would sound.

At two minutes after eight, the Duke pulled out his pocket-watch and turned to glare at the door. Precisely thirty seconds later, Gallagher came through it as if responding to a telepathic summons, making straight for his master's chair. He put his head down and murmured to the Duke, who listened, then waved the servant away in irritation. Gallagher gave his little bow and left; no gong sounded.

Five minutes later, the Duke repeated his act with the watch. He shook his head, jammed the device back into its pocket (Stuyvesant was aware of the room going quiet) and snapped: "Ging the ruddy wrong!"

Dubuque frowned; Patrick winced; the boy at the bar tittered;

those who knew the Duke eased away, and Gallagher braced himself like a man set to go over the top. The Duke's mouth came open again, ready to issue a loud command to servants, family, and guests alike, but at that very instant a swirl of movement at the door and a couple of brief exclamations of relief doused the flame of anger before it ignited the cord.

The woman who swept in the door had to be the missing Hurleigh, Lady Laura, doer of good works and close friend of that subject of official suspicions, Richard Bunsen. Tall for a woman, slim as a boy, thirty-three years old, the eldest Hurleigh of her generation, she seemed oddly familiar—and after a beat he realized why: Given long hair and archaic dress, she could pass for that Spanish ancestress of hers overlooking the stairway. She had the same dark coloring, same almond eyes, that authoritative nose over a Renaissance mouth that looked as if it had a sweet, or a secret, tucked into its corner. Beyond the surface resemblance, her head possessed the same tilt of inner amusement, and she moved with an air of regal certainty, sure beyond a doubt of her place in the world.

She was the most magnificent woman Harris Stuyvesant had ever laid eyes upon.

Lady Laura swept into the room, kissing her mother with affection and tossing remarks along the way as she moved towards her father. The Duke's rage subsided beneath the oil of her presence, and he greeted his daughter with a mild snap about her tardiness. She kissed his cheek, gave him a graceful and apparently sincere apology, accepted a glass of champagne from Deedee, and took a sip. On the count of three, as if her sip had been the signal the butler had been waiting for, the sound of the gong rose up from below, echoing throughout the ancient rooms and setting the crowd into motion.

It was a breathtaking performance: In forty seconds, Laura Hurleigh had mollified her father, conquered her mother, captured the attention of every person there, and shifted the entire ambiance of the gathering as surely as a change in wind direction. Before her entrance, the solar had contained several unrelated groups and a current of incipient contention; now, the dinner gathering was of one mind, from the undergraduate putting away his cocktail shaker to the Duke pushing himself out of his chair.

The groups and individuals fell into place behind the host, filing in good cheer out to the dining room. Rather to Stuyvesant's surprise, Sarah Grey appeared at his elbow and hooked her arm into his. "Would you care to take me through to dinner?" she asked.

No: not in the least like Helen. He pressed her arm warmly into his body. "I'd be honored."

She chortled at the fervency of his response.

They moved towards the door, following various Hurleighs and guests. Just inside the long gallery, Stuyvesant realized that Grey had not yet emerged; he slipped free of Sarah's arm to glance back at the room behind them.

He had a clear view of the fireplace, and the figures before it. Grey and Lady Laura stood on either side of the Duke's empty chair, their bodies outlined by the glow. She was taller than he, would be even without the inch of heels she wore, but neither of them seemed aware of it. Neither of them seemed aware of anything, outside themselves. As Stuyvesant watched, she reached out her left fingers, very tentatively, to touch the back of her companion's hand.

Neither spoke and their postures gave nothing away, but in a flash of perception worthy of Grey himself, Stuyvesant was in no doubt: Touchstone and the terrorist's mistress had been lovers.

Chapter Twenty-Seven

STUYVESANT WAS NOT SURE how he got through dinner, after that revelation. He wouldn't have been certain afterwards that he'd had dinner except he retained an impression of hours spent over white linen and a multiplicity of forks, and later, when he finally got Grey alone, he had that bloated and half-drunk feeling that came with a large and leisurely meal followed by too much alcohol.

He'd stood there in the gallery, feeling his case crumbling around him, undermined by old loyalties and resentments and swept away by complexity. He berated himself for not following his own command, to beware his own reactions to Bennett Grey, and his immediate impulse was to wrap his mitt through Grey's collar and haul him out of there, gong or no gong. Only the thought of the Duke's irritation stayed his hand. Afterwards, when the Duchess rose and the males were released to their entertainments, the impulse returned, but despite his earlier discomfort, Grey stuck to his dinner companions like a barnacle to its hull. Grimly, Stuyvesant stayed, too.

The evening went on, and on: dinner, then port and cigars with the suddenly dull young men until the women and life returned, followed by billiards and cards and dancing to the gramophone. The talk danced, too, from doings at Oxford to the politics in London,

but even with the amount of alcohol he put away, Stuyvesant noticed
that every time matters began to turn serious and talk of the revolution on the doorstep raised its head, Laura deftly turned it away with
an amusing story, or a passage read aloud from a book she just happened to have at hand, and lightness returned. He also couldn't help
noticing that Grey spent the evening torn between the pleasure of
Laura and Sarah and the pain some of the others inflicted on him. But
he would not leave, and neither did Stuyvesant.

It was well after midnight when people began to drift away to
their beds. Sarah left after a series of stifled yawns, but Laura waited
until most of the others had gone before she excused herself; with the
dousing of her light, the moths were freed to flutter off. Stuyvesant
simmered along behind Grey until they had climbed the barn stairway, at which unobserved point he seized the Englishman's arm and
yanked him inside the tree-house bedroom.

"Okay, what kind of damned stupid game are we playing here?"
he hissed, trying to keep his voice low while wanting to dig his Colt
out of the wardrobe and jam it against the man's temple.

Grey jerked his arm free. "What on earth are you talking about?"

"You and Laura Hurleigh is what I'm talking about. I saw how
you two made cow eyes at each other. Don't you think that's something you might have mentioned?"

" 'Cow eyes'? What an absolutely repulsive phrase. I'm fond of
Laura, I told you that. Or I was, when we were young."

"The look you two were giving each other didn't say 'fond,' it
said '*fuck*,' " Stuyvesant snapped, deliberately crude in an attempt to
knock Grey into a confession. Instead, he nearly succeeded in knocking Grey into violence.

Grey clenched both fists, and Stuyvesant was suddenly aware
that here was a man eight years younger, muscles hardened with labor, half-drunk, and about to smash him to the floor. He felt his usual
hard upsurge of glee that accompanied a fistfight, then caught himself
before things could become ridiculous, and held up a hand.

"Sorry, sorry. But Christ, man, if the two of you have that kind of
history, it's going to throw all kinds of hammers in the works."

"Spanners."

"What?"

"Throw a spanner in the works, not a hammer."

"What the hell does it matter? We can't go on with this."

"Why not? Oh, for heaven's sake, Stuyvesant, what difference does it make? So you didn't know at the beginning I'd had an affair with Laura. *I* knew, and I was willing to go on with this... intrigue of the Major's. What, are you afraid that I'll take her side? That I'll warn her that the Major is on to her?"

"No," Stuyvesant protested, meaning *yes*. Grey, inevitably, heard the lie, and shook his head.

"Of course you're concerned about what I might do, but truth to tell, you have no recourse here. I suppose you could shoot me—you have a gun, I know you do, it's a part of your smell. But even if you put a bullet in me, you couldn't be certain I hadn't already told her what you have in mind, could you?" He stood in the unlikely room just looking at the American, wearing an expression in which mild interest battled alcoholic let-down.

Stuyvesant made a little gesture of frustration, and Grey gave him a tired smile. "Despite everything, and most particularly despite its continued employ of one Major Aldous Carstairs, I love my country. I have been doing my best to serve my King since the day I enlisted. I will continue to serve him until I die. The Major no doubt thinks he's bullied me into helping you by threatening my sister, but in fact, if anyone else had asked me, I might have done so willingly. Not whole-heartedly, I will admit: Laura is an old friend, and you are asking me to betray her trust. But I will do so, if necessary, and beyond that will devote any strength left in my body to my King and my country."

As if suddenly reminded of the question of strength, Grey's legs gave way and he sat down on Stuyvesant's bed, running a hand down his haggard face. "Look. Clearly, the Major believes that Richard Bunsen is up to something, and that Laura is either involved, or at least knows what he is planning. However, I don't believe she does. I get no sense of her hiding a thing, from me or anyone else. And in any event, I rather doubt she would do anything extreme: Laura has always been a remarkably sensible person. Scarcely a Hurleigh at all, you might say," he added, with an attempt at humor.

"Still," Stuyvesant said, then stopped. Grey was right: What choice did he have? He needed an entrée into Bunsen's movement:

Grey was the one at hand. It would be very awkward to invent another excuse now.

But damn it, the instant he felt the momentum of the connection take over, he'd shove Grey on the train to Cornwall.

Grey saw the capitulation on the other's face, and nodded. "As you say: Still. Let me be clear. I am not in love with Laura Hurleigh. I may have been at one time, but I am not the man I was. The man who loved her died long ago. I doubt that Laura is the person she was then, either. I am, I repeat, fond of her. Full stop."

Grey stood, walking over to the door. But before it closed, he put his head back inside the room, his green eyes miraculously restored to life.

"But, Harris? Whilst we're on the topic of infatuation, I saw the way Dubuque was looking at you. If you don't want company tonight, I should suggest you put the chair under the knob."

The door slammed one instant before Stuyvesant's shoe hit the place where Grey's head had been.

And sure enough, an hour later, the frustrated working of the door-knob took him from a sound sleep. He raised his bleary head from the pillow and roared, *"Shove off!"*

No more was heard that night.

Chapter Twenty-Eight

SOMETHING WOKE Stuyvesant early, some shift of the beams or whisper of movement. He lifted his head free of the pillow and held it up for a long time, but there was no repeat.

The gray smudge at the base of the curtains told him that dawn was not far off, although he'd been up late, then lain awake for a good hour while his thoughts darted between drunken undergraduates on a train and the gentle touch of fingers on a hand.

And the night before, Thursday, first he'd walked across half of London, then similarly stared at the ceiling, thinking about a half-inch long, eye-lash-thin sliver of matchstick against a wall. Two interrupted nights in a row, with a demanding day ahead of him. However, the light outside and the whirl of thoughts in his head told him that he was not going back to sleep. He turned over and scratched the hair on his chest, wondering if he could possibly ring and ask for coffee. Reluctantly, he decided against it: Fresh air would have to do instead.

Moving on stockinged feet, he splashed his face with cold water and eased his way to the downstairs door, where he laced on his boots. He pulled on his coat, then let himself out into the cool, silent morning, a morning of luminous potential such as he'd only ever seen in this country. It was like standing inside a pearl: not flashy, just glowing with perfection, an ultimate expression of natural beauty.

A light shone at the back of the main house, accompanied by the clatter and voices of an active kitchen, but again he hesitated. Presenting himself there would involve him in the ritual of being parked somewhere while breakfast was hurriedly cooked. And this might be his last chance today for a quiet time to think.

He turned his back on the Siren call of the coffee pot, and in twenty minutes was climbing the side of Hurleigh Peak, grateful for his boots on the dew-covered grass. The sunlight reached the Peak before he did, but only by minutes. He made his way to the top of the knob, and sat down where Grey had sat the day before.

The valley was in shadow. A faint rumor of moving water rose from below; a drift of wood-smoke followed the stream, buoyed on motionless air.

The Peak here, in the heart of England; the Beacon near the end of the world down in Cornwall: Bennett Grey did like his high places for contemplation.

He could imagine Bennett Grey as a boy, escaping what sounded like an uncomfortable home situation to spend weeks of his summer holidays here, surrounded by the Hurleigh estate, caught up in the rough-and-tumble of a large family. He was between Thomas and Daniel in age, a year and a half younger than Laura. Playmates in childhood, lovers as adults, yet Grey claimed he would be willing to convert all that familiarity into a weapon against her pledged cause. A weapon against *her*.

Stuyvesant wasn't sure he could bet on it.

Maybe the key lay not in Grey and Lady Laura, but in the missing figure at the center of their tableau, Richard Bunsen.

Damn it, thought Stuyvesant—is that why Grey had come, to appraise Bunsen for himself? Looking back at their conversation on the Beacon rock, Stuyvesant could see that when he'd told Grey about Laura's affair, Grey had reacted not just as a childhood friend, but as a former lover. Which made his presence extremely suspect, and highly dangerous.

To say nothing of the fact that Aldous Carstairs almost certainly knew about it, and used Laura Hurleigh to tease Grey out of Cornwall. Making Harris Stuyvesant his patsy in the maneuver.

Not that Stuyvesant was certain Laura Hurleigh really was Bunsen's mistress—Carstairs could be wrong about that, or lying— but either way, the problem remained: Why had Grey come?

Jesus. You'd think a Bureau agent would be used to the complications of the job, but honestly, this one took the cake. He'd started out with a straightforward investigation—across an ocean and without backup, yes, but still. And here he was in a country house party with dukes and the rest of it, not knowing if he was the least bit closer to Bunsen than he had been two weeks ago. If Bunsen didn't appear, how long was it going to take him to get to him? His hands itched with the urge to pull the man close, to get around his neck and to rip his goddamn head off. Nothing more complicated than that, really.

He shook his head ruefully, and lit a cigarette.

The sun cleared the hill-top, and Stuyvesant undid the buttons on his coat, his hands going about the motions without his conscious awareness. Instead, he was remembering the naked look on Grey's face when Laura Hurleigh's hand made contact with his, and the echo of his regret: *I am not the man I was.*

Yearning had been there, no doubt about that, but also a discomfort that bordered on pain (and he'd seen enough pain on that man's face this past week to recognize it when he saw it). Grey had been startled when her fingers made contact, but after a brief twitch, he'd held his hand motionless. Thinking it over, Stuyvesant couldn't decide if Grey had been controlling an impulse to seize Laura's hand in response, or stilling a desire to snatch his hand away.

Odd, that Stuyvesant couldn't tell which it was.

A few years back, he'd spent three very solid months guarding a personal friend of Calvin Coolidge, shortly after Coolidge inherited the presidency. The friend was a businessman who happened to be in the wrong place in what, for the state of New York, was the right time, since he'd been witness to some serious wrong-doing. In the weeks running up to the trial at which Coolidge's friend was a key witness, Stuyvesant had glued himself to the man like a shadow, eating at his table, sleeping in his house sometimes, learning his habits so thoroughly they began to feel like his own. He'd gone into the assignment with a clear lack of enthusiasm, knowing how much of his life this guard duty was going to eat up, but he had come to regard it as one of his more important acts in a life of crime-fighting. The man's innate dignity, his determination to go ahead with his testimony in the face of some serious threat, had quieted Stuyvesant's protests at the baby-sitting. On the final morning, before the car came to take them to the courthouse, he'd helped the man on with his overcoat, feeling oddly like the valet dressing a knight in armor. He'd stood at the back of the room and listened to the man's even voice, proud as a parent.

(Stuyvesant noticed something moving on the hillside opposite, something small and gray against the shadowed stand of trees. A dog, maybe? No, it was a fox, picking its way down a fallen log.)

And he'd been deeply grateful that nobody had driven past the man on the street in the weeks that followed and filled him with lead: Stuyvesant would have felt obligated to go after the murderer—personal revenge, not as an officer of the law—and that would have been the end of everything.

But here he was again, playing valet to another knight, this one already badly wounded by life. But equally straight of spine and determined of purpose, and—

Motion seen at the corner of his eye jolted Stuyvesant from his reverie, a looming figure so close that he jerked around and off his perch, cigarette flying as his hands sought a weapon, any weapon.

"Jumpy, ain'tcha?" the Duke said. He peered down at him curiously, his eyebrows arched in that lugubrious face.

Stuyvesant, standing now, remembered the cigarette and slapped belatedly at the front of his coat. A black-edged hole lay over his right thigh; fortunately it had not burned through to the trousers below.

"I didn't hear you coming, sir," he said. He should, at least, have noticed the two dogs, who now left off their happy snuffling at the side of the path and came bounding over to see this new person. They looked like small, rough-haired greyhounds, with intelligent faces and the kind of walk that was more of a bounce.

"Obviously. Got a smoke?"

Obediently, Stuyvesant retrieved his hand from the dogs and offered his host the silver case, followed by the burning lighter. The Duke drew deep and sighed with pleasure, then lowered his aristocratic rump onto a nearby rock. His shoes and tweed coat looked older than the century, his plus fours had been mended more than once, his cap might have belonged to one of his tenant farmers, and he hadn't shaved that morning; from his bearing, he might have been clothed in ermine.

The Duke said nothing. Stuyvesant wasn't sure of the conventions here, but he vaguely thought that a commoner spoke only when spoken to. Or was that only with the royal family? Should he remain passive and standing until the Duke presented him with a topic of conversation? The scion of warriors, friend of kings seemed happy just to sit and smoke, paying Stuyvesant no more attention than he would a cigar-store Indian. Stuyvesant cleared his throat.

"What kind of dogs are those?"

"Deerhounds. From Scotland," he added, then went silent again. However, it was an amiable silence, and from a man quite capable of dismissing unwanted Americans with a glance—which indicated that he was satisfied for Stuyvesant to remain at his side. But if this was the case, what could the man want from him? To talk about car repair?

Stuyvesant decided that, whatever the Duke wanted, it might not require his standing at attention. He moved over to a lesser and slightly removed rock, paused before he sat in case this was not acceptable, then allowed his own common backside to come to rest. He sat, his back stiff with the knowledge that he was seated at the left hand of Uncle God.

"Don't tell my wife," the Duke said eventually.

He couldn't have been talking about the dogs. "About the cigarette?"

"No. The dog-fox opposite."

Stuyvesant glanced over at the fallen tree; sure enough, the animal was still there, its attention riveted by something in the bark, halfway along the trunk.

"The creature moved in going on two years ago, half dead. Some damned bugger'd shot him, his seg went leptic. I came across him one morning about this hour, thought he was a goner, but he somehow pulled through. He's a good sort, keeps the pests down. Never known him take a chicken. Prefers the taste of rabbit."

Stuyvesant wondered what comment he should make on this, but couldn't think of anything except, "I see."

"You ever looked into a wild creature's eyes?"

Stuyvesant's eyes slid sideways at this unexpected question; the old man's profile bore a resemblance to some kind of bird of prey himself—but Stuyvesant thought he was talking about mammalian wildlife, not avian. He decided to venture a small story. "I like to fish, sometimes," he began. "Once a few years ago I was in Oregon, following a stream about five miles from the nearest road, and I looked up to see a cougar watching me from the bank, wondering what the hell I was doing."

"Cougar. That's a kind of catamount." One of the dogs came up, sniffed at Stuyvesant's leg, and settled at his master's feet. The Duke's hand went out absently to knead the animal's ears.

"Like a panther, only brown. Yellow eyes with a world of speculation in them, and a voice like ripping silk. It's a hell of a sensation, feeling yourself being considered for dinner."

The Duke gave a bark of surprised laughter, and Stuyvesant took a draw from his cigarette to conceal the trace of self-satisfied smile he could feel on his mouth: Teamster or duke, it didn't matter—he could get on the good side of anyone, anywhere.

"What kind of fishing?"

"Fly, of course. Is there any other kind?" Stuyvesant said in mock surprise.

The Duke grunted in approval. "River here's no use at all. Too many cows. But I've a place in Scotland with a nice little stream for trout, fill your pan in no time at all."

The "place in Scotland" was, Stuyvesant's research had told him, a castle with twenty bedrooms, in one of which a very young Queen Elizabeth had slept. This in addition to Hurleigh House and the requisite house in London, plus assorted French vineyards, Italian olive groves, and an island in Greece.

"Sounds idyllic."

"Had Baldwin up there in the autumn. You know Baldwin?"

"Not, er, personally."

"Means well," he reflected, a damning statement on either side of the Atlantic. "Might be more likable if he wasn't so earnest."

"I know the type," seemed a safe comment.

"Any rate, if you're heading to Scotland, let us know. Even if we're not there, the servants are always happy to open a couple of rooms for a visitor."

"Good Lord. I mean, that's extraordinarily generous, sir."

"Not at all. You should meet the Scottish trout, I imagine he's a different creature from his American cousin."

Stuyvesant thanked him, and they went back to watching the fox for a while. The creature hopped without effort onto the tree trunk, sniffed around the snarl of roots, then jumped down on the other side and began to dig.

"So you're a friend of the boy's? Bennett's?" The Duke hadn't come up here to talk about car repair or fly-fishing, then.

"I am, sir, yes."

"Been knocked about some."

"So I understand, sir."

"He was sweet on my daughter. Oldest one . . . Laura," he added, the pause suggesting that he'd needed to retrieve the name from some distant store of memory. "Had hopes. Knew his family—good blood, common or not. But in the end, it fell apart. If I was to guess, I'd say it wasn't as entirely his say-so as they give out. Laura knows her own mind, like none other, and what's more she has a way of making others want to go along. She's a leader, not a follower—and the most stubborn girl I've ever met. Makes her mother look soft, and that's saying something. Had two sons in uniform this last war, both good, solid officers, but Laura—if she'd been a boy, she'd have made one of those colonels you send in when the odds are impossible and all you're hoping for is a tactical delay, only about half the time he'll manage to bring off a miracle and snatch victory from a place no one was looking. And bring his men home to boot. My father was like that—Crimean was his war, you know. Or she'd have made one of those powerful nuns of the Middle Ages, abbess who looks the Pope in the face."

"She certainly did an efficient job last night of keeping the various factions in order."

"Promised her mother no fights would break out while we were there. Not altogether certain the agreement covers tonight. You may have an interesting time of it."

"I'll do my part to protect the furniture," Stuyvesant said, unable to tell if the man was making a joke or not.

"You were in uniform."

"Two years. I was on one of the first troop ships to reach France, didn't leave until it was over."

"Good man. You Americans, you skipped the tale for us."

Tipped the scale? "It was already tipping."

"Jerry and us, we'd been battering each other so long it was down to a question of who ran out of bread first. Your guns brought it back to fighting, and that took care of it in no time."

"You may be right," Stuyvesant said, then remembered that the man himself had been decorated in another long and brutal war, this one in South Africa: He was better qualified than some stray American sergeant when it came to military tactics. But before he could retract his dismissive remark, the Duke had moved on.

"Too bad you lot weren't early enough to save the boy Bennett from that shell. Instead of a happy battlefield of a marriage, he walked off into the night and ended up in a hut with some chickens. A gentleman's act, and what Laura half wanted, but it left my girl up to her neck in Nod goes what all kind of politics." God knows what, Stuyvesant translated. He made an encouraging sound, hoping to evoke a few details, but all the Duke cared to add was, "Bad show, all of it."

Stuyvesant wasn't certain if the bad show was Grey's knocking-about, his parting from Laura, or the God-knows-what-all of Laura's politics, but before he could find out, the other man made a growling noise deep in his throat, then said, "And now she's made a liaison with this upstart Union man from Leeds. You know him?"

"Bunsen? I haven't met him yet, either." What was it with imagining that he knew everyone? It wasn't *that* small a country, surely?

"Not a bad brain," the Duke said, an unwilling admission. "A little smooth for my taste, neither fish nor fowl when it comes to class, but that's modern life. Pity about the grandfather."

"You mean the stone mason?"

"What? No, don't be ridiculous, nothing wrong with honest toil. No, I'm talking about the shoe salesman." Bunsen's paternal grandfather had made, then lost, a fortune shipping raw cowhides in one direction and expensive leather goods in the other. His knighthood had marked the height of his personal fortunes, and the beginning of a rapid slide downhill.

"I don't understand. What's wrong with, er, shoes?"

The Duke glanced at him. "Are all Americans slow, or is it just you? There's nothing wrong with shoes, I wear them all the time, myself. But the grandfather was a cheat at the horses. Sure sign of a through-and-through bounder."

Stuyvesant was tempted to ask if Bunsen owned horses, but clearly that was not the point. "Well, sir, I'd imagine your daughter will keep him in line."

"By God, you got that right," he declared. Stuyvesant felt exonerated from the charge of slowness.

The old man crushed his cigarette out against the rock he was sitting on, dropped the stub into a pocket, and turned to fix Stuyvesant with the beam of those dark Spanish eyes.

"You're his friend. The boy Bennett's."

"I ... yes."

"My girl was badly hurt last time. Didn't show it, but it changed her. She gives her all, to a cause or to a man. Nothing halfway. Don't let him hurt her again."

And with that command, it appeared that the audience was at an end. The Duke stood up with the ease of a man half his age, and settled his hat. "Breakfast is sure to be ready. Good of you not to disturb the servants before they'd had their own."

Then he walked away. The dogs bounded after him as he strode down the path, his stride sure and even. Stuyvesant, who had risen automatically when the Duke stood, settled back on the rock and watched the man's retreat.

So, that was what a Duke looked like. Absolutely sure of his footing, on a hillside or in a conversation.

Or anyway, that was how it appeared. Stuyvesant had seen no indication that this scion of an illustrious name was aware of how very fragile the Hurleigh future was, with two adult sons and no grandchild in sight. And even the daughters: two of them deeply immersed in every meaningless thing modern life had to offer, while the third was out to undermine the Hurleigh way of life.

Somehow, he did not think that the Duke, for all his surface dottiness, was anything but rock-hard in his fundamental beliefs, which meant that he must be very worried indeed. And if, as Grey had said, the Duke succumbed to verbal gymnastics when in the grip of strong emotion, there had been three obstacles sufficient to trip the Duke's tongue: the shooting of a fox, the American relief of the forces in 1918, and his daughter's politics.

On the heels of this thought came another: Looking past the ducal waffling, when it came to getting on the good side of someone, Harris Stuyvesant had just been handled by a real expert.

Chapter Twenty-Nine

BENNETT GREY, TOO, WOKE EARLY, with the soft closing of Stuyvesant's door and the subtle shift of the old building under the big man's weight. Was the American always up at this time of day, or was something preying on his mind? He'd certainly been disturbed the night before. Grey had to wonder if something other than the revelation of his ties to Laura had been at issue. Maybe it was the residual effect of Sarah, whose appearance had so astonished the man—Grey had felt the American's pulse shoot up from ten feet away: redheads, my foot. Grey couldn't quite tell now, by the mere feel of Stuyvesant's movements, if he was still angry. He thought about getting up to look out of the window—he'd know in a moment, by the pitch of the American's head and how he held his shoulders.

But Grey stayed where he was.

Pamela's two antiques-shop friends were snoring on the other side of the hallway. They had begun the night in separate rooms, but not long after they'd all retired, the younger one, Dubuque, had come out of his room and tip-toed along to Stuyvesant's door, only to be met by a rebuff of no uncertain terms. He had then retreated to his friend across the hall, who (Grey had been relieved to hear) had been too drunk or too blasé to do more than exchange a few words before falling back to sleep. Dubuque had begun to snore a few minutes later, leaving the barn to subside into its rest.

Sarah, in the room below, spoke a few dreaming words, turned over, and went quiet again. He lay, listening to the sounds of Hurleigh over the eternal whine in his left ear: Birds—seven, eight, nine of them within the confines of the garden—woke to song; the rooster down the valley produced a tentative crow; a young dog-fox two miles away yapped restlessly; the pack of hounds in the Hurleigh kennel across the stream grumbled from time to time. He could smell the family of mice that lived in the barn's attic, although they had fallen still a while earlier. The cold air trickling through the small gap at the bottom of the window had the texture of a brief rainfall by evening. The odor of lavender had begun to fade from the bedclothes and he could feel the start of a worn place in the linen under his left heel; in another few washes, the laundry-woman would discover a hole. Another set of footsteps trod softly through the garden, feet that knew the path intimately—an older man, a faint odor of cigars: the Duke. A faint breeze scratched a leaf across Sarah's window downstairs, half an inch then it stopped. Someone in the main house, a hundred yards away and through several thick walls, dropped a pan; the last man to sleep in this bed had worn a flowery hair-cream, and water ran through distant pipes and the rich tang of coffee wafted in under the window followed by the warm tendrils of baking bread and in a minute he would catch Laura's scent riding the dawn, taste a scrap of air she'd breathed out, across in the house. *I wish . . .*

Grey jerked up onto one elbow and reached for the flask on his bedside table. The sound it made as it sloshed told him precisely how much was inside, and the sound of metal against metal as he unscrewed the top grated on his feverish nerves. But that was exactly what he needed, one sensation that could overcome all the others. He listened with all his might to the symphony the flask top made: a scraping noise, going smooth as worn metal turned against worn metal; a faint hesitation was followed by an infinitesimal ting as the threads hit the tiny dent where he'd dropped it two weeks before; smooth again, loose and looser, and then a microscopic sigh as the top came free.

He placed the flask to his mouth (*the whistle tasted of brass*) tasting the worn silvering of the edge. The liquid within hit his teeth like a miniature wave beating the shore, washing in over his tongue, filling his sinus cavity, giving him its burst of tastes—clear and identifiable, although he'd told Stuyvesant he didn't know: Potatoes, yes, but his neighbor had then added a handful of dried cherries and some apples (which had been starting to spoil), and he'd cooked the mixture in a copper pot. The cool liquid coated Grey's mouth and throat, seared his esophagus, and punched his stomach with its force. He took another, deeper swallow of the poisonous stuff, then lay back on his pillow.

The intense concentration broke his mind's mad gnawing; the alcohol blunted the sensations, and on an empty stomach, with last night's drink still running through his veins, it didn't take long before the sounds and smells that picked and squabbled incessantly at his attention took a small step back. Slowly, the filtering mechanism of his mind went back into place, and he could begin to feel lawn take shape around him instead of a million distinct and clear-edged, clamoring blades of grass.

Once upon a time, he had felt safe here at Hurleigh. He had spent weeks of happiness, protected and in the company of friends. Now, he was all too aware that he was not in the safety of Cornwall, where he could see people coming. Here in the green heart of England the trees pressed in, the hills might hide a thousand men, and birdsong rose to conceal a stealthy approach. Here, the soft edges of easy agriculture and the smooth open vowels of the inhabitants threatened to weaken his defenses, make him forget his wariness.

And why shouldn't he? The War was over, the enemy driven back to his own fields to lick his wounds.

Don't believe it for a moment, Bennett told himself. You thought the convalescent hospital would be a retreat, until the Major found you and beguiled you away with encouraging words, with flattery and usefulness and before you knew it, you were standing beside him helping him inflict pain, looking on in interest while his victims gasped out their shame and terror.

Strangely enough, although he'd spent nineteen months with the Major's so-called Truth Project, he still was not absolutely certain what its purpose was. Probably he hadn't wanted to know—after all, when he had arrived at the clinic from his convalescent hospital, in August 1919, his legs could hold him and his mind could follow conversations, but it was all he could do to bear human company for more than a few minutes without curling into a shuddering heap.

It was Laura who had saved him, Laura and her infinite patience and her motorcar that carried him off to the unpeopled countryside. Laura with her caresses and her eager response that restored to him a sense of manhood, a rock on which he could cling when the world trembled around him. With Laura, with the clinic's doctors and physical therapists, by the spring he felt in himself the semblance of a human being.

It had been months before the Major entered his life. He was aware of the man, as a presence in the background who made him uncomfortable but wasn't around too much. Grey knew he had something to do with bringing him to the clinic, knew as well that the clinic was not simply another sanitarium, but again, he was too caught up in the work of building himself anew to think about it.

In the spring of 1920, however, the Major was there more and more often. Grey would be with the masseuse and the Major would stop in for a brief chat, then go, leaving Grey with the sensation of spiders creeping over his skin. Grey would be taking a meal in the dining room and become aware that uneasiness had settled in beside him; when he glanced at the doorway there would be the Major, casually studying the room at large. The Major would catch Grey's eye and nod, but when the doorway went empty, Grey's appetite would be gone and his bones would be tingling, as if he'd narrowly escaped stepping onto a gaping hole in a stairway.

Then in September, one of the clinic doctors asked Grey to observe a session with another patient, to give his impressions of the man's truthfulness. It was in the interest of therapy, he said, because there was some confusion as to the man's history, and they had noticed that Captain Grey could somehow put his finger on the truth. If the soldier was lying, that was one thing, but if he was actually delusional . . . to help the man . . . if Captain Grey was willing . . . ? And, if Grey didn't mind, they'd just attach a couple of wires to the man's hands, to read his responses . . .

Afterwards, the doctor had thanked him profusely, saying what a difference it had made in the patient's therapeutic process, to know for certain where the truth lay.

It started there. And God knew, it was a blessing to be of some small use to the world, since his body was nearly whole again but his nerves remained incapable of everyday social relations.

Except for Laura, of course: Laura the healer, Laura the bringer of joy, Laura the focus point that overcome the clamoring.

There were two similar interviews during the months that followed: both with twitchy soldiers, both conducted by the same doctor, both with fine wires attached to the men's fingers and wrists.

The next interview, Grey's fourth, was different in a number of ways: A doctor he'd never seen before conducted it; Grey saw no sign of war wounds on the man being interviewed; and Major Carstairs was there.

The Major's presence was at first distracting, then painful, and by the end of it, a torment. He wanted something, craved it so badly he was sweating desire from his pores, but the object of his desire fluctuated between the man in the chair and Grey. It was not mere physical lust: He wanted them—wanted them both—to do something, to respond in some way that Grey might have been able to figure out if the driving confusion hadn't brought on one of his blinding headaches.

The session left him cowering in a darkened room for days, unable to bear the presence of anyone but the orderly who brought his meals. For two weeks, he refused Laura entrance. There was no sign of the Major, no reference to the last interview; slowly he regained his equilibrium. A month later he was well enough to see his family on a brief Christmas visit home.

In the middle of January, the Major found him in the clinic's conservatory and asked if he would be willing to assist on another interview.

Grey had not yet learned to trust his perceptions. He still thought that if he fought the sensations, if he refused to be dominated by this bizarre variety of shell shock, he could get back on his feet and live some kind of normal life. So he denied the repulsion he felt for the Major and all his works, and let himself be talked into it.

And that one went well. This one was clearly a victim of the War:

Three years after his last battle, the spasms and stammers still racked him. Grey talked to him, watched him, and afterwards told the doctor where the man's truths lay and what calming pathways might reach beyond the nerves.

It was a relief, being able to help. It made Grey feel not so utterly useless. He even began to wonder if perhaps, with care, this damnable sensitivity that afflicted him might not be turned into a gift.

It was the last time he'd held that thought.

The Major reappeared in early February with a young man whose bruises and easy winces made it clear that he'd been beaten. The Major demanded that Grey sit in on a conversation that in no time at all became an interrogation. The Major wanted to know which of the man's circle were responsible—for what crime, Grey never learned, just: responsible. The headache came instantly, but this time the Major would not accept Grey's dismissal, not until the Major had his answers. And in desperation, Grey told him which name had caused the man to tense, just a fraction, to hold his breath, for just an instant.

The next day, the Major had come to explain, something about disruption and violence and the threat of mob rule; later, asking around, Grey learned that the outside world was in turmoil because of the coal industry, and he realized that the young man with the bruised face had been a Bolshevik.

The world was indeed in turmoil, and the Major appeared with two more of these sort of men in March, bullying and cajoling Grey into cooperation. Grey was trapped: He couldn't bear to pry into these men's minds; the Major's presence made him want to scream; on the other hand, the thought of leaving the clinic and trying to live outside frankly terrified him.

And everyone swore he was helping his country, keeping it safe against a threat every bit as real as the Kaiser's army.

He might still be there, eating himself away inside, if the Major hadn't allowed himself to be distracted by the troubles, and pushed Grey just a fraction too far. The nurse had no business being brought under that kind of scrutiny: Two minutes into the session Grey knew that, and what was more, he knew that the Major knew it. When the poor young woman broke, when she began sobbing out her shame at what her brother had done, Grey looked at the Major, and caught the Major watching, not the nurse, but Grey himself.

In that instant, Grey saw what awaited him if he stayed. Even if outright insanity seized him outside the clinic doors, it was preferable to this monstrosity.

He hit out against the Major and, inadvertently, won his release.

He tried, on the outside. He went home, summoned the self control to walk through the town, desperately clung to the fantasy of job, wife, home.

In less than a week, he knew his failure. He wrote Laura a letter, put some warm clothes into a rucksack, and walked out of his family's house on foot, in search of peace.

He had thought he would find it beneath the wheels of a train, or at the bottom of a cliff. Instead, he had tramped without aim through lanes and over fields, sleeping rough under trees and in barns, until with the end of summer he found himself circling Dartmoor and entering Cornwall. There he found his end of the world.

So no, he was still not completely certain what the Truth Project was all about. He thought it had begun, as he'd told Stuyvesant, as research into interrogation techniques, looking to measure when a person spoke the truth, and when he lied. Using Bennett's hypersensitivity to calibrate their machines, the Project's researchers thought they might duplicate his sure knowledge.

In theory, leaving the Major out of the equation, he could see their point: He'd never actually participated in interrogations during the War, but he'd been outside a farmhouse during the questioning of a captured German, and just thinking of the sounds that spilled out made him queasy. As far as Grey was concerned, anything that meant you didn't have to torture information from another human being was a good thing.

However, the Project's frustrations had mounted when they found that using a machine to measure human truth was far, far more complicated than they had originally suspected. And because this was not mere scientific pursuit, but a project with not only the Major, but the military itself looking on, the option of failure was unacceptable.

That was when the underlying question had changed from, How do we create a machine with the abilities of Bennett Grey? to, How can we use Bennett Grey? His role changed from paradigm to participant.

And then the question changed again, when the Major brought the nurse before him, and Grey saw the speculation in those black eyes: How can we create *more* Bennett Greys?

For years afterwards, his nights had been haunted by a dream that jerked him upright and sent him out into the Cornish night: He was walking down a cold, bright corridor, straight and endless, with doors on either side. The corridor was empty, but he became aware of a murmur of voices, and so he stopped and looked through the small window in the door to his right.

The room contained three people. One had his back to the door. The other two looked up at him: Major Carstairs, and a blond man with green eyes.

Sometimes, this was enough to startle him awake. Other nights he would go on to the next door, and then the next, and the next, and in every room, the faces looking back at him belonged to Major Carstairs and Bennett Grey, and he would wake not with surprise, but with horror.

Once he'd discovered the safety of Cornwall and burrowed into his hillside, Grey tried to convince himself that, without him, the Project had withered and died. In the early months he had been unable to think about it at all; later, time and distance had reassured him that his absence had robbed the Major of any authority, and if the man had turned to some other dark form of governmental manipulation, well, that was hardly Grey's responsibility.

Now it looked as if it wasn't that simple. The Major wanted him back, that much was clear. Which could only mean that the Project had survived. In fact, the Major's aura of confidence and hidden authority had grown even stronger, suggesting that the Project not only survived, but was thriving. Perhaps he'd convinced his masters—military or civilian—that another war was coming, for which they would need the machinery of truth-telling.

And if that war were to be on Britain's own soil, against Britain's own citizens? Wasn't a domestic enemy still an enemy?

In fact, if the enemy were one of Britain's own, so much the better. The Major and his Project did not exist, so what could be easier than to drop a troublemaker in and have him disappear for a while?

And with Bennett Grey to help identify precisely where a man's weaknesses lay, the Major would have the troublemaker in pieces in no time at all.

In Cornwall, Grey had been far enough away, the Major would have needed to mount a campaign to extract him. Now, thanks to Sarah's dangerous closeness to Richard Bunsen, he could feel the Major's gloved fingers insinuating themselves down the back of his collar.

Lying there in the still dawn, the thud of his heartbeat grew faster and harder, until he could feel the throb of pulse within his ears. Then the raw taste of brass crept onto his tongue, and he really couldn't bear to start the day with that.

So Bennett Grey, too, threw off his bed-clothes, dressed, and left the barn, although he walked in the opposite direction from Stuyvesant and the Duke, down the road to the ford. As Stuyvesant, up on the Peak, was being startled by the unheralded approach of the older man, Grey was leaning over the side of the foot-bridge, mesmerized by the water that teased and smoothed the mossy paving-stones of the ford, feeling it smooth his mind.

Bennett, he addressed himself, *why the hell did you come here?*

He could have written his sister a letter warning her away from Bunsen and gone back to his potatoes, doing his best to dismiss Harris Stuyvesant from his mind. He could have sent a telegram, even ridden his bicycle into Penzance and used the telephone. Instead, he'd returned to the one truly happy place of his childhood, knowing that he would come face to face with the woman he had loved and treated abominably. Knowing that the scent of her would make his skin rouse from its long slumber, that one gesture of her fingers would send a shudder down his spine, that the sound of her voice would make him want to seize her hair and cover her supple body and velvet skin with kisses. He wanted to drown in her, wanted to walk across to the house and climb into her bed and never come out, wanted to admit that he could not possibly continue to live without her.

He came here knowing that he would not do that, that he could not do that to her, not again.

He came knowing that laying eyes on her might make it impossible to resume his life in Cornwall, a satisfying life that had, overnight and with not a word of warning, become stifling.

He'd come up from Cornwall because Major Carstairs had stepped out of the car into his yard with the force of a howitzer, and blown him into the realization that he was sick unto death of being a slave to his nerves. He'd come with Harris Stuyvesant because the man's honest strength shamed him, made him decide that, like an amputee sweating every prosthetic step, it was time to pretend normality. Even if he had to use the crutch of drink to get over the worst of it, he would learn to face the world. His world.

He came here because it was unfair to his sister, to be burdened with the constant ache of a mentally crippled brother down at the far reaches of the land. He'd come because he was abruptly homesick, tired of the primitive starkness of Cornwall, longing for the rich midlands of his country, its summer smells and the embrace of its history. He came, he supposed, on a whim as impulsive as anything Sarah would do, when the American's request slid so neatly into the possibilities. He'd come—

Oh, Christ, *Bennett: Stop lying to yourself.*

You came in a moment's impulse worthy of Sarah, because you wanted to lay eyes on this new man of Laura's, the man who had taken your place in her life.

Underneath that, you came because you wanted to see Laura.

And what, now that you've seen her?

Only now does it occur to you that Laura might not wish to see you.

Chapter Thirty

IN THE ROOM BELOW Bennett Grey's empty bed, his sister's dreaming mind had been weaving together a convoluted tale of responsibility and friendship. There was a man in the dream, although when she half woke, Sarah could not be certain if it had been her brother or Richard Bunsen. The uncertainty troubled her, and brought her closer to wakefulness. The two were nothing alike, in looks or nature, so why confuse them? They said that dreams Meant Something. Perhaps this one was simply about a person who did not interest her as a man, and both Bennett and Richard fit that description.

So, a friend or brother. And one for whom she felt some degree of responsibility. That, too, was both of them.

No matter how much she read about shell shock, she came no closer to understanding Bennett's mental state than the week he'd come out of hospital. They'd always been close, as children, but after the War it seemed he could see things about her that no one else could, her doubts and worries and secret pleasures. Take today: It was almost as if he could feel the remnants of shakiness from the train incident in her body. And more than that—he'd known she didn't want to talk about it in front of the servants, and waited until they were alone—alone with that American friend of his, which itself had somehow been all right.

Although that was another oddity, Bennett asking a perfect stranger to a Hurleigh week-end. And he called her impetuous! Ridiculous, really, how what others called her *whims* and her *rash acts* always made perfect sense to Sarah, even if they were hard to explain. Maybe that was the same with Bennett, when it just seemed right to him to bring the American along.

Certainly, Mr. Stuyvesant had fit in better than she'd feared. She should have known it would be all right. Whatever else the War had done to Bennett, it had made him enormously sensitive. He'd know in an instant if the Hurleighs were put off by his friend, and he'd have invented an instantaneous excuse and made off.

It couldn't be easy, to be so sensitive to glances and minute raises of the eyebrow. And that was the word, *sensitive*—poor Bennett couldn't even bear it when too many things were going on at once. She'd been so proud of him today, seeing the enormous effort he was making to act sociable, this man who could go for days without speaking to anyone but the cow leaning across the wall. He'd once been the life of any party, before the War—she'd been old enough back then to remember that. But if it was now so distasteful to him, why do it?

And what about him and Laura? The tension between them had positively *crackled* last night, the moment they laid eyes on each other, but precisely what it stemmed from she could not be sure. She'd never known exactly what happened to push them apart, although she'd put together hints both had let drop over the years. She was only seventeen when Bennett went to war, but he had told her of the secret wartime engagement; she'd known that Laura had taken rooms near his sanitarium (a place that had struck Sarah like an upscale loony bin, the two times Mother had let her go there) and that Laura bought a motorcar to take him on outings; everyone had assumed the engagement was going ahead.

And then *blooey*, it was raining down on their heads: Laura was back in London and Bennett gone completely, and neither of them would talk about it. She'd thought the break was temporary—the

War had changed everyone, after all; it was to be expected that the nature of love would change, as well.

But before they could heal the rift, the Margolin baby died, and although his death was neither the first nor the last, that failure was personal, and had shaken everyone, badly. To distract Laura, as much as anything, Sarah had introduced her to Richard. Before the evening was over, she'd fervently wished that she'd never brought them together.

With Richard, Laura hardened. Or was it just being without Bennett? In any case, the spark of fun had gone out of Laura—and that was five years ago, long before the recent spats she'd had with Richard. Before Richard, Laura had been able to set work aside, have a good time, go to a party. Now, she was impatient with anyone unconnected with Look Forward or the clinics. She could occasionally be almost rigid, as if she'd grown a steel spine.

Not that Laura wasn't as friendly as ever, or didn't care about the families they served (if anything, she cared more than ever—although one couldn't say the same about her own family, to whom she was polite in public and impatient when outside their hearing). And it wasn't that she didn't go to parties, because she did, but no matter where she was, Laura always seemed to be working. She was competent and cheerful, passionate and calm, but at odd moments, Sarah caught brief glimpses of something cold, even desolate, underneath. Something sad.

Oh, Sarah, she told herself, Laura just grew up. Go back to sleep.

But she knew it was more than just growing up.

She knew it was losing Bennett, and the life Laura thought she had. Oh, *why* hadn't they managed to patch it together? There was still a powerful connection there—that crackle of tension she'd seen could almost have been the electricity of attraction. Or animosity, but that couldn't be, because afterwards they'd been easy and affectionate, like two old friends who had just grown apart. But if it wasn't attraction and it wasn't remembered dislike, what could it have been? Fear?

Fear made even less sense.

Oh, sometimes psychology could be so irritating.

However, she had all week-end to figure it out. And all week-end to see more of that nice American friend of Bennett's.

Beauty sleep might be a good idea.

Sarah turned on her side and pulled the bed-clothes up around her ears; soon, her breathing slowed.

Chapter Thirty-One

LAURA HURLEIGH DID NOT WAKE before dawn, as the others had. She had not even got into bed until nearly four A.M., having sat before the low-burning fire smoking one cigarette after another. It wasn't so much the effort of keeping the gathering amicable, as she'd promised her mother—although she often had trouble sleeping after that sort of tense balancing act. It was the unexpected reverberations of seeing Bennett after all these years that kept her up, listening to the quiet.

Hurleigh House was good for that. She couldn't think how many times she had retreated to this room, wounded and fighting tears, to feel soothed by the very stones around her. Her family seemed to her increasingly foreign, brittle and irrelevant, but the house itself was another matter entirely. It listened, it nurtured, it spoke to her bones.

Once upon a time, she had thought she loved Bennett—

No: Be honest. She *had* loved him. She'd been primed to love him before she met him, come to that, having overheard the adults talking about this poor lad with a sick mother and a drunk of a father. Then he came and he was fun, and the age difference was too slight to matter, because he understood her the way no one else did. And then came the War, and the hospital, and that bloody clinic run by that dark-eyed snake who had done something to change Bennett, what she'd never known. Until his letter had arrived, out of the blue, she'd believed that she could put him together again, bring him out of the state the War left him in, make him whole.

Her life had turned completely upside-down, five years ago—almost exactly five years, come to think of it. She'd been traveling along, secure in her path, and then the path had fallen out from under her: Bennett's letter and the frantic telegrams and telephone calls to his mother, followed three days later by the Margolin child's death and the uproar and self recriminations and a vision of dead children pouring unheeded through an hour-glass. A handful of days that had ripped away all of Laura's illusions, made her see once and for all that her world was built not of stone, but of the loosest, most flammable straw. She'd crept home to Hurleigh after that devastation, too, and sat here smoking and staring out of the window.

Then a few days later, shaky and without hope but back in London—which had been torn by strikes then, too—she had looked up to see Richard Bunsen standing before her, and the previous ten days, even the previous ten years, might have been arranged to aim her at that moment. She'd seen Richard, and known him instantly as someone she could use—no, not use, he was much more than a tool—someone she could influence and shape and work with, to stop up that endless stream of dying poor. Richard, who had clasped her hand and given her that crooked grin, and shown her the way to rebuild.

(She paused to wonder how things had gone during the day, Richard's meeting with Matthew Ruddle, a man she didn't much like, not least because following a meeting with his Union mentor, Richard always seemed to take on a degree of coarseness she found ... unnecessary. Like those trips he took with his other friends to places like Paris and Monte Carlo, that always turned him into a seventeen-year-old again. Infuriating.)

What if she'd managed to cling to Bennett? What if the door to marriage and children had not been slammed in her face? She might have been happy, but would she have moved into the world she inhabited now? Would she have found purpose and meaning, have been in a position to change so many lives, if not for Richard? She had been born for what she would do in these next few weeks, as if her role had been scripted before her conception by some all-seeing Playwright: This is what we need, this is when we need her, precisely this and no other.

It was strange, but sometimes she felt very close to her mad, trouble-making old grandmother. In her final years, Grandmamma had adopted a fervent and probably heretical Christian doctrine based on the unshakable belief that All Things Were Ordained To Be. The belief had covered anything from Connie's broken engagement ("He'd have proved a bad 'un in the end, you mark my words.") to the teapot one of the dogs had knocked onto the small Turkey carpet ("I'm so glad we have to take that up for cleaning, I felt the other day that it was going to trip me.").

Laura's own convictions had little of the Christian about them, but time and again she had seen events slip into place, watched minor acts coalesce into something important, until eventually she could deny the pattern no longer: Since being driven away from Bennett, she had grown into her own.

But that did not keep the affair from feeling dreadfully...unfinished.

And he felt the same. His face had been an open one even before the War, but afterwards he'd been incapable of hiding anything, especially from her. One glance at him in the solar last night and she'd known he was as much in love with her as ever he had been. She'd also known that he would do nothing about it: If there was a first step to be taken, it was up to her.

As things, large or small, always seemed to be up to her.

And why not? Wasn't that what Hurleighs did? Wasn't that what her father meant when he harped on the blood of England? The aristocracy as a whole might have degenerated into a class of economic parasites, but over the centuries, Hurleighs had given (as those early Americans put it) their lives, their fortunes, their sacred honor for their country. Hurleigh ancestors had stood up to kings at Runnymede, generations of Hurleigh sons had given their lives on fields of battle, Hurleighs had beggared their families for a cause.

And now a Hurleigh daughter spent her time in first class compartments, sweet-talked corrupt politicians and newspaper barons, and dutifully kept squabbles from her parents' drawing rooms.

Irritable, cold despite the fire, she crushed the stub end of the cigarette into the laden ash-tray and went to wipe her make-up, wash her face, brush her teeth, all the comforting rituals. At the end, she sat at her childhood dressing-table and took up her hair-brush.

In the looking-glass was Lady Laura Hurleigh, eldest child of an ancient and powerful family, her name and face instantly recognizable to half the nation, moneyed, respected, and not even hard to look on. Variations of the face before her had appeared in newspapers two or three times a year since the week of her birth: Little Lady Laura riding her pony; Lady Laura and mother with the hunt; the Lady Laura Hurleigh presented at court. Lady Laura, haughty before the Prime Minister.

In the looking-glass was also Laura Hurleigh, lover and partner to Labour's up-and-coming fair-haired boy, Richard Bunsen. This was the Laura Richard himself would have seen, had he been standing behind her with his hands on her shoulders: helpmeet, bed-mate, sounding-board, as useful at charming Britain's upper classes as she was with wowing the Americans.

Why were men who publicly espoused the rights of women so willing to overlook the women close to them? Richard had started out seeing her as a person in her own right, she was sure he had; he'd listened to her ideas, supported her proposals, respected her as a colleague. But in a few short years, the brilliant, wild man she'd tumbled into bed and into partnership with had evolved into a different sort of creature, one that ordered his suits from a tailor, knew what kind of wine to drink, and saw her as a highly useful, but necessarily secondary, adjunct to his male ambitions.

Oh, *why* hadn't she just been born a man? As far back as she could remember, she'd known that she was Not-a-Boy. When she was five and four-year-old Thomas nearly died of pneumonia, it was little Daniel everyone had turned their increased vigilance on, not Laura. Then Thomas did die, in the second year of the War, and she had seen them pat and coddle his new-born son Theodore with that same hunger for reassurance. And in the winter of 1919, when the epidemic took Teddy, yet again they passed over Laura to settle their hopes back on her brothers. Boys mattered: girls were there to bear them.

And unmarried at thirty-three, she hadn't even managed that.

Was this where her sense of incompleteness came from, the fact that she had no child of her own?

No, she decided; she'd felt that way long before she qualified for the withered identity of Spinster. She'd always felt it. Maybe that was why she always had to outrun her brothers, why she fought harder for what she wanted, why she always made things more difficult for herself than any man she knew. Women were always adjuncts to some man's ambitions; she should be old enough not to expect anything else from Richard, women's rights or no.

Things would be better if they could just get away for a while, to crawl into bed for a week and boff themselves limp. They said it was bad for a person accustomed to regular sex to stop suddenly—and God knew, under the current strain she ached for the release—but he'd been so touchy of late, with so much resting on the next days and weeks, that although they had sex, it seemed as mechanical for him as it was unsatisfying for her. No doubt he was just as happy to spend some days away from her, although that left a dangerous door open for other affections. Still, he'd had to deal with Lord Malcolm on his own today, with no one but Matthew Ruddle to smooth the old reprobate's tongue: Perhaps that would make him appreciate her, just a little.

Another decision she could feel looming above her: marriage. Even with passion's waning, she suspected that, before too long, Richard would ask her to marry him. It would have been unthinkable to the young radical she had first met, but Free Love had been buried under the trappings of success and adulation, and a rejection of the political and economic bonds of marriage had turned into an excuse for philandering.

(Why the word *philander*, she mused? Brotherly love of men, the word meant, but really it meant erotic lover of many women. Perhaps men who partner a string of women feel a strong bond with other men? And why, when a woman chose to give herself to a man outside the bonds of marriage, did she become not a *philanderess*, but a *whore*?)

What of Bennett? Which looking-glass Laura would Bennett see if he were the man standing behind her, his light head over her dark one, his hands resting on her shoulders? (Her body stirred inside its heavy silk negligeé, at the image of those hands descending, that mouth meeting her neck, to leisurely explore places where Richard's fingers ventured only to see if she was ready for him.)

She tore her mind away from the thought of Bennett's sure mouth and stared at the reflection. The Lady Laura Victoria Anne Christine Hurleigh gazed back at her, slightly flushed, pupils dark, but with all her thoughts and ambitions hidden, those thoughts and ambitions of the other Laura Hurleigh, the true one, the only one who mattered.

She had to remind herself of that fact, often: Only the inner person matters.

Everything but the inner person—everything, everyone—is sacrifice to the Cause.

Her mind had been denied a boy's formal education? That was no sacrifice at all, when she considered how much easier it made it to speak with the millions who had been offered no such luxury.

She'd been born Not-a-Boy? What did that childhood resentment matter, when she'd come to maturity at a time when men were going to soldier and women were needed to run the machinery of the nation?

Bennett had abandoned her? Yes, she had loved him, loved and pitied and been in awe of his strength, but within days of that devastation, she'd been given Richard Bunsen, a powerful man who both needed her and taught her everything he knew—certainly everything she needed to know, to invent herself anew.

She felt burdened by the unfair privileges of her birth? Yet she had recently begun to see how those very privileges could be a weapon, precisely what was needed to turn the system on its head.

Grandmamma's belief that All Things Were Ordained To Be had proved true time and again, to an extent that was almost eerie in its perfection.

Of course, she never talked about the idea of pre-ordination—she didn't want to sound like her sister Connie with her bare feet and her Doctrine of the Nude. Not even with Richard, since he would have thought she meant the will of God, and divine approval did not enter into his vision of their work.

But privately, half ashamedly, she clung to the belief. It was not entirely irrational, for the coincidences of her life were too many to explain as mere luck of the draw: God—whether God was a person or simply a name one gave to the machinery of the Universe—surely must have taken an interest in the life of Laura Hurleigh, to have given her all those nudges? She had even tested her theory once or twice, deliberately trying to perform some wrong act, only to have circumstances turn against her. The theory had come up shining, and left her even more serenely confident in the rightness of her path: If the road is made easy, it is the right one.

Which made Bennett's sudden re-appearance a puzzle. Why had he come back into her life, just at this crucial point? Clearly, it might simply be coincidence—she wasn't such a fanatic on the idea of pre-ordination that she would deny random chance outright. But because the structure of her life was such a living thing to her, because the last few years had given her a powerful sense of all the loose threads of her existence weaving together in purpose, she had at least to think about Bennett's re-appearance, and wonder if it might mean something.

If she'd been a heaven-and-hell Christian—if she'd even been much of a Christian at all—she might have considered his re-appearance some kind of a test, of her faith, her resolve, her understanding. But Laura's awareness of the Divine was closer to a pagan, bone-deep sense of Purpose than it was to any Christian doctrine, and so she looked for a personal significance in the event, not merely a challenge set by an authority figure: Did Bennett have something to offer the Movement? And if so, was it through her, or through Richard?

Bennett might even be a mere tool of the Fates. Designed perhaps to bring that tall and mysterious American into the mix? It was true, she and Richard had been talking only the week before about the need for another, broader form of contact with the Americans, one that wasn't limited to the radical minority. Would a man who sold motorcars be sufficiently working class for their needs? Stuyvesant's leisure for international travel suggested that he would side with owners, yet he acted like a man who had spent years with dirty hands. And his clothes the night before had been what one might expect of a working man who, though he had moved up a notch in the hierarchy, nonetheless retained a certain disdain for the trappings of wealth.

In the end, cold and cramped, she knew she needed to consult Richard on the matter. His sense of what was needed was occasionally startlingly acute, and he would not be distracted by any previous affections or romantic dreams. Let him meet Bennett and the American, let him get the feel of both.

Yes, she decided; she'd like to hear what Richard thought.

And if the road is made easy, then it is the right one.

With that thought, finally, she went to bed, and to sleep.

Chapter Thirty-Two

A HUNDRED MILES AWAY, in the northern reaches of London, Aldous Carstairs, like Laura Hurleigh, was taking late to his bed. All week he'd been tugged to and fro by the furies and frustrations of his work on the one hand and the intoxicating possibilities opened by Grey's return (*Grey's possible return,* he corrected himself) on the other. A memo would arrive from Downing Street regarding the arrest procedures for the Strike and he would think, *If only I had Grey to hand.* A conversation with Kell at MI5 would circle around the nagging problem of closing in on the ringleaders of the growing unrest, and he would bite his tongue to keep from saying, *Round them up and let my men question them.*

About the time Bennett Grey was arriving at Paddington that morning, Carstairs had realized that if he didn't make time for a visit to Monica's establishment—which he'd planned on his return from Cornwall and had to put off—he was going to murder someone. So he had picked up the telephone and placed a call to the woman's private number, and told her when to expect him.

The rest of Friday had passed in a delicious blend of intolerable frustration and impending relief, like some ten-hour version of the moments before climax. He'd gone about his work, aware every mo-

ment of the tantalizing proximity of Bennett Grey, on whom so much
rested yet who was as volatile as a room full of petrol, as uncontrollable as a falcon tossed into the air. Several times Carstairs had found
himself fingering the scar on his face, each time loosing a small thrill
of memory: the intense pleasure of breaking that stupid nurse; the
even greater pleasure of forcing Grey to assist at her breaking; and
then the icy shock of Grey coming at him, the flash of terror and the
easy slide of glass into skin followed by the building fire of the cut itself. And worst of all, the devastation two days later when he came
around in hospital to find that not only had Grey been released, but
that Aldous Carstairs, the Project's director, had insufficient authority to demand his return.

It was a bad time—these same damned coal miners, then and
now—and he'd had to fight with everything he had to keep the
Project from folding entirely: debts called in, a score of personal visits to deliver the ever-distasteful blackmail threats. In the end, he'd
managed, but without Grey the Project was like a summer house,
receiving just enough attention through the cold times to keep it intact. Carstairs walked quietly, turned his energies to other—lesser—
projects, but he had never allowed the moribund Project to shut
down entirely, just in case.

For years, the scar's tingle and itch had been a physical manifestation of the unscratchable itch that was Bennett Grey, whom his
hands could never decide if they wanted to beat or to caress.

And now, thanks to an oafish American and a young woman in-
fected with the feminist disease, the waiting was over.

Admittedly, Grey had only ventured a glance at the outside
world; admittedly, too, Carstairs had no idea how he was going to
use it, but it was a beginning.

Carstairs, looking through the taxicab's windows at the sleeping
city, felt cradled in the languor of physical release. (God, Monica's
new little flaxen-haired bitch was something—cropped hair, no
breasts to speak of, no more hips than an adolescent boy, but lus-
cious, welcoming buttocks: perfect. He glanced down at his gloves,
new a week ago, now torn and scarred by her panicking finger-nails.
He had frightened her badly, albeit deliberately, when she'd been unable to draw air. Granted, he allowed it to go on just a bit too long,

so he supposed the gloves were understandable. He made a mental note to send her a little something extra, to sweeten her for next time.)

The marvelous thing was, the ache of hunger was still there. His body's present warm satiation did not in the least lessen the sharp restlessness that Grey evoked. If anything, it made the eventual satisfaction of breaking Grey to his purposes all the more real, like the first *hors d'oeuvres* of a great feast.

And most delicious of all was knowing that in this case, pleasure and duty nestled right into each other.

Carstairs stepped out of the taxi in front of his house at a quarter after five in the morning. He was aware that on some level, as always after one of these episodes, he detested himself. But as Machiavelli would have reminded him, virtue in a ruler was a very different thing from the virtue of an ordinary man: A ruler must be prepared to commit evil on the way to building a greater good.

And Aldous Carstairs was born to be a ruler. Not out in public, not like that puffing idiot in the black shirt who had taken over the great Niccolò's homeland, or that other one assembling a private army in Germany, but the man who moved the forces behind the unchanging façade of government.

Still, what did a little self loathing matter? One might argue that a visit to Monica's was for his own individual sake, as indeed it had been in the past, but tonight had been another matter. Put simply, it was dangerous to allow pressures to build unchecked. Apart from any pleasure it brought him, this episode at Monica's had cleared his mind effectively for the delicate, highly demanding work of the coming days.

He was no longer on edge—

On edge . . .

Carstairs went absolutely still, the key frozen in the lock of his front door as the phrase reverberated in his mind, causing the machinery that had been turning there to sing in response. On edge. On the edge. Director Hoover, saying how close to the edge his agent was, his straying agent (*"Blames this guy Bunsen for his turning his brother into a vegetable"*) who had walked in from the rain and become a catalyst for the reaction now taking place in Aldous Carstairs' mind.

The glimmering suggestion of a plan that had moved at the edge of his vision for the past week blossomed into life, a plot within a plot unfolding, glorious and perfect.

"This guy Bunsen"; a rogue agent; a sapper-turned–Labour politician; the Strike building to a head. Even—my God, could it be any more perfect?—even Hurleigh House, the stage for his play to be acted upon. Hurleigh House, the Duke, Stanley Baldwin, and the key players in the Miners' Union drama.

The changes would be minimal, the benefits enormous: A clear and immediate threat was infinitely more effective than an inchoate sense of danger. The personal won over the anonymous, every time.

And the American? He was disposable, along with the others.

But, Grey. Could he put Bennett Grey in the path of danger? Might be best to remove him, first.

Yes, with one deft move, the Carstairs Proposal would be clasped to the breast of England's governing body in its time of need, and the Truth Project would become the jewel in its crown of achievement. And as part of the agreement, when Carstairs himself stepped modestly away from the spotlight and reclaimed the Project that was his own, Grey would be his, to have and to hold.

Britain would be safe from the saboteur within.

The only thing he might ask for was a Lorenzo to his Machiavelli, a third P, the *Principe* he could mold and direct. Not Baldwin, by any means, nor Churchill—the man was too set in his ways. Someone young, malleable. What about that promising boy Mosley? He came from the right background, and surely no man who married a daughter of Lord Curzon could possibly be serious about Socialism?

All of that—realization, confirmation, and a direction for the future—came in the space of one held breath. He let it out slowly, hesitantly, but the vision remained. He smiled, and finished turning the key. Upstairs, he stripped off his ravaged gloves and dropped them into the waste-paper basket, sitting in hat and overcoat to write a full coded page in his journal.

At the end, he laid the pen down on the desk and looked at what he had written.

The great Niccolò would shake his head in appreciation.

Pity about the American, he rather liked the fellow. Well, perhaps *liked* was too strong a word, but he found him amusing. But the end was all.

Carstairs stretched and got undressed, putting everything but his hat into the clothes hamper to be cleaned. He drew a bath almost too hot to bear, scrubbing himself clean of the smell of Monica's. He shaved his face smooth, glanced again at his diary, and with a sigh, folded himself between the crisp sheets of his bed.

Chapter Thirty-Three

AT NEARLY THE SAME TIME, and a mere seven miles away from Aldous Carstairs, another man waited impatiently for sleep. Richard Bunsen slept little at the best of times, so filled with energies that a few hours sufficed, but lately, his mind seemed incapable even of that brief respite. A thousand and ten things to do, so many possibilities to consider, such a burden of decisions that he alone could make. Yesterday he'd given two speeches, spent much of the evening in meetings, returned to his flat at midnight, worked on an article until the words wavered in front of his face, and finally took to his bed, cold to his bones, just before four.

Only to lie, staring at the ceiling, irritably wishing that Laura were with him instead of with that bloody family of hers in Gloucestershire: Laura could always make him sleep. But she had her role to play, and one of the elements of that role was maintaining the family connection.

A dozen times a day, he was aware—with emotions ranging from furious resentment to abject gratitude—of how much he owed to Laura. And to think at first he had nearly dismissed her out of hand as yet another titled dilettante. He'd gone to the effort of attracting her mostly through pique, setting himself a challenge, that *he* would be the one to turn *her* down, this latest in a string of frigid females who teased and flirted and belatedly discovered her morals when her blouse was half off.

Instead, he had found a woman who'd determinedly abandoned her class's professional virginity some years earlier, and held her head high about it, as if daring him to criticize. He'd never learned who her first was, or even if there had been more than one. In the end, he'd decided that she'd been one of the many who had given herself to a young officer during the War, a junior officer who died before he could make good his promise of marriage. London was full of them: not quite a virgin, hungry for comfort, like that secretary today, a little long in the tooth but her eyes promising entertainment, if he'd had more than three minutes to spare.

Laura was more than a bed-mate, however. She'd quickly become the partner he hadn't known he needed, one whose identity opened doors to him with an ease he'd never dreamed about. How utterly unlikely she was, how completely she had transformed his work, how much her presence had placed within grasp for the first time— her connections, her money, her passion.

And he had to admit, her brains. His thinking became clearer, discussing his ideas with her. With Laura as audience, his ideas became firmer, more practical, their focus more precise. She also had a woman's instinct for vulnerability and manipulation, and several of her suggestions had brought forth unexpected fruit.

He'd had to consider the alliance long and hard, knowing how it would look: Richard Bunsen, little better than middle class, attaching himself to the Hurleigh coattails. With any other family, he'd never have dared to raise his head in public. But the Hurleighs were not like other families: heroes, yes, established authority in the country, certainly, but iconoclasts as well, outside the normal requirements of titled families. The Hurleighs wrote their own script, and the country trusted them, and followed.

In the end, he had to admit, it was his hunger for the shortcut that decided him. This was three years after Armistice, and he was restless, feeling less sure every day of the wisdom in allying himself with rabble-rousing misfits. Their hearts were right, of that he was convinced, but the way they were going, he could see no victory. He wished he'd had the sense to make a clean break at the time, instead of letting himself be talked into helping the Americans; the weeks that followed his last trip there had been tense ones, as he waited for the knock at the door, waited to have his connections there laid out for the world to see.

What he really wanted, today as much as he had five years ago, was to feel how he'd felt during the War. Hours with your heart in your throat, cradling a packet of hellfire through the wormholes the men had so silently carved, hiding your fear as you rode their apprehension and respect—their *awe*—into the hole. And when you came out, everyone—everyone who mattered—knew who'd been responsible for driving the point of the wedge that tipped the battle. Bunsen and his men knew just who was important on the Front, and it wasn't the generals, and it wasn't the men up there in the fresh air.

When he'd emerged from the hellhole of France, when he was finally convinced that he'd never again be called upon to swallow sour terror and creep through the earth to lay a charge under Jerry, it was like the sun slowly breaking through after a long winter. It took years before he began to notice just how good life could be, and to realize that he never wanted to waste so much as a moment of his precious, too-short life. What he did with his life had to matter. Richard Bunsen had to make an impact on the world. And now, the time was nearly at hand.

(That part of his mind that was always at work played with the phrase *strike while the iron is hot* for a bit, and made mental note of using the word play in his next speech. Audiences liked a spot of cleverness.)

Part of the trouble had been those years it took to find his way. Out of uniform, he'd felt moved by currents he could neither predict nor begin to influence: Speeches to summon indignation in soldiers had slid into speeches to rouse the workers those soldiers had become, until three years later, in the coal strike of 1921, he'd been making speeches to miners. And although his speeches drew a gratifying response, and his public face had been serenely confident, secretly Richard had wondered what on earth he was doing.

Then he'd met Laura, and everything came into bright, sharp focus. With the force of her personality, backed by her family connections, he saw his purpose at last: Look Forward was born, lines of communication and cooperation laid with men in Britain and abroad, men who shared his vision and his frustration.

It was, at times, just a trifle humiliating to reflect on how a few short years with Laura had advanced the cause by decades, but Bunsen was scrupulous about all his emotions: Everything was placed beneath the needs of the Movement, be it love, pride, or humiliation—life itself, even. True, it was his sense of humiliation that escaped his control the most; and true, when it did, he took it out on Laura, but in the end, he always re-gained his perspective, and then he would relish the delicious irony of it, that her family's lofty position would contribute to the abolition of hierarchy.

Perfect. Pre-ordained, you might say, if you believed in such things.

Not that life with Laura was all beer and skittles. She was a stubborn woman, who had beaten her parents into submission when she was a girl and imagined that she could do the same with him. They'd gone through a rough patch during the past year, as she'd begun to resent the interest paid him by Labour and started to harp about the wrongness of, as she put it, joining his wagon to the political machine.

What she didn't see was that he wasn't joining his wagon to Labour any more than he'd joined it to the Americans—or to the Hurleigh name, for that matter: Very soon, within the next month if even half his efforts fell into place, the dust of revolution would settle and reveal: Richard Bunsen's wagon, standing alone in the rubble. Any politician who had thought him a malleable lad grateful for the attention was going to be badly taken aback.

Fortunately, Laura seemed to be calming down. Last year, after that pair of rows that had her going off on her own, he'd half expected her to pack her bags and go home to Mummy.

The possibility had him on the horns of a dilemma: He would be glad enough for the freedom, for not having to argue each minute part of the Movement, but at the same time, he'd bitterly miss the benefits of having her at his side. In the end, he'd agreed to curtail his affairs (although even Laura couldn't expect him to stop from responding to women entirely—a man had his needs, after all) in exchange for which she'd scale down her criticism of his plans. A degree of coolness entered their relationship, but he'd had to do it, had to let her know that he wasn't her rough-handed puppet.

Still, on a night like this, he missed her body, warm and willing, in his bed.

Chapter Thirty-Four

SATURDAY MORNING BREAKFAST at Hurleigh House was laid out on twelve feet of crisp white linen covered with hissing chafing-dishes filled with hearty foods, many of them foreign to the American sensibilities of Harris Stuyvesant. He worked his way down the row of lids, eyeing the contents, before he decided that morning was not the time to investigate unidentifiable lumps of spicy-smelling meat. He helped himself to eggs and sausages.

The only person in the breakfast room was the Duke, seated with his back to the room and his shoulders hunched over the morning newspaper. Stuyvesant took his host's posture as a disinvitation to companionship, so he picked up a paper of his own and carried his plate to a seat between the window and the crackling fireplace.

Twenty minutes passed. A gray-haired woman came in to check the buffet table and left again, clearing his empty plate; the Duke grumbled at something in the paper, stood up, and stalked out, the two deerhounds bouncing at his heels. Stuyvesant skimmed the newspapers: Mussolini was in Tripoli; the House had stayed up all night debating the Economy Bill under Churchill; a boy fishing in the Thames had caught what he thought was a "big 'un" that turned out to be a badly battered corpse; some schoolchildren presented an iron-faced Duchess with flowers; and the *Times* was at last showing some apprehension about the looming strike—their regular "Coal Crisis" piece had moved smack into the center of its page. The less sedate papers verged on hysteria, calling for "volunteers" for the Organisation for the Maintenance of Supplies, which sounded more and more like a tool for recruiting scabs.

In the Oxford *Bugle,* interviews were given with a local housewife (who denied that her purchase of six tins of salmon, three of corned beef, and twenty pounds of flour amounted to hoarding food); a city fireman (who gave a stern lecture on the inadvisability of storing quantities of petrol in the home); and two university undergraduates (hearty lads who eagerly anticipated the chance to man a London bus in defiance of the Strikers, and rather hoped to be given the opportunity to use their boxing skills, as well).

With relief, Stuyvesant heard someone else come into the room; with pleasure, he saw it was Sarah Grey.

"Good morning," she greeted him, making for the coffee samovar. "None of the others up yet?"

"Just the Duke."

"The Duchess will have been up and away long ago; there's a horse she's looking at near Cheltenham."

"Your brother warned me that I might be pressed into horsemanship, but nobody's said anything."

"A month ago we'd all be mounted and off by now, but the season's just ended. Which is probably why this gathering didn't take place a month ago." She dimpled.

"I had an aunt once who was mad for German opera, used to dragoon anyone within arm's reach to go with her. It got so the rest of the family would check the theater listings before we accepted a lunch invitation, because it could easily stretch on to midnight."

"Then you know the hazards. As it is, I shouldn't expect the others until much later—I heard them at one, going strong in the billiards room."

"It was well after two when they came through."

Her eyes sparkled at him over the rim of her cup. "And did they all end up in separate rooms?"

"I did my best to ignore the openings and closings of doors," he replied primly.

She chuckled. "Gilly's incorrigible. The Duchess only invites him because she and his mother were ladies-in-waiting together. The Duke goes wild."

"He's going to get himself arrested, if he's not a little more circumspect."

"Oh, Mr. Stuyvesant, we've loosened up a bit since the days of Oscar Wilde's arrest."

"I wouldn't count on that if I were Dubuque. And please, call me Harris."

"If you call me Sarah."

"With pleasure."

A short time later, Stuyvesant was surprised to see the two men themselves. Gilbert Dubuque and his chinless friend, last night's bartender, both in startling Fair Isle pull-overs, both looking somewhat the worse for wear. Dubuque shot Stuyvesant a bloodshot glance, taking in the American's proximity to Sarah and the unwelcoming glare on his face, and veered off for the shiny samovar.

"Morning, boys," Sarah chirped merrily. "Hope you slept well?"

Dubuque muttered a response, whose only recognizable word was "train," and walked to a table set up at the far end of the room; his friend flipped a hand in their direction but did not try to speak. Sarah's eyes sparkled with mischief, and she called, "Mrs. Bleaks made some of her famous curried kidneys, you must try them."

The sound Dubuque emitted was halfway to a retch; the other spilled his coffee. The two young men crept into a couple of chairs, huddling over their cups, and Stuyvesant leaned forward to murmur, "Sarah Grey, you are an evil woman."

Again came the laugh, sexy as hell emerging from a cute little blonde thing like Sarah Grey. Damn it, her brother had been right: She was just his type.

Which wasn't going to make using her any easier.

As if summoned by the thought, or the laugh, Laura Hurleigh appeared in the doorway. She checked briefly, taking in the tête-à-tête between Sarah and Stuyvesant, and her eyebrows rose.

But not, as Stuyvesant feared, from disapproval, because her expression was warm as she came over to their table.

He stood and pulled out a chair for her, offered to bring her coffee, then subsided when the gray-haired woman appeared with a tray carrying a setting of tea and an envelope.

"This came for you, my Lady."

"Thank you Mrs. Bleaks," Laura said, snatching the flimsy and ripping it open. She ran her eyes down the telegram, and went pink with pleasure before folding it into a pocket and telling Sarah, "Richard thinks he'll be able to make it, after all."

"Oh good."

Stuyvesant felt like shouting aloud. He'd planned a day of vamping the two girls, feeling more and more like a heel with every passing hour, but trading that for a chance at The Bastard himself, well, that was an unexpected bonus.

"Mr. Stuyvesant, I trust you slept well?"

"Thank you, Lady Laura, the room—"

"Please, I prefer not to use the title."

"Okay, Miss Hurleigh. Yes, the room's very comfortable, but boy oh boy, it's quiet out here. I kept waking up and thinking I'd gone deaf."

"You should have asked Gallagher to stand outside and bang a few pans for you."

"If I have the same problem tonight, I'll be sure to ring for him."

"Well, you needn't have risen so early. You'd find the breakfast things out until noon."

"Oh, I've been up for hours. In fact, I walked up to the Peak, I think you call it, and had a nice chat with your father."

"Yes, the Old Man starts his day before the roosters." Her voice put capitals on the title, as if at a family joke. "Perverse of him, I've always thought. What did you and—ah, Bennett. Good morning."

The figure walking towards them looked no more rested than he had twenty-four hours before, following a night's train trip. Still, he gave Laura Hurleigh an easy smile and tweaked his sister's hair as he went past her, so maybe he just needed coffee.

Stuyvesant had to wonder at the timing of his entrance, but

decided that if the former lovers had spent the night renewing their acquaintance, the innocence of their salutations was an act worthy of Broadway. Besides, Laura's smooth skin was rosy with nothing more than the morning warmth, and her lips showed no sign of passion's bruising, while the powerful out-of-doors air that Grey carried into the room was not the result of a mere two minutes in the garden.

Stuyvesant folded his suspicions back in their box and set about winning Laura Hurleigh's approval.

"I was just telling the ladies that I started the day with a nice chat with the Duke, up on the Peak."

"Let me guess: Romans and military history."

"Right on the mark. But look, I should ask," he said, turning to Laura. "Last night I offered to do something about the motor on the Morris. He seemed to think it a good idea, but maybe I should ask you, was that just some form of English manners too subtle for me?"

"Oh heavens, you don't want to spend the day bent over a dirty motor! Wouldn't you prefer a nice ride, or tennis? No doubt there'll be boats on the stretch as well, nothing like the Isis but it has its own charm."

"It won't be an all-day job, nothing like. And I enjoy working on engines, if no one objects."

"I imagine my father would be just tickled pink if you were to beat the thing into submission."

"Oh, not beat it. I am of the gentling school when it comes to coaxing proper behavior out of engines."

"I thought Bennett said you sold the things, not fixed them?"

"Nowadays I do. Mr. Ford sent me over here to see if my English colleagues could use any help in their sales techniques, but before I moved into sales, I was a mechanic. Learning the business from the ground up, as it were."

"Industry in general might be less wicked if everyone followed the same path to the board room," she said.

"Oh Lord," Grey groaned, and got to his feet. "Politics before breakfast? I need fortification before I can face that."

They were, indeed, getting right into the heart of the matter. Well, thought Stuyvesant; so be it. "Yes, you can't help thinking this Strike would be a non-starter if some of the owners had ever been down their own mines."

"Inherited wealth goes hand in hand with inequity," said the Duke's daughter, "just as lack of respect leads to lack of self respect."

The American sat back, frowning at his cup as he took careful aim. "Interesting opinion, from someone born in a house like this."

Sarah stirred, but Laura waved away any would-be defense. "It is because I was born in this house that I can see both sides so clearly, Mr. Stuyvesant. That Hurleigh House was built upon centuries of robbery makes its walls no less graceful, its garden no less lovely. However, this is a new age we live in. I believe it is time to return the wealth from the few to the many."

"I don't know that I'll talk about the writings of Mr. Marx to your father, though."

"You've read Karl Marx?"

"Sure. I don't fully agree with him, but he has some ideas worth bringing up. Why do you think this country's fling with Socialism a couple years back didn't work? I'd have thought it would catch on like a house afire."

"That's rather like saying you'd have expected us to have a lovely picnic out in the fields, while guns are pounding on either side. The half-hearted, imitation Socialism of the Labour Party did not succeed simply because there was nothing to differentiate it from the capitalist policies all around. If one accepts that all government is based on enslaving the worker, then one realizes that no government can be otherwise—democratic, Socialist, monarchical, or what have you. Trying to change the nature of government by replacing one party with another is little more than using rouge to enliven a corpse."

He blinked at the image. "So what would you do?"

"I, Mr. Stuyvesant? Fortunately the decision isn't up to me, although I will say that if laws were passed by the miners, farmers, and housewives who have to live under them, more sensible decisions might be reached."

"And where would that leave owners of houses like this one? Would your parents be given rooms over the kitchen and families of ten brought in to fill the rest?"

"Now you're teasing me, Mr. Stuyvesant," she scolded. "But yes, my family is like anyone else's. Of some members and their actions, I am inordinately proud. Other portions of my family tree fill me with shame. But no matter our history, we have outlived our function, and all that remains are the chains that bind us as well as our working-class brothers. A house like this could be a resource for the nation."

"So you wouldn't follow the example of the Russians and the French and just execute the upper classes?"

But with that, he'd gone too far. She sat back, looking down her aristocratic nose at him in a manner worthy of her mother. "Mr. Stuyvesant, the reason the working class turns on their oppressors with violence is that violence has been done to them—literally, but also figuratively, in the violence done to their self worth. I believe there is hope in this country for non-violent change. No birth is achieved without pain, but with care, bloodshed is unnecessary."

Grey had returned with a laden plate and paid no attention to their talk. Instead, he addressed himself to a glistening sausage, its crisp brown skin oozing juice. He eased his fork into it, then sliced it open with a knife, head bent over the plate. A rich aroma of spices and fatty pork rose up. Grey's nostrils flared and his eyes half shut as he lifted the sausage round to his mouth—and by this time, the other three were staring at him.

He closed his lips around the morsel, withdrew the fork, chewed twice, and moaned with pleasure.

Sarah burst out in laughter, but Laura Hurleigh flushed scarlet. Stuyvesant had to agree, the overt sensuality was a little unnerving—he had to wonder if Grey had done it deliberately, to break up the discussion.

"For heaven's sake, Bennett," Sarah scolded. "Nanny would smack you with her ruler for making a noise like that at the table."

"I've dreamt of Mrs. Bleaks' sausages every morning for the past twelve years. You Philistines are not going to spoil my pleasure."

"Nor am I going to share it. I have a letter to write."

Stuyvesant rose along with her. "And I'm off to tinker with an engine. I'll see you later, Bennett. Miss Hurleigh, Sarah." He would rather have stayed and explored Laura Hurleigh's political leanings, but long experience with undercover work had taught him the benefits of playing hard to get—or at least appearing marginally uninterested. If Laura Hurleigh was half as passionate about the matter as he thought, she would not let it rest.

As they left the breakfast room, Sarah Grey asked, "Shall I show you where the motors are kept?"

"One of the servants can show me," he protested, but she declared that she wanted a breath of air before writing her letter, and he allowed himself to be talked into it.

"Just give me two minutes," she said. "I'll meet you in the garden."

Chapter Thirty-Five

STUYVESANT PACED ALONG THE PATHS, too restless to sit down, too tired to relax. He marched twice the length of the garden without seeing so much as a flower before he noticed what he was doing and took himself in hand: Sit down, have a smoke, and enjoy the place by daylight, he ordered himself. You won't get to Bunsen any faster by champing at the bit.

He spotted a stone bench tucked beneath the white rose along the wall, and sat there. From that angle, he noticed that the house, its garden, and the stream below seemed to have an almost mathematical relationship, as if it had been laid out according to some Golden Mean: x to y; house to wall; wall to stream; height of house to height of wall and height of ridge behind. The result might have been cold and inhuman but for the warm color of the stones used, the naturalness of the setting, and the enormous rambling rose behind him, its green expanse revealing glimpses of a central trunk as thick as Stuyvesant's forearm.

Before half the cigarette was gone, Sarah came out of the house. He rose, but seeing her hand go up, he stayed where he was, enjoying the sight of her trotting down the steps and along the paths towards him.

She tipped her head back and fixed him with those stained-glass eyes. "Tell me something, Mr. Stuyvesant."

"I thought you agreed to call me Harris."

"Harris, do you have such a thing as a nice manly handkerchief, that you could use to clear a section of that bench for me?"

Solemnly, he took out his handkerchief and brushed away a few petals and leaves. The cloth came up pristine, testifying to the cleanliness of the stone itself, so he did not feel it necessary to spread out his coat to protect her dress.

She thanked him and sat down. He offered her a cigarette. She accepted, thanked him again, and lifted her face to the sun, eyes closed.

After a minute, he made himself look away from her throat and cast around for a conversational topic. "The garden looks as old as the house," he noted.

"This house, perhaps, although they say there's been some kind of dwelling here for two thousand years. The garden itself was taken in hand by a friend of the Duchess's named Jekyll, a rather famous landscape designer. Do you like gardens, Mr.—Harris?"

"Never had one. Although my mother had a wisteria trained over the front door of one of the houses we lived in. Used to have one great load of purple blossoms every year in the spring, then drop them all and never do anything the rest of the year. I remember asking her once why she didn't plant something that bloomed for longer, and she said that the whole point of it was the brevity of the beauty, that it made you think about it all year."

"Your mother sounds like a wise woman."

"She was a sickly woman, which meant she had a lot of time to sit and think. She died when I was eight."

"I'm sorry."

"Long time ago."

"Does the brevity of her life mean that you think about her all year?"

He looked down at her in surprise. "I never thought of it that way. I suppose you could say it does."

"My own mother is alive and going strong, and when I'm not at home, I doubt she comes to mind more than once in a week. Come, Mr. Stuyvesant, I shall show you the motorcar stables."

They left the garden by a gate hidden beneath the rose, strolling down the road in the spring sunlight. At the far side of the circle, with the small orchard to their left, the road's downhill angle grew suddenly steeper. At the beginning of the slope, Sarah turned to admire Hurleigh House; at this spot, one could just glimpse the Peak rising up behind the roof-line.

"Bennett says he used to come to Hurleigh for the summer holidays," Stuyvesant said.

"He did, lucky brat. I was so jealous—Mummy would bring us, and then take me away while he could stay on. Oh, I used to have such tantrums!"

"Paradise withheld. So you've known Lady—Miss Hurleigh—since you were small?"

"She's gorgeous, isn't she?" Sarah took it for granted that any male would instantly fall under Laura Hurleigh's spell.

"She's got a lot of . . . charisma, I guess you'd call it."

"And she's ever so smart, considering that she never had any formal schooling. Less than me, even, and I had little enough. She says she used to go around and suck the brains of the boys' tutors."

"Your lack of schooling doesn't seem to have slowed you down much—those clinics have to be a job to run, to say nothing of your political work with Richard Bunsen."

At the name, her face relaxed into pleasure. "I'm glad you're going to meet Richard. Do you know about him?"

Besides the violence that follows him across an ocean and the man's compelling presence in a crowded hall? "No," he lied.

"He's quite extraordinary. One grandfather was knighted, the other was a stone mason, killed in an accident when Richard was ten. His mother ran a boys' school in the village where she'd been born. He was wounded twice in the War, and while he was convalescing, he began to read about the inequity of the capitalist system. After the War, he decided to work for the benefit of the common man."

"How did you and Miss Hurleigh come in touch with him?"

Sarah tucked her arm loosely into his and they ambled down the drive. "I knew him first. One of my responsibilities in Women's Help is to set up educational programs for the mothers through their children's primary schools. Richard happened to be speaking at one of my schools when I was there, and he was so eloquent, so passionate, he struck me as someone Laura simply had to meet. For her work, you understand—I didn't anticipate a more personal connection. But Laura fell in love with his ideas, and then . . . well, she's more or less allied her cause to his."

"I look forward to meeting this paragon."

"Try not to be too disappointed if he doesn't make it—he has so much to do with this Strike coming up. And it sounds terrible, but the Strike could be a real opportunity for Richard to make his name known. He has political ambitions, but for a man without money, it is necessary to spend huge amounts of time making the right connections. Still, they say that by the next general election, he'll be a certainty."

"I can imagine he'd be too busy with Strike preparations to drop into a house in Gloucestershire for a drink."

"If it were anyone but Laura, he wouldn't, but he has tremendous respect for her parents, and will certainly come if he can get free. But in any event, he's not that involved with the everyday preparations for the Strike."

"Doesn't sound like anyone is."

"I'm sorry?"

"Oh, it occurred to me this morning that the papers are full of actions the government's taking, calling for volunteers to ensure that the lights don't go out and the food gets delivered and there are plenty of constables to keep troublemakers in line—"

"The O.M.S.," she said with distaste.

"That's the Maintenance of Supplies thing? Yeah, I heard of that, sounds like vigilantism to me. But it made me think that I haven't heard a thing about what the Unions are doing. They seem to be awfully quiet, considering the Strike's only two weeks away."

"I don't know about your American newspapers, Mr. Stuyvesant, but ours tend to print very little in support of the workers."

"So you think the Unions are planning, it's just not being talked about?" This was a question he'd chewed over ever since Carstairs had brought it up during their dinner on the train: If the Unions weren't summoning their forces, why the hell not? Back home, he was used to all-out brawls—one of the I.W.W.'s tricks was to bus in so many demonstrators the local jails were overwhelmed—but he'd caught not a scent of any similar response here, and it had struck him as odd. Either the Unions were deluded into thinking the Strike would run itself, or its plans were remarkably hush-hush.

Or, as Carstairs feared, they had some clandestine, no-fail card up their sleeves, to be played at the last minute.

"You know," she replied after a moment, "I'm actually a very low person in the organization. If it weren't for my long-time friendship with Laura, I'd be typing and fetching cups of tea. So although it looks as if I'm in the center of things, there's actually an awful lot that I'm not brought into.

"I do know that the Strike is going to make an impact on society far beyond winning the miners their demands. With all the workers in all the Unions linking arms to say, 'This is what we want, and now is when we want it,' the leisure classes won't have a choice. I mean to say, I love the Duke and Duchess, but people like them just can't see that they're at the top of a pyramid that's only held together because everyone underneath them agrees that it needs to be that way. Once the working people lift up their heads and refuse to carry them, the entire structure will crumble."

The idea of this pretty blonde thing linking arms against the zealous truncheons of amateur constables made him wince, but despite her self deprecation, she was clearly a person of more substance, and commitment, than her appearance would indicate. He took care only to nod.

"As Richard says, once equity takes place, once the barriers are down, society's unnecessary structures will just atrophy and die. The royal palaces will become museums to hold the beauty of art and craftsmanship, the churches will become places where the human spirit is worshipped, not the commands of a distant god."

"That's quite a vision."

"Isn't it just? Oh, Mr. Stuyvesant, what a time you chose to visit. These are exciting days."

He glanced down at her face, glowing with possibility unleashed, and said nothing. It was a pretty picture, but in his long experience, radicals and revolutionaries were rarely content to nudge events towards an end. Sooner or later, the fancy thinkers got tired of talk, and decided to rush the barricades.

He put on a thoughtful expression. "I like what you're saying. I'll think about it."

"Well, here's the stables—and I've really got to scramble and write this letter for Alex to drop in the post when he goes into town at noon. I'll come find you when I've finished. Have fun!"

Stuyvesant's eyes followed the jaunty figure retreating up the drive, bright hair reflecting the morning sun, before he turned to the problem of a duke's faulty engine.

He found a partial set of tools in the back of the Morris, and a more complete set on a shelf that had originally been designed for tack. The magneto problem was soon resolved, resolving the back-fire and the smoke, but he cocked his head and listened, and decided to adjust the valves as long as he was here.

Going back to the shelves he found some rags and a coverall nearly large enough for him, if he took care not to bend over.

Whistling happily, he laid out his tools on the cloth-covered fender, and got to work. He did, in fact, enjoy tinkering with machines. And the smell of the engines seemed to grease his thought process as well.

He had half the car's guts on the stable floor when he heard voices. He walked over to the doorway, wiping his hands on one of the rags, to see Grey and Laura Hurleigh coming down the road, both of them resplendent in formal riding gear, from polished boots to riding hats. The Cornish woodcutter had seemed more suited to the shabby garb he wore when Stuyvesant met him than he had to the proper clothes he'd worn since, but now, in this borrowed finery, he was revealed as what, in fact, he was: a gentleman, bred and born. Were it not for his light coloring, he might have been one of the Hurleighs.

Stuyvesant let loose with a wolf-whistle. "Well, ain't you the peachy pair?"

Grey halted, startled. "I can't say the same for you, I'm afraid."

Stuyvesant looked down at the grease-spotted garment straining across his chest and shrugged. "To each according to his abilities," he said.

"Mr. Stuyvesant," Laura said, "are you *sure* you want to do this? Wouldn't you rather come for a ride? Gallagher can outfit you."

"I like fixing motors, and horses and me, we never really clicked," he told her. It was not entirely true, but he did not think the benefits of a ride would outweigh either the credit he'd get with the Duke of Hurleigh or compensate for the state of his thighs after a day of horse-straddling in an English saddle. All in all, he thought it better to let Bennett have her on his own. "Besides, if the car's needed at noon, it doesn't give me much time to put her together again."

"Alex will happily take one of the other motors," she said. "Especially if you'd lend him yours. He adores new motorcars."

"Good to know. You two have a nice time."

The one-time lovers continued down the drive towards the stables proper, leaving Stuyvesant to wonder if he was making a mistake, not to glue himself to them. Then he shook his head: If he couldn't trust Grey, it was best to know it now.

He returned to his engine, and his thoughts.

Sometime during this week-end, he'd like to get Laura Hurleigh to himself for a bit, and burrow into her beliefs a little more closely. Nothing better in getting to know a suspect than to pick his girlfriend's brain.

And some of Laura Hurleigh's speechifying over the breakfast table hadn't been just the usual cant. At times she'd spoken in the rhythm of well-used rhetoric, although some of the phrases were new to Stuyvesant—"rouge to enliven a corpse" had a certain ring to it.

The thing was, some of the phrases Bunsen's two women had used struck him as being other than the straight Communist line. Sarah's "leadership is archaic" and Laura's "inherited wealth goes hand in hand with inequity" were, to his ear, less Communist than Anarchist.

Granted, radical theory was as tangled as a packrat nest, and the lines between Socialism and Communism or Marxism and Bolshevism were often drawn with a very fine and meandering pen. Add into it the tendency of isms to splinter, like factions in a large and argumentative family, and you had a state of affairs too damned complicated for someone like him to keep track of.

Still, working around radicals as much as he had, you picked up patterns of thought. Anarchists believed devoutly in the innate goodness of the individual and the innate evil of society's structures—religion, property, or government. Laura had described Hurleigh House as being built on robbery; the other night on the stage, Bunsen had declared, "Capitalism is theft." The idea of property being robbery was straight out of the French Anarchist, Proudhon. Stir in Sarah's vision of crumbling social structures, and he thought he could smell Anarchist influence in Richard Bunsen's thought.

Not that there was anything wrong with Anarchism per se. In fact, its philosophy of society without government sounded a lot like the early forms of Christianity, all goodness and love. Communists usually went on about economic theory, Socialists explored the middle ground, but Anarchists, now, they were the real dreamers: Utopia or nothing.

Which wouldn't matter a whole lot except that in his experience, with Reds at least you knew where you were. Reds spent most of their time bickering, with each other if no one else was handy, and when they struck out, it followed a pretty predictable route. It was the Anarchists who threw away the rules: Once they'd made up their minds that things were beyond fixing, God alone knew where they'd hit out.

Anarchism was theoretically opposed to violence, but dreamers have always tended to give their all. And when a man looked at his enemy and saw a master of violence, it wasn't a big step to decide that one had to address the enemy in a language he understood.

The first self-avowed Anarchist Harris Stuyvesant had met was a vibrant young woman with the well-mannered name of Ivy Sweethome. At the time, he didn't believe she was really an Anarchist—she was far too bright, too thrilled with ideas, too in love with life to be one of those pale-skinned, cigarette-smoking, back-room revolutionaries the name evoked.

And really, didn't all college students go through an Anarchist phase?

As it turned out, however, Ivy was the real thing: The year after she left college, she killed herself throwing a bomb at a federal judge, in protest against one of his rulings.

It was called *attentat*, or propaganda by action, and the idea was to rouse the people's conscience by a shocking act of self sacrifice. It was nothing new—early Christians called it bearing witness, and went to their martyrdoms singing prayers to God; centuries later, Emma Goldman's lover embraced trial and brutal imprisonment in order to draw attention to the inequities his industrialist target represented. *Voluntary Anarchist sacrifice to make the workingmen think deeply,* he'd called it. Of course, the young fool also claimed it was *the first terrorist act in America,* even though one could argue that the whole country was built upon acts of terror and self sacrifice.

Harris heard of Ivy's death during finals in his second, and what would be his last, year of university. He thought about her at odd moments in the years that followed: How had all that passion for life found rightness in death?

Four years later, when he heard about a job that sounded a lot more exciting than cashing checks behind a teller's window, he had all but forgotten Ivy's name. He was hired by the newly formed Bureau of Investigation because of his bank experience, but before long he was fighting Bolsheviks, Communists, and the I.W.W., often literally—sometimes he suspected that his height and his muscles had been a more important job qualification than his bank experience.

When he came home from the Front in 1919, he was twenty pounds lighter and a decade older than he'd been when he left. He drank too much, twitched at every loud noise, and went back to work as a way of saving his sanity.

Four months later, on June 2, 1919, a series of ten bombs went off, targeted at prominent Americans: judges, legislators, a factory owner, a Catholic priest. The man who committed suicide directly in front of the home of A. Mitchell Palmer, the United States Attorney General, was an Italian Anarchist.

That was the first time Harris Stuyvesant heard the word *attentat.* And he'd thought instantly of Ivy Sweethome.

After that mass bombing, the Bureau's interest abruptly turned to politics. In 1920, the twenty-four-year-old J. Edgar Hoover headed up the new Radical Division; when Helen died, Harris Stuyvesant joined them, in time for the Bureau to embark on its series of wholesale roundups. Communists and Anarchists alike were shoved on ships and sent back where they came from. The country dusted off its hands, and was happy.

The only problem was, the Red Threat proved to be almost completely empty. Even in the midst of it, when he had time to pause for thought, Stuyvesant wondered where all these highly organized and abundantly funded Communist cells he was searching for had sprung from, practically overnight.

Soon, the suspicion that ten bombs do not a Communist takeover make had begun to penetrate even the higher reaches of government, and the Bureau began to cast around for evidence to support its massive reaction against the Red Threat. They hit on the Unions, where Communists were indeed thick on the ground, and turned their wrath against labor: timber strikes, railroad strikes, bomb threats—the bloodier the better, since newspapers were always hungry for drama.

But in the passion for Reds, the country's great enemy of yesteryear was swept under the rug: Anarchists were reduced to a cartoon figure holding a globe with a lit fuse. Anarchists were old-fashioned; worse, they were *foreign*—look at Sacco and Vanzetti, look at Emma Goldman. We've got rid of the foreigners, we solved that problem, let's move on to the home-grown Bolshevists.

Except that Stuyvesant did not think that the earlier enemy was eradicated. He couldn't help wondering if the movement had just gone clever instead, biding their time after the mass arrests. He couldn't shake off Ivy Sweethome, and how her brilliance and her passion for justice had led her down the path to cold-blooded murder. No, he was not willing to give up his belief in the dangers of international Anarchism.

So when Lady Laura Hurleigh—and her pretty friend Sarah, who despite her unexpected flashes of depth did not strike him as intellectually sophisticated—recited phrases with a flavor of Anarchism, he took notice.

Oh, sure, he liked Sarah Grey just fine. And he thought Laura Hurleigh was just the bee's knees, and he'd probably even find something to like about Richard Bunsen, too, because that's what happened with the leaders of Causes, they were leaders because they were likable. And Harris Stuyvesant was as susceptible as any man to the pull of charisma; it was a force, like gravity or the tides.

But he had to say, he wasn't altogether happy with the direction this case of his was taking. It was one thing to follow a roundabout path to the goal, he was used to that, but this job—here he was, cooling his heels tinkering with a duke's car because everyone was waiting for a guy who might or might not show up, and because he wanted to make a good impression on the guy's girl-friend, in case he didn't show.

And while Stuyvesant was waiting for his own case to get under way, he could feel a whole other set of problems grappling to get their hooks into him: Bennett Grey's troubles and Sarah Grey's involvement and the fact that his confederate Carstairs looked to be a shithouse of the first degree.

All of which were highly distracting, but not his problems.

Not. His. Problems.

It was almost as bad as the time in June of '22, when he'd started an investigation washing dishes in a dive off Broadway and ended up sleeping with a police chief's wife (but only sleeping—she was so drunk that anything more would have felt like necrophilia) in order to convince the—

"I say—"

The voice came inches from his backside as he lay head-down in the belly of the Morris. He jerked and cracked his head, swore and cut the oath short, and slithered backwards over the fender, a task made no simpler by the snugness of the coveralls. He extricated his upper body and stood upright, hand pressed against skull.

"Miss Grey," he said, and hoped like hell that she wasn't a mind-reader like her brother.

Chapter Thirty-Six

"I APOLOGIZE," STUYVESANT SAID. "FOR THE LANGUAGE."

"No, it's my fault. I should have cleared my throat or something. Are you all right?"

He withdrew his hand, examined it, and saw just grease: no blood. "I'm fine. I wouldn't come any closer, if I were you. It's been a while since anyone's cleaned the insides of this automobile."

"So I see," she replied, trying hard to keep her face straight. He rubbed a hand across his sweaty face, realized he'd just made matters worse, and felt in his back pocket for the rag he'd shoved there. He took one look at it, and shoved it back unused.

She pulled out a handkerchief and offered it to him, but he looked from the scrap of white lacy stuff to his hands, and went to find a clean rag.

When he'd located one and worked it around enough to bring his face into visibility, he asked, "Was there something you were looking for?"

"No, I'd just got the letter off and thought I'd come and see how you're getting on. But look, can I give you a hand? I'm quite good with machinery."

"That's fine, it's sort of a one-man job, and anyway I'm nearly finished. Why don't you see if you can find a seat that doesn't leave you with a black skirt, and you can talk to me while I'm putting her back together?"

He picked up the wrench—the spanner—and stretched out again. It was pleasant, having a pretty girl watch him work.

A couple minutes later, she broke the silence.

"Why has he never mentioned you?"

Grey would have noticed the brief falter of Stuyvesant's hands; his sister did not. "Who, your brother?"

"Yes."

Stuyvesant twisted his head to peer up at her, then went back to his task. "I wonder. Would he have any reason to keep his friendships to himself?"

She was silent for a moment. "I don't know that he has any friends."

"Well, there you have it. Anyway, your brother's a rare bird. I guess that's one of the things I like about him."

The silence that fell might have been uncomfortable, but it was not. After a while, Sarah got up and fetched the car's traveling-rug, laying it across the other fender so she could lean in and watch his hands. "I took a class last year in elementary engine repair," she said.

"Really? I don't think I've ever met a girl mechanic."

"Oh, it never got that far, but Laura and I decided that if we were going to be driving at all hours of the day and night, it only made sense to be able to fix simple break-downs ourselves. Laura's far cleverer than I, but to my surprise, I discovered that I rather like fiddling with machines. What seems to be the problem with this one?"

So he told her, in basic terms. Then, seeing that she was following what he was saying, he told her in more detail, and she followed that, as well. Before he quite knew how it happened, she had her arm down beside his in the motor; she even managed to manipulate a connection that his large hand couldn't get at. She had small, neat hands, and although she did her manicure no good, to his surprise, she collected only one small smear on the rolled-up part of her sleeve.

When they had finished, he had her slide behind the wheel and start the engine. He listened with satisfaction, and latched the hood—no, the bonnet shut, then looked ruefully at his own black and bashed-up extremities.

"You're certainly tidier than I am with the thing," he told her.

"You had all the hard bits done before I got here. Let's see, there should be a tin of hand-cleaner here somewhere—yes, here it is."

She stretched to pluck a squat tin from a crowded shelf, pried off the lid, and dipped a finger inside, smearing the stuff onto her hands and working it into the stains. He followed her example.

"How'd you know this was here?"

"A place like Hurleigh, if there was a tin of hand-cleaner in the stables in 1910, there will be a tin of the exact same hand-cleaner in the converted stables in 1926. We used to play all kinds of messy games when we were here, some of which involved machinery. But we found that if we cleaned up sufficiently, no one ever caught on. Come, there's a tap around the back for the finish work."

She led him through a small door in the back of the garage, and if the result was far from drawing-room standards, at least he wouldn't leave black stains on the walls. He peeled off the coverall, resumed his tie and coat, and gave the fender an affectionate pat.

"All set to pick up your friend at his train."

"My friend—you mean Richard? Oh, Richard never takes the train—almost never. He all but lives in his motor—has it all arranged as a kind of mobile office, spends his travel time writing articles and practicing speeches."

"I hope he has a driver?"

"Oh, yes." Her answer told him she wasn't terribly fond of Bunsen's driver, a fact he tucked into the back of his mind for later consideration. "I say, would you care for a walk before luncheon?"

"I would indeed." Clearly, Bunsen wasn't about to appear at any minute; he might as well enjoy the day and the company. He shut the big front doors, then glanced across the valley, his attention caught by the approach of a pair of banged-up motorcars.

"This will be the first of the evening's guests," Sarah told him.

"Kind of early, isn't it?"

"It'll be the boys with the music. See the gramophone speaker sticking out of the back? They'll want to set up and check everything early. Although knowing them, it's just an excuse to hang on and stuff themselves silly before the evening starts."

"They're friends?"

"Friends of Patrick's, mostly. Two of them are undergraduates at Oxford, the other three try to make a living out of it, playing at dances and such."

The first car had crossed the ford and was accelerating up the hill; the second, with most of the equipment in the back, took the crossing more sedately. The first car's driver waved and slowed, but when the motor sputtered and threatened to die, the driver accelerated in a panic, waving as he sped past them towards the top of the hill, followed by the other.

"You want to go meet them?" she asked.

"Why not?" he said, although he would much rather have stayed and changed the tires on the cars with her—or re-built the entire engine.

They ambled up the road and found five young men piling out of the two cars and beginning with great energy to haul out musical instruments, the large gramophone, a crate of records, a reflective light-ball, and a megaphone. The driver of the first car spotted Sarah and came trotting down to meet her, a vision in jaunty boater, white club sweater, voluminous Oxford bags in a startling shade of yellow. His sleek hair was almost the same shade of yellow, although the thin moustache riding his lip was suspiciously dark. When he was still some distance away, he spread his arms and burst into loud song.

Sarah Grey, you've made my day,
I'd come all the way, for youuuuu!

He grabbed her and planted an equally loud and vulgar kiss on her right cheek, then began a vigorous Charleston with her on the uneven road surface, singing all the while. She turned pink and laughed aloud, and after a moment the young man dropped his arms and stood away. "Ah, Sarah Grey, I've missed that frabjous laugh of yours."

Stuyvesant was seized by a pulse of irritation, that this young fool should hit on one of what he himself had found one of her more attractive features: A person this loud and vulgar should prefer girly giggles, not Sarah's deep chortle.

The intruder turned to Stuyvesant, but before Sarah could make any introduction, he dipped his hand into a pocket and held out a set of keys. "You want to put the 'bus away for us, my good man? Be sure she goes under cover, that's a good fellow."

"Simon!" she interrupted sharply. "This is a friend of my brother's, Harris Stuyvesant. Harris, this is Simon Fforde-Morrison. He's providing the music for tonight."

"Oh, sorry old chap. I saw the hands and I thought, well."

"No offense," Stuyvesant said through gritted teeth, unclenching his fist and trying to keep from crushing the musician's hand in his. The man didn't even have the sense to appreciate that their positions were precisely the reverse of what he'd assumed: He was, it would seem, here for pay, while Stuyvesant was a friend of the family. Snooty bastard.

Fforde-Morrison turned to Sarah. "Is the family up and around?"

"Laura's gone riding with my brother. I don't know about the others."

"Your brother's here?" he asked, his eyebrows shooting upwards. "Your mystery-man of a brother?"

"Miracles may never cease," she told him. "Harris and I were just setting off for a walk. Gallagher will take care of you, though. We'll see you for luncheon, shall we?"

"Unless the Old Man has one of his tempers and throws us in the river."

Now *that*, Stuyvesant thought, I'd pay to see.

Fforde-Morrison wandered off to find someone else to take charge of the motorcar. When he had gone out of earshot, Sarah studied Stuyvesant's expression and said, "You see what Laura was talking about, that lack of others' respect does violence to one's self respect?"

"There's nothing wrong with that young pup's self respect."

"I am talking about you. Simon mistook you for a menial, and treated you as someone beneath him. And although you are fifteen years older than he is and immensely more competent, you reacted with resentment. You wanted to put him in his place, didn't you? I saw it in your face."

Where he'd wanted to put him was with that self-satisfied smirk to the ground. "I guess."

"It wasn't just his mistake that made you angry, it was because his attitude humiliated you; it did violence to your self respect. If you hadn't cared a fig for what he thought, you'd just have laughed him off. Isn't that true?"

It was both true and not true. The cocky musician had indeed cut him to the quick, but it had nothing to do with car keys and class warfare. He just hadn't liked the kid's familiar attitude towards Sarah Grey.

Damn it, Stuyvesant, he told himself: Bad enough you've fallen under her brother's spell; you must *not* get involved with this young woman.

Chapter Thirty-Seven

THEY ENCOUNTERED no other impertinent musicians on their way to the barn. Back in his room, Stuyvesant checked his freshly scrubbed finger-nails and studied his pink and glowing, moustache-free face in the mirror, then scowled at the dull neck-tie. He traded it for another, took that one off and tried a third. He combed his hair, took another run at his finger-nails with the nail-brush, and gave it up.

Before he left the room, he checked the alignment of the shoes in the wardrobe, but they had not been disturbed.

Downstairs, Sarah's door was standing open, and she popped out when she heard his feet on the stairs.

"I say, how would you feel about ducking out on the family luncheon? There's this adorable scruffy little inn down in the next village that was a part of my childhood, a place a visiting American really ought to experience."

"I wouldn't want you to miss your friend Bunsen," he said.

"No fear of that, he's in Manchester until at least four."

"Then sure, I can't think of anything I'd rather do than play hooky with you."

"That's good, 'cause I've already told Gallagher we wouldn't be there." She tucked her arm snugly into his for the four steps it took to reach the door, although to his disappointment, she did not resume the position once they were outside. For some time, his biceps tingled with the warmth of her breast.

They walked down the road again, past the garage and the stables, pausing at the ford to talk to the ducks. They did not cross on the foot-bridge, however, but kept following the stream as its valley narrowed and rose. Eventually, they climbed onto the surrounding level of countryside, where trees gave way to open fields and, in the distance, a cluster of low buildings. Back in the direction of Hurleigh House, across a field, over a stile, through another field dotted with sheep droppings, and then a gate. All the while, Sarah talked.

She was a champion talker, was Sarah Grey, her stories about growing up and about the poor women and children she worked with filled with passion and the telling detail. She told him about the health classes she and Laura were teaching, about her single attempt at university, about her childhood, about her brother.

"Anyway," she said, with an air of continuing a conversation, "I'm glad he's got at least one friend. Other than the Cornish farmers he lives among, none of whom seem to count."

"Because they're beneath his class?" he said in all innocence.

She half turned and punched his arm. "Don't you tease me, you American brute. I'll have my brother challenge you to a duel. He's a deadly fencer, you know."

"But what would that say about your rights as a woman, needing to be protected by a male?"

"It would say that I have as much scorn for the system as I have for your attempts at teasing," she retorted.

"Touché," he said.

"Are you a fencer as well, then?"

"Sure—I spent a whole summer once, pounding posts and stringing wire."

"Pounding...? Oh," she said, "terrible joke."

"I didn't think it was a joke at the time. However, if you're talking about swords and foils and such, then no, I'm more a six-shooter kind of a guy. But I like your brother a lot. I'm glad we don't have to meet at dawn."

"You really just happened to stroll into his yard, on your way to Land's End?"

Stuyvesant set off into a somewhat more detailed version of the story Grey had told her the previous afternoon, concocted to explain his presence on Grey's land two summers earlier. He was surprised at how distasteful the lie was, and the effort it took to stick to it.

"So," he finished up, "when Ford sent me over here this time, I took a few days' holiday to see your brother. Problem is, this whole trip has made me realize how fed up I am with the company. I've been with it on and off nearly ten years, and it's no fun any more. Too big."

"By which you mean, the workers and the management have little contact with each other."

"I suppose you're right. I'm a cog—a selling cog, connected to a service cog and an advertising cog and eventually to a whole lot of manufacturing cogs. I've got some savings. I was . . . Well, I was sort of thinking of going into business for myself."

"Doing what?"

"Running a garage, maybe. I like getting my hands on cars. Makes it feel real." Christ, he thought, I'm beginning to believe my own cover story.

"Where?"

"Oh, New York I guess. Maybe upstate, where it's quieter. The only place I've seen that I like as well is Cornwall, but there don't seem to be more than two dozen cars in the whole county."

"There's lots of motors in London," she offered. Then, as a blush rose through her freckles, she hurried to amend what might be taken as forward. "Although considering how popular rambling has become, before you know it, Bennett will be driving people like you off his land with a shotgun. Motor-tourists won't be far behind."

"Unless the revolution comes," Stuyvesant noted solemnly.

To his pleasure, she took the opportunity to punch him again, this time harder.

Another place, another girl, he'd have taken it as an invitation to grab her and kiss her, but not here, not now.

Instead, he squatted down and dug a couple of half-opened

dandelions out of the weeds and handed them to her. She tucked them into a button-hole in her sweater. Apology given and accepted.

And she tucked her arm through his for the rest of the way to the village, her breast very occasionally making contact with the back of his arm.

The village scarcely qualified as such, being six buildings and an old well. The inn was called the Dog and Pony, and Sarah came to a halt to look up at the sign. "You see it?"

"See what?" Stuyvesant asked. After a minute, he did.

The dog on the sign was one of the Duke's deerhounds, tongue lolling as if in laughter. The pony was a true pony, stumpy and glowering, but the straight-spined figure on its back could only be the Duchess of Hurleigh.

Sarah grinned at his surprise, and pulled him around a propped bicycle and through the door.

The inn might have been built by the prehistoric inhabitants of the British Isles, the people whose child-sized adult armor graced museums. Stuyvesant stooped double to enter, and even Sarah had to duck to keep her hat in place.

The interior was dark and smelled of centuries of wood and tobacco-smoke, the stones of the floor were polished by generations of sluiced beer, and the inhabitants might have been in a diorama labeled: *Early Britain*.

"You'll have to buy the beer," she told him. "It might give them all heart attacks if I tried to. And we'll have to go into the saloon bar to drink it."

"Feminism hasn't made much inroads here, I see?"

"They've probably never laid eyes on an actual Flapper, and if I lit a cigarette they'd take me for a witch and duck me in the pond. I'll be next door."

He asked the rotund gnome behind the bar for a pint, a half pint, and two lunches (which the man insisted were dinners). Keeping a close eye on the beams, he maneuvered through the wood and stone cavern to the doorway, where he found a far lighter, newer, tidier room with roof beams that he could nearly straighten up under. There were six tables ranging from twosomes to one that would hold a Stuyvesant family gathering, all of them empty except for where

Sarah sat. She had chosen one beneath a bow window of glass panes the size of his palm, most of them too wavery to see through to the street beyond.

"Don't you just adore the place?" she insisted.

"They'd never make it in New York," he told her. "Half the patrons would be knocked unconscious before they reached the bar."

"I only wanted you to see the room, which Daniel swears hasn't changed since it was built in the thirteenth century."

"But how was this a part of your childhood? I wouldn't have thought little girls were allowed in pubs."

"That's exactly why. This was The Forbidden Place, dark and mysterious, with a sorcerer to guard it and only the initiated permitted inside."

"I'd have thought the reality so disappointing, you'd never want to set foot here again."

"True, but by that time it was part of the tapestry of growing up. Laura used to write plays for us to perform, and half of them were about nefarious plots and acts of dark derring-do that went on here."

"Laura's quite a girl."

"When she was young, she was a tom-boy. Can you believe that?"

"Yes, I could see it."

"She used to lead Bennett and the two older boys on all sorts of outings. Maybe it's what comes from being first born, even if you're a girl. And then when she hit maturity and really couldn't run around like a wild Indian, she turned to romantic dreaming."

"A romantic, huh?"

"She doesn't look like that, either, does she? All competence and realism. But underneath all that, Laura's terribly squishy for the Grand Romantic Gesture—the first time I met her, when I was eleven and she was about to turn sixteen, she'd memorized the whole of *Romeo and Juliet,* and she used to go around with this little glass vial and pull it out to declaim the death scenes, both his and hers. I was terribly impressed."

"Bennett's very fond of her."

"Yes." A flat answer, from her.

"You don't sound too pleased about it."

"It's not that. It's just ... he and Laura were secretly engaged, the first year of the War. She was of age, but he was only twenty. Then when he finished at Oxford he enlisted, so they put it off again. When he was wounded, I'm sure she would have married him anyway—tragedy being an essential part of Romance, don't you know? She more or less lived in the village near his sanitarium, although at the time I couldn't understand why she didn't stay here at Hurleigh, it's not that far away. But in the end—and I don't know this for certain, because neither of them will talk about it—but I think that when Bennett realized he was never going to fully recover, he practiced a Grand Romantic Gesture of his own. He disappeared. To Cornwall, although we didn't know that for some time."

"Hard on both of them, I imagine," he remarked, since she seemed to be awaiting a comment.

"Certainly it was hard on her. That was in 1921—the world was on the brink of revolution then, too, or so it seemed—you know we had a strike in the spring of 1921? It might have succeeded if some of the Union leaders hadn't given in. Anyway, Laura was so down in the dumps, both with Bennett's leaving and some hard problems with her work, that the family was frankly worried for her health. I talked her into coming to London with me for a change of scenery, something to get interested in, you know? And along the line I introduced her to Richard, who was one of the miners' shining lights in the Strike, and he seemed to just, I don't know, pulse with energy. And of course he's very good-looking anyway, and she took one look at him and, well, Juliet had her new Romeo.

"To tell you the truth, I wasn't all that happy about it—I thought it was too soon, and in any event he wasn't my brother—but in the end I had to admit she was right. Richard was ... intoxicating, where Bennett was so dark and hard to be around after the War, and looking back, I can't say that Laura sticking it would have made a difference to him. However, that's why I said I was glad to see he had a friend like you—he seems almost his old self this week-end."

Was he imagining the note of uncertainty in her voice, at the idea of Bennett being his old self? Perhaps she should be concerned, considering Laura Hurleigh's conflicting ties with the founder of Look Forward.

"Tell me more about this Bunsen fellow," he suggested.

But as she burbled on about the founder of Look Forward, as they ate their surprisingly tasty meat-and-two-veg, and as he made his responses at all the proper places, he found himself wondering if perhaps he shouldn't just tell the Bureau to kiss his ass after all, and go into the car repair business in Penzance.

Or London, where there were, as she'd said, a lot of cars.

"Tell me about this Bunsen chap," Grey said. He and Laura Hurleigh were only two miles from the Dog and Pony, riding in amicable silence while the Duke's two deerhounds coursed back and forth between the horses and the surrounding countryside. The air was warm and the clean animal smell coming off the horses mingled with the odors of spring and the smell of the leather saddle. The jingle of tack, the shape of the hills, and Laura's knee near his brought back all the rides of his youth; for a moment, Bennett Grey had felt almost happy.

It was such an unnerving sensation, he instantly pushed it away, and Stuyvesant's quarry was the first thing that came to mind.

At the question, Laura's gelding snorted and jerked its head; Grey's skull throbbed in reaction to the sudden wave of tension from her body. Then she loosed her grip on the reins and answered in a voice in which all emotion was clamped down. "He's a great man, Bennett. I'm so glad you're going to meet him. He said he'd be here for drinks. Maybe even in time for tea."

He ordered his hands to stay on the reins and not betray the rising headache. She might as well have said, *"I fell in love with him, Bennett, but I'm afraid I'm falling out, and I'm too committed to leave."* He also heard notes of experience and exasperation in her voice, which told him that Bunsen would show up whenever he damn well pleased, be it noon or midnight. Or never.

"They say he's to be Labour's next leading light."

"They do, don't they?" she said.

"You don't sound at all sure about it."

"Oh, I have no doubt Labour adores him. What I can't decide is if he's right in thinking that siding with Labour is a justifiable compromise. It would give him authority and visibility; on the other hand, the more one knows about parliamentary democracy, the more corruption and deceit one sees. As I said to your American friend, the system is designed to keep workers enslaved. There's a real danger that by siding with it, even temporarily, his voice will be lost."

There were lies in her tone, her spine, the tilt of her head, lies that crept over him like the wet mud of France. *Please don't lie to me, Laura my love,* he pleaded. *You might as well drive a knife into my brain.*

She was not the least bit undecided: She believed Bunsen was wrong, completely wrong, wrong to the edge of treachery.

His hand came up to rub at his forehead, but he kept his voice mild. "It seems to me we've had this argument before, over compromise being a necessary evil."

"Haven't we just?" she said, her voice gone suddenly fond. "And it will no doubt please you to know that I have learned the art of concession. But it's so seductive, isn't it? So easy a habit to fall into. Look what happened to Labour, two years ago. They took the election— the Labour Party! Out of the blue, an opportunity to push forward some real, substantial *changes*! The Liberals would have gone with them, I know they would. But when the time came, they were afraid of being labeled extremists and so they ignored their conscience, and would not use the authority they'd been given. MacDonald and the rest of them took one small, compromising step back, and then another, and in no time at all they had nothing left."

Politics were safe; politics brought her to life and took the lies from her voice. For Laura, politics were life, and it was a comfort to Bennett, just to relax and enjoy her passion. He commented, "The Zinoviev letter didn't help matters any."

"Oh, even without it, Labour would have lost the election. The letter was just a dirty trick that toppled a doomed structure. It's happened a thousand times in history, that a revolutionary group becomes mainstream, led astray by the illusion of power."

"So what's the other option? Systematically chopping off every branch of political and economic organization?"

"A generation ago, that might have been seen as the only choice, but Richard believes that the power of the collective voice could be immense, if only the proper means of uniting the people could be found. Look at the Paris Commune—don't you wonder what France would look like now if the army had stayed away long enough to give it a chance? For two brief months, ordinary workers ran the city, with remarkable efficiency and fairness. For that short time, government was based on an equality of voice, authority came with experience—did you know, there were billions of francs right there in the national bank, and they didn't touch a *sou*? Children were fed and educated, women walked without their traditional chains—God, Bennett, you have to wonder, if they'd been given time...

"And now we're being given our own chance, to let righteousness flow down like water, and give true freedom a chance. Piecemeal change just doesn't seem to work—it's like patching a leaky dam."

"So Bunsen would blow the dam up and build a new one." Washing away the poor buggers downstream.

"More like blowing it up and let the river run without it. Any time there's a formal structure, it opens the door to corruption and inequality. *Any* hierarchy is unequal. Which wouldn't be so bad if everyone occupied positions with only slight variations of superiority, but, Bennett, we live in a country where children starve within two miles of Buckingham Palace. British children, so thin they look like wizened old men. Children starve, and they die of minor ailments, and their worn-out mothers die in child-birth, and their unemployed fathers drink themselves to death. Have you ever been down a mine?" she asked, in an abrupt change of subject.

"I live in Cornwall, remember?"

"Tin mines," she said dismissively. "Positively civilized compared to the coal pits. Day after day, men, some of them little more than children, drop themselves down a mile-long tube into the darkness to grovel away in the earth. Their skin turns black and their spines bend, and they die, either quickly in preventable accidents or slowly of lung diseases. They die doing filthy work, in terrible circumstances, all the while knowing their sons are condemned to the same deaths. And up in the sunshine, the men who build their houses over the bones of the dead now expect them to work a longer day, and for less than they live on now. I don't believe in God, Bennett, but I do believe in sin, and that is sin."

He allowed the silence to hold for a while, overcome by the

intensity of her vision. Oh, he could hear the rehearsal in her words, phrases honed and arranged and used in one speech after another, but he had no doubt of the passion behind them. Lady Laura Hurleigh had come a long way since she had signed on as a twenty-two-year-old V.A.D. nurse, eleven years ago.

"So what would you have us do, you and your friend the Great Man?"

She turned and gave him a radiant look. "Tonight? Meet Richard and listen to him. But right now? Right now I'd have you race me to the Snag."

So saying, she drove her heels into the horse and took off, Bennett following a length behind.

Laura won.

Chapter Thirty-Eight

SARAH LED Stuyvesant back to Hurleigh House by another route, across the fields and then down a gated path through the woods. They passed the Hurleigh chapel without stopping in, but paused for a few minutes at a hillside clearing designed to offer a panoramic view of the estate: servants' hall roof directly below, the lodge and drive beyond it, then the house itself, with the river valley framed by the ancient rose at the bottom and the top of the opposite hill above.

"So, so beautiful," Sarah said. She sounded oddly sad about it, and Stuyvesant thought she had the beginnings of tears in her eyes.

They completed their four-hour circle at Hurleigh House at half past three. Somewhere nearby rose playful shouts, and as they went past the kitchen they heard the clatter of pans.

"See you in the house later, for tea?" she asked.

"Wouldn't miss it."

"Thank you, Harris. I had a lovely afternoon."

"The pleasure was all mine."

She stepped forward to give his cheek a quick peck, then disappeared into the wave room.

Stuyvesant's feet took him up the stairs, without much contribution from his brain. He was, he reflected, having about as much luck at not getting involved with Sarah Grey as he'd had at keeping himself aloof from her brother.

Upstairs, he used the toilet, gave his dusty shoes and trouser legs a brush, then went down the hall to knock on Grey's door. There was no answer, and the knob turned. Stuyvesant stepped inside and found the room empty. The riding boots Grey had been wearing were standing upright in the corner.

He walked over to the house, and found the energy level building. Strange faces popped in and out of doors, a collection of freshly scrubbed tennis players talked in loud voices in the gallery, and a delegation of boatmen were straggling up through the garden, half of them drenched and weed-draped but laughing nonetheless.

Richard Bunsen had not arrived.

Bennett Grey was not in the house.

Back outside, Stuyvesant walked a circuit of the garden, wishing he could borrow a shotgun and blaze away at a bunch of cans— waiting periods were the parts of cases he hated most.

The Morris sped down the road opposite, crossed the ford, and came up the drive without a trace of smoke or hesitation. Gallagher stepped forward to open the door to the noisy crowd of passengers— but Bunsen would not be in the Morris; he had his own motor.

Stuyvesant turned away, strode through the garden and past the barn to the path that led uphill. Ten minutes later he spotted Grey sitting on the Peak, chin on knees and silver flask between his feet.

Stuyvesant sat down and took out his cigarettes. He held out the case to Grey, who gave a small shake of his head but didn't take his eyes off the roof-tops below. Stuyvesant glanced at the flask, wondering if it was empty, wondering how full it had been when Grey had come up here.

"If you ask me how drunk I am, I'll hit you," Grey snarled.

"You're a big boy. You don't need me to nag."

"Damned right."

"Besides, now I don't need to ask. You're drunk enough to be obstreperous but not far enough gone to pass out."

"It takes more than one flask of the stuff to knock me out."

"Even of that Cornish vodka?"

Grey looked at him then, an eyebrow raised. " 'Vodka'?"

"Isn't that what it is? You said it was made out of potatoes."

"You're right. I just never thought of it that way. Makes it sound far too exotic."

"You going to be able to handle tonight?"

"I don't know. Depends on how drunk everyone gets. It's easier then, oddly enough. Drunks are more honest."

"I'll make sure Gallagher spikes the punch."

"If I disappear early, it'll mean I found the going too hard and have gone to bed."

"Grey, look," Stuyvesant began, but couldn't decide how to go on. What can you say to a man who is eviscerating himself on your behalf? "If there's anything you want me to do, give me the high sign." After a minute, Grey picked up the flask and unscrewed the cap, taking a swallow: nearly empty, Stuyvesant saw.

"She loves him, doesn't she?" the American said.

Grey considered the object in his hand, took another gulp, and screwed down the top, dropping it to the ground. "Laura is completely and utterly committed to Look Forward and its founder. We'll find that Bunsen treats her abominably, but then he probably treats everyone the same way, unless there is something he wants from them. As for your own needs, yes, I managed to work you into our conversation as we rode back, and planted in her mind the possibility that you might be sympathetic to her beliefs, with an eye to your ingratiating yourself into her beloved Movement."

The bitterness of his speech grated on Stuyvesant, who was already feeling quite bitter enough about this particular operation. He stifled a sharp retort, which wouldn't help either of them, and instead remarked, "Your sister seems to be equally committed to the Movement."

The instant he said it, he realized that he had played into Grey's hands. Grey shot him a grin. "I told you she was the kind of girl you'd fall in love with."

"I don't know about that," Stuyvesant protested. "But yeah, she's a great girl. And I've let her see how much I like her ideas, too."

The smile faded; Grey shook his head. "It's a low thing to do, Stuyvesant, taking advantage of two women like this."

"I've spent most of my life worming my way into people's affections. I can't say you get used to it, but you can see that it's necessary."

"So why are you so tempted to throw it all in?"

"I never said..." He stopped. Jesus, no wonder the poor bastard had no friends: Being with him was like parading down a street in the nude. "Yeah, you're right. I've been doing this half my life. Partly it's a game, you see. You find a way inside an organization. You talk right, act right, day and night, never letting your act down. You spend months handing out pamphlets on the street to prove your sincerity, you make yourself useful, you work your way up." And sometimes instead of handing out pamphlets you were delivering guns or beating up one of the opposition, but you did it because that was the only way to get to the end, and afterwards you didn't talk about it. "It's a young man's game, and I'm forty years old. Maybe I'm just tired."

Grey picked up the flask and held it out; Stuyvesant took a swallow, feeling the burn all the way to his diaphragm. In exchange, he offered the silver case again; this time Grey took one.

"Where were you?" Grey asked.

From his tone, Stuyvesant knew instantly what he meant. "In France? Mostly Belleau Wood and with the French near Reims. You?"

"Here and there. Spent a long time near Ypres."

"Bad."

"Very."

"Did you ever take R and R in Paris?"

"Of course," Grey said.

"Ever get to a place called the Dutch Wife?"

"God, yes. Most gorgeous woman in the world ran the place, fifty years old if she was a day."

"My great-aunt Mathilde. She'll be pleased to know you thought she was fifty—she was sixty-three when the War started."

"Is she still alive?"

"Going strong."

"Send her my greetings. Tell her—tell her I was the officer who gave her the Belgian lace collar for Christmas in '17."

"Oh yeah? She was wearing it last time I saw her."

"Really?" Grey said in surprise, then his eyes narrowed. "You're lying."

"Yeah, but I had you there for a second, didn't I?"

Grey stared at him, then laughed. Stuyvesant let a smile play on his lips as he watched the laden Morris scuttle down the road opposite, yet again.

Grey reached out and gave him a light touch on the shoulder, the first time he had willingly made contact. "You're a good man, Harris Stuyvesant."

"Not very, but I try."

"That's all one can ask. Ah—you smell that?"

Grey's head was raised, his nostrils flared. Stuyvesant sniffed, but all he got was tobacco and booze. "What?"

"Mrs. Bleaks has made scones for tea."

"You can smell scones, all the way from the house?"

"This time of day, the breeze rises up from the stream," Grey explained mildly. He got to his feet. "Anyway, I haven't eaten since breakfast so I'd probably smell her cooking a mile off. You coming?"

"You go ahead, I'll be there in a while."

Stuyvesant watched the small man work his way across the uneven rocks to the path, and start downhill. Then, just before the path ducked under the branches, Grey's head jerked up. He stopped, moving to one side to peer among the trees. There were a lot of blue flowers growing among them, but that did not seem to be what interested him. After a moment, he shrugged, as if to settle his shoulders inside his coat, and continued down the hill.

Stuyvesant wondered what he had seen. The Duke's dog-fox? He could feel the place on his shoulder where Grey's hand had rested. Poor bloody bastard, he thought. Ypres explained a lot—it was a minor miracle he was on his feet.

He picked up the cigarette case, tracing the elaborate initials with his finger before his thumb-nail sought out the hidden latch. He unfolded Helen's photograph, touching the lock of hair pinned to its corner. Yes: blonde, not red. Why had that been the sticking point, where he simply had to deny Grey his omniscience?

Too close to home, that color; too close to everything that mattered.

He'd gone into the Bureau's political wing because of Helen. This meant that with each and every job, he felt her looking over his shoulder, reminding him of the bigger issues. It wasn't enough to throw a villain in jail; he also had to set aright the lives the man had smashed on his way. It was sometimes hard to finish a case and move on, with this attitude riding him. Like how, for the last three years, Stuyvesant had sent money to the kids of a man he hadn't been fast enough to save. And how twice, he'd felt obligated to find jobs for the widows of other innocent victims.

Now, it looked like he'd been saddled with another damned collateral responsibility: keeping Bennett Grey out of the hands of Aldous Carstairs.

Oh, and while he was at it, unhitching Sarah's wagon from that of Richard Bunsen.

Wouldn't it simplify matters just to ask Bunsen point blank—in Bennett Grey's presence—if he was the man who'd set the bombs?

Well, no, it wouldn't. For one thing, as evidence it would be laughable, as well as guaranteeing that Bunsen would never venture into the States again. But the real problem was, he wasn't all that sure he could trust Grey on the matter. Could Grey objectively judge guilt or innocence in the man Laura had replaced him with? And if he could, would he then tell Stuyvesant the truth, or would the temptation of using Stuyvesant to remove his rival be too great?

Nope. Carstairs might find the man's talents useful, but here? It would only confuse matters.

He folded Helen's picture and put it back into the case, slid it into his inner pocket, and stood up. Time for scones, tea, and Richard Bunsen.

The rocks of the Peak required some attention, to preserve both neck and the leather of one's shoes, so that Stuyvesant was nearly clear of the hazardous portion when he lifted his gaze to the path itself.

In front of the trees, as if conjured from the flowers by dark magic, stood Aldous Carstairs.

Chapter Thirty-Nine

"CHRIST JESUS," STUYVESANT BLURTED. The black eyes watched him approach. "What the hell are you doing here? Grey heard you in the bushes, do you really want him to know you're lurking around?"

"He will not know unless you tell him."

"How the hell did you get here, anyway? I didn't see any car but the Morris."

"My car is waiting on a farm track a mile away behind the ridge. I came down the back way, thinking I might find you in the house, but I spotted you here with Captain Grey. A pleasant conversation, I trust?"

"You expect me to believe you drove all the way from London on the chance of finding me wandering around the grounds?"

"Oh no, I was in the area, and thought it worth an hour's, hmm, gamble to try to see you rather than depend on the telephone. I wanted to tell you that your Mr. Bunsen will be here this evening."

"I know that. He sent Laura Hurleigh a telegram."

"When he comes, I suggest you try to get a look at the contents of his motorcar. He keeps much of his paperwork to hand as he travels. You might find some useful information there."

"I know that, too. Trust me, Carstairs: I know my job."

"So it would seem. May I further suggest, however, that you pay particular attention to any correspondence concerning a gentleman by the name of Lionel Waller."

"Who is he?"

"No one, as yet. Merely a name that came to my attention, that I pass on to you. Also, this."

Carstairs pulled an envelope out of his inner pocket and removed a photograph, handing it to Stuyvesant.

It showed a man and a woman standing on the street: She was dressed in a flowered dress, which blurred slightly with the motion of a breeze. The man wore a lounge suit and soft hat, and could have been her father. Stuyvesant shook his head.

"Never seen either of them."

Without comment, Carstairs retrieved the picture and struggled to get it back into the envelope, not easy with the gloves on his hands. When it was enclosed again, he returned it to his pocket.

"Let me know if they appear."

"You going to tell me who they are?"

"Not yet. They, too, may be of no importance."

And to Stuyvesant's astonishment, Carstairs settled his gloves and turned to walk into the trees, wading through the soft blue flowers until he vanished, as if he had never been.

What in hell was the man up to?

Chapter Forty

When Stuyvesant got back to the house, it was five o'clock and tea was set out in the long gallery. He loaded a plate with tiny crustless sandwiches and diminutive savory pies. He could have done with a nice cold beer—or even a tepid British one—but allowed Deedee to pour tea and milk into a small, frighteningly delicate cup, which he immediately drained and held out for a refill. She giggled, and poured again. He retreated to a pew-like bench washed in sun from the window, and addressed himself to the plate.

Despite his own tardiness, the others were still drifting in, one or two at a time. Some had clearly been out of doors, carrying with them pink cheeks and the robust smell of fresh air; others lounged through the door smelling of cigarettes and warmth; two of the band members showed evidence of a bottle. Once again Stuyvesant found himself between Patrick and Pamela Hurleigh, both of whom persisted in standing close to him and laughing loudly whenever he said anything that could be construed as humorous. He was relieved to see Sarah Grey come into the gallery.

" 'Scuse me," he said. "There is something I need to discuss with Miss Grey."

He did not look to see if they were offended, just made straight across the room with his empty plate and cup, and inserted himself beside her. "You and I have something really important to talk about," he told her in a low voice.

She paused in transferring a sandwich to a plate to look up at him. "I'm sorry?"

"Vitally important," he said, helping himself to another plateful of insubstantial morsels. "Something that keeps us so engrossed, nobody will interrupt us."

She gazed for a moment longer, puzzled, then she glanced at the direction from which he had come, and enlightenment dawned. "Ah. I understand."

"Are they staying put?"

"Well, I'd say they show signs of restlessness."

"Will it encourage them to find another victim if you and I were to head for a corner and turn our backs on the room?"

She stifled a laugh. "If we choose a place with only two chairs. Try the curry puffs, they've been a specialty of Hurleigh teas since the eighth Duke came back from India in 1832."

He obediently shoveled a few yellow objects on top of the two-bite sandwiches and one-bite ham pies, received a third cup of tea, and followed her to a pair of spindly-legged chairs in the far corner of the room.

He risked a glance back as he turned to sit down: The two Hurleighs had snagged a couple of the band members. He let loose a relieved sigh.

"Much longer, and I'd have been afraid that one or the other of them would drag me off behind the sofa."

"If not both of them."

"Lord. I hadn't thought of that."

"I shouldn't worry, they mostly do it to annoy, because they know it teases."

"So it wasn't one of them who tried my door-knob in the wee hours last night?"

"Ah, so the openings and closings of doors included your own?"

"Not quite, since it was locked. I shouted at whoever it was to go away, and they did."

"Then it certainly wasn't Pamela. And I shouldn't have thought

Patrick would make the cold dark trek to the barn unless it was a sure thing."

"No, I think it was Dubuque."

"Good thing you'd locked your door."

"Your brother suggested it."

Her sudden snort of laughter sent a dose of tea up her nose. When she had finished coughing, mopped her eyes and nose with his handkerchief, and finally retrieved her cup from Stuyvesant's rescuing hand, she turned on him a pair of dazzling green eyes brimming with mischief. "My brother speaks from experience."

"Oh, do tell."

"My lips are sealed. No, no—I promised him, long ago. I will merely say that Bennett no longer sleeps in the altogether, as he has vivid memories of what happens when one scrambles out of the window into the shrubbery without a layer of protective flannel."

"Worse than Cora Whatsis and the peonies?"

"Oh, far worse."

"That'll reform a person's habits, all right. I once had a similar experience," he said—then realized that not only had the experience been during one of his times undercover, but the details were hardly suitable for the present circumstances: He'd ended up in the snow wearing only the bottom half of his pajamas; he'd come out of a woman's bed; and he'd had a revolver in his hand.

"I extend the same promise to you, if you'll tell."

It was tempting, but instead he constructed a less vivid version of it. "In my case I was not, er, completely without covering, but it was four in the morning and there was a foot of snow on the ground. Have you ever been barefoot in the snow?" She shook her head. "You're hopping back and forth between one foot and the other like a *fakir* on a bed of coals—you hope to all get-out that somebody will come to the rescue and fast, but you're also wishing that they sort of don't see you when they arrive. However, the house whose window I had just jumped out of was burning down, so the snow melted pretty fast."

Her deep-throated laugh at the brief story's phlegmatic climax was both delighted and delightful.

A hand slid past Stuyvesant's shoulder to pluck one of the curry puffs off his plate. "What kind of nonsense are you filling my sister's ears with, Stuyvesant?"

"Tales of a misspent youth," he replied. "Hey, get your own plate. Hello, Miss Hurleigh," he added, rising politely as he noticed Laura Hurleigh at Bennett's side. "Can I get you a cup of tea?"

"In the absence of something stronger, thank you."

"Don't forget the scones," Grey said, around the mouthful of ducal curry puff.

When Stuyvesant came back with the cup and saucer in one hand and a plate piled high with jam-and cream-filled scones in the other, he found that Grey had carried over a small settee and settled in, holding Stuyvesant's plate. Stuyvesant set Laura's refreshments on the diminutive table, then reached for the empty plate on Grey's lap. Grey looked down at it, startled. "Sorry, old chap."

"Don't worry about it, there's plenty. You want something to wash it down?"

"No, I'm fine for tea."

But when Stuyvesant arrived back at the grouping the second time, a number of others had moved in, and Bennett was on his feet talking to three young men. He seemed little troubled by their presence, and only flinched when one of them playfully slapped him on the back. He covered his reaction by introducing Stuyvesant.

Over the course of the next forty minutes, Stuyvesant was introduced to a famous novelist (or perhaps *infamous* was a better term), an equally renowned playwright, a minor English royal, a very minor French royal, the owner of a string of fashionable restaurants, the various sons of one general, two dukes, three knights, and a maharaja, and close personal friends of Krishnamurti, Oscar Wilde, and T. E. Lawrence. Talk veered from the place of the biography in modern literature to music on the wireless to a show of Paris fashion, and there seemed to be an unspoken agreement to avoid mention of any faintly political topic.

Stuyvesant found it difficult to keep track of the people, much less the conversation. After a while, he excused himself and retreated to his room, only to find that Aldous Carstairs was with him as he walked through the rose garden—not in person, although he did find himself watching the shrubs for sign of the man. Why had Carstairs come here? What did he want?

He stretched out on his bed and stared at the ceiling, but the answer did not appear there. He turned over and told his brain to shut off, and managed to sleep for an hour. Voices and movement woke him, and although he could have stayed there until morning, he dragged himself upright and found the bath free. He soaked in the hot water, scrubbing the last traces of motor grease from his nails, and back in his room, wanting to be presentable, laid out his shaving equipment for the second time that day. As he watched the safety razor travel through the foam on his cheeks, his thoughts circled yet again to Aldous Carstairs.

Had he been checking up on Stuyvesant? Or reminding him that he was being watched? Surely there would be an easier way than driving all the way from...

The razor slowed, then stilled. *I was in the area,* the snake had said. Which Stuyvesant discounted as an obvious lie, but what if it wasn't? Sarah had said something about the sanitarium being nearby—and *sanitarium* could only mean the Truth Project.

If Aldous Carstairs was in the neighborhood, odds were fair to middling that he'd been at his so-called clinic. And if he was, did he have an ongoing reason to be there? Or could it be that he was readying the place for use once again?

The razor went back to work, although Stuyvesant's mind was not on the task.

He'd better keep a close eye on Grey, until he could send him back to the safety of Cornwall.

He'd put him on a train tonight, were it not for his need to meet Richard Bunsen.

Speaking of whom, had The Bastard arrived yet? Stuyvesant hadn't heard any new voices, but then, he had been asleep, and the two vacant bedrooms were downstairs. Would they give Bunsen the crypt room? He hoped so; he'd treasure that image, Bunsen sleeping among skulls.

And how would Bunsen be, face to face? The man was smart, there was no disguising that, but would he be clever with thinking on his feet, or was he just good at writing speeches? And his looks: Would he prove as handsome up close as he had seemed on a stage in Battersea?

(*Richard says,* Sarah had said dreamily—she might have been talking about Valentino. *He's so eloquent, so passionate—*)

Stop it, he told himself. *You can't get involved.*

But the next minute he found himself thinking of a story he could tell her, that she might laugh at, and at the same time wondering if she might like the smell of his Bay Rum after-shave lotion.

In disgust, he rinsed his razor and glared at himself in the mirror. *Stop it. Now.*

Chapter Forty-One

FOR THE SECOND TIME in twenty-four hours, Harris Stuyvesant climbed into evening wear. His one formal shirt had been taken away that morning and returned, clean and starched; his suit had been brushed, his shoes shined. As he dressed, Stuyvesant listened for the sounds of a new arrival, but he did not hear it. And when he joined the cocktail party in progress, again in the long gallery, Bunsen was not with them.

The Duke and Duchess were there, holding court to a group of hearty individuals who looked as if they'd climbed off their mounts at the door. At the opposite end of the room, the younger generation had gathered, among them Laura, clutching a half-full glass of some faintly yellow stuff and looking relieved at the long-awaited infusion of liquor. When he had exchanged pleasantries with his hosts, Stuyvesant circled around to her and said in her ear, "I'm glad to see you finally got something stronger than tea. Afternoon, Lady Pamela, Lord Pontforth."

Laura Hurleigh turned a dazzling smile on him—she was tall enough to look him nearly in the eye. "What is it about coming home that makes one crave strong drink?"

Personally, the idea of strong drink coupled with home made

Stuyvesant a little queasy, as there'd been far too much of the combination when he was growing up, but he nodded in sympathy and said, "Probably to remind yourself that you can, if you want to, without your parents firmly inviting you to have a nice glass of lemonade."

"Not that my mother isn't capable of doing that even now," she told him.

"A formidable lady, your mother. Did she buy her horse today, the one near Cheltenham?"

"I should think so. It has good lineage, which is generally enough for Mother. I believe she may have studied *Debrett's* like a form book before she agreed to marry Father."

He'd never heard a girl speak of a parent in quite such, well, biological terms, but he smiled gamely and changed the subject. "Has your friend Bunsen arrived yet?"

She responded with a deep swig from her glass. "Not yet, but since he hasn't rung, he's sure to be here. Richard had a meeting in Manchester today, which may have gone longer than he anticipated. He's sure to arrive eventually."

Her emphatic declaration was made through clenched teeth and rang as false as her gaiety: She was nowhere near certain that Bunsen would get here at all. Damn it, Stuyvesant thought: So much for the short-cut. Sounded like he was back to his original plan, working his way into Bunsen's circle through Sarah.

Then a familiar alto laugh reached out across the room, reminding Stuyvesant that there would be benefits to being forced to linger in Sarah's company.

"Can I get you another drink?" he asked Laura Hurleigh.

"Oh, you'd be a dear if you would—my mother will be counting the number of times I go to the bar, but if you went for me, she won't notice."

Stuyvesant wasn't at all convinced of that, but he took her glass and went back to the bar, asked for a White Lady, and tried to hold the drink possessively as he returned to Laura's side. The attempt at subterfuge was spoiled when she snatched the glass and took a hefty swallow, following it with a sigh of relief.

Her sister, with a thin attempt to cover the effect, asked,

"However do you manage it in America, Mr. Stuyvesant, being dry from coast to coast? I think I'd just die."

"Prohibition is more a theoretical fact than an actual one," he said. "The price has gone up and the selection's gone down, but there's no problem in finding booze if you want it."

"What a relief. I'd been putting off a trip to New York because I just couldn't bear going there sober."

"I wouldn't worry about it. Although I'd avoid any alcohol served in a really low-end dive. You might wake up blind."

She laughed, and Laura joined in, laughing much harder than the joke called for. He stepped back mentally and took a hard look at her. The regal figure of the night before, the friendly and passionate doer-of-good he'd seen over breakfast that morning, both had disappeared. In their place was a person who would have blended into any society party in New York or Chicago—or, no doubt, London: brittle, shallow, decorative, loud, and drunk.

Maybe *drunk* was the key here: Laura just couldn't handle her alcohol. Then again, how many White Ladies had she had? And what had she swallowed beforehand?

He removed the half-full glass from her hand and set it onto a nearby table, then took her elbow.

"Pardon us, Lady Pamela, your sister and I are going out for a little fresh air," he said, propelling her in the direction of the doorway.

"Mr. Stuyvesant!" Laura protested. "I—"

"Just a little turn in the garden, clear our heads a bit, watch the stairs, now—there you go. Can you get me a coat for my lady here, Patrick? Any coat—that'll do nicely. Now, more stairs, take my arm, there. Isn't that better?"

He kept an eye on her, concerned that the sudden cold air might make her faint—or vomit—but after some startled blinking and a gulping noise, she seemed braced rather than overcome. He settled her arm through his, finding her not quite as tall as he'd thought, although a glance at her feet explained why: She was wearing low heels tonight. In those, the drive should be safe enough, he decided, and led her in the direction of the gate.

They went down the gravel drive, Stuyvesant holding her arm firmly while maintaining an amiable patter of nothing at all: a dog he'd had as a boy (invented on the spot), a mildly amusing episode with a very tall horse that explained why he didn't like to ride (not entirely invented, but adapted from a tale he'd heard once).

Her only reaction was a shiver, which suggested that Stuyvesant might do well to get her out of the cold. He led her to the converted stables where he'd worked on the Morris that morning, found the car in residence, and opened its back door for her. He turned on the garage light, then went around to the other side and let himself into the front seat, so she could see him but not feel pressed by a stranger's familiarity. He lit two cigarettes, passed one back to her, and said, "Is there anything you want to talk about? I'm a pretty good listener."

She stared ahead of her, out the car's front window and into the night beyond, and then made a sudden choking noise. Stuyvesant jerked back with a curse, but it was not what he thought: Her hands went to her face, and as she slowly bent forward he hastily stretched over to pluck the burning cigarette away from her hair.

It was emotion coming out, not the contents of her stomach. She wept almost silently, without the wails of sorrow and regret that Stuyvesant was used to hearing from crying women. She wept as a release, with an air of something near to gratitude, her shoulders heaving with the great gulps of emotion unsuppressed. She wept whole-heartedly and without apology, as if he weren't even there, and went on without pause for several minutes.

And then she stopped. She sat up, drew a shaky breath, and said in wonder, "Good Lord, where did that all come from?"

He held out his clean handkerchief; she took it, and gave a juicy blow of her nose.

"Thank you."

"You're welcome."

She gave him a smile, bleary-eyed but true. "You Americans, you're so polite."

"Oh, I forgot, you Brits don't say 'You're welcome,' do you? Okay then: Don't mention it."

She sat back against the leather seat with a thump. He handed her the cigarette he had taken from her earlier, and she took a grate-

ful draw, letting the smoke curl out between her lips on a sigh of appreciation. "Oh my," she said. "I needed that."

The words and attitude joined with the gesture of the cigarette
brought a sharp memory of a similar declaration Stuyvesant had
once made to a woman, following a long absence of female company.
He narrowed his eyes, but she seemed unconscious of any salacious
overtones.

"I'm sorry you had to witness that," she said. "And I shouldn't
worry about it, if I were you; it doesn't really mean anything. When I
was a little girl, I used to launch into the most horrid screaming fits
that left me hoarse for days. Crying is much better. Or sex," she said
frankly.

He was startled at the last remark, but she didn't appear to be
asking him for any service beyond that of the handkerchief. He
cleared his throat. "I did mention that I was a good listener."

Then he shut up.

She rolled the ash end of the cigarette into the car's ash recepta-
cle, a deliberate gesture somewhere between thoughtful and drunken.
Then she began to talk.

"Do you know your grandparents, Mr. Stuyvesant?"

"They're dead, except for one grandmother."

"Your great-grandparents? Did you know who they were?"

"I know where they were from."

"It must be marvelous, to be free and unburdened from the eyes
of one's ancestors. You saw the ancestral window, over the stairs?
When I was a little girl, my father and I used to sit on the top step and
study the names on the branches, and he'd tell me their stories:
William the Ready, the second Duke, whose insomnia meant he
heard the enemy coming one night and saved his men; Richard the
Firm, who resisted the tortures of the Saracen when he was captured
in the Second Crusade. Another William, who distracted Cromwell's
men from their hunt for the fleeing King by deliberately tripping his
own horse at the full gallop. He broke half the bones in his body, but
the King escaped."

"A lot to live up to," he commented. What this had to do with
her spasm of tears, he couldn't imagine.

"And I was only a girl. I could never figure how Thomas could bear to get up in the morning with all those family members waiting for him, until I realized he had no more imagination than one of Father's dogs. I was the one they bothered. I used to have nightmares of being caught up in the arms of a tree, dangled off the ground."

He grunted, not knowing how else to respond.

"I know," she said, as if he had contributed something intelligent. "And I assure you, I did grow out of it, and came to be grateful that I had been born a woman, so no one expected heroism of me. Still, it is a considerable responsibility, being Richard's right-hand person. And that's what I am, no matter what the others think. People in the Movement look at me and see either a frivolous member of the governing classes who is playing games during her summer holidays and who is sure eventually to undermine the work of a great man, or else they see a member of the governing classes who has been brought down by her blood enemy, made to debase herself for his amusement and by way of proving the inadequacy of her class: All we're good for is keeping the men entertained."

When he said he was a good listener, he'd rather expected her to unload her love life onto him, the pressures of having Grey here and Bunsen on his way, or something of the sort. But no, this was a true child of the Movement: everything was politics: family was politics; love was politics; fear was love mixed with politics. God alone knew how the politics worked into her sex life.

It was disconcerting, but the all-pervasive presence of politics made the job of picking her mind that much easier. And it sure was sobering her up.

"Either way, they see me as a traitor to my class, and a traitor is never, ever trustworthy. But what they don't see is that I regard my work with Richard not as a denial of my history, but as its culmination. I am the result of centuries of aristocracy; Richard is the result of the same years of working-class values and ideas; together we are the essence of this country. I learn from him, but he learns from me, as well. That is what these men don't understand."

Grey had said they would find that Bunsen treated Laura abominably, which had made Stuyvesant think of Bunsen as one of those radical leaders whose impressive speeches about equality turned into petty tyranny behind closed doors—he'd sure met enough of those over the years. And there was no doubt that Bunsen had reason to feel demeaned by Laura, both her birth and her person.

However, he reminded himself, just because Bunsen doesn't show up for a party on time, that doesn't necessarily mean he was in the habit of treating her like dirt.

"Still," he said, "I suppose it's understandable, that his fellow workers would mistrust you. Asking them to accept a woman, especially one of your background, would be like asking them to suddenly start speaking Chinese. They could do it, but a little at a time."

To his gratification, she snapped at the bait. "Time is precisely what we don't have. Since before the War, we have been working towards a huge change in the social structure of this country. One strike after another, building all the time—if we hadn't been interrupted by the War and D.O.R.A., we'd have got there by now. You know about D.O.R.A.?" she asked, remembering his nationality.

He knew about D.O.R.A., but asked anyway, "Who is she?"

"Our so-called Defence of the Realm Act," she spat. "The straight path to a police state. During the War, D.O.R.A. put control into the hands of a very few men, under the excuse of national security. Parliament went its way, but in the background, for six solid years, the King's privy council moved this country around like pieces on a chess-board. And when D.O.R.A. expired in 1920, the same men came up with the Emergency Powers Act. That's what we're looking at now—all they need do is declare a state of emergency and the Act comes into play, so that again, two or three men and their pocket king become absolute rulers. Democratic rights are set aside, new classes of offence can be established without the approval of Parliament, harsher penalties set, wide-scale arrests and imprisonments easily justified. Just declare an emergency, and overnight, Britain becomes a police state."

She glared at him owlishly, looking so gorgeous it was all he could do not to make a pass at her. But instead, he got out his silver cigarette case and fiddled with it thoughtfully. "And the upcoming General Strike..."

"—will be the very definition of a state of emergency, with

nothing to keep the government from sweeping the boards and starting again, re-writing all the rules so many people have fought to es-
tablish. Nothing, except the words and actions of reason."

Stuyvesant swallowed his response to the idea of Richard Bunsen
as a paragon of reason. He said, "Well, I guess I can see why you
need to have a crying jag from time to time. Sounds like quite a load
on your shoulders."

"*My* shoulders?" she said in surprise. "It's mostly Richard's
work. He's the brilliant one, I just go along with him."

When he bothers to show up, he thought, then found himself
wondering, What does Richard Bunsen do when *he* needs to blow off
steam? Or should the question be, Who does he take it out on?
Again, questions he would not address to Bunsen's lover.

"So what does Bunsen have in mind to keep that from happening?" he asked. "If you're allowed to talk about it, that is."

"He's been working on it for months. And without going into the
details, I can tell you he's negotiating a very high-level meeting between the government and the Unions, which should have some positive results."

"From what I read, meetings haven't proved very productive
yet."

"The government feel themselves in a strong position, since
they've been preparing to undermine the workers since, well, one
could say since the Railway Strike in 1911. We need to show them
that their self confidence is without basis, that—"

She broke off. He looked up, and found her staring past him at
the open doorway. Following her gaze, he saw the twin head-lamps
cutting through the dusk on the other side of the valley. "Richard,"
she said to herself. Suddenly she was in motion. "I must look a sight!
Oh Lord, he mustn't see me like this, I must go freshen up. Bless you,
Mr. Stuyvesant, for allowing me to weep on your manly shoulder, I
must keep an American to hand for that express purpose. I'll see you
at dinner—and don't worry, I'm really much restored to myself,
thank you for everything."

"I think you should call me Harris," he said to her fleeing back.
He looked down at the sodden handkerchief she had pressed into his
hand, stained with powder and kohl, and folded it thoughtfully into

a pocket. He shut the doors of the Morris, twisted the switch for the overhead light, and moved over to the doorway.

Up the hill to the right, he could hear Laura Hurleigh's fast-retreating footsteps and a muffled chorus of voices from the house. From the left came the sound of a motorcar gearing down as it approached the ford.

Suddenly, he was hit by the need to see Richard Bunsen up close, before Bunsen had a chance to look at him. He hauled the stables door shut and sprinted up the drive in Laura's wake, dashing up the grassy verge and around the back of the lodge-house, hunched down to avoid notice from the servants' quarters beyond. He heard an exchange from the shade garden—Laura going into the house as Gallagher was coming out—just as he eased into the giant rhododendron at the front of the lodge. Thirty feet away, the butler stepped out of the iron gate and took up a position near the street-lamp.

As the car hit the drive's circle, the powerful head-lamps flared over Stuyvesant's hiding place before sweeping across the shaded north garden, the corner of the house, the waiting figure of Gallagher the butler, and the gate-way to the formal front garden. The harsh illumination finally came to rest on the long wall and its massive rose, then winked out. The hiding American pulled aside the leaves.

The street-lamp cast its beam across the car, revealing glimpses of the man in the back. It was a closed car; the man was in shadow. Gallagher stepped forward to open the door, and the man emerged.

Richard Bunsen was taller and slimmer than he'd appeared on the stage. He had changed into evening dress on the way, and wore the black garment as if born to the class for which it was designed. His dark hair, which on Thursday had been slightly rumpled, now lay in perfect obedience, and his spine was held straighter. Like then, however, even in profile his face inspired confidence.

Bunsen greeted Gallagher by name and told him he'd need the top bag in the front. A servant Stuyvesant had not seen before walked around the car to retrieve a bag from the seat beside the driver's. From where Stuyvesant stood, he could hear the butler telling him to take Mr. Bunsen's valise into the house, followed by Bunsen's response that he wasn't staying the night, he'd just need his shaving kit.

The house, not the barn: The daughter's lover was being given a room among the family.

Bunsen and Gallagher exchanged a few more words, their voices conversationally low and unintelligible. Then Bunsen seemed to stir himself into action, drawing upright in a gesture of dismissal. Gallagher gave him a short dip of the head and stepped back, and Bunsen addressed the burly man who had climbed out from the driver's door.

"Jimmy, Gallagher here will show you where you can have a snooze, if you like. Don't get to drinking, I need to leave around midnight."

The driver merely nodded, cast an eye over the house as if to say he'd seen better, and followed the butler. Bunsen, left alone, stretched luxuriously, showing the lines of his lean body, and spent a moment kneading the small of his back while his eyes (what color were they, anyway?) followed the two men, a slight frown on his face.

Stuyvesant took in his every move: the man of his witness drawings, the shipboard photograph, the grainy newspaper images, and the Battersea stage, brought here to life. The man he'd hunted for half a year, the man whose box of groceries had killed a woman, burned two city blocks and reduced a beloved younger brother and husband to a vegetable, whose china doll had nearly incinerated a judge, whose bottle of Bourbon had come within a hair's-breadth of crippling and killing a roomful of senators and officials. The man who was sleeping with the glorious woman whose tears were damp on Stuyvesant's handkerchief, a woman with whom his new friend with the peculiar gifts seemed still in love, a woman whose fire, intelligence, and heart suited her for the best in the land.

A man easy to hate.

Bunsen's hand came up to smooth the back of his head, as if he had felt a faint touch there; after a moment, he turned on his heels and passed through the gate to the house.

If Stuyvesant hadn't known better, he'd have thought this was the son and heir, returning to his ancestral home.

Chapter Forty-Two

STUYVESANT REACHED HIS ROOM without being seen. Behind its closed door, he sat on the edge of the bed, staring blankly at the wardrobe.

Okay: He'd seen the enemy, and The Bastard was even more formidable than he'd thought, every bit as handsome and confident and sharp as you'd expect of someone who'd re-invented himself, fooled two nations, and convinced Laura Hurleigh that his was the superior mind.

But what if he had? Harris Stuyvesant was good at what he did, too—no, damn it, he was the best when it came to pulling on another skin and going undercover. Better than this upstart Red, this sapper-turned-politician.

Time for the curtains-rising sensation for this performance he would put on for one man alone, its aim—nothing more, nothing less—than to bring him close to his quarry.

But what form would that act take? Stuyvesant had to be wearing a white collar, but feeling its pinch—a continuation of what he'd been giving out already to Bunsen's two women. Stuyvesant's teeth gnashed at the idea of Sarah Grey as one of that slick figure's women—and then he caught himself. What about that—not Sarah, of course, but Laura herself?

Most of the radicals he knew—the men, certainly—thought the idea of free love was just fine. Opposing the possessive claims of the marriage rites was noble, and meant the man never had to step up and marry. And funny thing: Such noble belief never seemed to have much effect on the possessive claims of the radicals themselves, who were generally as high-handed with their women-folk as a potentate with his harem.

Of course, to make everyone feel good about themselves, from time to time a woman was allowed to give a speech or perform an *attentat,* but the men didn't like to see too much of that. Not only did it take away from their own importance, but having too many of their women standing trial at once interfered with meal-times. In all the radical households he'd been in, he could count on one hand the number of men he'd seen scrubbing pans.

What about Richard Bunsen? Just how closely did he fit the mold, when it came to being possessive about that splendid Hurleigh woman? And if he was, how could Stuyvesant use that?

After a while, he got to his feet and went over to the wardrobe. The loose board came up readily under the point of his knife, and he withdrew the small gun. It wasn't that he wanted it tonight, not enough to risk having someone notice it, but when he needed a reminder of who he was and what he was after, there was nothing like a revolver to do the job. Cold, efficient, deadly, patient. Absolutely safe until a part of it snapped down on the tiny vulnerable spot of the bullet and burst its powder into flame, sending its deadly scrap of lead in the direction required.

He was Harris John Stuyvesant. He had killed men—not with this particular weapon, not yet—and he had trapped men, and there were men whose vulnerable spots he had snapped down upon, sending them in the direction required. Yes, he generally worked among men whose clothes stank of sweat and age, whose drink foamed into large glasses, whose faces and hands bore evidence of the work they did each day. Generally, he even looked like one of those men.

Here, he would wear spotless black and white, and his fingernails would be clean, if not exactly manicured. He would go over to the house and make conversation about New York society and London art galleries, he would present a likable and believable persona to the assembled members of a class that was foreign to him, and in the end he would find the vulnerable spot of Richard Bunsen and send him where he wanted him.

But where might his vulnerable spot be? Possibly Laura. But he must not forget: That handsome face belonged to a man with nerve enough to carry an explosive device through a tight, lonely, dangerous tunnel, with the enemy poised above, and still have rock-steady hands when he reached the tunnel's end. This was also a man who made much of his working-class origins while wearing a suit that cost more than Stuyvesant earned in months. A man comfortable in two worlds—

Stuyvesant caught himself: a man *apparently* comfortable in two worlds.

For the first time, it occurred to him that he and Bunsen were not dissimilar. He had more siblings, but their parents were dead, and both carried the knowledge of status and money a generation or two gone. Neither he nor Bunsen was purely working class, nor were they impoverished aristocracy.

In the States, except for a few small pockets of high society, this wasn't much of a problem—in New York, a cat could look at a king. Hell, a cat could get himself elected king. But in England, where people had windows reminding them of ancestors whose bones had long since gone to dust? In England, the country that had perfected the art of the devastating remark? In England, where the servants' entrance waited, where all ears were tuned for the tiniest wrong accent, where the exquisitely subtle vocabulary of Us and Them held ten thousand complicated traps, unspoken and unarguable?

Somewhere inside that self-assured figure in the pretty suit had to be a scared little boy, waiting for one of those nuanced traps to swing shut on him, condemning him forever to the cold outer reaches of eternal disdain. You'd have to be awfully cold-blooded not to hold some degree of uncertainty.

So how to tap Bunsen's pocket of uncertainty? And how to do it so Bunsen didn't simply pull away? Stuyvesant could hold the threat of shame over him, making it clear that if Bunsen ran, Laura would see it, but if he wanted Bunsen to allow him near, he couldn't be too open with it.

Much better to ride the line between harmless and puzzling—like the bumptious American act he'd pulled on Carstairs, but with thorns, to whet a sapper's appetite for danger.

He wanted Bunsen to be so interested in him, he couldn't bear to let him go.

A distant clamor rose up, which grew into the reverberation of the gong. He glanced at his wrist-watch, startled at how long he'd sat here staring into space: Time to get going. He turned the gun over between his palms, feeling its reassuring authority, lifting it to his face to breathe in the odor of the oil. Then he stood up from the bed and put the weapon back into its hiding place: He wouldn't be needing it any more tonight.

He washed his hands, studied his reflection in the mirror, and went to join the others for dinner.

Chapter Forty-Three

IT MIGHT HAVE BEEN EASIER if Bunsen didn't look like a Mediterranean Ivor Novello, smooth and handsome and oozing charm and good humor from every polished pore. He wasn't tall, no taller than Laura (ha! thought Stuyvesant—that's why she's in flat shoes tonight. And immediately pushed away the thought as petty.) and his eyes looked somehow amber, caught between light brown and hazel. His hair was perfect, and his moustache might have been painted on, its lines were so flawless. He made even Patrick Hurleigh look like a "before" picture in the advertisement pages, and Sarah's friend Simon Fforde-Morrison was sulking in the corner, shooting the newcomer dark glances.

The music man, however, seemed to be the only stand-out among the thirty or so people in the long gallery when Stuyvesant arrived. The group around Bunsen was laughing at some nicety, and even those in the other groups glanced over from time to time with amusement or interest.

Without knowing his history, Stuyvesant would have sworn that Bunsen was born to the life of cleverness and ease. Certainly he was the most vivid creature in the room, and it was extraordinary, and somewhat disturbing, to watch Laura Hurleigh pull into herself, deliberately dropping a basket over her own light so that Bunsen might shine the brighter.

Not that she needed to: As Stuyvesant had anticipated, the man possessed in large measure the knack of the successful politician—or the successful scam-artist—to make the person he was talking to feel the most important, most fascinating individual on the planet. Holding eye contact, Bunsen might as well have been saying aloud, *My entire attention is on you and you alone.* And when the eye contact was broken, that impression stayed on: Stuyvesant would bet that, after tonight, each person here would feel that he or she had been in close, prolonged conversation with the man.

That kind of animal magnetism was a gift, not a thing one could learn, and Bunsen had it in spades. Even the Duchess of Hurleigh was not immune: She had melted in the palm of Bunsen's long-fingered hand, and was responding to his overt act of flirtatious courtier with a similarly self-aware act of near-coquettishness: a game, and they were both agreeing to play it.

Stuyvesant circled around to where Sarah and Bennett Grey stood, and bent forward to say in her deliciously scented ear, "Your friend seems to have made a conquest of the resident dragon."

Sarah turned and said something to him in response, but Stuyvesant did not hear her words, for Bunsen's attention had been attracted, either by Stuyvesant's entrance or by the big man's proximity to Sarah Grey, and he turned his gaze on the American.

The jolt of that gaze was so tangible, the room's voices seemed to fade. But the crackle of energy between them was personal; he and Bunsen alone had gone still, and Stuyvesant stood with his head canted towards Sarah's voice, unhearing, his full attention locked on the light, oddly colored eyes of the man he had crossed an ocean to find.

The only one taking notice of the meeting was Bennett Grey, at Stuyvesant's elbow. Grey's hand had closed onto his arm, to convey some wordless comment. Encouragement? Protest? Stuyvesant could not tell without looking at him, and he did not wish to break away from Bunsen for another few seconds—but too late. Bunsen pulled away first, to make another comment to the Duchess and raise his nearly empty glass to his lips. Stuyvesant waited. Sure enough, on the count of seven, Bunsen glanced back at him. His eyes, Stuyvesant decided, were hazel-yellow with a green overtone. This time, Stuyvesant was the one to withdraw first. He turned back to Sarah.

"I'm sorry, honey," he said. "What was that?"

"I said, 'Do you want to meet Richard?'"

"Oh, he's busy just now. We'll have plenty of time after dinner to get to know each other."

Five minutes later, just before the second and final sounding of the gong, the Duke came in to claim his wife's arm. Out of the corner of his eye, Stuyvesant saw Bunsen come to attention and greet his host with a great deal more formality than he had demonstrated towards the man's wife. He then moved over to pick up something from a table in the corner and, with a formal little half bow and a deprecating gesture of his other hand, presented it to the Duke.

It was a small paperboard box held together with a twine tie. The Duke listened, and with a degree of reluctance pulled the twine and lifted the box top.

Whatever the contents, they caused his bushy eyebrows to rise. He tucked the top under the box and pulled aside the packing material. Bunsen continued to speak, shrugging to let his host know how relatively unimportant the gift was, but the older man was clearly captivated by the object, and Stuyvesant did not think him a man easily impressed by the efforts of his lessers.

The Duchess said something to her husband, causing him to push the contents down in the excelsior and replace the top. He appeared intent on carrying it in to dinner, but the Duchess took it, handed it to a nearby servant, and firmly put her arm through his. The Duke pointed at the packet and told the man something, and the servant immediately left the room, holding the crude box as if it were a diamond tiara. As the man went past, Stuyvesant looked to see what was in the box: a small, rather dull china dog, something that might sit in the garden of a child's doll-house.

Right: the Duke collected the things. Clever Bunsen.

Arms were linked into elbows and the guests and family began to move towards the stairway. Stuyvesant was pleased to be given Sarah's for the purpose, but he waited for her indication that it was time for them to move—the order and priority of guests at a country house Saturday dinner was a mystery too deep for a mere Bureau of Investigation agent to crack.

He followed the parade down the stairs, and found that tonight, dinner was to be in the Great Hall. He was seated across the table and down from Bunsen and—to his chagrin—down from Sarah Grey, who was at Bunsen's left. When the Duchess turned to the other side, Sarah leaned forward to speak to Bunsen. His gaze came down the table to touch on Stuyvesant—Sarah must have been introducing him in absentia, because Bunsen nodded—before returning to her.

To Bunsen's right was the Duchess herself. Stuyvesant watched the arrangement surreptitiously, wondering what it meant. Twenty years ago, he knew, the rigidity of society meant that every person at a dinner party had their seating clearly laid out for them—and if there were any doubts, priority was given in *Debrett's,* lest incompetent servants or an inexperienced hostess commit a career-shattering *faux pas.* But then the War had run its cart and horses through every level of society, and Stuyvesant did not know how far-reaching were its effects. Yes, there were thirty people here for a formal meal, but they were mostly either family or their young friends, and presumably rank was allowed to loosen its tie a notch. Hell, twenty years ago, a ducal family like the Hurleighs would not have shared a table with half the people here, including himself—the question of seating would never have arisen.

Was there even a salt any more, to sit below?

In any case, he was just an American, and a purveyor of motorcars at that, who shouldn't be expected to possess any awareness of subtle social hierarchies. So he would not.

He introduced himself to his neighbor, settling in for a demonstration that even American car salesmen were capable of civilized behavior.

As the meal wore on, civilized behavior became increasingly difficult. To his astonishment, Richard Bunsen had responded to their little staring contest by taking the lead, and was playing precisely the game Stuyvesant had considered playing with Laura Hurleigh. How he'd known Stuyvesant was at all interested in Sarah Grey, he didn't know, but Bunsen was clearly paying a closer attention to the young woman than she was accustomed to. She went from surprised over soup to flustered over fish, and by the time the beef was laid before them, she was pink with pleasure.

Despite his exasperation, Stuyvesant had to admire Bunsen's technique: The man managed to engage Sarah fully without giving the Duchess the least cause for complaint. If anything, he was more openly flirtatious with the older woman; it was only in Sarah's reaction that Stuyvesant saw anything out of the ordinary. The Bastard possessed the skills of a polygamist, he thought, giving a vicious stab to the meat on his plate: two-handed seduction, conducted right out in the open.

One time only, as the final course was being set on the linen, did Bunsen betray any awareness of the American down the table. He leaned over to murmur something to Sarah, and at her resultant laugh, his eyes flickered in Stuyvesant's direction.

Bunsen was already turning to the other object of his affections, the Duchess, so their eyes met only for the briefest moment. But that brief flash washed like a soothing balm across Stuyvesant's growing ill humor, and he picked up his fruit knife (was this the fourth knife?) feeling cool and purposeful once again. He did not so much as glance in Sarah's direction during the remainder of the meal, but entertained his table-mates with an embroidered tale of how he'd sold a fleet of very pricey Ford motorcars to an infamous New York crime lord, ending his story with, "And, I even managed to get his check to clear before the police raided his headquarters!"

As if he'd timed it, the laughter was still ringing when the Duchess rose, followed by the other ladies. Under the different timbre of male voices and masculine laughter, half the party moved upstairs, to take port and cigars before the fire in the solar and in the adjoining billiards room. Stuyvesant excused himself for a minute, and when he returned, positions had been taken up: Bunsen with the Duke at the center of things, the two Hurleigh sons to one side with a coterie of friends, ostensibly on their own but in fact more than half listening in. Bunsen had the voice of an experienced public speaker, capable of a carrying volume with no apparent effort. In this setting, his voice cut through cross-noise in a seemingly natural manner, as if he just happened to have that manner of speech. It was difficult not to listen to him, as he casually recounted to his host how he'd come across the china dog, in the grasp of a small child in a pram in Kensington Gardens.

Stuyvesant took a glass (brandy, not port—he'd experienced that alcoholic syrup before) and circled around to where Bennett Grey stood, in the cool air near the window. His face was pinched and the knuckles wrapped around his empty glass were white.

"You okay?" Stuyvesant asked.

"Do I look 'okay'?" Grey snapped. Stuyvesant exchanged glasses with him and watched him shoot the contents down in one swallow. He looked, if anything, worse after that. With a shock, Stuyvesant realized that the man was actually drunk.

"Is it one person in particular, or all of them?"

"All of them," Bennett said, then immediately, "Bunsen's the worst, but the accumulation...Are you going to get me another drink?"

"No, I'm going to take you out of here."

"I can't go yet."

"Why the hell not? You're a goddamn blown-up war hero, you're allowed to feel ill any time you like. Come on."

"I must at least take my leave of Uncle God."

"Uncle—oh, right, the Duke." Godlake Reginald Gryffin and so on. "Okay: ten seconds and then I'm dragging you away."

Grey walked up to the group around Bunsen as if approaching a firing squad: straight-backed, slightly unsteady on foot but unwavering of purpose. Keeping his eyes on the old man, he made his formal apologies, nodded to the others, and returned to Stuyvesant, definitely weaving.

While Grey was speaking with the Duke, Stuyvesant had been covertly watching Bunsen, who studied his glass, his face neutral. Did he know of the connection between Grey and Laura Hurleigh? Stuyvesant couldn't begin to tell.

He got Grey down the stairs without quite having to carry him, and had one of the servants show him the short way to the barn, a door beside the kitchen. Outside, the rain was gurgling in the downspouts and sheeting off the far end of the roof where a gutter was blocked, but when Stuyvesant would have laid a hand between

Grey's shoulders and hurried him in the direction of the barn, Grey stopped dead and lifted his face to the sky. There he stood, showing no sign of moving, so Stuyvesant took a step back under the eaves, lit a cigarette, and gave himself a thorough kicking for not managing to keep an eye on Grey's intake. Sarah would not be pleased.

The rain fell; the smoke swirled; the man got soaked through. At last he scrubbed his face with his hands and ran his fingers through his dripping hair, then looked around.

"Harris," he said. "Why din' you go back inside?"

"It's nice out here," he said, and crushed his stub under his heel. "C'mon, my old friend, let's put you to bed."

Grey leaned on him as they went up the stairs, then stood on the rug like a child as Stuyvesant peeled off the sodden garments. "See if you can get those buttons," he suggested as he knelt down to pick at the wet shoelaces. Grey's fingers, clumsy with drink and cold, managed about half of them, and Stuyvesant did the rest.

In the end, he got Grey down to his under-shorts. He pulled the bed-clothes over the man's savagely scarred leg, stuck a bath-towel under his head to protect the pillow, and went to the door.

"Thank you, Ster— Stew— Stoy— M'ol'fren' Harris." The man in the bed giggled, a sound that in a sober man would have been hair-raising.

"Any time, Bennett. Sleep well, old man, you've done a valiant job. And by the way, you're finished for the week-end. From here on in, I'm on my own."

The only answer was a ragged snore.

Chapter Forty-Four

BACK UPSTAIRS, STUYVESANT FOUND that a shuffling of personnel had taken place, and that more had been added. New arrivals, dressed less formally than if they had been dining, were spotted here and there, most of them young and with the look of students about them. And the ladies had returned from wherever ladies went after dinner, although neither the Duke nor Duchess were present; it occurred to Stuyvesant that apart from Gallagher, he was the oldest person in sight.

Drinks were again set up in the solar, with the doors that linked it, the billiards room, and the long gallery propped open to ease the flow of movement between the three spaces. There were a few people talking in front of the fire in the solar, including Bunsen, but most of the girls were draped around the billiards table with cigarettes and glasses, waiting for the music to begin. Several men had removed their jackets to concentrate on the game, and others were sitting down to cards on the other side of the room.

The band was taking its place at the far end of the gallery, putting down their drinks and tuning their instruments. Half a dozen eager dancers stood waiting, and shortly, Simon Fforde-Morrison stood up beneath the mirrored ball they had hung from the ceiling, and signaled to his musicians. On the downstroke of his arm they launched into "Five Foot Two, Eyes of Blue." The waiting couples began to gyrate; a number of those in the billiards room extinguished their cigarettes and hurried to join them.

Bunsen stayed where he was in the solar, leaning against the fireplace with an audience to hand. Stuyvesant slipped behind the others to fetch himself a drink, then took it to the doorway, where he could appear to be watching the dancers while he was listening to Bunsen's voice.

On the stage at Battersea, the man had looked and sounded like the educated son of a working man; his hair was slightly wrong, his suit had come off the peg, and his wide gestures were designed to reach to the farthest row back. Tonight, however, he wore an accent as expensive as his suit, and the motions of his hands were controlled and subtle.

Still magnetic, still compellingly intelligent, just working a different class of crowd.

He felt a touch at his elbow: Sarah.

"Is my brother all right?"

"Oh yeah, just plastered. I put him to bed; he'll have a head on him in the morning but he's fine."

"I wish he wouldn't do it."

"He hurts," Stuyvesant said bluntly. "And booze is the world's oldest pain reliever."

She took a metaphorical step back to look at him. "You are a remarkably sensible sort of a person, Harris Stuyvesant. Come, you must meet Richard properly."

Slipping her hand into his, she began to pull him across the room. Stuyvesant wished her grasp felt more like a woman conscious of her skin against his and less like that of an eager acolyte: "Sensible" was little threat against a sleek-haired firebrand with eyes like chips of amber and a face like Ivor Novello.

Sarah pushed him forward into Bunsen's admirers, and Harris Stuyvesant held out his hand to the man, showing no sign that his entire body hungered to beat his brother's destroyer to a bloody pulp.

As soon as they started in his direction, Bunsen had turned the search-light of his attention on them, drowning them in his brilliance.

He hesitated now for the briefest of instants, looking down at Stuyvesant's hand, before removing his shoulder from the mantel-piece and returning the handshake. His clasp was experimentally firm, although the man's fingers would be more suited to the delicate work of attaching wires to blasting caps than to wrenching off stub-born engine bolts. If it came to a squeezing contest, Stuyvesant knew he could make Bunsen wince. But that game was far too childish for what he had in mind.

"So you're Sarah's American." Bunsen's voice was amused and therefore dismissive; in that instant, Stuyvesant's role became clear.

"I'd like to think so," he replied, meeting the hazel gaze with all the confidence he could muster. Set out baldly like that, it could be taken either as brash American humor, or as a declaration of intent. Bunsen's eyes narrowed briefly as he tried to decide which; Stuyvesant gave him no help, merely maintaining his air of open, firm friendliness. *Yeah, I'm a Yank, buddy, and we can beat you so easy, we don't even got to say it.*

Their hand-clasp had gone on for just a bit too long; Bunsen ended it, with a brief squeeze before relaxation. Stuyvesant widened his smile, and looked down at Sarah, who had a little frown line be-tween her brows. "You didn't tell me your friend here looked like a movie actor."

No one could take it as an insult, but at some level, Bunsen had to wonder. Stuyvesant barrelled on. "Sarah tells me you're something with the government. I have to say, I sure chose an interesting time to come over here, didn't I?" Another, double-handed slight—"some-thing with the government"—but again impossible to pin down as anything but amiable stupidity.

"Indeed you did, Mr. Stuyvesant. Although in fact I'm not with the gov—"

"Oh, call me Harris. Any friend of Sarah's, and all that."

The interruption threw Bunsen off track, although he was experi-enced enough at the tooth-and-nail techniques of British debate that he didn't show it. He nodded, and said, "I spent the day with a group of miners who would say we are looking at interesting times, indeed."

"You ever worked down the mines, Richard? You don't mind if I call you Richard, do you?" He glanced around and admitted, "Never much caught on to the shades of English formality. We Yanks are always putting our feet in it."

Bunsen gritted his teeth genially at the familiarity. "No, I've not worked down the mines. Been down, of course, a number of times. How else to understand the lives of the miners?"

"Good plan. And shoveling coal isn't to be recommended, really, as a permanent way of life."

"You've worked..." Bunsen began in surprise, before he could help himself.

"Oh yeah," Stuyvesant said. "Just for a few months, back when I was fourteen or fifteen. A cousin got injured and needed someone to help out, so I put on his clothes and took his place until he was back on his feet. 'Course, by that time I was already nearly six feet, constantly hitting my head. But you being a government man and all, maybe you can tell me, I hear that one of the demands your coal miners are making is for seven-hour days. Seven hours sounds pretty cushy to me."

Bunsen's mouth compressed at the idea of being a government man, but his voice stayed even. "In this country, the miners' workday is determined exclusive of winding time. That's the time it takes to deliver the man to the coal face itself," he explained, less for Stuyvesant's benefit than the rest of the ears. "In Europe, the statutory eight hours is from the time they leave the surface until they re-emerge. Considering the depth of some of our mines, men often end up with considerably longer than eight hours below in order to spend their seven hours at the face."

"That makes sense," Stuyvesant agreed amiably. "Thanks for clearing that up. You play billiards?"

"Not just now, thank you."

"Maybe later, then. Sarah, you must dance? Even Red Emma was a prize hoofer, when she was young."

Reaction to the name rippled through the room—Stuyvesant had made sure he'd spoken loudly enough to be heard.

"You know Emma Goldman?" Laura asked.

"Met her a couple times. Quite a woman. Not much to look at, but she knew how to have a good time—'course, this was before the War."

Sarah stared up at him. "You—did you dance with her?"

She'd have been less surprised if he'd claimed to have done the Charleston with the Queen. "Sure. 'Course she's getting on in years, but she used to be a terrific dancer. Full of..." Deliberately, he looked over at Bunsen before he finished the thought, and half lowered one eyelid. "...enthusiasm."

And then he seized Sarah and whirled her onto the impromptu dance floor, not waiting to see the thought hit Bunsen: When it came to Red Emma's appetites, "enthusiasm" might readily describe something more intimate than dancing.

Stuyvesant was not a bad dancer, and he'd picked up some of the latest steps on the ship from New York. His pleasure at having Sarah to himself was intensified by the waves of frustration coming from Bunsen's corner: sniping at Bunsen but giving him no target in return had definitely got the man's attention. Especially when there were pretty girls in the vicinity.

But looking at Sarah, seeing her face go pink with exertion and happiness, was bittersweet. She was the one vulnerable place that he'd shown Richard Bunsen, and Stuyvesant had no doubt that Bunsen would seize the weapon he'd offered. Sarah was not going to have an easy time, before this was over.

Sometimes, he really hated his job.

"Yes, Sir, That's My Baby" bounced and jangled to an end, after which Simon Fforde-Morrison, with more sensitivity than Stuyvesant would have expected, slipped into the slower "It Had to Be You." Stuyvesant did not hesitate, but wrapped his arms around the girl and swung her into the dance.

Blonde hair smelled different from other shades, he reflected. All too soon the song was over, and Sarah was tugging him back in the direction of the solar.

Bunsen was waiting. He looked as if he'd been chatting with his friends, but Stuyvesant could tell he'd been waiting for him to return. "Did you know that Emma Goldman now lives in London?" Bunsen asked, his voice silky: Anyone could claim to know a person, it said, but not everyone could back their claim up.

Stuyvesant looked Bunsen in the eye. "Yeah, so I heard, giving speeches on modern drama, isn't it? I'm glad she got out of Russia before she froze to death. But if you're asking if I'm going to look her up, no, she probably wouldn't remember me. This had to be twelve, fifteen years ago." In fact, the Goldman meeting happened during the first political outing for big, young Harris Stuyvesant, who'd been brought in when the Bureau needed an agent able to pass for a working-class tough. "She and I got arrested together, if you must know." He took a swallow of his drink, making sure that everyone in earshot was hanging on his words, then admitted, "I got picked up by mistake, really, one of those wrong place wrong time situations. But she was a nice old girl, tons of fun as we got ourselves driven in and booked, and she told me to look her up later. So I did."

"Why were you arrested?" This was from Laura.

He summoned a look of embarrassment. "Well, there was this demonstration of garment workers. I wasn't involved in it, but I worked down the street and was going by when the police charged the crowd, on horseback, their nightsticks flailing. I saw one of the bas—one of them aiming straight at this skinny little girl, couldn't have been older than seventeen, and I, well, I stopped him."

"What did you do?" Sarah asked, enthralled. Stuyvesant did not look to see the effect of all this twaddle on Bunsen; he didn't have to.

"I didn't do anything to him, not really. I mean, I'm not about to get charged with assaulting an officer—but I had this tube in my hand, just a cardboard tube with some papers rolled up in it, and the horse's . . . er, a sensitive part of the horse was right there in front of me, so I waited until the creature was, what do you call it, tipped up-wards?"

"Rearing?" supplied Laura.

"Exactly, rearing a little, which meant it couldn't kick back-wards, and I just sort of, poked it. Distracted the cop no end."

The group around him erupted with laughter. Even Laura's dark eyes were dancing. Stuyvesant shrugged modestly and drained his glass. "Anyway, Emma and I were hauled in, we struck up a conver-sation, then later I did look her up once or twice. That's it."

"So, what, are you a Red, too?" This slurred question came from the doorway to the billiards room, where the burst of laughter had attracted several of the players. The boy who spoke was one of the evening's latecomers, drifting in after dinner in an ordinary lounge suit and a definite lack of focus to his eyes. Stuyvesant hoped for the sake of the felt on the tables that the tipsy idiot didn't try to play billiards tonight.

"Nope," Stuyvesant answered, "just a working stiff. Not, I think, like you."

The young man heard the insult in Stuyvesant's tone if not in his words, but before he could do more than bristle, his friends had come forward *en masse*. In a practiced set of moves, one placed a cue in his hand and told him it was his turn while another offered him a drink, and the young drunk was hustled away.

Stuyvesant glanced at Laura. "At a guess I'd say that's not one of your friends."

She shook her head, both vexed and amused. "Patrick's."

"I wouldn't want to be inside his skull tomorrow."

"I wouldn't want to be there tonight," she said repressively, then turned to her sister Constance and asked about the dress she wore.

The evening went on in the same vein, with Stuyvesant and Bunsen like a pair of jousting chameleons, taking on each other's colors as they aimed their jabs. Stuyvesant played his American face for all it was worth—gullible, self assured, competent in a score of areas, mature but energetic, uninformed politically but clearly on the side of the angels, brash but forgivable because he meant no harm. He flirted with the girls and acted the buddy with the men, sent the occasional innocent but stinging remark in Bunsen's direction while giving nothing to grasp in return.

Except for the one. By the end of the evening, everyone there including Sarah herself knew how smitten Harris Stuyvesant was with her. And everyone there could see how hopeless it was, because Richard Bunsen already had her.

It was crystal clear to Stuyvesant that Bunsen had not laid claim on Sarah Grey before that night: If Sarah's earlier surprise at Bunsen's attentions during dinner hadn't already shown him, Laura Hurleigh's growing puzzled resentment would have proved it.

He had marked Bunsen on the nose: Like many leaders of causes, Bunsen was possessive about his women, even those he did not intend to make use of.

And beyond that, Stuyvesant thought Bunsen would be a believer in the dictum *Keep your enemies near.* In fact, he was putting all his chips on it, waiting on the result with increasing anxiety as the night progressed.

Any sensible man would take his possessions and walk away from a potential threat. Anyone but a man filled with his own grandeur would suggest to Laura Hurleigh and her friend Sarah that they should have nothing to do with this American stranger, who could prove dangerously untrustworthy. They would do that, both of them, drop him in a flash if Bunsen asked. However, to give that order, Bunsen would have to admit, to himself and to Stuyvesant, that the American was a threat.

Better to hold a snake close, behind the head, than to leave it loose to bite.

But Sarah would be in for a hard time, he thought, and cursed The Bastard from behind clenched and smiling teeth.

The night grew late, then early. The musicians took a break every hour, twice coming back from a turn in the garden smelling faintly of marijuana, but eventually Fforde-Morrison's voice gave out and he traded the megaphone for the gramophone, opening up his crate of records. Half the young latecomers piled in their cars to weave down the drive, headed for a party they'd heard of in Oxford. Their companions either cavorted to the recorded music, squabbled over the rules to some arcane card game, or sobered up and edged towards their more formally clad elders. Stuyvesant's young accuser had been propped into a chair with a pool cue, and was snoring over the din.

Stuyvesant had a hard head for the booze, but even he was feeling the effects. He perched on the arm of a sofa with Sarah at his side—Bunsen, to his surprise, had slumped into the deep cushions of the other sofa rather than claiming the Duke's chair. That chair had been taken by the Lady Constance; the other family and guests were scattered in a wide circle around the fire. Stuyvesant nursed his drink, listening passively to three separate but occasionally overlapping conversations, a Babel of talk that ebbed and flowed around him like waves on a beach.

"—sun on the flesh like a warm"—(here Lady Constance giggled like a young girl)—"milk bath, restoring one to—" She had yet to strip off her clothing for a demonstration, although Stuyvesant had not given up hope. Her audience was Gilbert Dubuque, too sozzled to do more than gape at her with a glass drooping in one hand. Lady Constance was facing away from the circle around Richard Bunsen and was speaking with some determination, refusing to acknowledge the unsavory discussion of politics going on literally behind her back.

"—for example, the wage issue of the Samuel Report which, despite all promises to abide by the Report, was simply buried beneath—" Bunsen was pontificating to Lord Daniel, Lord Patrick, a monocled Oxford don named Baxter who had been invited by Patrick, and, of course, Laura and Sarah. Except that in all fairness, he wasn't pontificating, he was speaking with reason, compassion, and sobriety; the slight dishevelment to his hair and loosening of his collar only added to the effect.

"—all of Hyde Park just wall to wall with vehicles, it was the wildest thing to come across without expecting it." Lady Pamela was droning on to Dubuque's chinless friend, whose name Stuyvesant never had caught, and to Lady Evelyn about the terrible state of affairs in London.

Constance: "—New Gymnosophy Society, *gymnosophy* meaning 'naked philosophy,' you know, and we're looking—"

Bunsen: "—like poor old Comrade Pollitt last year, kidnapped by the bloody Fascists of the O.M.S.—Maintenance of Supplies, I ask you, as if the Unions would even consider starving the country into submis—"

Pamela: "I understand Harrods' shooting range is busy 'round the clock, everyone preparing to keep the revolting masses at bay. Or was that Selfridges'?" Pamela's painted eyebrows arched together in a frown.

Constance: "—sandals, of course, to allow air between the—" Constance giggled again, a habit that seemed unrelated to the topic or even any natural pauses in speech.

Bunsen: "—and charges were dropped, both for the kidnapping and the theft of the van, they were dismissed as a light-hearted romp. Can you imagine the sentence Communists would have got in the same circ—"

Pamela: "—torn between going to their place in Surrey or holding out in Town to watch the show, only Edwina is convinced they'll be ripped from their beds by the mob and Harry is—"

Constance: "—of course, spring is just the most *enticing* time of year, one finds oneself wanting to throw off restraints although it's still so terribly chilly, and—"

Bunsen: "—and you heard about the Fascists' wholesale buying-up of *Workers' Weekly,* an issue with an article of mine that they didn't like on—"

Pamela: "—so in the end they've decided to send the dogs and the children to Surrey and stay in Town themselves, only now they're worried that the cook will join the Strike and put poison in—"

Constance: "—such a pity we had to close the Moonella club in Essex, some horrid building project nearby and they did protest so, how ridiculous to be so stifled that a glimpse of nude—"

Stuyvesant found himself wondering if the two Hurleigh sisters who were fighting so hard to deny Bunsen an uncontested audience were doing so because of aristocratic sensibilities, dislike of politics in general, or a disapproval of Bunsen in particular.

Bunsen: "—typical of their approach, they're so caught up in protecting their interests that they can't see their interests would actually be better served by overhauling the entire system and turning the Parliament buildings over—"

Pamela: "Poor Johnny, he's lost two teeth right in the front and they were such pretty teeth, but he's certainly learnt not to shout at large men with signs in their—"

Constance: "—all have club names, of course, we have to be careful to preserve our privacy. Mine is Byff, with a Y you see, and there's—"

Of course, it could simply be that the two women couldn't bear to cede the floor to anyone, be he commoner, blue-blood, or royal.

Bunsen: "—while the boys who should be helping us are practicing as constables—"

Pamela: "—the railway could possibly want with Buffles I can't imagine, I certainly wouldn't trust him not to send the whole train off a bridge or—"

Constance: "—my friends in the Folk Dance Society that we should come down and entertain the strike-breakers in Kensington—"

Bunsen: "—unless the General Council and the owners reach an agreement, which we'll have to make sure doesn't happen—"

Certainly neither Hurleigh sister—and then the import of Bunsen's monologue penetrated Stuyvesant's fog and he snapped to attention, but the next words were drowned by one of Constance's loud, girly giggles, and in fact, he couldn't have been sure of what he had heard, because Bunsen continued, "—because the Strike is going to be just devastating for the workers, of course. The Unions have funds, but they won't go far with several million men out on strike."

Without warning, a growl rose up in the room, sounding as if one of the Duke's hounds were closing for the kill. Conversation died. The faces looking behind Stuyvesant took on expressions of horror; Bunsen started to fight his way out of the cushions, Laura dropped her glass, and Stuyvesant whirled to confront whatever was coming at him from behind the back he'd dared to turn.

The growl became words: "—want to turn the country over to the Bolshies, we'll deal with your types, one crack of the whip'll send your working-class mutts back to their holes. Who do you think you are, you Red pansy, coming here?"

The drunken boy had roused and was lurching forward with the pool cue held aloft.

Stuyvesant raised himself up to his full six foot two and planted his feet. The boy staggered to a halt, confused by the sudden apparition of a black and white wall. His squinting eyes traveled up the waistcoat studs until they located Stuyvesant's face.

Bunsen, Laura, and other voices were coming from somewhere, but Stuyvesant paid them no mind. He reached for the pool cue, but either he was more drunk than he'd thought or the boy less, because the cue jerked just out of his reach.

"Come on, kid," Stuyvesant said. "I think it's about time you called it a night."

But the kid had focused on his face, and scowled. "You're that other one. The working stiff. Well, some of us are stiff where it matters."

"I say," Bunsen protested, and the older women in the room, those who understood the reference, tittered in embarrassment.

"Now, that really is enough," Stuyvesant said sharply. He turned to put his glass on the arm of the sofa, and although he heard the sharp cries from the onlookers, he didn't want to spill the drink on the pretty carpet, and how much trouble could this drunken prig be, anyway?

But he had not figured in the effects of long years of sport in the raising of the upper class British male, and grunted at the crack of the cue across his shoulders—had he been six inches shorter he'd have been knocked cold. The drink flew in the air and drenched Constance Hurleigh, who squealed in protest; Stuyvesant was aware that others were closing in but he kept his eye on the cue. It rose and spun again through the air back-handed—although this time it seemed to be aimed to one side of Stuyvesant.

He flung out an arm to seize it, and realized only when the stick had slapped hard into his stinging palm that the boy's target had been not him, but Richard Bunsen, who had moved forward to help.

Stuyvesant jerked the stick from the boy's hand and jabbed him in his rumpled chest, sending him backwards into the arms of a friend—except that the friend seemed more interested in joining the fray than stopping it. "Hey," Stuyvesant shouted loudly, at the same instant bringing the cue down smartly across the new man's wrist. With a yelp, the newcomer sprang back, cradling his injured hand, but the first one just ducked down his head and came on as if in a rugby scrum.

Stuyvesant lowered the butt end of the cue, aiming it at the kid's belly, and allowed the boy to run full into it.

That got his attention. He staggered back again (why the hell didn't he just fall down?) with his hands over his belly. Stuyvesant dropped the cue, snapped his fingers at the nearest person and ordered, "Hand me that waste-basket," while keeping an eye on the kid. Who must have been numb with drink because he dropped his hands and hunched for yet another run at his enemies.

Stuyvesant felt the leather object hit his fingers. He switched it into his left hand, stepped forward, and met the kid's charge with a right to the gut.

That, finally, stopped him cold. The kid bent over, coughed, and vomited a great quantity of liquid into the waste-basket. Stuyvesant waited until he was finished, then grabbed the back of his collar and propelled him out of the room into the long gallery.

"You, and you," he snapped in passing. "Take this idiot out and put him to sleep in the stables. And if he vomits over the cars, I'll make you clean it yourselves in the morning. Now, *scram*!"

The boy's friends looked at him, looked at their vanquished compatriot, then wisely chose discretion.

Stuyvesant gave them the reeking waste-basket to take with them.

He came back in the room sucking a knuckle—the same one he'd broken open on the miner in London eight days ago—to find that for the first time that night, the party's entire attention was on someone other than Richard Bunsen—whose skull, Stuyvesant realized belatedly, he had saved by grabbing the stick. If he'd moved just a trifle more slowly, the kid's blow might have scrambled Bunsen's brains for him.

"Neatly done," Bunsen said, sounding frankly admiring.

"What, slugging it out like a couple of twelve-year-olds?"

"I meant the trick with the waste-basket."

"Oh, that. Comes from a lifetime hanging around the wrong kinds of bars."

"You're fast, for a big man."

"You're not bad, yourself," Stuyvesant replied.

Bunsen lifted an eyebrow and shot Stuyvesant a look of pure camaraderie. "Not bad, for a 'Red pansy'?"

And then he laughed. Bunsen's laugh was a full-bodied expression of masculine delight, utterly unforced and instantly contagious. In an flash, the room's tension was swept up in a paroxysm of humor.

Reluctantly, honestly, Stuyvesant had to join in.

But when the laughter ended, when the room had gathered itself to refill its glasses and take surreptitious glances at the clock, he stifled a sigh. Yeah, this really would have been a whole lot easier if he'd neither liked nor respected the man. If he could have kept calling him The Bastard.

Laura and her brother Daniel moved towards the billiards table, playing a desultory game. The gramophone shut down next door, the musicians packed up, the last of the latecomers drifted away into the night. Bunsen seemed content to talk about lesser matters such as rain and the oddities of Prohibition in America, and Stuyvesant did his part, trying to ease the sharp pang of the bruise across his shoulders.

The billiards game came to a close, with Daniel winning by a thin margin, and the two eldest Hurleigh children returned their cues to the rack and wandered over to the fire. Laura took a seat on the long settee between Sarah and Bunsen, draping her slender arms along the back of it in a position eerily similar to that of her ancestress in the painting. One finger stretched out to brush Bunsen's collar, then returned to the settee back; Stuyvesant was grateful that Grey hadn't been forced to witness the gesture.

"Are you sure you have to go back to Town tonight, Richard?" she said, clearly expecting the answer to be Yes.

"Actually," he said, "I think I'll stay the night, after all. Since there's a room ready for me in any case."

Her face lit up, as much with surprise as pleasure. "Oh, that's lovely, Richard. I don't—we don't see enough of you these days. I'll tell Gallagher you're staying."

Stuyvesant tossed back the final drops in his glass to hide his own triumph. *Gotcha!* he thought.

Chapter Forty-Five

HARRIS STUYVESANT WATCHED the self-satisfied man in the mirror brush his teeth. He stripped to his shorts, then dressed again in dark wool trousers, black pull-over sweater, and thick stockings. He drew back the bed-clothes and climbed into the feather bed, lying on the crisp linen with his hands tucked behind his head, staring at the dark ceiling. He thought about Sarah and her brother, and about the play of emotions beneath the well-controlled skin of Richard Bunsen's face, and about the age of the house and the generations of men who had influenced the life of the nation from this place, and about what that age and that influence might mean to Richard Bunsen. Then he thought about how Sarah's warm hair had smelled like honey when he danced with her in his arms, how he'd wanted to whirl her right out the door into the garden and put his mouth on hers and then let it wander down to taste those freckles at the base of her throat, Sarah Grey in a moonlit garden.

He dragged himself upright, wincing: It was a beautiful dream and he craved sleep to his very bones, but his day was not over yet, not by a long shot.

He moved to the hard chair where discomfort and cold would keep him awake. For an hour, he sat in the dark and listened to the barn. At first, it shifted beneath the steps of the guests upstairs and down, and although he could not hear voices, he felt that someone was speaking, from time to time. After a while, the last closing door vibrated through the building. The stones and wood grew still.

While Harris Stuyvesant stood watching his self-satisfied reflection in the glass, downstairs from him and at the other end of the building, Sarah Grey sat watching the puzzled young woman in her looking-glass. She was brushing her hair, giving it her customary nightly hundred strokes, while her mind dwelt on her drunken brother in the room overhead.

She truly couldn't see why Bennett had ventured out of his self-imposed exile. And she had to say, as an experiment in normal life it didn't look to be wildly successful. The last few times she had been to see him, he had been happy, closer to his old self than she could have hoped. Not, however, this evening.

Growing up, Bennett had been a good brother, affectionate and willing to listen. He still was—apolitical himself but happy to let her give voice to her thoughts, hopes, and frustrations. There'd been a night on one of her trips to Cornwall, two or three summers before. She'd gone on a—what else?—whim, following a bad disappointment with a local official who had encouraged her to think he supported a project, kept her dangling for months, and finally told her it was impossible. She blew up in his face and called him something childish like "repulsive little corpuscle," which, of course, was terribly foolish and only made everything worse—even as she was saying it she knew she was creating an enormous mess for Laura to clean up.

And when she got home to her dull little flat that afternoon, she'd looked at the contents of her cupboards and simply couldn't face any of it. She'd thrown some clothes in a bag—and then rung Laura to say she was leaving town and would Laura cover her appointments, the only sensible thing she did all day. She didn't even send Bennett a telegram to warn him that she was coming. Of course, one thing about having a hermit for a brother, one knew he'd be home.

" 'Too Red,' " she'd stormed at Bennett that night. "I ask you, one small dental clinic to treat the rotting teeth of poor children, deemed a part of the Bolshevik takeover because it would be run by volunteers! Bennett, what is this country coming to? We can't treat the poor that way, it's unnecessary and utterly cruel."

As she'd paced up and down his small sitting room, Bennett smoked his pipe and watched her, saying nothing much. Finally she'd dropped into a chair and picked up the glass of good single-malt he'd poured for her twenty minutes before.

"Feel better?" he asked.

"Oh, my dear brother, I *so* wish you didn't live at the far end of an entire day's journey."

"You could move to Penzance. There are poor people there in need of help."

"I need to be in London. I need to feel useful."

"I, on the other hand, am tired unto death of being useful."

He sounded it, too, exhausted with life itself, and she blurted out the question that had been so long on her tongue. "Bennett, what *happened* to you? I don't mean in France, but afterwards, that... mental place where you lived after the hospital. Mother said it would help you, but it just made your heebie-jeebies worse, didn't it? Oh, I'm sorry, you don't like to talk about it, but I don't even know what was wrong with you!"

She didn't think he would answer, but after a while he said, "I lost myself, Sal. After I was blown up, I became someone else. And in the clinic, they tried to put me back together again, in a fashion that might be useful, to myself and to them. But they were killing me. So I left, and wandered around until I came to a place where I could listen to nothing. The clinic was like... Remember old Mackelby, my maths tutor?"

"Oh, crumbs, I was so grateful when you left home and I didn't have to have him any more! He gave me a permanent phobia about maths—I break into a sweat whenever anyone says the word *accounts*."

"Exactly: He'd give one a problem, and then before the poor pupil could even read through it, there would be Mackelby growling away at his shoulder, harassing him and building up to shouts— 'Come, boy, let's see some action from that pencil, the problem isn't going to solve itself, do we have to begin again with the times-twos?'

And so on, until the stick came out and he'd start in on one's knuckles. I suppose the idea was to help one perform under pressure, and it did that. In fact, I used to find myself doing trigonometry in my head in the trenches, waiting for the signal to go over the top. But later, I lost the ability to narrow my focus and think only about the problem at hand. In the clinic, I felt as if there were ten Mackelbys standing at my shoulder shouting all day, every day."

"And that was supposed to help you heal?" she exclaimed. "You must've been driven mad!"

"Precisely." She remembered how he'd said that word: *Precisely.* Dry and grim, a signpost to the end of the world. She never had learned just what they did to him there. But after that conversation, she no longer complained at his quirky choice of domicile.

She was sorry he'd come to Hurleigh. She should have put him off, knowing there was a chance Richard would come, knowing what Laura had once meant to Bennett. She was glad that Laura had never told Richard about Bennett. They'd talked about it, she and Laura, whether or not she should tell him: True freedom included freedom from society's conventions, from the burdens of personal history, from the complications of one's past. And although Sarah certainly agreed in principle with the idea of complete disclosure, at the same time she'd wondered aloud if it wouldn't prove a distraction to Richard.

Until tonight, she hadn't been sure if Laura had told Richard or not. But she knew him well enough to be certain that, if he'd known, he'd never have overlooked Bennett as he had this evening.

Although, come to think of it, maybe she didn't know Richard as well as she thought she did. After all this time, why choose tonight to flirt with her?

Maybe he *did* know about Bennett, and he'd been trying to make Laura jealous?

Or maybe he'd been trying to get Harris Stuyvesant's goat? But why? He didn't even know Harris. And even if he did, why would he care if Sarah liked the American or not? He'd never before tonight expressed an interest in her apart from her role in the Movement. Oh, he'd occasionally come out with a flirtatious comment or mildly risqué suggestion, but it was always as if he needed to remind everyone including himself that he was a man, and not just a mind. She'd tended to treat him as an older brother, until tonight.

Maybe she was imagining it all. She had to admit that Harris Stuyvesant was stirring up feelings she'd nearly forgotten she had, and maybe the effects of that disturbance were spilling over into other parts of her life.

In which case, she should add another maybe: Maybe it was time to step back from the big, tasty American before things grew any more complicated.

Was that what Richard was trying to teach her, by his unaccustomed attentions? That she wasn't big enough to divide her loyalties?

The Movement mattered: She knew that with an absolute and unquestioning certainty of body and mind. And in any enterprise as vital as the one to which she and Laura and Richard were devoted, sacrifice was built into its very bones. The world could simply not go on as it was; change had to come on all levels. Men had to sacrifice their expectations of inherited power, women had to give up the expectations of another age.

Maybe that's what Richard was trying to tell her, that the Movement couldn't afford for her to get any deeper with Harris Stuyvesant.

It was, she decided sadly, the only interpretation of Richard's behavior tonight that made any sense.

Sacrifices would be required, without a doubt. The sacrifice of Harris Stuyvesant might be the least of them.

Chapter Forty-Six

WHEN THE BARN HAD HELD ITS SILENCE for half an hour, Harris Stuyvesant stood. With slow and cautious steps, he moved across the room, taking his kit from the table near the door: soft leather bedroom slippers, a small electric flash-light and extra batteries, some twice-folded sheets of paper and a pencil, and a pair of old, supple black gloves. The big man crept out of his room, down the stairs, and out of the door.

Outside, he pulled the slippers from his trouser pocket and put them on—bedroom slippers were not only silent on gravel, they were disarming, should he be discovered. Who could suspect a man in bedroom slippers of any worse sin than insomnia?

In his ornate room in the main house, lighted only by a bedside candle, Richard Bunsen studied the naked man in the looking-glass. Two weeks past his thirty-second birthday, and as fit as he'd been during the War—the firm outlines of his body were clear despite the flecks and tarnish of the two-hundred-year-old mirroring.

His mind lingered over the image: *New Man seen through the patina of history.* How to use it in a speech, how to work it so it

sounded natural? He walked over to the desk, relishing the Hurleigh
air drifting against his bare skin, to write the idea down on a piece of
house stationery.

He stood, frowning down at the page. Too cumbersome, really,
for a speech. But the image could be used somewhere. Maybe invent
a story to go with it? He made another note, then capped the pen and
dropped it onto the desk.

It had been a hard day in Manchester with Lord-bloody-
Almighty-Malcolm followed by an evening of tricky self control
among the Hurleighs, and he wanted another drink. Two or three
more drinks, for that matter, but he'd had enough for one night, especially if he was going to talk to the old man first thing. And meet with
Ruddle about the P.M. in the afternoon. No drink.

Restless, he circled the sumptuous room, feeling his toes dig into
the thick carpet, running his hand across the velvet and the polish.
He pulled aside the curtains to throw open the heavy glass. Cold,
damp air swept over his skin, bringing up goose-flesh. Bringing up
other flesh, as well.

Standing naked in the open window was weirdly stimulating, as
if he were about to fuck the house itself. He angled his hips forward
until his half-erect cock was brushing the sill, and found himself
wishing that someone were standing in the garden below—the window's lower edge came just below his umbilicus, so he would be
showing nothing unseemly, just the firm outline of a man younger
than his age.

And if it was that mouthy American out there, he'd have no way
of knowing what lay hidden: Men over six feet tall had an unfair advantage over normal males, and there was no need to give the fellow
illusions.

Abruptly, the cold air ceased to be stimulating. Bunsen banged
the window shut and jerked the curtains across it, walking back to
the center of the room, running his hand over his smooth chest and
belly, then down to cup the mild ache in his balls.

Why had he told Laura that he'd stay? She had been irritatingly
aloof recently, as if he'd disappointed her in some way. And distressingly willing to vamp the most unlikely men, men he was absolutely
positive that she had no interest in, but who could be useful to the

Movement. Although he had to admit that tonight she'd met his eyes with the old affection and openness. Perhaps he just needed to make her feel more useful, and if that meant dragging himself halfway across England to bow and scrape to the old horrors who were her parents, that's what he'd do.

Oh, he liked them well enough, the mother at least, but surely people like that should realize when their kind was dead? However, until that class had their last vestiges of power wrested from their hands by the new age (*New Age/New Man/through a glass, darkly*— no, people might think he was making reference to that bloody Alice story), until then, he'd have to keep working on her father, keeping him sweet. Not long now, he told himself, before the world could do without the Duke of Hurleigh, leaving commoners like little Dickie Bunsen free to walk openly down the corridor of this ancient house to have his way, loudly and often, with the Duke's daughter.

He'd intended to be traveling back to London by now, working in his wheeled office while Jimmy drove, then sleeping for a couple of hours before setting off for his afternoon meetings, and in the evening finishing off two speeches and an article. Instead, here he was in Gloucestershire while in London events were building—vulnerable events, requiring his constant touch on the reins.

Another phrase with a certain ring to it: *events that require a constant touch on the reins.* Use it with Ruddle? Or save it for Baldwin?

He held out his own hands to study them. His mother, long ago, had once called them surgeon's hands. Not that he would have wished to become a doctor, even if the money had been there: If you're going to be up to your elbows in blood, it had better be for something more important than catching a squalling brat or repairing some old sot's ruptured gut. No, his hands were repairing something much larger than could be brought to a surgery: attending the birth of a new age, cutting into the body politic.

"A surgeon for the body politic," he said aloud, trying it out, then walked over to write that phrase beneath the other.

He looked at the bed, looked at the decanter, then wandered back to the looking-glass. *Through a glass, darkly. Through the glass of history, darkly?* What about, *New Man glimpsed through a glass, darkly?*

None of those were quite right, but he did like the image. Liked, too, what his eyes saw: He really was not a bad-looking man, even if that damned American had compared him to a bloody film actor. (What about that American? Intriguing fellow, competent and bright, but it was almost as if he'd been trying to irritate.) Well, why not a film actor? He'd been talking to a man in Liverpool during this last trip, on how to make movies work for the Movement. *Birth of a Nation,* without the half-naked girls. Or maybe with them, and a few half-naked boys, as well. Artistically done, of course, but didn't propaganda encompass many forms? And why couldn't that include the bourgeoisie's favored forms of entertainment?

Why did the bourgeoisie put up with the limitations around them? Why go to gawk at scantily clad females on flickering screens when the world was full of women?

Then again, he was one to talk, standing here in the nude, playing with himself in front of the mirror and trying to get up his courage to creep down the hallway. If only the Duke were out of the way, he'd have no problems. If—

A small movement in the looking-glass caught his attention: the door-knob. He whirled; the door began to open.

Chapter Forty-Seven

STUYVESANT REACHED THE GARAGE unseen, although he'd had a bad moment in the garden when he'd realized someone was standing in a dimly lit upstairs window. But whoever it was had been looking out into the darkness, and had not seen him. In a moment, the figure had banged the window shut and closed the curtains.

Stuyvesant went on, making no more noise than a cat.

Laura Hurleigh did not stare into her own looking-glass, although she was sitting on the chair directly in front of it. Instead, she had spent the past quarter of an hour searching through the detritus of her past.

Specifically, she was sorting through the contents of her jewelry box. There was nothing of value in it—the rubies her grandmother had left her lay locked in the safe downstairs, along with two or three other pieces that would bring something at the pawn-broker's. The Hurleigh servants were trustworthy, but it was not nice to lay temptation before them. And jewelry was wicked anyway; when Mother asked yesterday if she wanted to wear the rubies for dinner, Laura had been adamant that, if she wasn't allowed to sell them, she was

damned if she was going to flaunt them around her neck. The one
time she'd sold a necklace, to buy desperately needed equipment for
the clinics, it had created hell's own uproar when her father had to
buy it back.

No, the jewelry box contained treasures with little market value:
a ring she'd bought at the St. Giles Fair when she was ten or eleven,
thought to be turquoise until the blue paint had begun to peel; a tiny
fresh-water pearl on a tarnished chain, one of a matching trio exchanged by three sixteen-year-old friends for life, who now hadn't
seen each other in years; six pair of decorative hair-combs, useless to
a modern woman with short hair.

On the dressing-table next to the box were the two objects she
had spent a quarter-hour extricating from the tangle inside.

One was a thumb-nail-sized cockle shell with a slightly off-center
hole in it, drilled by some hungry predator. A string made out of
black silk sewing thread, laboriously braided then braided again, had
been threaded through the hole: the hand-made cord was frayed
where it passed through the shell.

Bennett Grey had made the necklace for her the first summer he
had spent here, when Laura was eleven, Thomas and Bennett around
ten. One August day, Bennett's father had come to take the two boys
to the seashore; she could no longer recall the details of why he had
come, or why more of the Hurleigh children had not gone with them;
what she remembered were the hot tears of rage when the Greys'
touring car had pulled away, leaving her, the oldest but a girl, behind.

Bennett had seen her tears, and instead of flaunting his privilege
or making fun of her, he had brought the shell back from the
seashore, then spent hours plaiting and twisting the cord from a
spool of sewing floss. She fell in love with him then, and she'd worn
the shell every day for years, until she noticed the wear on the cord
and feared it would be lost.

The other object was a small tarnished brass ring incorporating a
tiny heart, but it possessed an oddly similar history. Bennett had
made this for her, too, over a period of many weeks, huddled in the
trenches of northern France. Its raw material was also a shell, but of
a very different sort, the shell of the first bullet he had fired in the heat
of battle, thrust in a pocket and come across when the dazed survivor

had finally reached a calm place again. He had snipped the brass into strips and laboriously bent and woven it into a ring. It would never be a lovely object, but it was an eloquent one.

Ten years after the first gift, in the summer of 1914, Bennett had promised his mother that he would complete his degree at Oxford before he enlisted—hard to remember, but that first summer they'd all been convinced the War would be over by Christmas. Three weeks after War was declared, he and Laura happened to meet for the first time in years, at a garden party dominated by uniforms. Five days later, he had formally written for permission to call the next time her family was in London, although by then she was twenty-one and able to answer for herself. In any case, he was known to the family, and the answer had been Yes.

The following ten months had been fraught with the knowledge that time was short, that life would never be the same, that their friends and family were being swallowed up in the carnage across the Channel. And finally, in July 1915, Bennett had come to her house, wearing his uniform and an expression of manly apprehension. She had wept; he had laid his hand across her shoulders and pulled her to his woolen chest, then given her a clean handkerchief and vowed that he would come back to her.

He made the ring a few weeks later, and sent it as a birthday gift in October.

All terribly ordinary, really; a play acted out tens of thousands of times during those years.

But what had happened to him four years later had been in no sense ordinary.

Sarah had rung with news of her brother's injury. Laura found out when he would arrive in England and drove through the bright dawn of a late May morning to be there when he landed. She found a bundle of moaning bandage, drugged to high heaven, but she was a V.A.D. nurse, and there was little she hadn't seen by them in the way of ripped bodies and battered minds. She went back again, and again, for since the death of manners in 1914, there was no one to stop her.

With Laura's help, Captain Bennett Grey was hobbling by July, and by August able to move himself from the Bath chair to her motorcar. She took him for long drives through the fields of summer, buying and begging petrol from all directions, once even stealing it. For most of these expeditions, Bennett sat motionless and mute as the warm wind played through their hair.

It only rained once during these outings. They had brought a picnic tea, and Laura, determined to have her hard-fought rationed delicacies, hunkered under the umbrella he held out of the motorcar's window, boiling water on the small camp-stove. In triumph she had made the tea and poured it, handed him the two cups through the window, then run laughing through the downpour to the driver's side. He had laughed, too, and dried her hair with their checked table-cloth. They had drunk their tea with decorum, eaten the two petit-fours she had located in Piccadilly, and when they were finished, he had taken her empty cup, stretched an arm into the rain to place it on the bonnet, followed by his. Then he had kissed her, and undressed her, and had finally taken her virginity in the cramped confines of her Tin Lizzie.

From that September day until the first week of March, Bennett had been hers. At least once a week, in out-of-the-way hotels all over the south of England, she had been Mrs. Grey and worn this ring. At the end of each such outing, she had relished the green shadow on her finger, scrubbing it away only at the last minute.

From the beginning, and now more so, the object had brought mixed feelings. Love, yes, but from a thing used to kill a man? (And it probably had: Bennett was as careful and methodical at his marksmanship as he was in other things.)

When spring came and Bennett had his break-down, coming near to murdering the horrid Aldous Carstairs, she went to his family's house and begged him to marry her.

He refused. White and shaking and in terrible pain, he would not let her in. He told her how sorry he was, told her it was impossible, then shut the door in her face.

She went back to London, and to her work, and to Sarah Grey and Mary Margolin, who were more sisters to her than silly Connie or brittle Pam. Three mornings later, Bennett's letter reached her. And two days after that, the infant Christopher Margolin had died, and been wrapped in a luxurious shroud.

She slipped the tarnished ring onto her finger. Bennett had been right, she knew that now. Her presence had only made matters worse for him, and their union would lead nowhere. Not like Richard, who loved her and needed her, who challenged her and demanded that she grow and learn and find her strength, who confused her and only explained his ideas, never his feelings, and who sometimes grew furious with her and had twice hit her, only to fall to his knees immediately and beg her forgiveness.

Bennett Grey had been a gentle lover and a wounded hero, but Richard Bunsen was a flame: lover, teacher, father, son. She yearned after him even when he was with her, longing to touch him in public, reveling in his magnificent speaking voice. She loved to drown in his words, to burn with his passion, to support him in his unexpected moments of uncertainty, to lie beside him and listen to him breathe. He was not as attentive in bed as Bennett had been—at the memory of Bennett's touch, the room felt suddenly warmer—but at the same time, the process didn't seem to tear him between pleasure and agony the way it had Bennett.

If only he didn't embrace the idea of free love with quite so much abandon. Faithfulness was a concept for the bourgeoisie, small and limited, and she felt petty every time the complaint came to mind. (Although really—*Sarah!* That was a bit much.)

She pulled off the ring and put it away, placing the shell necklace beside it. Poor, poor Bennett, she thought, rubbing the green from her finger; it had been a mistake allowing Sarah to bring him here to witness his replacement.

She closed the top of the jewelry box and slid it back in the drawer of her dressing-table, then looked at her reflection in the glass. If the road is made easy, it is the right one.

The house had long since subsided into the night-time creaks of its age; Laura rose and snugged the tie of the dressing gown, letting herself out of the door and padding barefoot down the familiar carpet of her family home. No one saw her, no voice questioned her passing— she'd been avoiding detection in this house since she was nine years old, when she'd mapped out where each squeaky floorboard was.

She opened the door at the far end of the hallway, and looked at the naked, semi-aroused man standing in front of the looking-glass. She shut the door silently, then murmured, "It looks like I got here just in time."

Chapter Forty-Eight

STUYVESANT WENT THROUGH the small rear door into the converted stables, moving with care across the rough grit floor. But the drunken boy seemed to have been stashed elsewhere, and Bunsen's driver was not napping in his car, suggesting that, despite his size, his duties did not include those of guard.

Another small fact to tuck away.

Stuyvesant checked that the stables' door was securely shut, then opened the car's rear door.

The car was a Humber, large and remarkably staid for a young man with radical leanings, but one glance inside and Stuyvesant could see why the car had been chosen.

It was, in fact, a mobile office, the transportation of a man who did not wish to waste a minute of his life on the road. The left half of the back had been converted to contain a filing cabinet on the floor, a set of purpose-built wooden cubby-holes fitted across the seat, and a swing-out wooden desk complete with blotter. The entire structure would break down for easy removal, if the owner had a passenger he didn't want to put up beside the driver or on the little fold-down seat in front of him.

There was even a reading lamp, fixed to shine on Bunsen's lap, but Stuyvesant did not want to risk draining the car's batteries, so he propped his flash-light in the empty crystal glass sitting in a holder on the door, and lowered himself onto the worn leather where Richard Bunsen sat. He breathed in the air Bunsen breathed, touched the edge of the glass, settled his shoulders into the seat back where Bunsen rested his shoulders.

How difficult would it be to put a triggering device into the seat below his trousers, he wondered, as Bunsen had done to the judge's car back in November? Run a slow fuse from the trigger to a little flask of flammable liquid, let the car go up in flames. A touch of rough justice.

He shook his head: You're a Bureau agent, not an assassin, he reminded himself. Get to work.

He started with the cubby-holes, Bunsen's current projects. Most of the files there appeared to be speeches, some of which had the target audience written on the file. His eye caught on the word *Battersea,* and he opened that one, reading almost verbatim the speech that he'd thought Bunsen gave off the cuff. Even the two preliminary remarks that had been made to answer the audience questions were there— which meant that Bunsen knew the questions were coming. That he had arranged for them to be shouted aloud.

Stuyvesant shook his head in admiration. Sapper or politician, the man left nothing to chance.

He went through the other files, finding the speeches clever but the basic ideas repetitive, to be expected from a man who gave a dozen or more speeches every week. The handwriting was neater than he'd have thought, for notes written in a moving car. A few had been transcribed on a type-writer, although he also found a manila envelope containing scraps of paper with nothing but catchy phrases on them: "Tory toadies"; "strike while the coal is hot"; "brothers and sisters under the skin"; "Black Friday and the domino action of capitulation." And yes, "rouge on a corpse." The phrases had been written by two or three different hands and half a dozen pens and pencils, indicating an ingrained habit of scribbling down inspiration.

He reached the bottom cubby-hole without revelation. Both filing cabinet drawers were locked, but the mechanism gave him no more problems than the car door had, and he slid open the top drawer and reached into its first file.

At four A.M., he was still on that first file of the first drawer: It had held a book, on the leather cover of which was stamped:

DIARY 1926

Every day had its page, and every single page had something written on it, even if only the rare notation *Day off*. The top few lines Bunsen used as an appointments book, some days only one or two, growing to six or seven in the past weeks, all in pencil. The bottom part of the page had other notes, written mostly in pen; on some pages he had run out of room, and either spilled over to the next page or used adhesive tape to fasten on a loose sheet.

Stuyvesant turned to the beginning of the book. Five days in he found:

11:00 to S'hampton for NY

The next two weeks held only the penciled note:

NY

Nothing about meeting the hotel maid, nothing about building a bomb out of gelignite and nails to cripple a roomful of important men. Nothing at all until the appointments began again on the first of February.

Bunsen's native caution kept him from incriminating notes.

Either that, or the man kept another diary, outside of the car.

In the end, although he copied names and dates onto the paper he had brought, there was far more here than he could possibly follow up. Some pages went a third of the way down with his dates. Looking at the past Thursday, for example:

9:00 Breakfast Laura
10:15 T. Bros (fitting)
12:30 Gibson's (Chum, Riley, O'C.)

5:00 drinks (B., C., S.?)
7:00 Battersea hall

The 5:00 initials matched those of the other speakers, Stuyvesant noted, but in the end, he put down his pencil and skimmed over Bunsen's notes, since he had no way of knowing who half these people were. Some of the names he recognized—there'd been a meeting with Baldwin ten days earlier, although the Prime Minister was just the first in a list of names, one of whom was Matthew Ruddle, Bunsen's Union mentor and one-time employer. Stuyvesant figured Bunsen had done little more at the meeting with Baldwin than hold Ruddle's hat.

Reluctantly, Stuyvesant closed the diary. At this rate, he would still be here reading away when Jimmy the driver came to get the car out. Short of stealing the book outright, he had to admit he wasn't going to get any more from it.

He slid the diary back into its place, reached for the second file, and hit gold.

Death threats. Fourteen of them.

Chapter Forty-Nine

IN THE THIN HOURS WHEN SATURDAY GAVE WAY TO Sunday, Aldous Carstairs sat in his suite of rooms at the Truth Project, thinking. The building was utterly still, so still he could hear the scuffle of some small creature in the leaf mold outside the open window.

The American agent he'd spoken with that afternoon near the Peak was not the same man who had bumbled into his office two weeks before. This man had been sleek and intense and sure of himself, with nary a stumble or blank look in sight. Even his accent had grown sharper.

It was hard to credit, but it would appear that Harris Stuyvesant had been playing him along—him, Aldous Carstairs. Which was not only offensive, but troubling. What else had he missed, while distracted from the man's true competence?

Before, he'd thought to make use of the man more for the satisfaction of crushing an insect than through any real need, but now, he had second thoughts. What he had seen as a minor amusement was, perhaps, a more urgent necessity.

He stretched out one arm for the telephone. "Mr. Snow? We may need to re-consider our strategy concerning Mr. Stuyvesant."

* * *

When Stuyvesant laid eyes on Richard Bunsen Sunday morning, he thought, Funny, you don't look like a man carrying around a file of death threats.

Instead, Bunsen looked like the cat who'd been at the cream. And when Laura came into the breakfast room a few minutes later and glanced at Bunsen with the same whisker-licking air about her, Stuyvesant knew why.

Had the man got an extra jolt of pleasure from the act by doing it while her father slept down the hall? Probably. Maybe he justified it as a form of the re-distribution of wealth. Bunsen stood at Laura's entrance, poured her a cup of tea, took her hand, and turned it over to give the palm a lingering kiss.

Damn good thing her parents weren't there to see that, Stuyvesant thought sourly; they'd have had little doubt about what had gone on under their roof last night.

He was grateful, too, that Bennett Grey had not been required to witness the possessive and sensual gesture, either.

The glow of self-satisfied energy from the other table made him feel very old and very tired; his shoulders and fist hurt from the fight, his spine ached from a night spent hunched over files, and his eyes felt as if someone had flicked sand in them. How long had it been since his last full night's sleep?

But the game that he played had its own pleasures, and having Richard Bunsen in his sights was more invigorating than eight hours in the sack. He knew precisely where to step now; indeed, he'd already set things into motion.

The other people in the breakfast room were Gilbert Dubuque and his don friend Baxter, who had taken seats in the dimmest corner, muttering something to Stuyvesant about having to be in Oxford by noon: By the looks of things, they planned to float there on coffee. Dubuque had seen Bunsen's bit with the hand and looked quickly away, but Stuyvesant finished his plate of bacon and eggs, picked up his half-full coffee cup, and headed over to the window table: big, blunt, a little pushy, but friendly as all get-out: Harris Stuyvesant, human Labrador retriever at your service.

"Ah, the merry warrior," Bunsen said, not sounding altogether pleased at the intrusion.

Stuyvesant remained oblivious to the thread of rebuff. "You mind if I join you? Our friends over there are a little incoherent this morning."

"Please," Laura said, drawing herself into a hostess posture reminiscent of her mother.

"Can I get you anything, while I'm up? Your cup's empty."

"Thank you," she told him, pushing it towards him.

He went to fill it, whistling a tune from the previous evening—"It Had to Be You," he realized, remembering the honey scent of Sarah's hair.

He placed the cup on the table in front of Laura Hurleigh, turning it by the saucer so the handle was pointing to her right hand. The swell of the thumb had a red patch on it, he noticed: Bunsen hadn't just kissed the hand, he had given it a sharp little bite. But then, looking at those long, thin fingers picking up the little spoon, he reflected that hers was a hand he wouldn't mind nibbling, himself.

"Haven't seen Bennett yet this morning," he told his companions. "He'll probably be out 'til noon."

"Laura tells me you're a friend of Sarah's brother?" This morning Bunsen's eyes were a light olive color, and his shave was immaculate, his energy level undimmed by a long and no doubt energetic night. He looked at Stuyvesant with good humor and curiosity, as if he just couldn't wait to see what this American would do next.

"That's right, I met him a couple years ago, and I try to see him whenever I'm in the country. This is the first time I've known him to come out of Cornwall, however. He sure likes that place."

"And you, you work selling motorcars?"

"Now I do, yeah. When I first started at Ford I was on assembly, then repairs, but after the War they had a fair number of vacancies, and I sure knew the cars inside out. So I bought a suit and interviewed for a job in one of their showrooms, and did pretty well there. I'd probably still be doing that except the English division was having some problems that lay sort of halfway between sales and service, and needed someone who knew both. I clean up good, so they sent me."

The account he'd crafted sacrificed impeccable working-class credentials for a story that made his presence here believable—but Henry Ford wouldn't have sent one of his dirty-handed mechanics over to England, so it had to be a compromise between worker and management. Like Bunsen himself, suspended between classes.

"But Sarah says that you're considering a return to your beginnings."

"My—oh yeah, as a mechanic. Nice to hear she's been talking about me." Bunsen's complacency sagged just a touch, having had his dart turned back on him—he'd no doubt mentioned Sarah to illustrate how the young woman reported to him, not to suggest that she'd been gushing about a potential beau. "I like England, a whole lot. And I wouldn't say this to everyone here, but I'm liking what your Unions are doing. The workers here seem to have considerably more clout than they do in the States. Between the Pinkertons, the cops, and the Feds, there's little chance of getting together and presenting a united front. I hope our workers're paying attention to what's going on here."

"Oh, I should think they are," Bunsen said.

Stuyvesant lowered his voice. "Those kids last night, talking about being Strike volunteers for the O.M.S.?"

Bunsen's face went dark and he drew his hands off the table and onto his lap, leaving Laura's by themselves on the white cloth. "The Organisation for the Maintenance of Supplies," he spat.

"I wanted to ask you—this is a government group of strike-breakers?"

"At root, that is its function, although it's only semi-official. 'Working with the government,' they say."

"Scabs, or vigilantes?"

"Both, and more. The O.M.S. is nothing less than legalized Fascism, prettied up by its ties to lords and retired admirals, all terribly respectable. It sounds as if you've had experience with strike-breakers."

Now it was Stuyvesant's turn to study his hands. He pulled out Helen's cigarette case, and glanced up at Laura. "You mind?"

"Please do."

He took out a cigarette and tamped it on the case a couple of times, acting hesitant as he prepared to play his card. "I probably shouldn't tell you this—if it got back to my bosses I'd be well and truly done for. But you're a friend of Sarah's, and I think you're on the side of the angels. So yeah, I know some things about strike-breakers. A couple years ago I took a few weeks off work to help out a buddy. I told my boss I'd broken a bone in my foot, but actually, I was standing in as a sort of bodyguard during a particularly, shall we say, *active* sort of a strike."

"You mean a violent one?"

"It ended up that way. This was out in Washington State, logging problems that sound a little like what your miners are looking at now—profits are dropping, so take it out on the working man. This friend of mine was one of the organizers, and first he started getting death threats, then he heard a rumor that the owners had put a price on his head. His dead head, you understand? So I offered to stand around next to him and look big. I got him through the worst of it, but at the end he had to move on, because he had family and the owners were pretty upset. He didn't need me any more, so I went back to Ford."

"That must have seemed very dull," Laura remarked.

He grinned. "Sure did. And it took some explaining how I'd managed to break my nose and get two spectacular black eyes while I was home nursing a broken foot."

"Who was your friend?" Bunsen asked it mildly, as if the question was of no importance. However, Stuyvesant had felt the man tense up at the mention of death threats.

Stuyvesant told him the name, and Bunsen blinked. "You were involved in that strike?"

"Only at the end. And a few weeks later he got himself arrested anyway, so there wasn't much more I could do for him."

And it was true, pretty much every word, once you left the Ford company out of it. He'd befriended a prominent Union official and acted as bodyguard in a series of violent strikes in 1923; he'd spirited the man's family out of harm's way, taken a beating for him, and then been far away when the Bureau raid had picked the man up, right where Stuyvesant's information had placed him. Bunsen could send a dozen telegrams to his American Union friends, and every one of them would confirm that this Wobbly leader had been protected for a while by a big, blue-eyed New Yorker named Harris Smith.

It had been one of Stuyvesant's more successful operations.

And now Bunsen and Laura Hurleigh were both looking at him with speculation in their eyes. He gazed back at them, a large, friendly, competent man who'd just laid his cards on the table; the next move had to be theirs.

Bunsen's move was to pick up his cup, drain the last drops, and stand, sticking his hand across the table at Stuyvesant.

"It's been interesting to meet you, Mr. Stuyvesant, but I need to have a word with Lord Hurleigh, and after that, events are calling me to London. I hope to meet again, soon."

Sooner than you imagine, bud, Stuyvesant said to himself. "Are you going, too, Miss Hurleigh?"

"No, I won't be going back until tomorrow morning, so I shall see you later today."

He watched them leave the morning room, Bunsen striding in confidence, Laura following behind. He'd have given a lot to know what they needed to talk to the Duke about.

Since he couldn't think of a way to find out, he wandered outside and, as he'd expected, found Bunsen's motor standing in the drive. Jimmy the driver was resting his backside against the car, reading a newspaper—not, he noticed with amusement, the *Workers' Weekly,* but a racing sheet.

"Morning," he said to the man. "You Bunsen's driver?"

The paper came down a fraction as the man scowled at him and grunted a response. Stuyvesant introduced himself, thrust his hand under the man's nose so he couldn't avoid shaking it, then asked him if he'd ever had any problems with his gas filters.

"Can't say as I have," the driver said. So Stuyvesant reeled off a long story about how the Ford company had received a number of complaints about their filter in England, and it had occurred to him that maybe the gas—or petrol—here was different, somehow, and he wondered if the driver had ever heard of that.

The man was patently less interested in fuel filters than the contents of his racing paper. After waffling on for a while, Stuyvesant let him get back to it.

Not a bodyguard, or even a guard in general, and for sure not much of a mechanic: Jimmy was a driver, period. Which meant he wouldn't notice the little modification Stuyvesant had made to the wires from the spark-plug coil the night before, until it was too late.

As he walked back towards the barn, Gallagher emerged from the house with a folded note on a silver tray. "Telephone message for you, sir. The gentleman did not wish to wait for me to find you."

Stuyvesant didn't imagine he would, with a houseful of servants and half a dozen exchange operators listening in—he'd been pretty cautious, when he'd phoned Carstairs' number early that morning, about his own end of the conversation. Fortunately, the voice on the other end of the line had understood the purpose of cautious wording, and merely said he would pass the message on. He took the precisely folded half-sheet of paper from the tray and read:

Yes.

The bells of the Hurleigh chapel clanged at precisely ten o'clock. The doors closed against the spectacular spring morning, the small procession followed the cross up the aisle, and the assembled Hurleigh party, washed, polished, and in various degrees of hangover, prepared to meet their God.

Not Harris Stuyvesant. He was a Roman Catholic, after all, and no more expected in the chapel than if his name had been Jacob Cohen.

Instead, Stuyvesant walked up the path that led to the Peak, whistling softly. At the place where the path opened out, the place where Bennett Grey had stared into the woods the day before, he turned right, through the trees. He avoided as many of the soft, knee-high flowers as he could, although they were thick on the ground.

Twenty minutes later he dropped down over the ridge, adjusting his angle towards the parked motorcar. The back door opened and Aldous Carstairs got out, tugging at his gloves as he walked to meet him.

"You wanted to see me, Mr. Stuyvesant?"

Stuyvesant held out a lumpy, oversized manila envelope.

"Don't worry, I wore gloves," he told Carstairs. The man's own black gloves hesitated, then reached out for the object. He had an odd expression on his face.

"My way in's going to be through Bunsen's driver," Stuyvesant told him. "You'll find some Automobile Club papers and the little identity doodad from the front of Bunsen's car—I don't want to destroy them, but I wouldn't want them found in my suitcase, either. I fiddled the car so it'll break down, probably somewhere between here and Oxford. He's not going to fly off the road and burst into flames or anything, the car will just die. I don't think the driver will be able to fix it, he doesn't seem to be much of a mechanic, so they'll flag down an Automobile Club man to help them, only they won't have any proof that they're members, because it seems as though the clumsy driver's misplaced his papers. Plus that, he hasn't noticed the car's badge is missing. As I say, nothing dramatic. Just a series of irritations for a man aiming to get back to London for a meeting.

"The driver's name is in there, too. See what information you can get on him—if I'm going to replace him, it'd help to know his weak spots."

"You . . . propose to take the place of Bunsen's driver." It was said flatly; the quizzical expression had become faintly ironic.

"What's wrong with that?"

"Nothing. Nothing at all. Would you like him, hmm, removed?" His tone of voice made his meaning clear.

"What are you talking about, 'removed'? Is this England, or Russia? Of course I don't want him 'removed,' I just want to find something that'll persuade him to quit, or get him fired. 'Removed.' Jesus."

"Very well. Anything else?"

"Yeah. There's a bunch of names and dates in there I got from Bunsen's diary, which only goes back to January. Nothing about the name you told me to look for, Lionel Waller. Most of the names don't mean a thing to me, but I thought you might know them. And I didn't have time to make a copy of all this for you, but I want it back. Okay?"

"Is that all?"

"Bunsen met with the Duke this morning, I don't know about what. And there's nothing in the diary about his trip to the States in January other than he made it. He may have another diary in his actual office."

"I will see what I can do about this," Carstairs said, holding up the envelope.

"You'll give it back when I see you?" The man hadn't actually agreed to it.

"Yes, Mr. Stuyvesant, I will return it to you, every scrap and wrinkle. Telephone me in the morning, I should have some information by then. And might I suggest that you make an early night of it this evening? The house-party week-end can be strenuous for those, shall we say, not accustomed to it."

In other words, these aristos are drinking you under the table and you look like hell. Which wasn't surprising, considering he'd had maybe eight hours' sleep over the last seventy-two. "I'll phone you tomorrow," Stuyvesant said, and began to turn away.

"Mr. Stuyvesant?"

"Yeah?"

"How is Captain Grey holding up?"

"Oh, he's just hunky-dory, thanks. Hey, Carstairs, tell me something. Did you guys find anything when you searched my hotel room?"

The faintest reaction flitted through those black eyes, so controlled Stuyvesant wouldn't have seen it if he hadn't been watching. He winked, and sauntered away.

When he reached the top of the ridge, he hadn't heard the car start or its door shut. He shot a look over his shoulder, and saw Carstairs reaching for the handle.

Points to the U.S. of A., he thought.

Still, all in all, he'd rather work alongside a Red.

When Stuyvesant reached the path again, the breeze carried a sound of distant voices, raised in song. He peeled back his cuff to check his wrist-watch: He'd been gone from the house a scant twenty minutes. Church services were still under way. He could go back to his room, or sit in the garden, but in either case, he was afraid he'd fall asleep.

He went uphill instead of down, up to the Peak and a smoke.

The blue sky of the early morning was withdrawing behind a high gray haze, so he left his jacket on, pulling his knees to his chest. No dog-fox this morning, and the Roman ruins Grey had claimed to see were nothing but a rock on a hillside. But even without the bright sunshine, very, very calm and pretty.

A far cry from the outside world, with its university hooligans knocking around pretty girls on trains and its manipulative Truth Projects and its O.M.S. strike-breakers and the frank despotism of the Emergency Powers Act. Maybe he should go home and turn his mind to fighting nice honest criminals. Or take his hat in his hand and ask the Duke for a job right here, keeping all the Hurleigh engines running, making friends with the foxes, and never reading another newspaper in his whole damn life.

Yeah, and be so bored, he'd put his Colt to his head inside of a week.

What the devil was Carstairs playing at, anyway? He was up to something, Stuyvesant could smell it, and although it might have nothing whatsoever to do with Richard Bunsen or Harris Stuyvesant, not knowing what the man was up to made him twitchy. Like stepping into a dark room, knowing there was a rattlesnake in there somewhere: The snake wasn't after you, but that didn't make your leg any better if it bit.

Like the Bible said, subtler than the other creatures, that was Aldous Carstairs to a T. Whatever he was up to, it would have more layers to it than a snake's skin.

As he stretched to slip the cold cigarette stub into his pocket, it suddenly occurred to him that, at some point in the past twenty-four hours, he'd made a decision about Bennett Grey.

Simply put, he wasn't going to let Carstairs have him. Not for his entertainment, and not for his damned Project, not if Harris Stuyvesant had anything to say in the matter. And if it meant this pretty country got just a little more overrun with Bolshies, well, maybe a country that gave an Aldous Carstairs free rein deserved a little boot up its ass.

He'd cooperate just so far as he had to, to get a rope around Richard Bunsen, but he'd draw the line at snaring Grey.

And in the meantime, he thought, he'd take advantage of his final free time at Hurleigh to go look at some mighty fine paintings, down there in the long gallery.

Chapter Fifty

STUYVESANT HAD THE HURLEIGH ART COLLECTION to himself for nearly an hour before he heard the first house guests come into the breakfast room downstairs, where the aroma of coffee had been rising for a while. He tore himself away from the Constable and went down, finding the others glowing with righteousness but happily changed from their church clothes into casual dress. Grey came in with Laura and Sarah. He looked as tired as Stuyvesant felt, and took a swallow of the coffee from his cup before he had sat down at the table.

Stuyvesant went to join them.

"I'm glad to see that left-wing politics doesn't interfere with Morning Prayer."

"Not even with Communion," Sarah told him.

"The Church may make some bad decisions," Laura added, "but the beauty of the ritual makes it difficult to condemn it outright."

"Does Bunsen feel the same way?"

"Fortunately, Richard had to return to London, so he wasn't faced with that decision. He has a meeting at Downing Street this afternoon."

Which he may not make, Stuyvesant thought with satisfaction, picturing a red-faced Ivor Novello standing by the roadside shouting at his driver while trying to flag down an Automobile Club man.

"I had a very satisfactory Communion myself, with Nature and with Art. I took a walk," he explained, "then spent some time in the long gallery. Boy, your family has some beautiful pieces there."

"Generations of aristocratic privilege will turn out to have some benefit for the people," Laura replied.

"Any time you want to park one of the paintings on a commoner's wall for a while, you're welcome to use mine. But look, I'm sorry, I'm going to have to get back to London myself this afternoon. I've got a meeting tomorrow, and I don't think I should risk the drive in the morning."

"Will you stay for lunch, at least?"

"I can do that, sure. But, Grey, you want me to drop you at the station in Oxford as I go by, or you want someone to drive you later?"

"Actually," he said, "I believe I'll go with you. I could use a day in Town, if nothing else than for the bookstores."

Maybe it hadn't been a good idea to tell him in front of the two women, after all.

"I thought you wanted to get back to Cornwall?" Stuyvesant said, fixing Grey with a compelling gaze.

The green eyes met his, not in the least compelled. "Maybe after a day or two."

"Lovely!" exclaimed Sarah, all but clapping her hands with pleasure. "Perhaps we could meet for a meal, or coffee. Or I could show you the free clinic, Bennett, you've never seen our new building."

Stuyvesant wanted to stand up and slam his cup on the table. *I can't protect you in London, you fool. Go home, pull up your drawbridges, leave Carstairs to me.*

But he could only glower his disapproval at Grey, and agree that they didn't need to leave until after luncheon.

Grey put down his cup and said that he would go and pack his bag. Sarah stood, too, and said she'd keep him company. Which left Stuyvesant talking about art with Laura, not at all a bad way to spend a half-hour.

Family and friends continued to drift in for refreshment and out in search of entertainment. Lord Daniel came in with a young woman whom he introduced with a touching degree of pride as his fiancée.

Stuyvesant was talking to the fiancée, who seemed to him awfully young and naïve for a woman on whose womb an ancient house might rest, when he felt a touch on his arm. Without thinking, he not only knew who it was, but he reached across to lay his hand on hers until the girl came to a pausing place.

He apologized to the earnest young woman for not knowing if the Macy's linen department was superior to that of Gordon Selfridge's London department store, then looked down into Sarah's green eyes.

"Bennett said to tell you that when you're finished here, he'd like to show you the chapel. He'll meet you over there." She made no move to pull her fingers out from under his; on the contrary, she parted them slightly, to let his fingers settle in between them. He thought this a gesture of charming innocence until he looked more closely at her eyes, and saw the spark of mischief, deep within.

"You little minx!" he said, as startled as he was pleased; the fiancée looked more than a little confused, but Sarah gave him her lovely laugh and withdrew her touch.

"Go talk to my brother, Harris," she told him.

"I hear, and obey, my lady," he replied, and abandoned the long gallery for the chapel.

It had begun to rain. Stuyvesant accepted an umbrella from Gallagher and reversed his steps along the path he and Sarah had followed the day before, returning from their lunch at the Dog and Pony: across the rose garden, through a gap in the hedge, and up a winding path that climbed the hill behind the lodge-house and the servants' quarters. The path was of white gravel gone green at the sides, firm even where it was sliced into a patch of steep hillside behind the kitchen garden.

When all the roof-tops but that of the chapel were below, the path widened into a level viewing platform, with a wrought iron bench and a railing that kept the viewer from tumbling face-first into the back of the servants' hall. Stuyvesant looked down over the drive's circle, then out over the valley for a minute, finally turning his back on the view to follow the smaller foot-path.

The white gravel led to three rustic steps through a lych gate, with a little cemetery of tilting headstones, many of them illegible with age. The chapel had a small wooden porch attached to it, with an iron loop in one corner for dripping umbrellas. He left his there, removed his hat, and turned the latch on the heavy wooden door.

It was warm inside from the morning services, the air fragrant with incense. The smell reminded him of the churches of his childhood, but this building looked more like the miniature cathedral of some exotic Eastern sect, ornate and brilliant. Every inch of the lower walls was decorated with tile or carvings, and the tiles on the floor had a random scatter of white spots, like petals blown from some flowering tree. Where the walls had neither tile nor wood, the glass was stained. Gold and lapis-blue, maroon and touches of bright green dominated. He turned on his heels and whistled, only afterwards thinking that a whistle perhaps wasn't an appropriate expression within a church.

"Extraordinary, isn't it?" Grey was half hidden by one of the church's four pillars, standing before a ten-foot-long carving on the wall, made of a wood so black it rendered the figures invisible. Black with age, Stuyvesant decided—even the metal strips used to mend a long crack near the bottom looked ancient.

"Feels like standing inside a tapestry," Stuyvesant said. "Down to the flowers underfoot."

Grey did not answer, just stood gazing into the carving. He looked bone-tired, with stains beneath his eyes; one day in London and he'd be ready to go back to Cornwall for sure, Stuyvesant thought, then wandered off to look at the church.

At the back, a high window faced west, in order to pick up the afternoon sun and splash it around inside. This afternoon the sun was nowhere in sight, but the window was still a swirl of blues and oranges surrounding a descending dove.

The altar at the front of the church, the east end, was covered with a golden cloth and had another dove on the wall behind it, this one carved of wood and intertwined with some flowering vine. The tall candles on the cloth of gold added the odor of honey to the underlying incense. Along the east wall he found a long Coptic-style painting of the flight into Egypt. When he had reached its end, he was back to where Bennett Grey still stood.

Grey had stretched up both hands and laid them on the carved wooden panel. His eyes were open but fixed on the black wood; his fingers, infinitely slow and light of touch, explored the surface; his lips moved as if puzzling out half-known words.

Stuyvesant went still.

Touchstone, Aldous Carstairs had called him. From what Stuyvesant had seen, this awful gift Grey had been given seemed less a matter of being drawn to gold than it was being repelled by dross, often with a violence that shook the man to his core. But for the moment, he could glimpse the coin's other face. As Grey's fingertips caressed the ancient shapes, his entire body seemed to rise up and yearn for the surface, as if a blind man were exploring the face of God. Stuyvesant found himself wondering what would happen if he were to touch Grey: Would an electric current smash Stuyvesant to the floor? Would Grey faint dead away? Would they both burst into flame?

Fanciful thoughts, dispersed when Grey spoke.

"You can talk," he said. "I'm not going to break."

"Glad to hear that. What's the carving?"

"In a strong light, you can see it's a composite story of various events in the life of Christ that involve water. In the left corner is the story of the loaves and fishes. This here"—he traced a finger across an oval shape—"is Christ walking on the water. And down there is the baptism."

Stuyvesant approached to peer closely at the panel, and now that they were pointed out to him, he could make out the figures. On a bright enough day, he might even be able to distinguish Jesus from a fish. "Looks old," he commented.

"Extremely. A seventeenth-century Hurleigh brought it back from the Holy Land, but it's a lot older than that. When this was carved, England was in the dark times after Rome withdrew. The man who carved this put his soul into it. There was something exquisitely personal to him about these stories. The marks his tool made in the wood pulsate with age and life and truth."

He made no move to pull away from the panel. Stuyvesant chose a pew and pulled his damp coat around him, wishing a man could smoke in church. It was restful, to sit in that quiet stone and wood tapestry with a man caught up in worship of the artistic spirit. Being denied tobacco, he pulled one of the substantial, much-used volumes from the pocket in front of him: *Book of Common Prayer.*

"I always thought prayer books were little things you could slip in your pocket," he commented.

"The old Duchess refused to wear reading glasses, but she couldn't read without them. So she had a special edition printed for the chapel, with large print."

Stuyvesant could sympathize with the old lady: He often squinted furiously rather than put his on. But the larger print in this one made it easy to read the words. Not that he could make much sense of the confusion of services and texts. He grew weary of incomprehension and slid the book back into its pocket, propping his elbows on the back of the pew and letting his eyes roam along the mingled birds and flowers behind the altar.

"St. Columbine's chapel," Grey remarked. "*Columba* is dove, for the Holy Spirit. The columbine flower is supposed to look like a flock of doves."

Stuyvesant couldn't see it himself, but they were pretty. He looked around, and found several more doves on airy flowers.

After a while, the Catholic in him began to feel the urge for confession—wasn't that what churches were for? First, he looked to see that the door was still closed, and even then, he spoke in a low voice.

"I may have found a way to get myself close to Bunsen."

"Mmm?"

"Don't know if you noticed, but he has a driver."

"He would. Sarah says he spends his life traveling across the country giving speeches. Having a driver would be the only way he'd get any sleep."

"Or keep from killing himself behind the wheel."

Grey took his hands off the panel. "You don't have to sound so regretful."

Stuyvesant gave a rueful laugh. "Yeah, that would solve a number of our problems." He gave a half-guilty glance at the altar, and wondered if that might be taken for a prayer. "But the driver's not much of a mechanic, and he doesn't look like a bodyguard. It seemed to me like Bunsen could use both."

"So, what, you're going to put in for the driver's job?"

"I might have to encourage things a little."

Grey had left the black panel at last, moving to a small framed painting of a dark-skinned mother and infant sitting on a donkey. He turned and frowned at Stuyvesant.

"By kidnapping the driver? Cornering him in a dark alley?"

"I won't go anywhere near him."

Grey picked up on the faint stress on Stuyvesant's first word. "The Major," he said in a flat voice.

"He has resources I don't."

"You'd be party to that?"

"I'm not a party to anything, just asking for information. He's not going to put the driver in the hospital or anything. If nothing else, it would be stupid—Bunsen's a clever boy, he might get suspicious."

"You don't think Bunsen has a whole platoon of drivers to choose from?"

"He may. In which case it'll be back to the drawing board."

Grey studied him, but whatever he saw in Stuyvesant's face satisfied him, and he removed his reproving gaze, continuing his drift towards the front of the church. Once there, he tried to kneel on a cushion before the railing, but his left leg rebelled, leaving him to prop himself up sideways, arms stretched out across the altar rail for balance.

"Laura and Bunsen sure make a handsome pair," Stuyvesant sent in the direction of Grey's back.

After a time, long enough to recite a quick Hail Mary, Grey answered. "I am all right, Stuyvesant. Honestly. She was the love of my life, but that life, as I told you, is over. Laura has moved on, I have moved away, and I will never approach her as anything other than a friend; never. Please don't worry. And you're right; they are an extraordinarily handsome couple. Extraordinarily gifted as well."

"So, what did you think of Bunsen?"

Grey struggled out of his uncomfortable perch to sit facing the church. "Are you asking as Harris Stuyvesant the man, or the Bureau of Investigation agent?"

"I'm not asking you to do my work for me, Grey. If he's not the man I'm after, I'll deal with it."

"Well, in either case, I can't tell you if he's your terrorist or not. I will say, he's every bit as magnetic as I'd expected. Bunsen's the kind of man one would either shoot at sight, or follow off a cliff."

He was talking about Laura, Stuyvesant could hear it in his voice. He was saying that he understood Laura's commitment to the man, understood it with all his mind.

And it was true: Bunsen's blazing charisma and intelligence made him a man either to follow absolutely, or to rise up and murder; few people would respond to him with any lesser emotions. Even Stuyvesant had felt the man's magnetism, although he'd spent so much of his life in the company of one charismatic crook or politician after another, he would have thought himself immune.

"No, er, turmoil? Dissonance?"

"The little time I spent with him, he felt as true as a bell."

Which, Stuyvesant reminded himself, didn't mean Bunsen wasn't bad through; it merely meant that his nature was not at war with itself. Having met the man, he'd have said the same thing himself.

"Okay, well, thanks. And, Bennett? Thank you, for all your help. I know this trip has been tough on you, and I'm grateful."

Bennett Grey nodded, then said, "There's one more thing you need to see, here at Hurleigh. One more exquisite Hurleigh treasure."

He led Stuyvesant out of the chapel and deeper into the woods. There were more of the blue flowers, but unlike near the Peak, where they had been scattered among trees, here they filled a clearing, brighter than the sky. "The Hurleigh bluebell wood."

Before them was half an acre of solid, intense blue: summer's day blue; high-mountain-lake blue. Helen's eyes blue.

No, thought Stuyvesant: the Hurleigh unicorn doesn't live under the white rose, or even in the chapel. It lives here, with the elves.

The two men stood there for a long time, listening to the rain dripping off the trees and the umbrella over their heads.

"That girl I knew," Stuyvesant said. "Her name was Helen. Her favorite flower was the larkspur, that same color. She'd have loved this. And yeah, you were right," he told Grey. "She was a blonde."

Stuyvesant flipped open the hidden compartment of his cigarette case and took out the picture with the lock of hair pinned to its corner. The pin had gone rusty, he noticed as he unfolded the photograph. He gave it to Grey.

"You loved her," Grey said, studying her face.

"Yeah. And all the other stuff you said, too."

Grey handed the picture back. "What happened to her?"

Stuyvesant concentrated on putting the photograph away, tucking in a straying golden hair. When it was safely away in his breast pocket he looked at the bluebells, the trees rising out of them. "Summer of 1920. Guy drives a cart and horse up to the front door of J. P. Morgan's bank, corner of Wall and Broad streets, walks away. A few minutes later, on the stroke of noon, a hundred pounds of dynamite packed inside five hundred pounds of scrap metal goes off in the cart. Nothing left of the horse but his feet. Thirty-some people dead then and there, hundreds bleeding, maimed. Only explanation given was a circular dropped into a nearby mailbox, talking about political prisoners and signed by the 'American Anarchist Fighters.' This was five days after Sacco and Vanzetti were indicted, and we still haven't arrested anyone for it."

He cleared his throat, staring at sky-blue but seeing an acre of scarlet and flesh, floating scraps of white paper and a shimmering frost of broken glass over everything. "Helen," he began, and had to clear his throat again. "Helen was a secretary, worked across the street from Morgan's bank. I was meeting her for lunch, but I was running late. Five minutes. Just five minutes. She was waiting for me in the foyer. Big glass walls. She bled to death before I got there."

The two men stood and listened to the rain. After a while, they made their way back down the rain-soaked path to the house, their arms occasionally brushing under the sheltering umbrella. They ate lunch, then took their leave of Hurleigh.

To Stuyvesant, the high part of the day, better even than the bluebells, was knowing that he was not saying good-bye to Grey's sister.

BOOK FOUR

London

Chapter Fifty-One

THE DRIVE TO LONDON was long and hard, coming on top of a number of long, hard days. In the car outside Hurleigh House, with Stuyvesant's hand on the key, he'd glanced over at Grey and asked, "I don't suppose you want to drive?"

"I don't suppose you want to end up in the ditch?" Grey replied.

Stuyvesant pressed the starter and put the Ford into gear.

It rained hard the whole way, and one of the side-curtains dripped no matter what adjustments he made to it. Oncoming traffic loomed up at him from the gloom, and on the far side of Oxford, he got tangled in a convoy of Army lorries bearing down on London. Darkness fell early, and the head-lamps turned the sheet of raindrops into a tunnel, hypnotic to a man with as little sleep as Stuyvesant had managed; he fought it by driving faster than he should, to keep himself on edge.

Grey slept, murmuring and twitching.

Stuyvesant made it as far as London before he got lost. After casting back and forth for the main road and failing to come across it, he pulled to the side of a silent row of warehouses and took out his map and flash-light.

"You want directions?" Grey's voice came.

"You have them?" Stuyvesant snapped.

"If you go two or three streets up, you'll find a big road. Go right."

Stuyvesant threw the map into the back and ground the gears.

Three streets ahead he found the main road, and turned right.

Traffic was light this rainy Sunday evening, although they came through inexplicable knots of cars and taxis, separated by dark emptiness.

"What street is the hotel on?" Grey asked.

Stuyvesant told him, adding its nearest large cross-street; he felt Grey nod.

They came through the fog to another build-up of street-lamps and traffic, with a few fast-walking pedestrians under umbrellas. Was it just his imagination, or had London's tensions ratcheted up a few notches since he'd driven away on Friday? It might have been simply the contrast between the bucolic setting of Hurleigh House and this cold, ugly labyrinth of stone and brick, but the people scurrying under umbrellas and folded newspapers all seemed about to go for one another's throats. He glanced to his side and found that Grey had shut his eyes again, although he was not sleeping: Under the noise of the rain and the engine, Stuyvesant could hear his passenger humming tunelessly, as if attempting to drown out the echoes inside his skull.

"I really think I ought to take you straight to Paddington," he said.

Grey's eyes opened, then jerked wide and Stuyvesant looked back at the road with his foot already stamping at the brakes, nearly sending them both through the wind-screen. A taxi ahead had clipped the fender of a private motorcar, and the two drivers were standing chest to chest, drenched and screaming, given wide berth by the other inhabitants. The taxi driver was wearing a cloth cap and an oil-cloth slicker; his opponent wore a bowler, a thick black overcoat, and leather gloves; both had bellies mounding their disparate clothing.

All of a sudden the two men tangled, a burst of fury as vicious as a dog-fight. Stuyvesant cursed and fumbled with the door-latch, but just as suddenly they separated, stalking off to their separate cars and pulling away with much racing of engines and spinning of tires.

"A classic illustration of the meeting of worker and management," Stuyvesant commented, an uneasy joke.

Grey said nothing.

They found the hotel, just short of four hours after leaving Hurleigh House. Stuyvesant turned the final corner, pulled over to the entrance, and dragged up the hand-brake. His hands vibrated with fatigue and tension, and he nearly fell onto the street when the doorman opened the car door.

"Good evening, sir," the desk man said.

"Not a damned thing good about it, except we made it in one piece."

"A terrible night indeed, sir. Would you like me to have your coat hung in the drying room overnight?"

Stuyvesant stripped off the garment, the right half of which was sodden through from the drip, and turned to see Grey coming through the door, moving as if he wasn't at all certain about the relationship between his feet and the ground.

"Do you by any chance have a room for my friend here?" he asked the desk man. The man's face brightened.

"Certainly, sir. We can put your friend in the room next to yours."

"That's very convenient."

"Yes, well, people seem to be keeping away from London just at present." The man held out the pen for Grey to sign. "The dining room will be open shortly, if you two gentlemen would care for dinner."

"Mostly I need a drink." Stuyvesant didn't need to consult Grey about the matter—he'd emptied his flask long before.

"The saloon parlor is open as well," the man said, "and there's a fire."

"Show us the way," Stuyvesant said, and they followed a bell boy into the quiet warm cave.

They asked for a bottle, and pulled their chairs close to the hot fire. Both men slugged down the first glass. Slowly, life returned. The vibrating sensation faded in Stuyvesant's arms; Grey's color improved until it no longer matched his name.

Half an hour later, with less than a dozen words exchanged, a man Stuyvesant recognized as one of the waiters came in and offered to set up a table for them there before the fire.

The waiter said, "There's a piping hot cockaleekie soup, if you're so inclined."

"Bring us a couple bowls of that." Stuyvesant was not particularly interested in food, but it might help settle their nerves.

An hour later, the two men were dry, fed, comforted, and half drunk. Stuyvesant led the way upstairs, stripped off his clothes, upended his valise in the middle of the floor and dug out his revolver, sticking it under the pillow, then crawled into bed after it.

He was asleep in seconds.

The telephone beside his bed rang at six o'clock in the morning. He fumbled around, picked it up, and immediately broke the connection, without speaking.

Some time later, he heard a rustle from the doorway. He roused just enough to be sure no one was actually coming in, then put his head back on the pillow and took his hand out from under it.

At seven-thirty, one eye came open. No bells, no rustles, no rain, just the sound of traffic two streets over. He squinted at the clock sitting on the bedside table, scrubbed at his face, and pulled the bed-clothes back up to his ears.

Then he recalled the rustle at the doorway in the early hours of the morning, and he threw back the covers and went to see.

The hotel envelope contained a piece of hotel stationery, on which was written:

Mr Carstairs requests that you telephone
him at your earliest convenience.

Stuyvesant sat down on the bed, picked up the phone, and gave Carstairs' number.

"Carstairs," came the familiar smooth voice—the man himself, not his assistant.

"You wanted me to call?"

"Perhaps this afternoon, if that is convenient. I should have some information for you by then."

"But why—oh. I mean, you asked me to 'phone you?" Stuyvesant said irritably. This damned language: *Call* here meant to show up.

"Yes. Did it go well in Gloucestershire?"

"Progress was made. You really want me to go into it on the telephone?"

"I merely need to know if the proposal you made to me still stands."

"So far."

"Because I am led to believe that our friend had some considerable difficulties getting back to Town yesterday."

"What a pity," Stuyvesant said cheerfully.

"As you say. So, will you come to my office this afternoon? Say, two o'clock?"

"I'd like my list back as soon as possible."

"I have a meeting this morning. If you want the list before that, you can come to the office at your convenience and get it from Mr. Lakely."

"That's your assistant?" Pasty face, nervous eyes.

"My secretary, yes."

"Tell him I'll be there."

Carstairs simply hung up. Stuyvesant held the earpiece out and stared at it for a minute, then laid it in the hooks. Rude bastard.

He picked up the telephone again to ask for a pot of coffee. "Maybe you should send two cups," he added. "And could you bring me up the morning papers? Thanks."

He dry-washed his face again, walked next door to use the toilet, then bent over the heap of clothes he'd dumped out of the valise the night before. He found his pajama bottoms and put those on, then his robe, and a knock came at the door.

He dropped the armful of clothing on the bed, glanced to make sure the Colt wasn't lying in plain view, and opened the door to a man with a tray. The man greeted him with the news that it should be a pretty day, put the tray on the desk, laid the newspapers out beside it, accepted Stuyvesant's coin, and left. The door was caught before it shut, and Grey came in, fully dressed and shaved, the dark circles under his eyes slightly less exaggerated than the night before.

"I got you some coffee," Stuyvesant told him. Grey poured two cups and settled in a chair by the window with the papers while Stuyvesant made a rapid sort of his clothes, hanging up two unworn shirts, bundling most of the others into a bag to be cleaned, and tossing the empty valise on top of the wardrobe.

He took his cup and the other chair, glancing over the headlines, but they were much as before: the *Times* controlled in its reporting of impending doom and chaos, the other papers in varying degrees of panic.

"You're seeing the Major today?" Grey asked.

Stuyvesant looked into the green eyes, as calm as a *Times* headline. "Yeah, this afternoon. This morning I have to go look up some names in the library."

"Anything I can help you with?"

"Thanks for the offer. If I get stuck, I'll call on you."

"Feel free. I plan to spend the day lost in the stacks of booksellers—it's the one thing I crave, in Cornwall. We'll both need alcohol by late afternoon. Shall we meet back here and go for a drink? I'd suggest a place, but between the bombing and natural attrition, those I knew may no longer be in existence."

"Here is good. Leave a message at the desk if there's a change."

"Fine. And, Harris?"

"Yeah."

"Tell the Major that the price of my assistance is that no innocents are hurt."

"Innocents? You mean the driver? I told you, we're not going to touch him. The most that happens is he gets fired."

"The Major may have other ideas. But if ever he requires my help again, this is my price."

"You sure you want to make that offer?"

Grey fixed him with a pitying look. "The Major controls my sister's fate. Do you honestly think I have any choice?"

"Shit. Look, Grey, I . . ." What was there to say? "God, you must hate me."

"I did, at first. And then you said you had only just met the Major, and I could see that you meant well."

Most damning of phrases: He meant well. And Grey knew, that first day—five minutes after they'd met, and Grey had seen it all coming. Felt the trap closing on him.

No wonder the poor bastard looked twice his age.

"Sarah's not to know," Grey said. "She must never suspect that her actions brought the Major back onto me."

Stuyvesant swallowed, and nodded.

Grey picked up his cup and drank the last of his coffee, folded the newspapers, and went to the door.

"Grey?" The small man stopped, his hand on the knob. "I'm sorry. I really am. I'd never have agreed to any of this, if I'd known."

The green eyes met his. "That is why I don't hate you." And he left.

Hell and damnation, thought Stuyvesant. I sail across here with my nice tidy problem and end up putting that poor bastard's nuts in Aldous Carstairs' hand. Oh, Carstairs would have found a way at Grey sooner or later, but still, here he was, caught between his sister and that snake-pit of a Project.

And the only solution he could see to Grey's dilemma was the Gordian one: Grey could always cut his own throat.

Or Carstairs' . . .

Stuyvesant poured the last of the coffee into his cup, rescued his cigarette case from his jacket pocket, and went to the small window-seat overlooking the street, where he sat smoking and thinking about life, love, work, and the man who'd just left. Bunsen and Laura, Grey and Carstairs, and Sarah: Things were getting just a bit complicated for his taste, but he couldn't for the life of him see how to strip them down to a controllable level, not at the moment.

First things first. Number one, get Bunsen's driver out of the picture.

Number two, get Grey on the train to Cornwall, and hope Carstairs was too busy to go after him.

Three, figure out just how closely Sarah Grey was involved with Bunsen's criminal activities. Which meant figuring out Bunsen's criminal activities, as well.

And four, sometime today—maybe after his meeting with Aldous Carstairs, to take the bad taste out of his mouth—ring Sarah Grey and ask her for dinner later in the week, trying to pull Laura Hurleigh into it as well.

But of absolute priority, before anything else, he thought, scowling at the disgusting fag-end in his hand: Locate some decent American cigarettes in this benighted war zone of a city.

Chapter Fifty-Two

AT 2:25 MONDAY AFTERNOON, Aldous Carstairs sat at his desk eyeing the big American across from him. He wanted to murder the man. Personally.

How much effort over the years had he, Aldous Carstairs, put into Bennett Grey? How many hours, how much painstaking thought, had he devoted to penetrating Grey's defenses, and he'd never come anywhere *near* what this man had in a handful of days. He'd positively *bled* to make Grey trust him, talk to him, and in all those months, what he'd been given would barely fill a page. And this great clumsy Yank, this idiotic thug of a Bureau agent, had come bumbling in and had Grey eating out of his hand.

The whole thing was so bloody unfair, Carstairs wanted to pull his automatic pistol from his desk drawer and empty it into the sneaky blue-eyed oaf's manly chest.

But he sat calmly and listened, showing no indication of the sour burn of loathing, making the occasional note. He wondered what Stuyvesant was failing to tell him about the doings at Hurleigh House—and there was another source of indignation, that Harris Stuyvesant should be welcomed to that ancient place with open arms while he, the man working day and night to preserve the system under which the Hurleighs flourished, was left behind in London, knowing that if he turned up at the Hurleigh door, he would be sent around to the trade entrance.

He shook himself mentally and returned to what the man was saying: that he wished he'd been able to find out what business Bunsen had with the Duke.

Well, Carstairs thought, at least I'm ahead of you there.

"Did you get anything on the driver?" Stuyvesant asked.

Carstairs picked up a thin file and slid it across the desk for him to read. The American pulled out a pair of tortoise-shell reading glasses—thank God there was *some* weakness to the man!—and scanned the pages.

As he had begun to suspect on Saturday night, the American was indeed a better operative then he'd first appeared—either that or he was freakishly lucky. In the space of forty-eight hours, he had not only brought Grey over to his side, he had befriended the major players in their little drama, identified a path into Bunsen's organization, and laid the groundwork for putting the plan into action. The list of Bunsen's contacts, which Stuyvesant had retrieved that morning, included a number of important politicians, financiers, and newspapermen—to be fair, one could not fault a foreigner for not knowing all of them. Certainly, between the time the man had picked up the list and the time he'd walked back in a quarter of an hour ago, he'd done a good job of bringing himself up to speed regarding the Empire's key players.

The man's unexpected competence was both reassuring and worrying. He would need to be kept on a tight lead.

Carstairs tapped his pen on the blotter in a methodical tattoo, then caught himself, and reached instead for the ornate box, given him by Benito Mussolini, in which he kept his cigarillos.

"After we spoke yesterday," he said, "I set enquiries under way about Mr. James Balham, born James Bosch. And just before you arrived, I received that report. It would seem although our Mr. Balham works for Richard Bunsen, he is not what one might call a pure revolutionary. He enjoys regular visits to one particular unlicensed house of chance. Gambling," he clarified for the man on the other side of the desk.

"How regular?"

"Most weeks, when he's in London. Generally Monday or Tuesday nights."

"How close are your ties to the police?"

"I have ties."

"Could you arrange to have the place raided, while Balham is there?"

"Given half a day, I could."

"Do it."

"If it's tonight, it may be too late, but I'll see what I can do."

"But make it clear to your colleagues, Balham isn't to be harmed. Like I said yesterday, we don't want to kill the guy. And I should tell you, Grey won't like it one little bit if his sister tells him that Richard's poor driver had his skull cracked."

"Keeping Captain Grey happy is not terribly high on my list of priorities, but in fact, there is no need to take a, hmm, physical approach to the problem. If nothing else, it lacks finesse. I shall speak to my city colleagues as soon as you have left."

"Okay, another thing. I've been thinking about some letters I saw in Bunsen's car. Threat letters."

"Of what sort?"

"The usual thing, vague and badly spelled. We'll bash your pretty face, you better shut up if you know what's good for you. Generic, so although they have his home address and know where he's been speaking, they don't seem to know about his private life. There's nothing about Laura Hurleigh, for one thing. But he's kept the letters, which means he's concerned. So I stuck another one in the post today, with similar sentiments, directly connected to the upcoming Strike. However, I think it would be a good idea to throw in an actual physical threat, some time in the next two days, preferably when one or the other of Bunsen's circle is with me, so no one could possibly find me to blame. Could you arrange that?"

"I don't imagine you want Mr. Bunsen actually to come to harm?"

"I was thinking along the lines of a brick through his office window or a rotten tomato thrown at his car. He's cold-blooded enough that it might not scare him, but when Lady Laura hears about it, she'll urge him to take precautions."

"You being the precaution."

"After yesterday, he'll be convinced Balham's useless as a chauffeur. If we can convince him that a bodyguard isn't a bad idea, just until the Strike is past—hey, presto! Why not hire a man who can do both jobs at once? Okay, that's all I needed. Are we all set, then?"

"I have something for you, Agent Stuyvesant. That meeting between Richard Bunsen and the Duke, yesterday morning? Would you like to know the purpose of it?" Carstairs examined the end of his cigar.

Stuyvesant paused, his body half lifted from the seat of his chair. "Okay, I'll bite."

"As you may know, ten days from now, the General Council of the Trades Union Congress are due to convene here in London, for the formal vote to approve the General Strike."

Stuyvesant took his hands off the chair's arms: another of Carstairs' "oblique" responses.

"Before that, on Monday—a week today—Mr. Baldwin has set a tentative appointment with the Miners' Union representatives—that is, if no settlement to the dispute has been reached in the interim. And before that meeting, this coming Thursday, the Miners' Union and the owners will meet here in London, at the insistence of Mr. Baldwin."

"Time is short; I get that."

"Yesterday morning, Mr. Bunsen was asked to convey a joint message, from Prime Minister Baldwin and from Herbert Smith, president of the Miners' Union, to the Duke of Hurleigh, asking if the Duke might both oversee and provide a venue for an informal and private—the emphasis being on private—conference between the Union and the mine owners, that they might talk like, hmm, reasonable men, outside the glare of the newsmen's flash-bulbs.

"This is, I repeat, a private undertaking, about which very few people know. I need hardly add that were you to let this information out, you would find yourself asked to leave the country immediately. The entire purpose is to allow Mr. Baldwin and a few chosen representatives of both sides of the dispute to meet as gentlemen, without the need for speech-making and posturing."

Stuyvesant slowly crossed his legs, staring at Carstairs. "I'll be damned."

"Quite."

"Whose idea was that?"

"Does it matter?"

"It might. When do they propose to meet?"

"Friday afternoon. At Hurleigh House."

"What, *this* Friday? Four days from now?"

"Correct."

"It takes people in this country four days to decide to offer you a cup of tea. You're sure about this?"

"Yes."

"Shit. I don't have a chance."

"If you say so."

The man wore a look of disdain, as if to say, *You never had a chance*. Bastard, Stuyvesant thought; I'll show you up if it's the last thing I do. "Well, I'll certainly never get it done sitting here. I'd better get to work."

"As had I. Is there anything else I can do for you?"

Stuyvesant stood before the desk, fiddling with the coins in his pocket, then cocked his head at the other man. "Yeah," he said, flat-faced. "You could take care of this damned miners' dispute. It's making my life hell."

The black-eyed man said, "I shall see what I can do about the matter, Agent Stuyvesant."

Outside of the non-descript building that housed Aldous Carstairs, Harris Stuyvesant stopped and said aloud, "Finesse, my ass." He hawked loudly and spat.

Feeling somewhat better, he headed for the Underground station that would take him back to the hotel.

Grey had not returned from his raid on the bookshops of London, so Stuyvesant, after eyeing the bottle on his dresser, sent for coffee and settled in with a copy of the *Workers' Weekly* that he'd picked up from a street vendor. The Communist rag was nearing hysteria, trying to work its readers into a slavering frenzy of outrage.

From what Stuyvesant had seen on the London streets, it wasn't going to take a whole lot more effort.

The coffee was gone and he'd worked his way through half a

dozen other papers when Stuyvesant heard sounds from the next room. A few minutes later, there was a tap at the door.

"C'mon in!" Stuyvesant called. He pulled off his reading glasses to examine his visitor; oddly, Grey looked no more exhausted than he had that morning. "How're you doing?"

"Books are restorative," Grey said. "They're honest, which is rare in life. I now have a year's reading material on its way to Cornwall. And your meeting—no, don't bother, I can see that it went about as you expected. I had lunch with my sister—who sends her greetings, by the way, and asked you to 'phone her tonight." He smiled at Stuyvesant's reaction. "Shall we adjourn for refreshment? I spotted one of the places whose owner kept a good bitter, about ten minutes' walk."

From the smell of him, Grey had paused for refreshment at least once already, and the air of deliberate good cheer seemed to go about as deep as a papier mâché mask. But as he'd told Sarah, alcohol was just a pain-killer, and if Grey wanted the pain deadened, Stuyvesant couldn't hold him to blame. He shoveled the newspapers aside and grabbed his overcoat.

The rain was light, little more than a mist filling the street. They followed quiet side-streets, a zig-zag that kept them off the main thoroughfares, and the sidewalks were so sparsely populated that the two men could walk shoulder to shoulder most of the time.

"I liked London, when I came here after the War," Stuyvesant said, breaking the silence. The moment the words left his mouth he wondered if they were a mistake, since the days after the War were hardly a sympathetic memory for his companion. But Grey nodded in agreement.

"Before the War, I had a friend whose family lived near here. The summer before he and I went up to Oxford, I spent a month with him, and we used to walk all over the City, letting ourselves be seduced by her charms. I don't imagine New York to be at all like London."

"There's areas that feel surprisingly similar, but on the whole, it's true, New York runs in a different gear. Although I was thinking earlier that London feels a little like downtown Manhattan on a hot day, this time around. You've got some angry people here."

"The whole City seems to be standing at the edge of an abyss," Grey agreed.

"And then some of those papers I was looking at make the whole thing sound like a lark, grown men playing at train drivers and dressing up as policem—"

He was cut off as Grey's outstretched arm slammed across his chest, keeping him from stepping down onto the roadway. "What's this madman up to?"

The madman in question was behind the wheel of a large, elderly motor lorry, and having a problem with its gears. The engine roared as the driver—the would-be driver—clamped down on the accelerator; it gave a horrible clash and strangling noise, leapt forward six feet to precisely where the American had been about to step, coughed, and died. In the quiet could be heard the sound of a young man cursing.

Stuyvesant walked around and yanked back the lorry's raincurtain. The startled driver looked like a schoolboy, no more than eighteen; his companion might have been twenty.

"What the hell are you two idiots doing?" Stuyvesant demanded. "You could have killed us."

The boy stared at the two men, and Stuyvesant could see the sharp realization come into his eyes. "Lord!" he said in plummy accents. "I was so engrossed—I'm ever so sorry, I just, these gears, they're like nothing under the sun."

"So what are you doing with it? If this is a prank, I could think of better things to steal."

"Oh no," said the boy. "It's no prank. We're volunteer drivers. For the Strike? London will starve without help, and we promised we'd be able to drive this thing by the first of May."

His passenger leaned forward. "We were just given the keys and told where it was. At this rate, when the Strike begins we won't have got beyond Regent Street."

"There appears to be something wrong with the gear-box," the driver complained.

Stuyvesant ran his hand through his hair, replaced his hat, and glanced at Grey. "You mind if I sort this out so they don't kill someone?"

"If one of Sarah's crew spots you assisting a blackleg, it'll be all over for you," Grey pointed out with amusement.

"I'll risk it. Move over," he ordered the driver.

The two lads perched on the other seat and Stuyvesant climbed behind the wheel. The truck—lorry—was old but its cleanliness suggested it had been cared for, and indeed, when he pushed the starter, it caught readily enough, considering how violently it had died moments before. He worked the clutch, glanced around to make sure he wasn't going to mow down any pedestrians himself, and gave it just a little gas. The lorry moved down the quiet street, smooth as cream.

He circled the block, showing the two would-be heroes what he was doing and describing the differences between the motors they were used to and the heavy-duty engine they faced here. He then traded seats to repeat the circuit, two sides with one lad at the wheel, the remainder with the other. At the end he climbed out and interrupted their thanks with the statement that they had a friend of the Miners' Union to thank for their strike-breaking skills. They gaped at him, open-mouthed.

"Scram, now," he ordered. "Get it out of here."

The gears clashed and with a race of the engine and a juddering motion, the vehicle moved away. It didn't die, and the driver didn't run anyone down in the first hundred yards.

Stuyvesant brushed off his hands. "Those kids are going to be hugely disappointed if the Strike gets settled before they can save London from starvation and barbarism."

"The Strike won't be settled," Grey replied.

"You don't think they'll find a compromise?"

"The government, especially Churchill, have been eating humiliation since last summer, and are telling themselves that if a stand is not made, the Bolsheviks will be at the door. And the Unions persist in their starry-eyed illusions. They'll strike because they have to, but they won't win."

"Your sister wouldn't like to hear you say that."

"Nonetheless, it is true. Why should a London bus driver lose his job to protect a Yorkshire coal miner? Coal is dirty and faraway and a dying industry anyway, and no urban worker is going to sacrifice his own livelihood just to nurse it along for a few more years."

"So our boys there will have their chance to save the city."

Grey snorted, a sentiment Stuyvesant could agree with.

They found Grey's remembered house of refreshment and passed an enjoyable couple of hours there, drinking just enough to maintain a degree of open-armed amiability without actually descending into drunkenness. By eight o'clock, they adjourned to the restaurant down the street and polished off three satisfactory courses and a quantity of more than satisfactory wine. By ten o'clock, Stuyvesant was prepared to return to the hotel, but Grey looked at his pocket-watch and suggested a night-cap.

Stuyvesant shook his head, then stopped at the spinning of the room: French wine was stronger than he'd thought.

"Christ," he said. "Your sister wanted me to 'phone her."

"Do it tomorrow."

"She said tonight."

"So do it from here."

Stuyvesant thought about it, and decided that he might as well. He asked for a telephone and dialed the number she had given him. When her voice responded, he opened his mouth and only then realized that he was too drunk for this.

"Sorry," he told her.

"I beg your—Harris? Is that you?"

"I think so."

"You sound—have you been drinking?"

"I fear so, my lady."

She laughed, and the sound traveled down his spine to stir some interesting sensations. "Are you sober enough that you'll remember this conversation in the morning? Because if not, I'm going to ring off now."

"I could never forget words shared with you."

"You are indeed feeling no pain," she said. But she did not sound resentful about it, so he took courage and went on.

"I've been entertaining your hollow-legged brother."

"He didn't go home to Cornwall, then?"

"He has not."

"Damn," she swore. "He said he was thinking about it, when I saw him at lunch-time."

"Well," Stuyvesant said, "he did not. He spent the day buying books."

"I know. Is he all right?"

"He is feeling no pain."

"I can imagine. Has he told you when he's leaving?"

"No."

"London will not do him any good at all. Oh well. In any case, Harris, I asked my brother to have you 'phone so I could offer to show you the women's clinic Laura and I run. Since you expressed an interest."

"I'd like that. And come to lunch with me before we visit your ladies. Or to dinner afterwards. Or both. And," he added, belatedly remembering the plan he'd laid before Carstairs, "if your friend Laura wants to join us, I'd be happy to see her, as well."

"I'm awfully busy tomorrow. Would Wednesday do?"

"I shall pine for you until Wednesday," he said, and the laugh came again. He wasn't happy about delaying another twenty-four hours, but surely by Wednesday he could convince Grey to retreat to his quiet corner of the world, leaving Stuyvesant to focus on his job. Tomorrow Grey might still be here, and be tempted into joining any luncheon that involved Laura Hurleigh. A complication Stuyvesant would rather avoid, just now. "Wednesday would be superb."

"Give me your number and I'll ring you in the morning to say when and where. And I'll let you know then if Laura will join us."

He retrieved the hotel's number and read it out to her, then said, "I could 'phone you, if you'd rather."

"Oh no. This way I don't have to wonder if you've remembered tonight's conversation. Good night, Harris. Take good care of my brother."

"Good night, Sarah," he said, but she had already gone.

He paid the check for the dinner, and they went for a night-cap. By the time the pubs closed, they'd had quite a few.

Chapter Fifty-Three

AT ONE-THIRTY IN THE MORNING, Harris Stuyvesant walked through his hotel room, strewing garments across the floor and furniture, to fall between the bed-clothes. He slept there like the drunken man he was until the hounds of hell began to clamor at his door at some ungodly hour the following morning.

He fell out of bed, fumbled his dressing gown out from the back of the bath-room door, and snugged the tie around him as if it might squeeze his brain into action. He went to the door, running his hands vigorously over his bristled face; the pounding came again, louder than ever.

"Jesus wept," he grumbled. "Give a man a chance."

The man in the hallway was someone he might have known, later in the day and with a pot of coffee in him. As it was, Stuyvesant screwed up his face against the light and wondered where he'd seen this scrawny, balding customer in the shiny-kneed suit before.

"Major Carstairs requires your presence," the stranger informed him. After a minute, Stuyvesant's brain began to turn over, reluctant as a winter engine. Carstairs: a weedy male secretary in his outer office; *this* weedy male secretary.

He squinted at the intruder. "Lackey?"

"Lakely," the fellow corrected him.

"Right. Carstairs. Wants to see me."

"Yes. It is urgent."

"Yeah, I sorta guessed. What's it about?"

"I wouldn't know."

Stuyvesant eyed him, knowing it was a lie, knowing too that the man wasn't about to tell him.

"Twenty minutes," he told the secretary. "I'll meet you down-stairs."

"It is truly urgent."

"Twenty-five minutes, then." He shut the door in the man's face and stood for a while trying to rub some life into his skin. What the hell had he drunk last night, anyway? The damn Prohibition regula-tions meant he was out of practice with tying one on. God. Coffee.

He spoke an order into the telephone and went to set the cold taps running into the bath-tub, glad to find the hall-way empty. He yelped as he stepped in, scrubbed himself until he was shivering, then pulled out the plug and exchanged cold water for hot. At the end of it his skin was awake and his hands steady enough for a razor.

A light but insistent rapping at the bath-room door reminded him that he had asked for coffee, so he slung a towel around his hips and cracked the door open. Bennett Grey stood in the hall-way, a tray in his hand. He eyed Stuyvesant's garment.

"A good thing I intercepted the young lady with your coffee," he said. "She'd have been rather taken aback."

Stuyvesant glanced down. "Young ladies need some kind of thrill to make the job worth-while," he said. "I hope you don't expect me to give you her tip."

"No, just a cup of my own will do nicely, thank you."

Stuyvesant retreated to his shaving mug. Grey balanced the tray on the edge of the tub and poured, placing one cup within reach of the man at the looking-glass. The other he raised to his lips, leaning against the frame of the open door. The green eyes traveled over the American's bare back, taking in the stripe from the pool cue, reviewing as well the signs of scars going back to childhood. Belt, he'd thought in the Oxford Turkish baths. The buckle end, he now decided.

"Is it going yellow yet?" Stuyvesant asked. Grey transferred his gaze to the mirror, noticing the shadows of metal shard that had hit in a spray, from chest to temple.

"A little greenish around the edges. The lad sure caught you a good one."

"I deserved it, turning my back on him."

"Lucky he didn't land it across your neck."

Stuyvesant grunted, squinted at the bloodshot eyes in the glass, then moved his gaze over to the reflection of the clean, rested-looking person in the doorway. "Why don't you look as pissing awful as I do? You put away as much as I did, last night."

"Because I haven't tried to sober up. Haven't been truly sober since Robbie's brother drove me to Penzance five days ago, come to that."

"You drink like that all the time?"

"Heavens no, I'll climb back onto the wagon when I go home."

"I don't envy you your head then."

"Robbie's mother is the local witch, she has a brew that takes the top of your skull gently off and sets it back down again. I believe it's mostly opium—she has a suspicious fondness for poppies in her herbaceous border. Was that a summons from the Major?"

Stuyvesant paused to pick up the cup, which had cooled enough that he could swallow half of it at one go. He did so, then started on his left cheek. "He's got a burr in his blanket, sent his secretary to fetch me, but the guy wouldn't tell me what it was about. You want me to 'phone here as soon as I find out what's going on? What train were you planning on catching?"

"I had thought to stay on another day."

Stuyvesant met the green eyes in the mirror, razor poised over his neck. "Why?"

"My dear Stuyvesant, a person would think you were trying to get rid of me."

"Why the hell would you want to stay in a place that makes you drink in order to keep from screaming?"

"Perhaps to prove to myself that I can."

Stuyvesant shook his head. He finished without shedding too much blood, drained his cup, took one bite of the cold toast the kitchen had sent along, then went to find a clean shirt.

As he did his tie, he glanced out the window (raining again) then at the other man.

"Grey, you don't have anything to prove. You've got more guts than any ten men I know. There's no shame at going home to Cornwall, no more than a fish should feel at needing to be in the water."

"A noble speech, my friend," Grey said lightly. "And I will go back, soon. Just not today."

Light dawned in Stuyvesant's head. "It's Laura, isn't it?"

"I beg your pardon?" Grey said, but not quickly enough.

"It's to prove yourself to her."

"Certainly not—"

"Ah, damn it, I should've known. Bennett, she's moved on. It doesn't matter if you sprout wings and fly, she's with Bunsen now, she's not going to come back to you."

Grey's face went cold with fury, and he clattered his cup and saucer down on the tray before turning for the door. "Ring me when you've found what the Major wants," he ordered, and was gone.

"Shit," Stuyvesant said into the empty room.

Halfway across London, Stuyvesant began to wonder if the weedy secretary's appearance might not be a disguise. Certainly it was belied by his driving, which was that of a race-car driver, dodging in and out of traffic and using his horn indiscriminately when beer wagon, omnibus, perambulator, or schoolboy came into range. At the end of it, Stuyvesant peeled his fingers out of the leather and flung open his door, not waiting for the man to lead him.

"Aldous Carstairs," he shot at the building's watch-dog, the same one who'd been there that first day. This time he didn't call up, just detached himself from the desk and took Stuyvesant to the lift, folding back the outer door and pushing open the inner one for Stuyvesant to enter. The secretary slipped in, and the lift rode upwards.

"What took you so long?" Aldous Carstairs demanded.

Stuyvesant overrode the secretary's attempt at explanation by saying, "You got me out of bed, what d'you want?"

Carstairs transferred his scowl from the secretary to Stuyvesant, then jerked his head to dismiss the man. When the door was closed, he reached for his box of cigarillos.

"Something's come up."

"I sure as hell hope so," Stuyvesant snapped, dropping into a chair without waiting for an invitation. "Look, can we get some coffee here? Your man dragged me away before I could drink mine," he lied.

Carstairs picked up the telephone on his desk and said, "Lakely? Bring my guest a pot of strong coffee, and some toast or muffins or something."

Stuyvesant didn't know whether to feel mollified or disquieted at this clear indication that Carstairs intended to keep him here for long enough to eat toast. He put on his poker face, and prepared to listen.

"The proposed meeting at Hurleigh House between the miners and the Prime Minister has been approved. Unless word of it leaks out to the press, it will go ahead."

"Okay."

"Hurleigh House, as you have seen, is ideally suited for such a gathering, being private land with severely limited access—the one road and, if necessary, flat ground behind the ridge that can be used as an air strip. Once the representatives are in, there is no way for the public or the newspapers to spy on them."

"Seems a pretty fancy place to talk about coal mining."

"You'll find that the miners' representatives have come a long way since they worked in the pits themselves," Carstairs said dryly.

There was a knock at the door and the race-driver secretary came in with a tray. He filled two cups, placed one in front of his boss and one in front of Stuyvesant, then shifted the tray towards the guest's side of the desk so Stuyvesant could help himself to the traditional cold toast and lumps of what looked like gray rocks.

"Scotch eggs," Lakely said, then turned on his heel and left.

Stuyvesant ignored the plates but took the beverage, hoping that before too long his brain would begin to fire, and Carstairs might explain why it was so damned urgent.

"The parties coming together are five: the Prime Minister, two representatives for the miners, and two for the mine owners. Each side approved its opposite members, so that all five are men who might be expected to listen to reason. Each will be permitted a staff of three, be they secretaries, valets, bodyguards, or strolling minstrels. The conference will begin informally on Friday evening, meet in more formal settings throughout the day Saturday, dine at Hurleigh Saturday night, and join in a church service in the Hurleigh chapel on Sunday. The idea being that, given the format of a weekend house party, talk will be less constrained and consensus more possible."

"It's worth a try," Stuyvesant commented.

Carstairs ignored him. "It has come to my attention that one of the two Union representatives will be Matthew Ruddle, M.P."

"Bunsen's mentor."

"Ruddle is a member of the Trades Union Committee, assistant secretary of the T.U.C.'s General Council. He is in public a firebrand, popular with the Unions in general and his electrical Union in particular, but in private given to reason. And as you know, he is a friend and mentor of Richard Bunsen in the Unions. Bunsen will almost certainly be one of his three permitted assistants."

"Okay," Stuyvesant said.

"I want you to be one of the other two."

"Never gonna happen. I haven't even got close to Bunsen, yet, much less his boss."

"You will have a clear opportunity tomorrow. The gambling club James Balham goes to will be raided tonight."

"Fine," Stuyvesant said, knowing full well how many things could go wrong with that plan. "I'm having lunch with Sarah Grey tomorrow, and possibly Laura Hurleigh, as well."

"You must convince Bunsen to take you on."

"I probably won't even see him."

"Try," Carstairs urged.

Stuyvesant set down his cup so as not to throw it at the man. "Look. Up to now, I've been working on this all by my lonesome. Why the sudden interest? They're never going to take along a newly hired driver, and not even Ruddle's driver, at that."

"You can try."

"I will try, of course I will. But you haven't told me what you

want me to do if I manage to get dragged into it. Listen at the key-
hole? Snap incriminating pictures?" Carstairs fiddled with his thin
brown cigar, and Stuyvesant eyed him narrowly. "What the hell are
you not telling me?"

Carstairs sighed, and gave it to him at last. "There may be, hmm,
a bomb."

Chapter Fifty-Four

THE DIM OFFICE SEEMED TO FLASH and sparkle: glass and screams; a small woman with blood matting her floss-blonde hair. He went very still.

"A bomb. You utter shit bastard. How long have you known?"

"I said 'may'; we don't 'know' a thing. We merely confirmed the possibility this morning. When I asked you on Saturday to look for the name Lionel Waller, it was merely a rumor we were following."

Which meant he'd been pretty sure about it even then. Stuyvesant's fist ached, wanting to smash into the smug black-eyed sadist; his shoulders longed to upend the heavy desk into the man's face. In a long life of concealing his feelings, sitting in his chair without an act of violence was one of the hardest acts he'd pulled off. He deliberately pulled his cigarette case out of his breast pocket and got one going, pleased that his hands did not betray him.

"You going to tell me who this Waller is, or do I have to play Twenty fucking Questions with you?"

"I'm sure you know how these things develop. One hears a rumor, and by the time one follows it to its source, it has accrued so many dubious variations that one begins to mistrust the whole thing."

Stuyvesant just sat and smoked and glared.

"Two weeks ago, one of my men in the Midlands submitted a report. In it, he made passing mention of a conversation in a public house with a man named Lionel Waller, who worked in the Army supply depot and had been suspected on two or three occasions of supplying stolen munitions. Nothing major, just the odd sidearm here, a handful of bullets there. We'd have arrested him, but sometimes it's better to let these types have a bit of slack to see if one can reel in something bigger, namely, the person up the line who is interested in buying the weapons."

Again, Stuyvesant gave no indication of agreement. Carstairs continued.

"However, this report mentioned that the man seemed particularly animated, and over the course of the evening my man received the clear impression that Waller believed he had got away with a bit of a coup. He gave no details, but two days later, the Army depot in question reported the loss of a distressing quantity of an experimental high explosive, a concentrated form of, hmm, gelignite. Easy to handle, remarkably stable, compact, its explosive force, shall we say, devastating."

"When you say 'compact' . . . ?"

"Two ounces would utterly destroy this room."

"Got to love modern science. How much is missing?"

"Twenty ounces."

"Twenty—Jesus, are they planning on leveling Buckingham Palace or something? I hope you picked him up."

"He is in custody, yes. He proved something of an amateur lawyer, and dragged his heels with both the civilian and military police interrogations, but yesterday I suggested that he be transferred to London. And early this morning, he talked."

Stuyvesant glanced sharply up. He hadn't noticed before, but beneath the pristine collar and freshly shaved face, Carstairs looked tired—not a grim exhaustion like Bennett Grey's, but a complacent fatigue. Like a man who'd been up half the night in pursuit of a difficult, but ultimately pliable, female conquest.

"And?"

"The man who bought the explosive from Waller lives in Manchester."

"Manchester. Where Bunsen was, on Saturday."

"That is what brought Waller to my—"

"You swear to me you just found this out? Because if you've been holding back on me—"

"Mr. Stuyvesant, I finished my interrogation of Mr. Waller at four-thirty this morning. I went home to bath and change my clothes. I came here to review the files. When I confirmed the connection, I sent my secretary to bring you here. Seeing as how yesterday I experienced some difficulties in getting a response from you."

"So what is the connection?"

"I have had Richard Bunsen under surveillance since the day after you brought him to my attention—ten days now. While in Manchester, Bunsen was seen with a man named Marcus Shiffley. Shiffley was a friend of Bunsen's at university until he was sent down for threatening a professor. He migrated to the radical fringe, writes occasionally for the *Workers' Weekly* and other Communist papers, and he has been questioned twice concerning acts of violence associated with industrial action—once for an epidemic of broken windows in clothing stores during a garment worker's strike, the other for a Molotov cocktail thrown through the open door of a bank from a passing motor-cycle. In both cases, he was let go when he came up with friends who swore he was with them. Since in neither case was there more than property damage, we keep a file on him, but don't have him under active surveillance.

"However, when he was seen with Bunsen on Saturday, I recalled mention of a man fitting his description having a drink with Mr. Waller, a month before the theft from the armory."

"Not a very strong connection."

"I thought it strong enough to encourage a closer look. I sent the photographs taken in Manchester on Saturday to the man who knew Waller. He confirmed that Shiffley was the man who had been in the pub with Waller, last month."

Carstairs opened a desk drawer, pulled out a crisp new manila folder, and laid it in front of Stuyvesant.

The folder contained three items. First was a photograph showing five people in a restaurant. "This photograph was taken the middle of last week." Facing the camera was Richard Bunsen. The two other men were strangers, though one of those Stuyvesant had seen before. Carstairs tapped the familiar figure. "That's Shiffley. Whom, by the way, we have been unable to locate."

"You showed me his photo the other day, with a woman."

"That was his mistress, a known Bolshevik. The other man is Comrade Peter Markovitch, visiting from Russia. And of course Lady Laura you know."

The last person, sitting with her back to the camera, he knew as well: That blonde head could only belong to Sarah Grey, up to her pretty neck in it. Whatever *it* was.

Shit, he thought. *Oh, shit.*

His face must have given something away, because he felt Carstairs' eyes lock onto him. He did not look up, just turned the photo over.

The next document was a Photostat copy of a page from a surveillance log, neat handwriting giving details of time, location, and names. The man who had written it had noted only the names of Shiffley, Bunsen, and Laura Hurleigh; not of Markovitch or Sarah.

The last page was another photograph, this of two men, one in the uniform of a sergeant. "Waller?" he asked.

"Yes."

Stuyvesant shook his head to indicate that he'd never seen them before, closed the file, and slid it across the desk.

He took a deep breath, and said, "The other woman in the photograph? You probably know that's Sarah Grey." No choice, really, but to drive that particular knife into his own vital parts. But judging by Carstairs' lack of reaction, he did know.

Was it a test, Stuyvesant wondered? Did Carstairs suspect what had taken place between Stuyvesant and the young woman up in Gloucestershire? Not that anything had taken place, not exactly. Did he have a spy within Hurleigh House? Guest or servant? Or could he merely be working from the finely honed instincts of a skilled interrogator?

Not that it mattered. Stuyvesant had no choice but to say her name, when his every instinct was to tear the photograph to pieces. He drank the dregs of his cold, bitter coffee, and waited for the rest of it.

"After I had elicited the information from Mr. Waller, and confirmed the links between Waller, Shiffley, and Bunsen, I rang Downing Street and asked a question."

"You wanted to know who suggested the private meeting at Hurleigh."

Carstairs blinked. "Quite. And since you seem a devotee of guessing games, would you like to venture a guess on who made the suggestion?"

"I'd say the Duke of Hurleigh rang up his old buddy Baldwin on Sunday night and said that he'd just come up with a smashing idea to settle this bothersome Strike."

"First thing Monday, in fact. But yes, it came from the Duke."

"Jesus Christ," Stuyvesant breathed, as the chain of events linked together in his mind. And what a pretty chain it was, to build a stranglehold on a nation: An Anarchist trained as a sapper gets his hands on some high explosive; the following day, he arranges to meet his mistress's father, a man whose voice would be heard by the highest in the land; in the course of their casual, Sunday morning talk, the Anarchist plants a suggestion that quiet, private conversations such as the one they were having right now could do so much more good than formal meetings overseen by furious assistants and the spectacle-producing press; and finally, somehow or other, the careful Anarchist would be one of that select group, one of those voices of reason whose decisions would shape the nation's future.

Except that what would be heard might not be gentle reason, but twenty ounces of deadly explosive that would blast a schism through society and split every faction from its neighbor. There would be no possibility of unity in a nation ruled by vicious hatred and mistrust. Anarchy would move in. Anarchy would prevail.

He dropped his head into his hands, no longer caring if Aldous Carstairs was looking on. "I should've stayed in New York."

"But you did not. And now, Mr. Stuyvesant, it would appear that I require your assistance."

"Hell's bells. You do, don't you?"

"We shall search the bags of the representatives and staff, of course, but it's going to be delicate, since trust is the entire *raison d'être* for the meeting. And as I said, the explosive is quite compact; a man could carry a sufficient quantity on his person to punch a hole in a ship's hull, much less effect an assassination."

"Have them cancel the meeting."

"A forum that could well avert open class warfare on British soil? Without more concrete evidence, I will not do that."

"You'd trust me to find your explosive?"

"You have done so in the past. And frankly, I have no man at present who knows more about bombs than you."

It was a disturbing admission—not that Carstairs didn't have a bomb expert among his men, because why would he? But it indicated that, although he was happy enough to make use of the police to stage a raid, when it came to bombs, he so craved playing it close to his chest, that he'd risk using a stranger over bringing in colleagues from another force.

Did Carstairs have some reason not to trust them? Did he suspect a traitor in the ranks—of Scotland Yard, maybe, or Military Intelligence? Or was he just making sure this outsider stayed outside, keeping him busy beating away a cloud of smoke?

Or, did bringing Stuyvesant into his circle mean that Carstairs was playing a game with rules all his own? A game that, if those others—Intelligence, police—caught wind of, they would try to shut down. A game that could leave a stray American very badly burned.

Stuyvesant pictured himself sitting across the desk from his Scotland Yard acquaintance, the man who had inadvertently given him Carstairs in the first place, telling him how he'd spent the last week. What would the Yard man do, hearing that the mysterious (and remember: somewhat distasteful) Major Carstairs was up to no good?

First thing he'd do was ensure that Stuyvesant had no contact whatsoever with any of the principals in the case, not Carstairs, not Grey, and certainly not Richard Bunsen. And Sarah and Laura would be way off limits.

Nope, Stuyvesant thought. I didn't come here to dangle my legs from a chair.

The thought process, from speculation to decision, took Stuyvesant no more than five seconds: something to be said for a life of having to think under pressure.

"You're pretty sure they'll arrest the driver tonight?" he now asked Carstairs.

"So I am told."

"How long can they keep him?"

"More than twenty-four hours may be a problem. Unless he is injured during the course of—"

"No. Twenty-four hours is plenty to inconvenience Bunsen. I'll see Miss Grey and possibly Miss Hurleigh tomorrow." He thought for a minute, then shook his head. "I've got to be honest: I can't say there's more than a slim chance I'll get taken on as replacement driver. And even if I were, the closest I'd get to the actual meeting would be when I dropped Bunsen off at the door. You've got to regard this as a real long shot."

"I have the authority to cancel the meeting, if things do not go satisfactorily."

"Just so you're not betting the house on my being there."

"Not just you."

"Who—" Stuyvesant stopped. "You want Grey there."

"Who better, to sense which man is plotting murder in his heart?"

"No. Absolutely not."

Carstairs looked, if anything, amused. "Are you telling me that you, an American agent of the Bureau of Investigation, forbid me from requiring service of one of His Majesty's servants?"

"Yeah, I am. You're not going to do that to him. Let him go home, he's done enough."

"Agent Stuyvesant, I will overlook your offensive overstepping of bounds because I have reason to be grateful for the affection the man Grey has developed for you. However, even you must see that with the life of a Prime Minister and the peace of a nation at stake, I may have to draw in all possible assistance."

"Then pick up Bunsen now. Grill him."

"Is that what you would do, Agent Stuyvesant?"

The question brought him up short. It was tempting, but

the problems were enormous. If a bomb did exist, there was no saying who had it, or who its target might be. Better to follow the spoor
they had than to go off half cocked and lose track of the explosive. Besides, much as a dark corner of him would like to see what
Aldous Carstairs could do with the smooth-faced Richard Bunsen, it
would be an interrogation of a very different order from the questioning of a pilfering supply sergeant. Breaking a man like Bunsen, a
committed believer in a cause, was the slowest thing in the world.
Frankly, he wouldn't lay money on it, not even with Carstairs in
charge.

"Yeah," he said after a while. "Yeah, I can see the problems.
But let's not bring Grey in right away. I'll talk to him, ask him to
be ready to get on the train from Cornwall, but let me see what I can
do first. I can wire him and ask him to come Saturday if I turn up
zilch."

"It would be better if I were to arrange for his transport,"
Carstairs said. "A telegram would not reach him in time, considering
that dinner Saturday would be the prime target of opportunity, with
all the guests gathered together. And under those circumstances,
Captain Grey would locate in moments the one who exhibits undue
disquiet."

It was true; it was all true, God damn it. But it was all so tenuous:
If Richard Bunsen had a bomb; *if* he intended to use it at this meeting
and not, say, in the House of Lords next week; *if* the driver went
gambling and got picked up; *if* Bunsen didn't already have another
man to hand, and *if* he offered Stuyvesant the job of driver-cum-
bodyguard. And even then, *if* he could convince Bunsen that a driver-
bodyguard would be useful at the Hurleigh meeting. If, if, if.

Still, he'd known this kind of job before, cases that depended on
a weird and uncontrollable momentum all their own—it was un-
canny how often the sheer unlikeliness of a plan seemed to glue it together. Like one of those modern stage plays that consisted of
unrelated events and segments of conversation, which came together
in a kind of dreamlike logic at the end.

No, the plan to get Harris Stuyvesant into Hurleigh that week-
end would almost surely come to pieces—but as Carstairs said, if it

didn't pan out, they could always cancel it. Or they could let it go ahead, then go through every object coming into Hurleigh with a nit-comb, and require full body searches of everyone. Although Carstairs might draw a line with the Prime Minister's person.

In a way, that plan might be for the better. If they found the stuff on Bunsen, it would leave one Yank Bureau agent out in the cold, but it would mean one terrorist off the street. And if Bunsen came out of the meeting as blameless as he'd gone onto it, well, Stuyvesant would still be positioned to work his way into the man's circle.

Too, going the search-and-watch method would keep Grey clear of the whole thing.

He nodded, his mind made up. "Leave me a message at the hotel with the word *book* in it if you've succeeded in removing Balham from play. And I'll be in touch tomorrow after I see the two women. We'll decide then how it stands."

Carstairs rose, holding out his hand. Stuyvesant gave it a brief clasp, concealing his distaste, and picked up his hat and coat.

Aldous Carstairs listened to the American's footsteps recede across the outer office. When the outer door had closed, he took out his note-book and wrote in it for a minute, then sat back, frowning over what he had written.

Sometimes, it was just a matter of giving a person what he was hoping to find. He had no doubt that Stuyvesant accepted what he told him, and would do as he had asked. The man had no reason not to.

Grey, however, was a different story. They were fast approaching the time when Grey's intuition would be too dangerous. Best to re-move him from the action, for a time.

Stuyvesant walked, head down, through the busy streets, and was halfway to the hotel before he thought of who awaited him there, and what that meant.

He couldn't go straight from Aldous Carstairs to Bennett Grey with the knowledge of Carstairs' plan still raw on his face. He veered into a tea shop and sat until the cup in front of him was stone cold, then went to find a public telephone.

The hotel operator connected him to Grey's room, and Stuyvesant held the receiver away from his mouth and lifted a piece of stiff paper, slowly crinkling it.

"Grey? That you? Don't know what's up with these machines, I think they're working on the lines down the street. Grey, you there?" *Crinkle crinkle.* "Where's the operator, anyway? Look, I better make this short before we're cut off entirely. Everything's fine, it's just that a meeting's been called for this week-end, made some decisions urgent. Nothing really—you there?" Grey's raised voice came clear over the earpiece, and Stuyvesant crushed the paper in his fist. "I've got some things to take care of here, and I don't want to go over it on the telephone, anyway. How about I meet you at the same place we started out last night, at, say, five? What's that?" Grey's voice was at a shout, and Stuyvesant half-covered the mouthpiece with the fist holding the paper. "This is nuts," he said in the direction of the receiver. "I'll see you at five."

He hung up on Grey's protestations.

He spent the remainder of the morning in the library, reading about the men who would be at Hurleigh; the middle part of the day in a Turkish baths, sweating out the previous night's poisons; and the afternoon in a strange hotel room, catching up on a few hours of sleep. Between the library and the baths he found a map store, and bought a highly detailed Ordnance Survey map of the area around Hurleigh. He asked his temporary hotel to wake him at five-fifteen, so he would arrive forty minutes late: the pub would be crowded and noisy, and Grey would be on his second or third drink.

Bennett Grey was the trickiest confederate Stuyvesant had ever had to keep happy, worse than any gin-soaked, itchy-fingered gun-for-hire. He'd be so glad when the man admitted defeat and skulked home to Cornwall.

With luck, tonight would do the trick.

Grey was waiting at the public house, and lifted his glass by way of greeting as the big American threaded his way through the noisy crowd. Stuyvesant could see from the gesture that this was at least his third. He waved back, detoured past the bar to give his order "and a refill for my friend," and finally slipped into the chair Grey had guarded for him. He took off his hat, putting it on his lap under the edge of the table, and unbuttoned his overcoat.

"Sorry I'm late," he told Grey. "I fell asleep, believe it or not. Your libraries are soporific places."

Grey did not react to the half lie, Stuyvesant was interested to see. The distractions of the room battered at him, so that the two statements, which were actually true when taken separately, elided into the suggestion that Stuyvesant had fallen asleep over his books. To distract him further, Stuyvesant pulled the folded Ordnance Survey map out of his breast pocket.

"One thing I love about this country is its maps."

"Is that of Hurleigh?"

"Yep." Stuyvesant leaned forward to speak into Grey's ear, not only for security, but for the added advantage that Grey could not see his face. "There's going to be a private meeting this week-end at Hurleigh, between the principals of the Strike. Union and owners, with the Prime Minister in attendance. It might just be possible to get me in on it. That's what Carstairs wanted to see me about."

With another man, Stuyvesant would have immediately launched off on some distracting behavior: taking off his coat, craning around for their drinks, anything to keep from having to meet his companion's eyes. But Grey would see the actions for what they were, so instead, Stuyvesant met his green gaze openly, and allowed him to see what he could.

He's not psychic—but despite the noise in the room, Grey knew something was up.

"You are trying to get rid of me," he said to Stuyvesant.

"Of course I'm trying to get rid of you. No offense, I like you a whole lot, but I've got a job to do and pretty soon you're going to be in my way."

"But the Major..."

"You're right, Carstairs would love me to hang on to you. Hell, if I could hog-tie you and dump you on his desk, he'd put me on the Honours List for a Sir. But while his mind's on you, he's not focusing on the problems with Bunsen."

Stuyvesant waited for the tell-tale rubbing of the forehead, but it did not come. It would appear that, given a distracting enough environment, Touchstone would react to the given truth, and miss the real truth hiding behind it. Had Grey been rested, sober, and sitting in a place where a man could hear himself think, Stuyvesant wouldn't get away with deception.

"So you'll go?"

"Tomorrow," Grey promised.

Stuyvesant felt a burst of relief, then told himself he couldn't count on it until he watched the train pull out of Paddington. Not that it would matter all that much—the more he'd thought about Carstairs' plan during the day, the more he'd suspected that the only way he'd be joining that secret Hurleigh conclave was if he held a gun to someone's head. Stuyvesant was a veteran of so many investigative cock-ups over the years, he knew the farther a plan got from simplicity, the smaller the chance of success. An idea like this one, there were just too many opportunities for the gods of fate to step in and have a good laugh.

And anyway, he wasn't altogether certain that he believed in Carstairs' mythical bomb plot. It was just too neat: that chain of supply sergeant to university friend to Bunsen; Carstairs just happening to remember the description of a man in a pub from a month before. Frankly, it stank of the man's deviousness. Although for the life of him, he couldn't imagine what Carstairs could be working toward.

Still, the Hurleigh meeting did not replace the substitute-driver plan, which was more reasonably within his grasp. But he wasn't sure, when the topic of the driver's unreliability came up at lunch tomorrow, that he would do anything to remind Bunsen of his skills as a bodyguard. His aim with Bunsen was in the longer term, and if it meant Carstairs had to draw a line through this secret meeting, even if the consequences were that Britain's General Strike went ahead, he didn't much care.

The States had survived its Civil War, Britain had survived theirs; maybe it was time for this country to have another one.

His target was Bunsen, and he mustn't get distracted by British politics. Sooner or later, if he wasn't arrested here, Bunsen would return to the States, and when he did, Stuyvesant intended to have sufficient information to slap on the handcuffs the moment his polished shoes hit the docks.

Everything on this end was Carstairs' problem.

Stuyvesant lifted his glass to Bennett Grey, and set about getting his friend absolutely roaring smashed.

Chapter Fifty-Five

WEDNESDAY WAS A FULL DAY.

For Bennett Grey, it began before dawn when the full life of this terrible city crashed down around him. Literally crashed, with dustbins being collected on the street below. Three sets of snores rose up from the rooms around him, including that of Harris Stuyvesant through the wall. The sheets were damp and stank of sweated drink and fear—the whole room stank of his state of mind; the heat from the ticking radiators made it worse, close and suffocating; the feather pillow seemed to creep up around his skull as if it had been made of mud. There was tension in the voices, anger in the dust-bins, distress in the heels hitting the pavement, and his mouth tasted of brass, tasted as if all his teeth had been coated with the stuff.

He fought free from the grasp of the bed-clothes and lurched to the window, fighting with the latch until he could fling it open. Even then, the stifling atmosphere inside seemed more to absorb and transmute the miasma of the city than be diluted by it, and it took a long time, standing at the window, panting and feeling the pull of the pavement thirty feet below, before he could bring his head and shoulders back inside.

A cold bath and a hard, all-over scrub with the face-cloth

removed some of the feeling of disgust. Shaving was harder. Every
time he picked up the straight razor, his hand began to tremble with
desire, lusting just to slide the blade across his throat and be done
with it. In the end, he folded it away and told himself he'd see a
barber.

But he knew he wouldn't.

He would be going home.

He couldn't do this for one more day.

He had failed.

Bennett Grey pushed his clothing any which way into his case,
forced the latch to hold, and went to bounce his fist off his neighbor's
door.

For Sarah Grey, the day began almost as early. For the past two or
three weeks (and it was only going to get worse in the weeks to come)
Richard Bunsen's work had taken an increasing amount of her time.
This meant that the clinics had to be fit in around the edges of
Richard's day.

She was at the office of the main clinic at six o'clock, drinking tea
and working her way through the letters, queries, complaints, and
proposals that had accumulated since the previous morning.
Fortunately, she had dependable assistants, and the day-to-day business of Women's Help had not suffered. In the long term, such an
arrangement was impossible, but she expected that once the Strike
was settled, life would return to normal.

By nine, the pile of papers had been sorted for their designated
workers, and Sarah permitted herself the first cigarette of the
morning.

It was, as it turned out, her only cigarette of the morning, and she
only managed to smoke half of that before Richard's problems came
crashing down on her: His driver, a man she'd never been all that
fond of anyway, had failed to show up at eight to take Richard to the
first of six urgent meetings that day—the P.M. was to meet with the
mine owners that afternoon, and Richard needed to lay the ground
first. He'd waited for a quarter-hour before running for a cab, telling
his secretary that Jones was waiting for him and to let Sarah and

Laura know the problem. In other words, handing the problem over to Sarah.

Five minutes later, the phone rang again, with Richard's secretary phoning back all in a flutter to say he'd heard from the driver's wife, that Jim Balham had been arrested the night before in a raid, and not to expect him until Thursday, that he couldn't find Laura Hurleigh, and that he just didn't know *what* to do.

Sarah listened, said that they could no doubt find another car if they needed to, but suggested that, since Richard was in Town all that day, perhaps he could just use taxis for once. The secretary agreed, unhappily, then handed to Sarah the task of telling Richard, and while she was at it would she take him enough money to pay for his day's gallivanting?

And of course, when she located Richard (who had finished with one appointment and gone to the next) to give him the information and the little purse full of money, he had pressed upon her several urgent tasks that only she could do, and in the end, she never managed to make it home to change into a nicer dress for her lunch with Harris Stuyvesant.

To make matters worse, when she got to the restaurant, she found that Laura had spent the morning on one of her rare shopping expeditions, and had a fresh hair-cut, polished nails, and a rested air about her, unlike the rumpled and rushed person of Sarah Grey.

Still, she had to admit later, Harris didn't seem to have noticed the shortcomings in her appearance.

And later, too, although she couldn't quite remember just whose idea it had been—Laura's probably, as good ideas usually were—but somehow talk had come around to the sins of Mr. Balham, and like the sun coming through the clouds, it became obvious that Harris was the solution to all their problems. Temporarily, at any rate.

They managed to collect the car and converge with Richard's hectic schedule, snatching him from Piccadilly where he stood trying to flag down a cab. Harris aimed the car across the busy street, cutting off a taxi and coming to a halt at Richard's feet. He sure looked surprised, Richard did, to see his familiar car pull up in front of him.

She jumped out, and got no further than, "Mr. Stuyvesant volunteered to step in for Mr. Balham today, you may have to help him find his way but—" when Richard gave her an approving kiss on the cheek, handed her the considerably thinner money-purse, and slid into his accustomed place in the back.

She waved at Harris, and he pulled out, as smooth as any London cab driver.

So there was that, anyway.

Of course, it meant that he'd be far too busy with Richard to have dinner or lunch with her, but it was only for a few days, until they got it settled, and so it had all worked out for the best: Richard and Harris would get to know each other a little, and by the time they found another driver, things should be settling down for Sarah, as well.

Even Laura seemed happy at the solution, especially because it meant sending Richard out into the current troubles with someone who'd guarded a man before. And Sarah had to agree: It was reassuring, to think of Harris at Richard's side.

For Harris Stuyvesant, that Wednesday morning began at 7:40, when Richard Bunsen's would-be driver was wakened from a sound if alcohol-induced sleep by Grey's fist on the door.

At 8:20, on his way through the hotel lobby, Stuyvesant was handed a message informing him that his books were ready for delivery: Balham was off the page.

At 8:40, Stuyvesant and Grey were eating bacon and eggs and drinking a great deal of coffee.

At 9:50, Stuyvesant carried Grey's bulging valise down to the lobby and watched Grey check out, scarcely able to believe his luck.

At 10:45, he stood on the platform at Paddington and watched the Penzance train pull away in a swirl of smoke and whistles, carrying Bennett Grey away from the city.

At 12:31, he sat down at a beautifully laid table between two gorgeous dolls, both of whom he dared to greet with a kiss on the cheek.

At 12:33, he heard that Richard's driver, who had been increasingly unreliable anyway, hadn't shown up for work that morning, because he'd been arrested.

At 12:35, Laura admitted that she hated to have Richard wandering around London just now, because the day before someone had thrown a rotten tomato at him as he'd come out of his office. This on top of the letters, she added. It was the first Sarah had heard of any threat letters, and Laura's telling her took a few minutes to explain that no, Richard didn't take them seriously, that he hadn't reported them, that he hadn't wanted to make a fuss.

At 12:47, as Stuyvesant was about to open his mouth to say, If he could be of any help . . . Laura Hurleigh beat him to it, asking Dear Mr. Stuyvesant if he wouldn't like to help them all out of a pinch and take over the wheel of Richard's car, just for a few days, until they could find a replacement? Sarah clapped her hands at his agreement, then looked at her wrist-watch and said that if he was going to take over, they'd better finish lunch quickly.

At 1:15, Stuyvesant slid into the driver's seat of Richard Bunsen's car, precisely where he'd sat in the wee hours of Sunday morning to rifle the driver's papers and remove the Automobile Club documents from the packet. The motor started smoothly, re-assuring him that someone had fixed the little adjustment he'd made to the wires.

At 2:07, Sarah, at his side, spotted Bunsen standing on the street looking harassed and irritated. Stuyvesant closed his eyes and shot across the unfamiliar traffic to cut off the taxi that had begun to slow in front of Bunsen. His reward, when Bunsen had shut his door, was a manly clap on the shoulder and a thanks for helping out. Bunsen told him where he needed to go and asked if Stuyvesant could find it. On being told yes, he thought so, Bunsen pulled over his swiveling desk-top and addressed himself to some papers from his brief-case.

At 7:31, Stuyvesant dropped his passenger at the club where he was dining, and went to find a telephone box. He rang both the numbers he had been given for Aldous Carstairs, and at the second was merely told that Mr. Carstairs was not available.

He hung up, frowning at the instrument. Wasn't there some kind of a bomb investigation going on here, for Christ sake? Did he expect Stuyvesant to believe that he'd learned nothing new, all that day?

At 11:53, Stuyvesant pulled up in front of Richard Bunsen's flat to let him out. Bunsen gathered his papers, switched off the light he'd been reading by, and leaned forward. "You're willing to help with tomorrow, then?"

"Happy to," Stuyvesant told him.

"I've very grateful. And look, why don't you take the car tonight, if you have someplace secure you can leave it? The buses have stopped running, and you'll never get a taxi from here. And I'll need you back at seven, sharp."

Stuyvesant thanked him, assured him the car would be safe, and waited until Bunsen had disappeared into the apartment house.

He gazed at the mobile office in the back seat with a look of loathing on his face: He'd much rather take a run at Bunsen's actual office, where he might find last year's diary and all kinds of interesting bits of paper. However, if he had to be back here at seven, shaved and in a clean shirt, that would give him less than five hours to break in and do the job. And once he'd broken in, he doubted he'd get a second chance.

Better leave the office for another night.

At 2:40 Thursday morning, Stuyvesant folded his glasses and put the folder he was reading back into Bunsen's file drawer, locking it in disgust. He hadn't reached an end, but in two and a half hours had found precisely nothing of any interest. And he had to pick Bunsen up at 7:00 Thursday morning, sharp.

At 3:45, Stuyvesant ordered his mind to think about something, anything but his problems with Richard Bunsen. Think about Grey, home and snug in his little white cottage on the cliffs, three hundred miles from Aldous Carstairs, three hundred miles from strike negotiations and speechifying. Think about nothing, and go to sleep.

Which wasn't easy. He just couldn't shake the feeling that time was getting short.

And that when it came to evidence, he was looking in all the wrong places.

At 10:03 on Wednesday morning, Aldous Carstairs received news that Grey and Stuyvesant had just entered a taxi with one suitcase, and given the command for Paddington. He cursed the man on the other end of the line, broke the connection mid-explanation, and placed a call of his own, followed immediately by two others. Sliding his cigar case into one pocket and a small hand-gun into the other, he took out his personal keys and moved over to the filing cabinets in the corner. He took out a folder, removed an envelope, checked the contents, then put the envelope in his inner pocket and the folder back in the cabinet, which he closed and locked.

He gathered his hat, coat, and gloves, telling Lakely he wasn't sure when he would return, that if Lakely hadn't heard from him by one o'clock he should cancel the afternoon appointments and close up at the usual time.

He moved quickly, and bribed the taxi driver to ignore the rules of the road, but he reached Paddington too late.

However, he was Aldous Carstairs. He reached out to catch the sleeve of a passing Great Western official, and asked him for the station master's office.

Captain Bennett Grey was not entirely surprised when the train he was on slowed, forty-six minutes after leaving Paddington, and changed tracks for an unscheduled stop in Reading. He was even less surprised when the man came through to announce that there was some minor trouble on the tracks, but they would be on their way shortly.

Three trains pulled up and pulled away; the Penzance train sat motionless.

Not for long, however. Half an hour after they'd stopped, Grey's compartment door opened and Aldous Carstairs stepped in. As if a switch had been turned, a headache flared to life in Bennett Grey's skull, and Cornwall vanished from the map.

The other man brushed off the seat across from Grey and settled into it. His gloved hands dipped into his breast pocket, coming out with a photograph. He stretched out to place it on Grey's knee.

Five people. Two strangers, Richard Bunsen, Laura, and Sarah.

"One of those men is currently being sought for the possession of a quantity of stolen explosive. He sold it to Richard Bunsen. I can keep your sister out of this." Grey said nothing, and did not move. After a minute, Carstairs added, "I can do my best to keep Laura Hurleigh out of it, as well."

Grey stood up and walked out of the compartment, half blind with pain, letting the photograph fall to the floor, leaving his valise and his coat. He knew Carstairs would have a man to retrieve things, just outside the door, and he did. He knew Carstairs would have a second man to make sure Grey didn't make a break for it or fling himself under a train; he, too, was there.

Neither of them mattered. Not even the photograph mattered, not in itself. What mattered was the Major's conviction that whatever he had, it was enough to get Grey to go with him, and Bennett had seen that conviction in the angle of the gloved hands as they came through the door.

There was really nothing to say.

BOOK FIVE

Hurleigh House

THURSDAY, APRIL 22, 1926
TO
SUNDAY, APRIL 25, 1926

Chapter Fifty-Six

STUYVESANT SPENT THURSDAY HARING to and fro across the face of London behind the wheel of Bunsen's car, desperately racking his brain to recall the maps of this, one of the world's least gridlike cities. Main streets possessed half a dozen names within a mile, roads that shrank and expanded with no rhyme nor reason either trailed into nothing, or gathered themselves and flew off rapidly for the hinterlands.

After a while he discovered the knack of following taxis—when they dove off the straightaway, more often than not they were following convoluted short-cuts to the next artery. Twice the technique got him caught in the backwaters, when the taxi disgorged a passenger and turned around again, but on the whole, it saved him time.

While Bunsen was in meetings, Stuyvesant would study the maps and scribble down the route to their next stop.

He also phoned Carstairs' office, to be told that the man was unavailable. Six times. And blowing up at the secretary didn't get him anywhere.

The afternoon was enlivened by a nicely aimed chunk of wood bouncing off the side window six inches from Bunsen's head. Stuyvesant allowed himself to react strongly, with a squeal of brakes and a cacophony of horns that traced his fast dodge to the side of the road and his even faster abandoning of the car. The man who'd thrown the missile went suddenly wide-eyed, not expecting pursuit from a large, apparently angry American, and whirled on his heels to sprint away. Stuyvesant gained until the man went around a corner, then he slowed and allowed Carstairs' man to get away.

When he got back to the car, which had become the center of a clot of traffic and an angry constable, he apologized to his passenger for losing the man. Bunsen did, he was pleased to see, look just a bit shaken.

Lunch was three boiled eggs from a pub. Tea was carried out to him where he sat in the car, by a secretary, at Bunsen's request. (Damn it, Stuyvesant thought, the man can't go all thoughtful on me now. But he thanked the secretary, and drank his tea.)

Dinner was on a park bench with Sarah, out of a picnic hamper, while Bunsen and Laura Hurleigh ate five courses at a very posh-looking club with various Union heads. It had been decided that the two Union representatives for the Hurleigh week-end would be Herbert Smith, president of the Miners' Union, and Matthew Ruddle, Labour M.P. and Bunsen mentor. Bunsen would be one of Ruddle's three permitted assistants. The choice of mine owners was down to three, with the final decision due later that night.

Stuyvesant didn't know about it, of course, since it was all highly secret. Except that Sarah told him when she brought him dinner.

"You mustn't say anything to anyone," she told him for the third time. "If the newspapers got wind of it, Richard would never speak to me again."

The temptation of that alone was great, but he promised.

"However, it seems to me," she went on, "that if he's trusting you to guard his life, he can surely trust you to keep mum over a secret meeting."

"Will you be going?"

"Oh no. Tell you the truth, I'm looking forward to catching up on my work while Richard is occupied up at Hurleigh."

"And maybe if he doesn't need me there, I can take you to dinner Friday."

She pinked nicely, and said primly that she'd have to see what her calendar permitted. Stuyvesant came very near to kissing her.

Later, when she was long gone, when even Laura had left in a taxi an hour before, Bunsen came out from the club and found Stuyvesant reading a novel by the light of the back seat reading lamp.

"Have to make sure it doesn't drain the battery," he grumbled.

"Yes, sir," Stuyvesant said, putting a salute in his voice.

"Sorry," Bunsen said. "Sorry. It's just that I simply can't afford to get stuck somewhere, and it's happened to me before, that the battery ran down."

"I've been keeping an eye on the charge, and it's only been on half an hour. Where to now?"

"Home, I think," he said. The son of a bitch still looked fresh as a daisy—he seemed to thrive on a day like this. "Tomorrow I'll need you to drive me to Hurleigh. Come at about ten. I'll ring your hotel if there's a change of timing."

"Is this just a day trip?"

"I'll be staying at Hurleigh until Sunday, but I shan't be needing you. You're welcome to come back to Town, or stay in Oxford if you'd rather."

"Okay. If you don't need me first thing, I'll change the oil. Looks to me like it's been a while. And the spare tire has a slow leak, I'll have that looked at, too."

"Good idea."

Harris Stuyvesant, full-service garage-hand to a terrorist, he thought darkly.

He was glad to confirm that neither woman would be going to Hurleigh with Bunsen, not when twenty ounces of high explosive were floating around out there, somewhere. Bad enough to think they might be stashed behind him on the drive up. "Fine," he said. "I'll be there at ten."

But at five minutes past three on Friday morning, the telephone beside his bed went off, shooting him from sound sleep to pure panic in a second flat. He snatched up the instrument. "What!"

"I'm terribly sorry, sir," said a voice. "This is the night manager, and you have a telephone call from a lady who was most insistent. She said to tell you her name is Sarah."

The name did nothing to calm his heart rate. "Put her through."

"Harris?"

"Sarah. What's wrong?"

"We're fine, we're all fine. But there's been a little change of plans."

Stuyvesant didn't care at all for that word *little,* and he was right.

Shortly after midnight, Matthew Ruddle, M.P., had been seized by a terrible spasm of illness. When he recovered enough to phone to his assistant's room and ask the man to bring him some bicarbonate of soda, he got no answer. It turned out the assistant was ill also. And Ruddle's secretary, who was slated to be the second of his permitted three at Hurleigh. Also spending the night huddled around porcelain were half the members of the Union dinner.

Not Bunsen. Not Laura Hurleigh. Herbert Smith and two of his three designated assistants seemed to be unscathed, as of twenty minutes earlier.

The hotel doctor urged that the men be transferred to the hospital; Ruddle was holding out, declaring that he would be fine on the morrow.

"But Mr. Smith, the head of the Union delegation for the weekend, said that we can't very well ask that it be delayed a week, and in case they haven't recovered by tomorrow, we'd better be prepared to field a full team, as it were. Richard will take Mr. Ruddle's place, and take along the one man of Mr. Ruddle's who seems to be all right— he's a vegetarian, which may have something to do with it. The other two places will be filled by Laura and"—Stuyvesant's beleaguered heart clenched at the thought of Sarah going, but she finished the sentence—"oh, Harris, would you at all consider being the third? I know you're an outsider to all this, but Richard's permitted to choose anyone, and Laura has got it in her head that those men were all poisoned, and she says she wants someone there who can do something more than take shorthand."

"She thinks Richard needs a bodyguard?"

"I don't know what she thinks, she's not entirely rational and it's the middle of the night, and—"

"Whoa, honey, that's fine, I'm happy to do it."

"Really?"

"Well, I'll be sorry to miss dinner with you tomorrow night—or tonight, I guess—but save me a slot next week, okay?"

"I could take the train up and see you at Hurleigh."

"No! I mean, I'll have to keep my mind on the job, won't I? I'm sure to see you next week."

"Okay. Well, I'll tell Laura it's set, then. You go back to sleep now."

"I'll try. Tell them I'll be at Bunsen's flat at ten in the morning, unless I hear otherwise."

"Thank you, Harris. I... Thank you."

Stuyvesant hung up, staring at the telephone, shaking his head at the deviousness—and ruthless efficiency—of Aldous Carstairs. How the hell had the son of a bitch managed it?

He could only hope it was nothing worse than food poisoning: Surely Carstairs would keep in mind Grey's injunction against injuring the innocents? Although Stuyvesant wouldn't have put it past Carstairs to burn down a couple of houses with the inhabitants inside, if it did the job.

Next morning, Stuyvesant got to Bunsen's flat half an hour early. When he rang the bell, it was Sarah who came out.

"Oh, good," she said. "You're here early. I somehow thought you might be, I told Richard as much, but he left about six 'phone messages for you."

"I left the hotel hours ago. What's up?"

"It's just that we need to dismantle his office from the back of the motor."

"That's why I'm here early. Where does he want me to put the things?"

She gazed at him with frank adoration. "Harris, when you compare how much of a tussle this would have been with his old driver, all I can say is, bless you."

Don't get used to it, Stuyvesant thought: I'm not Bunsen's new driver. But he said nothing, just drove around the back of the building so she could show him where to stow the fittings. And it was still before ten when they returned to the flat's entrance.

He helped carry and stow Bunsen's cases, then Bunsen remembered a book he'd meant to bring and went back inside. Sarah waited with Stuyvesant at the car, standing there in her spring dress looking delicious.

"You haven't heard from Bennett, have you?" she asked.

"No. Why?"

"I just thought he might drop a line to say he'd got back safely."

"Even if he mailed it when he first reached Penzance, it wouldn't be here yet."

"That's true."

There was a pause.

"You should have nice weather," she said. "For the drive."

"Better than Sunday night, anyway," he agreed.

"I hope next weekend is as nice," she went on. "I was just thinking, if they manage to settle this strike business at Hurleigh, wouldn't it be lovely to be able to show you London in April, without having to think about politics?"

"I'd like that a lot," he said.

"Harris, I—oh, rats," she said, and rose up on her toes to kiss him.

It started with lips, and progressed to a faint brush of teeth before it ended, far too soon, but it took his breath away. He looked down at her and grinned at the flush that rose through the freckles. He leaned down to give her a quick, soft kiss in return, little more than a promise. "A *whole* lot," he said.

The small frown of uncertainty vanished, and she laughed, that irresistible sound.

Then the door opened and Bunsen came out. Stuyvesant held the door for his temporary boss, winked at Sarah, and drove off to get Laura.

The trip to Hurleigh took little more than two hours, through a sparkling spring day. Every mile along the way Harris Stuyvesant spent veering wildly between the champagne-bubble happiness of that kiss (she was a whole lot more experienced than she gave across, he'd bet on that) and the ice-in-the-gut memory of Helen's yellow curls matted with blood.

If it's Bunsen, he knows what he's doing, the thing won't go off while we're driving across the countryside.

But if it's Bunsen, it's got to be in the car, how else would he move the stuff to Hurleigh?

This isn't liquid nitro we're talking about here, it's as stable as can be.

And once we get there, what then?

Then we worry about it. But while Laura's sitting in the back, this car is about the safest place in England.

Thank God Sarah's staying in London, I don't think I could be so free and easy with her here.

For any number of reasons! Yes siree, that girl knows how to wake a man right up.

She's not a toy. You can't play with her like you could Louise or Phoebe or, well, any woman other than Helen.

Yeah, that's going to be a problem. Then again maybe I'll be lucky and get blown up myself, not have to worry about things.

Let's see if we can arrange to be standing next to Aldous Carstairs when that happens, eh?

Maybe Bunsen, as well.

If Bunsen's responsible.

If it's Bunsen—

And so on, across the green and open countryside. Between the threat and the promise, the hairs on the back of his neck stood up the whole way.

They drove through Hurleigh village, along the valley road and across the ford, and Stuyvesant had made the sharp left turn leading back to the house itself when he was forced to brake by the sight of a young tree lying across the road. It was accompanied by a fit, sharp-eyed man in his sixties who looked like no tenant farmer Stuyvesant had ever seen, and who indeed, moved forward to the car like a gate guard.

Laura put her head out of her window. "Hallo, Mr. Mackey, I didn't know you'd be dragged in. How've you been?"

Mackey touched his hat and brought his heels together. "Good day, Lady Laura, nice to see you. I'm fine, and the wife sends her greetings. Always happy to lend a hand." And so saying, he trotted over and moved the tree from the drive. Stuyvesant put the car back into gear; Laura waved as they went past.

"One of my father's men," she explained.

"Looked a match for any London newsman," Stuyvesant commented.

Today, the servants who waited at the head of the drive would not be mistaken for family members: Gallagher looked like a butler from the movies, black and white, stiff-lipped, and efficient.

Their bags vanished in seconds, Bunsen's and Laura's at any rate, carried in the direction of the house.

Gallagher looked at Stuyvesant, and hesitated infinitesimally at the conundrum of a driver who, the previous week, had been a family guest. The professional challenge would have broken a lesser man, but Gallagher showed his mettle. Arranging a bland face, he said, "If you would be so good as to drive the motor into the pasture behind the stables, someone will show you to your room."

Stuyvesant nodded, and pretended he did not see Gallagher's relief. He parked the car and carried his own bag to the servants' quarters, the long, two-story building at the base of the hill on which the chapel stood, all but hidden from the drive by the lodge-house and its attendant shrubs. The rooms he was given were the size of a broom closet but comfortable enough, and Alex—all business today— showed him the two downstairs rooms set aside for servants' use, a sitting room with a wireless set and gramophone, next to what he called the buttery, where Stuyvesant could get a cup of coffee or a sandwich. Alex, too, seemed puzzled at the change in status, but Stuyvesant didn't help him out, just listened and thanked him for his help.

He looked at his wrist-watch. Two hours to tea-time, when the assembled enemies would come together and begin their prickly machinations, wary as lovemaking porcupines. He would begin out of doors, and see just how many old friends of the Duke there were, standing guard over Hurleigh House.

In the end he met five more elderly soldiers with sharp eyes, although he knew there would be more, up at the Peak and down near the river. Their perimeter followed the ridge-line, with all the Hurleigh buildings inside, and he took care to introduce himself as Mr. Bunsen's driver and bodyguard.

He trotted down the steep path from the chapel, moving quickly because his reconnaissance had taken longer than he'd planned. When he came off the hill he was moving at a fast trot, aimed at the shaded garden to the side of the house itself.

His pace and the slope made it hard to stop when a man stepped out and pointed a gun at him.

Chapter Fifty-Seven

IT COULD HAVE BEEN AN AWKWARD MOMENT, with Stuyvesant trying to dig in his heels even as he threw up both hands in a declaration of innocence. But he'd managed to skid to a halt before his momentum had him plowing into the man, and fortunately, the fellow wasn't trigger-happy.

"Here I was just thinking," Stuyvesant said, over the barrel of the man's gun, "at the top of the hill, that the place seems well guarded."

The guy was clearly not interested in conversation, but Stuyvesant could forgive tactiturnity in a man who'd passed up the chance to shoot him, so he said, "Name's Stuyvesant. I'm with Mr. Bunsen."

The man with the gun finally spoke. "What were you doing up there?"

"Wanted some fresh air. And wanted to see the set-up."

After a minute, the gun lowered a fraction. "You're the Yank."

"I guess."

"You armed?"

"Do I need to be?"

"Reason I ask is, there's no guns allowed inside the garden walls. They got a lock-box you can leave it in, when you need to come in."

"Makes sense," Stuyvesant said, and it did, he supposed. "But I didn't bring it with me. Thought I'd see what's what, before I go pulling guns on strangers."

The man looked at his weapon, and tucked it away inside his coat. "Sorry about that, mate, I heard you running and it took me by surprise, like."

"No harm done." He hesitated, then offered his hand. "Harris Stuyvesant, New York."

"Gwilhem Jones, Cardiff."

"Are you a friend of the Duke as well?"

"We go back a ways," Jones admitted.

The Duke of Hurleigh's own private army, gray of hair but sharp of eye. "Any idea where I might find Mr. Bunsen?"

"Through that door, past the kitchen and to the right, you'll find someone to ask."

"Thank you, Mr. Jones, and I'll be seeing you around."

The house was warm to a man in outdoor clothing coming in from a hike through the cold woods, and he took off his overcoat. Past the kitchen, he found a man seated at a desk. This one was not a retired soldier, or at least, not one of the Duke's retired soldiers. He was about forty, with a dark suit so non-descript that it might have been a uniform; the expectant look on his face was equally professional: mid-level civil servant.

"I'm looking for Mr. Bunsen."

"Mr. Stuyvesant?" the man asked, rising and putting out his hand. "I'm Julian Exeter. Come, right this way."

On the other side of the next door there was another man, a slightly less polished version of the first. He got up from his chair and slipped into the room that had just gone vacant.

Exeter led him through the house, using a route Stuyvesant hadn't known was there, along the northern side and up some narrow and poorly lit stairs. Eventually they went through a door into the family's realm. Here the walls were wood, the air was warm, and the floorboards underfoot were polished.

One more jog of a hallway and Stuyvesant's guide rapped on a closed door, opened it a few inches, and said, "Mr. Stuyvesant is here."

"Bring him in," said a woman: Laura Hurleigh.

Laura and Richard Bunsen were alone in the room, a small office or study with a desk and a fireplace. She had a note-pad in her hand and was sitting near the fire; Bunsen was on his feet near the window.

"Stuyvesant, good," he said, sounding distracted. "Look, Laura, I must run—Baldwin wants a word before we meet the others."

"Fine, there's nothing that can't wait."

"See you for tea, then."

The room seemed smaller and slightly shabby when he had left. Stuyvesant went over to glance out of the window, which looked out on the garden, then went to sit on the other side of the fire from Laura Hurleigh.

"Do you want something to drink?" she asked. "Coffee?"

"I'm fine. Your father has men in the woods all around."

"The Retirees' Brigade," she told him, sounding indulgent. "They love it."

"Look," he said, "do you honestly think you need a bodyguard here?"

"Here? No. But the others have them, so Richard should."

Stuyvesant had to laugh. "So you're just keeping up with the Baldwins?"

"More or less. I hope you're not offended?"

"That my presence is strictly cosmetic? Why should I be? He's paying me, isn't he?"

"Of course."

"Okay. But you don't mind if I actually do my job?"

"I expect no less of you, Mr. Stuyvesant."

"Maybe we should begin with your telling me exactly what's going on here." Since he was only supposed to have the sketchiest idea about the week-end, from Sarah.

"It is a meeting, Mr. Stuyvesant. Private, kept out of the press at all costs, and among men who were asked because they may actually listen to each other's words."

"It's an attempt to defuse the Strike?"

"It may be an attempt to defuse a revolution," she said, sounding remarkably sanguine about it.

"I see. How many will be here?"

"Two mine owners—Mr. Branning and Lord Stalfield, with three assistants each. Richard's colleague, Herbert Smith, the president of the Miners' Union, with his three, and of course, Mr. Baldwin."

"Why here? Why not meet in a back room of Downing Street, or Buckingham Palace? Or the Prime Minister's country home, what do they call it, Chequers?"

"Hurleigh is neutral ground, far from the eyes of the press. It provides an opportunity for the five individuals to meet as men rather than as figureheads. Take them out of their familiar settings, put a drink in their hands, let them loosen their collars and come together over the billiards table, and they can begin to look at each other as reasonable men with reasonable grievances."

"I'd have thought they'd be just as likely to break their billiards cues over each other's heads," he said, his back still giving him the occasional twinge from just that.

"Yes, well, that's why I'm here," she said.

"You? Not your father?"

"It's been decided that his presence might prove more distracting than useful. He and Mother will come to dinner Friday evening, and to church on Sunday, but apart from that, he will be absent."

"So if it comes to breaking up a fight, you're it?"

"There will be no fights, and I have to concur that a woman can serve better to encourage five powerful men to keep their manners."

Stuyvesant had to shake his head in admiration: Laura Hurleigh's presence here was a stroke of pure genius. It was not just that she possessed impeccable credentials on both sides, with a history of supporting the workers while the bluest of blood pumped through her veins. It was Laura Hurleigh herself that made the choice brilliant— intelligent, warm, regal, and feminine; a woman among men drilled from childhood to respect women, particularly aristocratic women; confident but never pushy. Her skills at controlling her parents could have taught Machiavelli a thing or two. Laura Hurleigh: eight hundred years of British blood in a cloche hat.

He began to laugh, and said, "Miss Hurleigh, when you get this little strike of yours straightened out, perhaps you'd like to come back to the States with me and sort out a few of our problems, as well."

She blushed and shook her head. "I'm only here to remind them of their manners."

"Sometimes, I think that would be enough for the world," Stuyvesant told her. "So, if I'm to be a bodyguard, can I get a run-down on the various personnel?"

She went to the papers on her desk, coming back with a sheaf of clipped-together carbon copies. The first page showed twenty names and their assigned rooms; the following pages had diagrams of seating arrangements for meals, for the formal discussions, and for the chapel on Sunday morning: Nothing left to chance.

He was halfway down the main stairway before he remembered the servants' entrance, but he didn't think it worth turning around again. He raised his eyes to the window showing the Hurleigh family tree: William the Ready, Richard the Firm. The Royalist who'd shattered half the bones in his body to distract Cromwell.

The weight of this week-end gathering was beginning to feel heavy across Stuyvesant's shoulders. On the one hand, he was an outsider here, a temporary driver, nothing but hired muscle, who even Laura Hurleigh admitted was there mostly for show. Add to that his actual reason for being here, which was, ultimately, looking for evidence to hang Richard Bunsen with, and what he ought to do was drive back to the phone box he'd seen coming through Hurleigh village and find out what the hell was happening with Carstairs.

On the other hand, he was a sworn law enforcement agent, who was in a unique position here by being, as far as he could tell, the only person on the place to know of twenty ounces of missing high explosive. If he drove into Hurleigh to see why Carstairs had gone off the horn, he could not also examine the rooms where the men would be meeting. If he drove to the village and the place blew up while his back was turned, he'd feel responsible.

He would, in fact, be responsible.

Shit. How'd he get into this mess, anyway? It was the sort of thing his kid brother would laugh himself half sick about. If Tim ever laughed again.

He heard footsteps come up a few stairs, then stop; he looked over the stair rail into the face of the government man, Julian Exeter.

"Was there something you needed, Mr. Stuyvesant?"

"Yeah. You and I need to have a talk."

He told Exeter as little as he could, and most of that between the lines. He said that Exeter probably knew that Bunsen had been a sapper during the War, so he tended to have explosives on the brain. He said that although he personally didn't know Bunsen well, they had friends in common (not entirely untrue, although he'd met those friends at the same time). And he said that he, Stuyvesant, had a pretty good eye for a booby trap, although they really didn't want to go using the word *bomb* in front of anyone else, did they? Because it would get back to the delegates, and there's nothing like cutting into your ability to relax and focus on the job at hand when you were afraid your chair was going to go up underneath you.

He'd chosen his man well: Exeter understood (at least, he understood the story Stuyvesant was giving him) and agreed, silence was paramount.

"Let me be clear," Stuyvesant said. "I have no scrap of evidence that there's so much as a faint rumor of a story of One of Those Things. But my boss, he's a worry-wart, and so I look carefully."

"And you'd know what you were looking at?"

"I've found one or two," Stuyvesant answered, the first half of which was literally true—the man might not be reassured by the whole truth.

"What do you want me to do?"

"Tell me who's here, what the set-up is, and let's go look at where they're meeting."

As Exeter led the way back up the stairs, he told Stuyvesant, "Four of the five delegates have arrived. Mr. Baldwin is still en route but is expected soon. The next forty-eight hours are arranged to be both formal and unstructured. After tea, there will be drinks, dinner, and then cards or billiards, for those who wish it. Tomorrow after breakfast they will assemble for a formal meeting in the Great Hall, primarily to air grievances. Then there will be an hour's break, followed by lunch, then two afternoon sessions of ninety minutes each.

In between times there are any number of entertainments available— tennis, croquet, there's even a lawn-bowling court near the barn. And after luncheon, anyone who wishes an excuse for walking will be given a shotgun to pot a few rabbits. Not the same as a proper shoot, but gentlemen often enjoy blasting away at small creatures when they've had a tense morning."

Stuyvesant glanced sharply at the man, but saw no glimmer of humor.

"This is where they'll take tea."

It was the long gallery, and the information was rendered unnecessary by the sight of servants laying out tables at the far end.

"So," Stuyvesant said. "The common rooms will be the long gallery, the solar, and the billiards room upstairs, and downstairs the breakfast room for meals and the Great Hall for more formal meetings."

"The Hall will also be used for dinner both nights. And, of course, the chapel on Sunday morning, if they manage to work out the details of how to do a joint service, Anglican and Chapel. It may just be a prayer meeting, not Communion."

As a Catholic who hadn't been to church since his father's funeral eleven years before, Stuyvesant figured the exact disagreements that existed between the various factions of Protestant were beyond him. Enough to help check the place for bombs.

Although in truth, Stuyvesant had absolutely zero expectation of finding anything untoward. Certainly not this early in the week-end, especially since the Prime Minister wasn't even here yet. Nonetheless, he ran his eyes over the familiar paintings and sculptures in the gallery, then opened the door leading into the solar. Exeter followed, watching his every move.

The room was empty, the fire unlit, although the servants had brought in two crates of various drinks. He started there, found all the bottles sealed, then started to work his way around the room, lifting furniture, peering behind the books on the shelves, taking the lids off decorative jars and looking inside.

The first guests came into the gallery, and were offered tea. Exeter shut the door.

"You don't have to stay here," Stuyvesant told him, and climbed up on a chair to look at a particularly ugly Chinese vase on a high shelf.

"You're right, I should probably get back to work. You sure I can't help you?"

"Only if I find anything," he said. "I'll let you know if I do."

"I'd appreciate that," Exeter said, a second near-invisible trace of humor, and let himself out of the solar.

Stuyvesant finished with the solar minutes before the servants opened the doors and started setting out the drinks trolley. The billiards room, although larger than the solar, was easier to search, being less crowded with decorative knickknacks and furniture.

And being a bigger room, it would require a larger quantity of explosive to destroy.

He found nothing.

Which could mean there was nothing to find, and Aldous Carstairs had gone off for a week-end in Paris and neglected to mention that the Army had found their missing explosive. Or it could mean Carstairs was lying unconscious in the hospital after a road accident, and Harris Stuyvesant was on his own.

It could also mean Richard Bunsen hadn't put his bomb into place yet.

As he moved into the long gallery, heading for the stairs, he saw Laura Hurleigh and her father, in a group with Bunsen and four others. Laura caught Stuyvesant's eye, making a small hand gesture to indicate that he should join them.

He shook his head and would have moved on, but her look grew more emphatic, one eyebrow raised in a manner that instantly evoked his mother saying, "Don't make me come get you, Harris Stuyvesant."

A look like that, a man had no choice: Stuyvesant walked over to join them.

As he drew near, he realized that one of the men was Stanley Baldwin. The Prime Minister was a placid man with a high forehead, a large nose, and a slight look of eyebrow-cocked disbelief that lent his face more humor than one would expect. He had a reputation for being a fair-minded plodder, which Stuyvesant didn't think at all a bad thing to be, for a government official, and although he had been through Cambridge and was a cousin of Rudyard Kipling, he'd managed the family iron works before running for Parliament. The Prime Minister was listening to something Laura was saying, and when she finished, he and the others laughed.

They called it "breaking the ice," Stuyvesant reflected; he could only pray that once the ice broke, it wouldn't drop them all into deadly cold waters below.

Laura reached out and pulled him in. "Mr. Baldwin, I don't believe you've met Richard's friend from America, Harris Stuyvesant? Mr. Stuyvesant is a particularly appropriate addition to this little get-together, not only bringing the outsider's point of view, but because he can claim membership in both the working class and management. Harris, Mr. Baldwin."

She made it sound as if the Prime Minister of Britain should be just delighted to make his acquaintance, and to Stuyvesant's astonishment, Baldwin was. Or acted as though he was. She gave the conversation a couple of gentle nudges and then stood back as five men—Britain's Prime Minister; a recently elevated Ford Motor consultant; the charismatic Union representative with the film-star looks; a mine owner with a face like a bulldog; and a slim young male secretary on his longest trip out of London in his whole life—began to argue genially about cricket.

After a bit, Laura rested her hand briefly on the Prime Minister's sleeve, murmured something, and faded backwards out of the circle.

Five minutes later, Stuyvesant pulled the same self effacement, and walked towards the tea samovar. Laura detached herself from another group, this one centered around her father, and slipped her arm through his to continue in the direction of the refreshments.

"It seems to be starting off well," he said.

"It was heavy going for the first few minutes, but a bit of oil has spilt on the gears and it's moving more easily now."

"Is that your job, spilling oil?"

"We aristos have to be good for something."

"Well, better oil than blood."

"Hmm," she said, distracted by the pouring of tea out of the samovar, and Stuyvesant decided she hadn't heard him. She was, he noticed, one of two women (other than the maids) in a room full of powerful men, the other being the iron-faced lady secretary of the miners' president, Herbert Smith.

"Can I ask," he said, lowering his voice for her ears only, "is it going to be a problem for you, being Bunsen's . . ."

"Associate?" She completed his sentence, one eyebrow arched with amusement. "I am openly an advocate of the working class, Mr. Stuyvesant. Anything further, well, they may have heard rumors, but the British are far too polite to believe rumors. Here, I am no one's mistress but my own. One lump or two?"

She held out a cup and saucer that looked as if they might have come from a London museum, and he closed his big fingers gingerly on the saucer. "No sugar, thanks."

"Really? Well, you must have one of the cheese savories, they're divine, and one of these little purply things, for after. Now, my dear Mr. Stuyvesant, please tell me you know something about the sport of boxing?"

"I've been in the ring once or twice, in my youth," he admitted.

"Oh, bless you! Come," she ordered, and propelled him across the room to where a gruff old man and a nervous-looking young man were planted. "Mr. Smith, this is a friend of Richard's from America, Harris Stuyvesant, who was telling me that he used to box when he was a boy. Harris, this is Herbert Smith, who as you know is the president of the Miners' Federation. Mr. Smith was a prize fighter when he was a lad in the fields, weren't you, Mr. Smith? And this is his associate, Tom Decater, who's interested in baseball."

Smith was a stolid old Yorkshire miner who looked as if he could still manage a hard right to the chin if he had to. Born in a work-house, orphaned not much later, he'd gone into the pits at the age of ten. He gazed calmly at the American over a pair of wire spectacles, and seemed to have summed him up in two seconds flat—not, the American was relieved to see, disapprovingly. The men did as they'd been told, and talked about boxing for a few minutes, then moved to cricket, and baseball, and to life in New York.

As they talked, Stuyvesant watched out of the corner of his eye as Laura closed in on the next group, all miners' representatives, and abducted two of the men—one thin and with an office stoop, the other who would look more at home in front of a punching bag—in a manner that was halfway between flirtatious and maternal. She deposited the two in a group of the Prime Minister's men and started them talking, then performed the same exchange with a pair of that group, returning them to the miners' representatives. She spent the next hour stirring the mixture, providing constant variety, planting conversational seeds and waiting until they had begun to germinate, then moved on to the next flagging group. She touched and patted, laughed and admired, stepped in the instant any voices were raised and soothed, distracted, and amused.

He was exhausted just watching her.

At half-past five the platters were allowed to go empty, and Laura began to circumnavigate the room with the suggestion that drinks would be served in the room next door in an hour, if any of the gentlemen wished to change for dinner.

Stuyvesant waited until he saw Bunsen leave, and drifted away behind him until he turned into his bedroom, at which point the American moved rapidly to intercept the closing door. Bunsen looked around, surprised, when the door didn't shut.

"Oh, it's you. Come in," he said, although Stuyvesant was already in and the door shutting behind him. "I hope you brought your D.J. We didn't have much time to warn you what you'd need here."

Stuyvesant assured him that he was well set for dinner jackets, then asked him, "How close do you want me to stick to you?"

"Sorry?"

"As your bodyguard, that is. Yesterday in London, I made it a point to be at your shoulder in a crowd, but I don't imagine that's what you'd want here."

"Certainly not. You probably ought to talk to Laura about that, she's the one who thought I should have a bodyguard."

"I will. But as far as you're concerned, you'd like me to be discreet?"

"Discreet would be good."

"That's fine. But we should have a signal if you want me to back away for a while. Perhaps lifting two fingers, like you're holding a cigarette only without the cigarette?" It was a gesture unnatural enough not to be made by accident, but easy enough to work into a conversation's normal hand gestures—he'd used it before, with men he was guarding.

Bunsen stretched his index and middle fingers out from his other fingers experimentally, and said, "Sure, that's easy to remember."

"Just try to forget I'm there. If you go for a walk, I'll be behind you, but you can ignore me. If you're in a room with a few others, I'll probably be nearby rather than inside, although in a crowd like this afternoon, I'll stick closer. And whenever you're in here, I'll be right outside the door."

"Is that really necessary?"

"Yes," he said firmly. And didn't add, *And if you'd thought of sneaking off to Laura Hurleigh's rooms during the night, you'll just have to keep it in your pants.*

"If you say so."

"Now, I have to go and talk with Laura for a few minutes, but I should be back before you're ready to go down. I'd appreciate it if you wouldn't go out of your rooms or let anyone in while I'm away." It was absolutely unnecessary, would have been unnecessary even if Bunsen was one of the good guys, but if it discouraged him from wandering, fine.

"Very well," he said, beginning to sound irritated. It was a phase most people went through, who weren't accustomed to a tight guard.

"Thank you. So if you'd lock your door now, I'll be off."

He stood outside until he heard the key turn in the lock, and went to find Laura Hurleigh.

She was not in her room, nor in the solar, nor in the Great Hall. He finally located her under the portico where he had sheltered while watching the rain fall on Grey. When Stuyvesant came out, she was fumbling through the pockets of her skirt for a somewhat crumpled packet of cigarettes.

Stuyvesant snapped his lighter into life and held it to her; she guided his hand with hers until the cigarette was going, and nodded her thanks. She pushed her dark hair away from her face and leaned back against the wall, smoke drifting from her narrow Spanish nose. He took off his jacket and eased it between the thin fabric of her dress and the stones.

"You must feel like you've been run through a mangle," he said.

"What, from a tea-party?"

"That was no tea-party, that was a major phase of negotiations. I've got to hand it to you—I wouldn't have thought anyone could keep that group of men from each other's throats for an entire hour."

"And the week-end is young," she remarked, sounding a touch grim.

"It'll get easier, now that you've set the tone."

"It never ceases to amaze me, the extent to which this country will defer to my kind of people."

"C'mon, don't short-change yourself. It's not *what* you are that pulled it off, it's who."

"That's very sweet of you to say, Mr. Stuyvesant."

"You called me 'Harris' in there, you're welcome to go on with it. And I say nothing but the truth. They should elect you Queen and toss out the rest of the system."

"Now, there is a political arrangement I've not heard mooted. An elected monarchy."

"Make it an absolute monarchy, all or nothing."

"I shall try to bring up your proposal over this week-end."

"Seriously," he said. "That was an impressive job of oil-pouring in there. And I think you ought to go put up your feet for a few minutes before it starts again."

She took a last draw of tobacco and planted the butt in a bowl of sand laid there for the purpose. He held the door for her; she handed him his jacket.

"I need to know," he said. "How close do you want me to stick to Bunsen?"

"I'm not sure I understand."

"I'm here as his bodyguard, although as you say, it's mostly as decoration. Still, don't you think I should go through the motions? Not on the level of pushing him through a crowd and watching for rotten tomatoes; just keeping a discreet eye."

"We shall assume that here the rotten tomatoes will be strictly verbal. Just use your judgment, Harris."

"Well, if I'm not going to be glued to his hip, maybe you should take my name off the dinner lists. I may stick my head in, but it's better not to be nailed down to one place."

"As you wish."

"And, let me know if there's anything I can help you with," he told her. Her smile was warm as she went inside, leaving him thinking that Laura Hurleigh was one heck of a lady.

Dinner that night lacked the ease of the tea-time gathering, either because the setting was more formal, or because Laura Hurleigh was not permitted to circulate and turn matters to her satisfaction. Watching the currents in the room, Stuyvesant thought it a good thing that, for this time anyway, the three groups had been seated to themselves.

During dinner the Duke was at his most formal and the air of the Great Hall pressed down on all sides. Everyone breathed an exhalation of relief when the final course was cleared and they could adjourn to the billiards room and its neighboring library for brandy and cigars. Laura and the lady secretary disappeared for a very few minutes, the scantest of recognition to the traditional withdrawal of the ladies.

Laura came into the billiards room and re-inserted herself into the group, allowing one mine owner to get her a brandy and soda, permitting young Tom Decater to light her cigarette. To Stuyvesant's interest, a short time later the Duke stood up and left, as if for a brief visit to the restroom. Except that he did not come back, and Laura's presence ruled.

The next three hours passed like tea-time had, but smoothed further by alcohol, gramophone music, and the bonhomie of the billiards table. Laura kept in the background, but seemed to know the very moment when constraint would re-appear or two men would recall that they were opponents, when she would appear at their elbow with a question, a story, or some entertaining distraction. Once she told a joke that sounded perfectly innocent until one thought about it, then stood with a surprised look on her lovely face when the men around her began to snort with laughter. Later, she recited a conversation she'd overheard between Chancellor Churchill and his wife about water-colors, a duet of a woman's voice alternating with a gruff, pompous man that had even the Prime Minister hiding his amusement. And before the evening was over, she succeeded in snaring nine assorted males for a game of charades, thus providing Harris Stuyvesant with the lifetime memory of the Prime Minister of Britain crawling on the carpet and yapping in an illustration of the phrase "barking mad."

Weaving through it all, Lady Laura Hurleigh glowed, luminous with purpose as she moved through the roomful of implacable foes and soothed their raised hackles beneath her aristocratic hands, convincing them of their shared interests, reminding them that they were human beings, and British, before they were supporters of an unyielding position.

As the foundation for an agreement, it was unlikely, it was unhurried, and it was brilliant.

It was also a huge amount of work. By the time the party broke up at a quarter to one in the morning, Stuyvesant wondered if he'd have to carry the poor woman upstairs. But she managed to walk under her own power, charming to her last good-night wave, having planted chaste, almost motherly kisses on the late-night bristle of the two mine owners and one of the Prime Minister's assistants.

Stuyvesant watched Bunsen's door shut, heard the lock turn, and went to take up his place at the meeting of the corridors. To his surprise, Laura's door came open a minute later and she leaned out.

"I just wanted to thank you, Harris, for all you've done."

He walked down the corridor, so as not to have to raise his voice and disturb the other inmates. "I haven't done much of anything except drink good booze and watch a beautiful lady work her heart out."

He succeeded in making her blush again. "Good night, Mr. Stuyvesant."

"Sleep well, Miss Hurleigh."

The night passed without event, Stuyvesant sitting in his chair until he felt sleep creeping up on him, at which point he would get up and go search one or another of the rooms. Each time he returned to his chair, the tiny scrap of carpet fiber he'd shoved between the door and the jamb was still there, assuring him that Bunsen had not left his room—even if he'd brought climbing ropes in his suitcase, going out of the window wouldn't get him past the guards.

At three o'clock, he snapped awake at the first fall of a foot on the bottom stair. He watched as the guard who'd pointed a gun at him the previous afternoon appeared up the stairs. This time, his hands were empty.

"Mr. Jones," he murmured in greeting.

"Mr. Stuyvesant. All quiet here?"

"Not a stir."

"I just came to see if you'd like a spell off. I just came back on duty, and I can give you a few hours if you'd like a kip."

Kip probably meant nap. "No, I'm fine. Maybe in the morning when they're having breakfast and their morning session."

"That'd be eight to eleven or thereabouts. You sure that's enough?"

"Should be fine."

"Can I bring you some coffee?"

To trust him or not? Normally on guard duty, Stuyvesant would have touched nothing he didn't see poured out, but this was the Duke's man.

Yeah, he thought, and Aldous Carstairs' machine, whatever its purpose, is ticking away in the background.

"I don't think so. It'll just make me need to piss. But thanks."

"Have it your way. I'll be through again in an hour or so, I can bring you something then if you want."

Stuyvesant thanked him, and Jones went away.

The night passed that way, completing a close examination of all the public rooms, punctuated by the occasional meaningless noise and by Gwilhem Jones's hourly visits. At seven in the morning, Stuyvesant saw a light go on under Bunsen's door. Seven minutes later, one of the maids brought up a tray. Stuyvesant took it from her, checked it perfunctorily, and tapped on Bunsen's door.

Bunsen was up, looking like a character in a play—the romantic lead, in velvet dressing gown. He was surprised at the face behind the tray. "Stuyvesant, hello."

"Shall I put this on the desk?"

"Certainly," Bunsen said, stepping back to let him in.

"I thought I'd tell you that once things are under way, I'll be going off duty for a few hours. It might be good if you stay with the others until I'm there to watch your back."

"I hardly think that's necessary, Stuyvesant. No one here is about to come after me with a club in their hand."

"Whatever you like," he said, and let himself out. This time, Bunsen did not lock the door after him.

He'd known from the beginning that proper guard duty was utterly impossible under these circumstances. If anyone were wanting just to assassinate Bunsen, they could do so ten times over—poison in his breakfast tea, a sniper's bullet as he took a walk outside, shinnying up the drain-pipe to knife him in his bed, you name it. Three men and complete control over Bunsen's every action was the minimum; neither requirement had any chance of being met.

But after all, his guard duty was primarily an act, on two fronts. Bunsen needed a burly assistant to keep face in front of the other men with burly assistants; and Stuyvesant needed an excuse to be here and sniffing for any indication of a bomb. He'd examined every inch of the breakfast and meeting rooms during his night-time prowls, and was satisfied that the only way an explosive device could lie there would be if it had been inserted behind the wallpaper thirty years before.

Which didn't mean that one of the participants wouldn't bring one in with him, but brief-cases were being checked, and really, damn it, if Aldous Carstairs seriously believed a bomb might go off near his Prime Minister, he'd have done something more than hijack a stray American for the purpose of finding it.

At half past eight, the delegates were well settled into their first formal session. Stuyvesant stood outside the doors and listened for a few minutes. By now he knew most of the voices well enough to identify the speakers. Herbert Smith's dogged Yorkshire accents came clear through the heavy wood.

"—what some of my colleagues say, we are not out to overthrow Capitalism. You say that miners have got to accept a cut in pay or risk permanent mine closures across the country, but I say to you that the miners need to feel that the owners are taking a pay cut as well."

The Prime Minister spoke up. "Despite my respected colleague's protestations, I have to point out that there are among the Miners' Union those who openly profess scorn of Parliament, who wish to wield power over a rightful and constitutional government, and who threaten, in point of fact, to hold the nation to ransom with their General Strike."

Smith retorted, "It is the owners who threaten to lock out—"

He was cut off by Richard Bunsen. "It is difficult not to sympathize with those who see Parliament as an empty façade, when we have only recently watched a single newspaper dismantle a legally elected government."

Voices rose, but above the men's voices came that of Laura Hurleigh. "Mr. Bunsen," she said firmly. "We do not encourage name-calling here."

Stuyvesant nodded in satisfaction, and took his gritty eyes and heavy limbs off to bed—round-the-clock bodyguarding was all well and good, but if he didn't get some sleep, he'd be in no shape to recognize a bomb if he was handed one with a fizzing ignition cord.

He found Exeter (who looked disgustingly well rested) and told him he was going to sleep for a few hours, tacked a Do Not Disturb note on the door of the broom-closet bedroom, stripped to his shorts, and fell into bliss.

Chapter Fifty-Eight

THE VOICE CAME from a great distance. A voice speaking a foreign language. He was in the trenches; the Germans must have overrun them. He pulled the pillow over his head, in hopes they would pass him by, and the voice retreated.

Then a rat landed on his shoulder, and in a whirl of movement he was upright with his revolver on the German.

Not a German. A young woman. What was a young woman doing in the trenches? A terrified young woman, white, wide-eyed, her hands up and out. A familiar, terrified young woman. *Honey.*

"Deedee," he croaked.

"Sir?" The maid's voice climbed and broke.

He looked at the thing in his hand, shoved it under the pillow, and twitched the covers over his bare, dangling legs. "Sorry, hon— Sorry, Deedee, you surprised me. What is it?"

"I'm sorry, sir, I—That is to say, Mr. Gallagher—There was a—"

"Kid: Spit it out."

"Sorry sir. There was a message. She said it was urgent."

"Who?" At the word *urgent,* he flung the blankets aside and stood up: Deedee took a quick step back. *"Who?"*

"Miss Grey, sir." Finally, the girl recalled the envelope in her left hand, and held it out to him.

He ripped it open, and read:

Harris, I'm terribly sorry to interrupt, but if you have a minute, could you come to the chapel? It's about Bennett.
Sarah

"Okay, thanks," he said, and reached for the trousers on the back of the chair. Deedee fled.

He left the building by way of what Gallagher had called the buttery, which some thoughtful person had designed for the needs of stray men hungry at odd times. The coffee was hot, and he drank one cup while hacking slices from a slab of cold roast beef, slapping it onto some bread, and smearing the whole with horseradish and mustard. He filled his cup again, picked up the crude sandwich, and walked out.

He finished the sandwich before he was halfway up the side of the hill, drained the cup and left it on the bench in the small porch, and pushed open the door to the Hurleigh chapel.

It was frigid inside, the stone walls wintry. Sarah was up behind the altar, dressed in coat, hat, and gloves, looking at a small painting. Not gloves plural, he saw as he came near, but glove; in one bare hand she grasped a soft, leather-bound book, whose oversized pages she had been consulting.

"Harris! My, that was quick."

Instantly, Stuyvesant's driving anxiety vanished: If it was truly urgent, she wouldn't be perusing the art like a tourist, nor would she look so perky and rested. If anything, she seemed more embarrassed than worried. He went up the aisle towards her, feeling his fear turn over and go back to sleep.

"The mere mention of your name sets me flying," he said.

"They woke you up, didn't they? I can tell by the wrinkles in your face."

"You told them it was urgent."

"Not *that* urgent. I am sorry, Harris, I didn't imagine you'd be sleeping at this hour."

"Just a nap. Hey, this wasn't here last Sunday."

The painting Sarah had been looking at was not much larger than a sheet of foolscap; on Sunday, there had been a larger, fairly ordinary nineteenth-century Madonna hanging here. This one was older, and far from ordinary.

"It's one of the Duke's favorites, so they only put it in the chapel for special occasions. I haven't seen it in years."

He let himself through the small gate in the railing that divided the body of the chapel from the altar area. A candle suspended in a hanging glass protector flickered gently, then calmed as the stir of his entrance subsided.

The small painting was dark and exquisite, done with a brush so fine one must have been able to number its hairs. The subject was a mother and child, both with faint golden marks radiating from their heads. Mary was sitting on some stones beneath a twisted tree that he guessed was an olive, her back to a faint panorama of dry hillsides and a city below—little more than a few lines, but enough to indicate that she was on the top of a hill. The baby was teetering on her thighs, kept upright by his mother's strong young hands. He was leaning back to gaze into his mother's face, and he was laughing, an infant's crow of delight. Mary smiled back at him, but she also appeared not far from tears. Stuyvesant moved closer to look at the dim surface, thinking that her expression was due to the ravages of time, but no, he could discern no ease and amusement on the mother's face: The infant might drink in the joy of living, but the mother was having a harder time of it.

"Is this a Tiepolo?" he asked.

"Very good," she said, then her surprise turned to suspicion. "Did you read the description?" She gestured with the book in her hand, and Stuyvesant reached out and took it from her.

The page she had kept open with her thumb read: *Mother and Child*, Giovanni Battista Tiepolo, probably 1756, brought from Venice in 1864.

"Some people bring back bits of Venetian glass as souvenirs," he commented.

"Isn't it the most gorgeous thing you've ever seen? The baby's laugh, and yet Mary is so sad."

"She knows what's coming."

Sarah was silent, as if his statement had layers of meaning. She was standing so close, he could smell the scent she'd put on in London that morning. He took a casual step away, bending over the sad Virgin.

"Would you want to know?" she asked suddenly.

"What, if I were Mary?"

"Anyone. Would you want to go through life knowing what was coming your way? I don't know that I would."

"It wouldn't make things easy," he agreed.

"My brother wears that expression, sometimes," she said, gazing at the Virgin's face. "He meets someone, and it's as if he's listening to a voice saying how horrible things are going to be for this person."

"He's been through a lot," Stuyvesant said, feeling stupid.

"Bennett loves high places, I don't know if you've noticed. He used to spend hours on the Peak above Hurleigh House when he was a boy, and now there's his beloved Beacon in Cornwall. At home, he used to climb up into a tree we had in the back garden. It used to drive Mother wild, worrying that he would break his neck."

"But he's—"

"I can't find him, Harris," she said abruptly, "he didn't make it home Wednesday night."

"Are you sure?"

She took an envelope out of her pocket and held it out to him. It was addressed to Sarah in London; inside was a brief letter, in the deliberate hand of a person unused to writing:

Dear Miss Grey,
I write to ask if you have news of your brother, Mr Bennett Grey. I was suposed to meet him at Penzance station on Weds night but he did not make it. So I thought maybe there had been a change of plans but if there was, could you please writ to me and let me know when I am to meet his train?
Yours,
Samuel Trevalian (Robbies brother)

Stuyvesant felt a stir of unease as he folded the page and put it back into its envelope. He squinted at the cancellation, then handed the note back. "It was mailed Thursday. He probably decided to get off along the way. See the sights, stretch his legs overnight. He doesn't seem to like trains all that much."

"Why wouldn't he let Samuel know?"

"Maybe he did. Telegrams get lost."

"He's not there. I sent a telegram last night to be sure, and Samuel 'phoned me at seven this morning to say he wasn't there, so I drove up here."

"Why? You should have 'phoned."

"Well, I thought . . . I don't know why, actually, other than I felt unhappy about it and you're his friend. I just . . . I thought it would help to see you. And I thought perhaps when you took him to the train, he might have said something."

Stuyvesant stared at her, hearing only her statement that she wanted to see him. Then he cleared his throat. "Far as I know, he was going to Penzance." But even as he voiced the thought, he was hit by another: Aldous Carstairs, too, had been incommunicado since Wednesday. He immediately tried to push that knowledge out of his mind. What: abduction, from a train, in broad daylight?

"Well, he didn't."

"Where would he have gone, if not there?"

She looked surprised. "Nowhere. I mean, why would he go elsewhere?"

"Because he's a grown man, having had his first taste of the outside world in years. Maybe he wanted to delay Cornwall just a bit longer." She seemed to think it possible, although to his ear, the words echoed falsely through the chapel. "What about your mother? Did you ask there?"

"No," she admitted. "Oh, Harris, do you think . . . ?"

"Let's go down to the house and 'phone your mother."

"Actually," she said, "I'd rather not poke my face down there, while Laura's so occupied. I already 'phoned her once about it last night; if I ask her again, she'll start to worry about Bennett, on top of everything else."

"You didn't bring your car?"

"I left it at the Dog and Pony, where we had lunch last week, and walked from there."

"Okay. Well, what about the servants' quarters? There's a 'phone, and Laura won't catch sight of you."

"How do you know there's a telephone there?"

"That's where I'm staying. I'm Mr. Bunsen's driver, remember?"

"Oh," she said. "Yes."

"Let's go down and use the 'phone, see if he's paying a dutiful visit home. Okay?"

She nodded, and then, standing there between the altar and the cross, she stepped forward to lean against him.

She was small, smaller than her great vitality made one expect. Her straw cloche rested under his chin; her hands, the bare one still clutching the letter, came together beneath the lapels of his greatcoat. He held her, intensely aware of the size of his chest, filling and deflating, and of the beat of her heart; his hands, motionless against her back, memorized the shape of her bones. And then she shuddered, and it took him a moment to realize that it was not an emotion, but a physical reaction: Those bare fingers were blue with cold.

"Hey," he said, "you're freezing. We need to get some hot tea into you."

She tipped back her upper body to laugh into his face, a position weirdly like that of the baby in the painting. "Good heavens, Harris, are we turning you into an Englishman, offering cups of tea?"

"Well, a hot toddy would do better, but I figured you wouldn't take one at this hour of the day. Don't you have a heavier coat?"

"I do," she said, sounding both exasperated and resigned. "But it's supposed to be spring. And besides, it's generally thought that when we're representing the working classes, it's best to leave our furs at home."

"That's just dumb," he told her. "You don't think a miner's wife would wear a fur if she had one?"

"Truly, one cannot win," she admitted, and allowed herself to be escorted firmly out of the chapel.

Down at the servants' quarters, he poured them both cups of coffee from the bottomless pot, settled her at the telephone, and went to change into a less formal suit. The operator was remarkably efficient for a Saturday morning, and Sarah came back while he was knotting his tie.

"She hasn't seen him," Sarah said, although he'd heard enough of her tone of voice coming up the stairs to be prepared for the news.

"I may have an idea," he told her. "Can you give me ten minutes, just to see that all is well over at the house?"

"Yes," she said, and he wanted to kiss her, for not delaying him with questions.

He walked rapidly through the gardens to the servants' door in the house. Exeter was there again, and looked up.

"Quick nap," he commented.

"Yeah," Stuyvesant said, and continued into the house.

They were gathered in the solar, making it warm and a little crowded, but the windows stood open and no one seemed uncomfortable. Herbert Smith was talking, slow, gruff, and sensible; Laura saw Stuyvesant and slipped out, her eyebrows raised in a question.

"Just checking," Stuyvesant told her. "All going okay?"

"Better than I'd expected."

"I just wanted to let you know, I'm going to slip into Oxford in a while to pick up a part for the car. I didn't like a noise I heard, on the way up, but I've got it identified and I can fix it before we have to drive back."

"That's fine."

"If you need anything, Mr. Exeter seems capable enough."

"We're fine, Harris. Thank you."

And she went back to work, making a comment about something Smith had said, asking one of the mine owners to clarify a point.

He trotted back downstairs, told Exeter he'd be off the premises for a few hours, and went to the servants' hall to fetch Sarah. First, however, he went to his room, and retrieved his gun from beneath the pillow.

She popped to her feet when he entered the buttery. "Where are we going?"

"We'll need your car."

"Are you going to tell me then?"

"No, you're going to tell me."

They saw one of the Duke's men on the path near the chapel, and another at the gate on the ridge where the path ended. Once they were in the open fields, Sarah turned to Stuyvesant.

"How are things progressing down there?"

"It's amazing. I wouldn't have believed it possible, for enemies to sit and listen to each other like that. Your friend Laura might single-handedly haul them into an agreement."

"Isn't she something?" Sarah said. "Laura always knows exactly what to say, and exactly how to say it. Have you noticed, she almost seems to put on separate voices for each person she's talking to, so they feel more at home with her? Where do you get a talent like that?"

"If she could bottle it, there'd never be another war."

"I sometimes wish she'd been in charge at Versailles. They ought to give her a medal, when this is over."

"You think anyone will admit to this week-end?"

She sighed. "Probably not."

Twenty-five minutes after leaving the buttery, they were at Sarah's motor, standing where she'd left it before the Medieval inn. The same bicycle stood against the wall. She stood at the car and looked at him expectantly.

"So, where are we going?"

If she'd been another woman, he'd have left her behind. As it was, he was tempted to take the keys and tell her he would be back, but he knew that talking her into giving him the directions would make for a delay, and he thought he could trust her not to lose her head in a tight place.

"You remember how to get to the clinic Bennett stayed at, somewhere near here?"

"That horrible place? Of course I can get there, but why? Bennett would never go there."

"Maybe not by choice."

She stared at him. Without a word, she opened the door and slid behind the wheel.

Chapter Fifty-Nine

SARAH WAS A QUICK, ATTENTIVE DRIVER. She also knew the area very well, and twice dove into short-cuts between the major roads, merging from farm track back into paved road without a blink, but Stuyvesant could see the tension in her, and kept silent so as not to distract her.

After twenty minutes, she asked, "Do you want me to motor up to the front door?"

"Is there another way?"

"Yes. Laura was driving, but I think I can find it. That way is shorter, but I have to go off here."

"Then go off here."

The road deteriorated, but she kept the speed up, traveling occasionally on the shoulder to save the tires from bad ruts.

"Tell me the layout of the place," he asked.

"I'll go with you, that would be easier."

"No. And not because you're a girl," he added, not entirely truthfully. "It's just possible I'll have to send Bennett out and stay behind, to talk to the people there. If that's the case, I want you to be there to meet him and get him away. Take him . . . where would you take him?"

"The Dog and Pony lets rooms," she suggested. "And the innkeeper is a great friend of the Hurleighs, he wouldn't say a word."

"Fine. Now, tell me what you know about the layout." He found a scrap of paper and the stub of a pencil in his coat pocket, and sketched in the information she gave him.

From the inside, she'd only seen the public rooms at the front, but she had once been upstairs, to her brother's room, and she'd spent both her visits here walking through the grounds, so she could describe the outside in detail. He listened, asked questions, corrected the sketch, and felt he knew it as well as he could.

Forty minutes after getting into the car, she steered hesitantly off the road, aiming directly at some low branches. They gave way, dragging against the car (Sarah clamped her hat on with one hand) with the sound of a witch's finger-nail before revealing an overgrown track that clearly hadn't been used in months, if not years.

"Well done," he said. "How far are we from the place now?"

"About half a mile."

"I'll get out here. Any closer and the engine will attract attention. Now, is this more or less accurate?"

She studied his rough drawing, made a couple of minor corrections, and handed it back to him.

"Harris, do you honestly think . . . ?" She couldn't complete the sentence, nor did Stuyvesant want her to.

"I think Bennett is fine, just a little stuck. But if he and I don't come back within an hour, we may both be stuck. In that case, I want you to promise you won't come after us. The best thing would be to go talk to Laura—no, not Laura, the Duke. He likes Bennett, and he is well equipped to ride to the rescue."

"I promise. And, Harris? Thank you."

"He's my friend, like you said."

"You be careful."

"Piece of cake, lady," he said, and gave her cheek a quick peck before getting out of the car.

Twenty yards away, he stopped to shift his gun from pocket to belt, and heard the car engine start up again. Puzzled, he looked back, and realized she was maneuvering it to face the opposite direction, for a quick getaway. He grinned: *That's my girl.*

* * *

Stuyvesant worked his way among the trees until he could see brick walls. It had been a country house, he thought, built by some Victorian who had cornered the market in wool blankets or pottery clay, then sold either when the bottom dropped out, or when all the sons died in one war or another. From the back it was an ugly building, although he doubted that the front was much more appealing.

The bricks could use a repointing, the grass needed mowing, and weeds grew between the stones paving the yard behind the house. The doors to the garage behind the house stood open, showing two cars; a beat-up delivery van stood outside. The door to the house stood open as well, two steps up to a hallway, and probably a kitchen. No sign of life, other than the open doors.

One advantage of a run-down house was, the shrubs near the walls hadn't been pruned in a long time. He'd be able to hear a lot, once he was under them, and the day's mild breeze would cover his movements.

It was an easy matter to slip behind the garage, follow the fence that hid the clothes-line from sight, and cross ten feet to the corner of the house.

Problem was, the house was silent. Not a voice, not a footstep, not even through the windows that stood open. There had to be people inside, but he couldn't begin to guess where they were.

Except for Grey, and that wasn't in the upstairs room Sarah had visited. Several of the ground-floor windows had bars across them, but in one of those, the moving curtains billowed back far enough to show a desk littered with objects, one of which was a silver flask very like Grey's. And although in the States pretty much every pocket had its flask, in this country, where booze was to be had for the asking, the pocket-flask was not as ubiquitous.

He moved back around the house to the kitchen yard, found it still empty, its door standing open at the same angle as before. He took his gun from the small of his back and moved cautiously across the exposed wall and through the door. The sensation of being watched was strong, but then he was as exposed as a pea on a plate, so the sensation was inescapable.

Once inside the thick walls, he could hear movement: someone walking across an upstairs room, water running into a vessel of some kind, nearer by. Holding the revolver up in front of him, he went down the hallway, passing an open doorway, then two closed doors.

The door marking the end of the servants' realm was propped open. Stuyvesant put his head around, and saw the expected jog in the hallway (Victorian builders didn't like to inflict on their clients any view of the servants at work). He went down it, fully expecting at any second that Carstairs or one of his men would step out and raise the alarm, but the gentle impress of his shoes on the worn carpet was all he heard.

Several doors, thick wooden affairs that would never give way to a heel, had been decorated with sturdy iron bolts on the outside, none of them new. Only the last of these, which roughly corresponded to the room with the silver flask, had the bolt pushed to.

With his back to the door and the gun out to cover the hallway, Stuyvesant eased the bolt over with his left hand. He flattened his palm against the door to push it open, then stopped, patted his pockets, and came out with the pencil stub. He inserted it into the drilled bolt-hole in the jamb, shoving it in with his thumb. There: He wasn't too keen on the idea of being locked inside a room with bars on its windows.

Now he pushed on the door, which opened without so much as a creak. He took a last glance down the hallway in both directions, and stepped inside.

Being outside of London made Tom Lakely feel uneasy at the best of times, but the deserted countryside around the clinic always struck him as downright sinister. The only animal within miles that he could recognize with comfort as not about to attack him was the cat that lived in the garage, and even that he'd had to shoo away that morning, for fear it would make him sneeze.

Because this morning, Major Carstairs wanted silence. Major Carstairs wanted him to sit inside the garage's storage room and stare out of the small, dirty window at the back of the house. He'd been there for hours, his bladder was killing him, and he'd been eyeing the various bins and containers on the shelves around him for a likely impromptu *pissoir* when out of the blue, the man appeared.

Lakely was so surprised he let out a noise, fortunately too small to be heard. His heart began to pound so wildly he thought the American would hear that, across the kitchen yard—or maybe it would beat so hard he'd pass out, crashing into the canisters and bins, and Mr. Carstairs would become very angry indeed.

The American disappeared down the side of the house, and Lakely swallowed, trying to get himself under control. Major Carstairs needed him, he'd said so. And all he had to do was wait until the American went inside the house, and then walk in a completely normal fashion around the house (the other side of the house) and let Mr. Carstairs know.

The wait was interminable. Lakely thought his bladder was going to explode, but he didn't take his eyes off the house, and eventually the man came back around the corner. The intruder then took out a gun and fiddled with it for a minute, before creeping along the bricks to the door, and slipping inside.

Lakely let out a breath, then grabbed the first bucket that came to hand and took care of his bladder. Only when that danger was out of the way did he leave the garage.

He strolled along the house as if admiring the blue sky, the green grass. He might have whistled to illustrate his nonchalance if his mouth hadn't been dust-dry. Only when he'd rounded the front corner of the house did he drop all pretense, scampering up the wide steps and fumbling with the knob until he got it open, then quick-stepping down the hallway to Major Carstairs' office.

He rapped on the door then flung it open so hard it bounced back at him. Carstairs looked up, startled at the dramatic entrance, and Lakely swallowed.

"He's here!" he squeaked, then cleared his throat. "The American, he's here. He went through the kitchen door not two minutes ago." An exaggeration: add three minutes to pee, since his bladder had responded to the sudden permission by seizing up entirely. But no need to tell Major Carstairs that.

Carstairs nodded and put the cap on his pen, then pushed himself up from the desk. "Very well, Snow and I will take it from here. You can finish up the letter to Steel-Maitland."

He took a pair of gloves from the top drawer of the desk and pulled them on, dropped a small revolver into his coat pocket, and left the room.

When the door closed, Tom Lakely collapsed into the nearest chair as if his tendons had been cut. He mopped his forehead, and swore he'd never leave London again.

Bennett Grey was sitting in a chair. Not reading, not listening to the wireless, not even looking out of the window, just sitting in front of the cold fireplace, hands slack over the chair's arms. He did not seem surprised at the sudden apparition of a man through his door. Stuyvesant, on the other hand, stopped dead at the sight of him.

"Jesus, Grey, are you all right?"

The man's first name might have been Dorian rather than Bennett—the muscular woodcutter Stuyvesant had met just twelve days earlier had been replaced by a small, gaunt figure with dull eyes and four days of beard. He did not respond, just watched as Stuyvesant carefully shut the door and walked over to draw the gauze curtains together.

On the table next to Grey was a breakfast tray; the contents of the tray were untouched. Stuyvesant put down the gun to scoop a cold fried egg onto the limp toast, thrusting it at the other man. "Eat this."

"Why?"

"Because I don't want to carry you to the car after you pass out from hunger."

"I'm not going with you."

"Of course you're going with me. You knew I would come. You were waiting for me."

Grey studied the object in Stuyvesant's hand as if it contained some message. A slight grimace passed over his face. "The body's hope is a terrible thing."

"Ain't that the truth? Eat."

"There's no point."

"Grey, listen to me. Carstairs is using Sarah against you, isn't he? Threatening to expose her involvement in—something."

"I can't risk her life."

"What did he tell you she'd done?"

"I . . . I don't remember. A conspiracy? Tell you the truth, I had a headache and so I wasn't listening. I could see he believed it, so I went with him."

"She is innocent, Grey."

"You don't know that."

"I do."

"Carstairs knows otherwise."

"Carstairs is wrong." The green eyes left the food to travel to Stuyvesant's face; a small frown line appeared. "Oh, it's possible Carstairs believes he's right. But I think it's just as possible that Carstairs knows how to get around you. That he knows what his presence does to you, and he knows you won't be able to see through him, not right away. What you're seeing is his satisfaction, not his conviction. It doesn't matter. Whatever he says she's done, Sarah's innocent."

"How do you know?"

"I know. Now, do I have to shove this down your throat?"

Grey took the thing, looked at it dubiously, then nibbled a corner.

A thud came from somewhere in the house, as if someone had dropped a heavy object or slammed a door. Stuyvesant moved over to the door to listen, but it was not repeated; still, it was hard not to rush the man away.

Instead, he went back to the breakfast tray and poured out a cup of tepid coffee, dosing it with cream and sugar. He put the cup on the desk next to Grey, then sat in the chair on the other side of the fireplace, watching the man eat.

Grey finished the food and drank the coffee, and although at the end of it he gulped and Stuyvesant thought he would be sick, he was not. Stuyvesant sat for another minute, just to be certain, then got to his feet and went to find Grey's coat—the woods were cool, for a man in this condition, and he hadn't seen a rug in Sarah's car, either.

He was standing at the wardrobe when he caught Grey's quick motion out of the corner of his eye, at the same instant a sound came from the doorway. He dropped the coat and whirled towards the door, but it slammed open and a man stood there, pointing a gun at him—two men, since Aldous Carstairs was behind the man's shoulder. There was a gun in his hand, as well.

Stuyvesant spread the fingers of both hands, palms out, even as his head was turning towards Grey, to plead with him not to shoot. The words died in his throat. Grey had the revolver, yes, and his finger rested on the trigger, but he was not aiming it at the men in the doorway.

Grey was pressing the barrel of the Colt into his own right temple.

Half a mile away, Sarah Grey stood next to the car, smoking. At her feet was a scattering of cigarette ends, testifying more to the state of her nerves than the length of time she'd stood here. She looked at her watch again, held it to her ear to make sure it hadn't stopped since she'd listened to it three minutes earlier, and dropped the cigarette to the ground, crushing it under her shoe as if it was the face of one of those clinic doctors. Or that man Carstairs, whom she'd met once and that was enough. He was probably behind this somehow, he seemed just the sort.

She stopped twisting her heel, her head coming up like a frightened deer: Was that a gunshot?

After a minute, she decided it wasn't. She resumed smashing the object into the ground, took a circuit around the car, and looked at her cigarettes: two left. She looked at her watch: eighteen minutes more would make an hour.

And what then? Could she just motor away? Knowing that Harris and Bennett were, as Harris had put it, "stuck there"? She couldn't imagine what it would take to keep the American in a place he didn't want to be—or rather, she *could* imagine, but she didn't want to.

Come, now, Sarah, she chided herself: This is England, not some despotic country where men vanish overnight. What can happen to a British citizen and his American friend, here in the heart of England?

She lit her next-to-last cigarette, clinging to the distant comfort of the Duke of Hurleigh, standing ready to come to her aid.

Chapter Sixty

IN THE HURLEIGH GREAT HALL, under beams harvested by men whose fathers could have known Chaucer, lifted into place when the sons of the house were fighting the Hundred Years' War, one of the mine owners snapped. Despite everything Laura Hurleigh could do to present herself as unbiased, her preferences for the working man invariably crept in, and finally, the red-faced Mr. Branning lived up to his complexion and lumbered to his feet, pounding his fist onto the table and sending the crystal bouncing and tipping onto the linen cloth.

"We haven't gone back on a single one of our agreements!" he shouted. "Not a one, even those that were forced down our throats by the government. We've lived up to our word and now we're looking to be punished yet again for giving way last year and the year before that and every year since 1911. Well, it's not going to happen, we swallowed those losses because we were asked to and they're getting bigger every day, until it's got to the point of standing firm or closing the mines and leaving the country to depend on German coal. And how long will that last, I ask you? No!" He shook off Laura's supplicating hand on his arm. "I'll not be patted and cajoled into bankruptcy. I'm a reasonable man, but this has gone too far."

And that was when the other side of Laura Hurleigh's heritage came into play. She drew herself to her full height, a scant quarter-inch less than the angry man in front of her. "Mr. Branning, will you please come and talk with me?"

"I'll not—"

"Please."

Her voice, not raised in the least, cracked like the end of a whip in his face. She moved not a hair, just waited, rock-hard and implacable, until his chest deflated and his eyes went to the side. She immediately lost half an inch in height as she reached to take the table napkin from his left hand, dropped it on the table, and tucked her arm through his. As they strolled out of the dining room, her voice murmured words inaudible to the others.

Mr. Branning had been raised by a no-nonsense nanny; the habits of obedience were in his bones.

They came back in over the pudding course, Branning looking only faintly defiant, Laura with her customary regal friendliness back in place.

The meeting went on.

The sight of Bennett Grey holding the gun to his head put a whole different complexion on the matter of men with guns. The first man in the doorway had his weapon on Stuyvesant, and held it there, but in seconds, Carstairs had followed Stuyvesant's horrified gaze and saw Grey.

"Hold it," Carstairs said to his man. The man didn't move, because Stuyvesant hadn't moved. "Snow," Carstairs said, and reached around him to push the gun down. The man called Snow resisted the push and glanced back at Carstairs, then over at Grey. After a moment's thought, he permitted his gun to be pushed away from Stuyvesant, although he held it ready as Carstairs slipped past him into the room.

"Captain Grey, what do you think you're doing?"

Stuyvesant answered for Grey. "You can see what he's doing, Carstairs. He's telling you that he's leaving this place, one way or another."

"Don't be ridiculous. He's just getting settled in."

"You sure you want to do this in front of your man, here?" Stuyvesant asked.

Carstairs glanced at the man Snow. "Wait in the hallway for me."

"Sir, I—"

"Are you questioning me, Mr. Snow?"

"Sir," he said, and stepped into the hall. Carstairs closed the door, not turning his back to the room, and took a step in the direction of Grey. Grey fixed him with a look, and gave an infinitesimal shake of the head. Carstairs stopped, then moved sideways to a chair and sat down, his revolver held loosely between his knees. Stuyvesant stayed where he was. The gun Grey held stayed where it was. Stuyvesant broke the silence.

"Seems to me you've got a choice here, Mr. Carstairs. You can either let Grey walk out of here, or you can have his corpse. Up to you."

"Dear boy," Carstairs, speaking to Grey, "you don't want to do anything rash. What would your sister say?"

The gun settled itself more firmly into the skin, and from where Stuyvesant stood he could see the finger tighten a fraction on the trigger. "Now now now," he said loudly, "threatening his sister isn't going to do it, Carstairs. Without Grey, that would be just revenge, and we all know your heart wouldn't be in it. Not with Sarah being a personal friend of the Hurleigh family, and all."

Slowly, the finger relaxed. Stuyvesant drew a relieved breath.

"Carstairs, you've lost this round. And even if I hadn't come and provided Grey with a weapon, you'd have had the same problem within a few days. You knew it, too—I'd bet he hasn't been within grabbing distance of a knife or a rope since you took him off the train. By now you have to be asking yourself how long it takes, for a man to starve himself to death."

Carstairs said nothing, his face stony.

"But even if you stuck a feeding tube down his throat, what the hell good would it do you? He'd refuse to help you, or he'd mess with your experiments until they were useless. He'd make your Truth Project a laughingstock."

Carstairs still said nothing, but he began to look like Grey had when the food hit his stomach.

Stuyvesant forced himself to turn his back on the man with the gun, and looked into Grey's eyes.

"Bennett, listen to me. You don't have to shoot yourself. I'm going to take you away. And after that, I promise, I will keep Sarah safe. Killing yourself will not protect her. But let me just ask you something.

"This 'gift' of yours, the ability to see the truth, it's not a thing I would wish on an enemy. If I knew any way you could get rid of it, I'd tell you in a second. You believe me?"

He waited until Grey gave a brief nod.

"You've been dealt a hand nobody should have to take. But. But—and don't panic here, I promise I'll back you up, whatever you decide. *If* you could find a way to make this 'gift' of yours useful to your King and country, without Carstairs and without being trapped here, would you?"

He didn't give Grey a chance to answer, but went on. "What I'm wondering is, could you bear to make yourself available to the Project scientists for maybe two days, a couple times a year? Letting them run their tests, giving them results that they can think about for a while, then get roaring drunk and go home to Cornwall. Two days, twice a year, no Aldous Carstairs in sight, and the chance to help your country come up with a machine that reads truth instead of you."

Grey said nothing, did not move, but Stuyvesant, sitting at arm's length from him, saw the unmistakable trickle of hope coming into his eyes.

He sat back and turned to Carstairs. "Mr. Carstairs, that leaves the decision with you. You can have the personal satisfaction of keeping Grey under your control, either behind bars or by holding his sister's safety over his head, when every hour you do so risks his life, your safety, and the future of your Project. Or you can take your hands off him, and preserve your Project.

"I think the Project is important to you. And I think, despite everything, you want to serve your country."

As solutions went, it was simple and it was obvious, but it required the people involved to put their own interests to the side. Which meant that Stuyvesant wasn't sure he wouldn't have to shoot his way out of the place until he saw Carstairs sit back and slip his gun into his coat pocket.

Grey immediately let the gun fall away and gasped, as if a hand had been taken from his mouth and nose. Stuyvesant grabbed the weapon, turning it on Carstairs, just in case.

"Get your things, we're going now."

It took Grey two tries, but he made it to his feet, and walked shakily over to where Stuyvesant had dropped the overcoat.

Stuyvesant kept his eye on Carstairs, and kept the gun at the ready. If the man opened his mouth to say something about bombs, Stuyvesant would have to knock him out: The last thing he needed was to get Bennett Grey all hot and bothered over twenty ounces of missing explosive—he was sure to learn about the Hurleigh House meeting, and he'd put the two together in a flash, and no doubt insist on turning the people there upside down, negotiations be damned.

But Carstairs said nothing, just watched Grey limp across the room to the table and stuff his possessions into various pockets.

"I'm ready."

Carstairs stirred. "You and I have unfinished business, Mr. Stuyvesant."

In response, Stuyvesant raised the gun, aimed at the spot where the silken tie disappeared behind the charcoal waistcoat, and pulled the trigger.

Sarah Grey looked at her watch: Harris had said to leave in an hour, and that was ten minutes past. But she couldn't just leave, not without being sure.

She studied the treetops as if there might be a note from him, wafting out of the blue, and then she settled her hat and turned to the woods.

She wasn't going after him. She was just making sure that she didn't leave ten seconds before he came out from the trees.

It seemed a long, long walk through the house and past the out-buildings to the woods. When they had reached the line of trees, Stuyvesant stopped to let Grey catch his breath. He cracked open the revolver and loaded it with a handful of bullets from his pocket, putting it back into his belt. Then he looked at his companion with a slightly sickly grin.

"When did you know the gun had no bullets in it?" he asked Grey.

"I suspected when you left it on the table next to me. I wasn't sure until I picked it up. It was too light."

"I couldn't take a chance that you would use it."

"I might have done, at that."

"And you'd have missed the chance to see Aldous Carstairs practically shitting himself."

"Yes," Grey replied. "Moments like that make it almost worthwhile."

Stuyvesant had pulled the trigger, and the click rang loud. Carstairs blinked fast, many times, as Stuyvesant walked over and bent down before him, seeing his own face in the black eyes. "Never doubt," he said. "Never. Grey would have pulled the trigger. And if the gun failed, he would have found another way. Send the rest of his things to Cornwall, Mr. Carstairs. And I suggest you write him there, when your scientists are ready for him. I'll phone you this afternoon. And now you can tell your man outside that we're leaving."

Now, safe from pursuit, Stuyvesant looked at his watch. "Damn, that took longer than I expected. Can you go now?"

They moved deeper into the trees, Grey walking more easily, although with few reserves of energy.

"Do you think he'll stick to his side of the bargain?" he asked.

"I think that when it comes down to it, he'll choose power over controlling you. Want to know how I came up with it?"

"How?"

"I asked myself what Laura would do. Last night I watched her walk into a roomful of men who hate each other's guts, and in no time flat she had them all moving from their sides onto her side. And so when I thought about your problem, and asked myself how Laura

Hurleigh would handle it, I realized that it was time for a third point of view. Neither wins, neither loses—offering your limited participation was obvious, once I'd thought about it. The tricky bit was to be certain that Sarah couldn't be used as a weapon against you in the meantime."

"And you are certain of that? That she's done nothing to put herself at risk of arrest?"

"Absolutely."

"Do you have any evidence?"

"Not a blessed thing. Someone could claim she set those three American bombs all on her lonesome and I couldn't *prove* otherwise. But you can't fake her kind of goodness. There's not a jury in the land that would convict her of anything but naïveté. I'd bet my life on it."

And as if his praise had summoned her from the trees like a naiad, she was there, running down the faint pathway to fling herself first at her brother, then at Harris.

Back at the car, Stuyvesant folded himself into the narrow back seat, and fell asleep listening to Sarah's cheerful chatter.

the newspapers. However, those who mattered knew. Laura's deliberate self sacrifice, following two brilliant days when she had guided the nation's powers to the brink of agreement, had forced her friends, her family, and her colleagues to think long and hard about what it had meant. About what it meant when a woman like that chose to lay down her life to make a statement about responsibility.

Her death may not have become the stopper to poverty that she would have wished, but behind the scenes, it was changing, directing, even slowing the flow. A Hurleigh had made the statement: That meant something.

But Grey had not heard Stuyvesant's cut-off question. He stood, perched at the edge of the world, swaying gently with some unheard rhythm: to and fro, to and fro.

Stuyvesant made his way alone down the hill to the lighted cottage.

Grey came back to the cottage well after darkness had fallen. The two men ate, and when the dishes were put away Stuyvesant took a bottle from his rucksack and put it on the table.

"I have to admit, the thought of that hooch of yours made me hesitate to come. So I brought you this instead."

Grey picked up the well-aged Scotch in one hand, pinched two glasses from his shelf in the other, and led the way to the sitting room. Fire laid, drinks poured, Stuyvesant took out his cigarette case and offered one to Grey.

Grey took a cigarette. Then he asked, "Do you still have your girl's picture in there?"

"Helen? No," Stuyvesant said. "I...I said good-bye to her back in May. Put a match to her picture and dropped it into the Thames. The sort of romantic gesture she would have appreciated. Why do you ask?"

By way of answer, Grey stood up and took an envelope from the mantel, handing it to Stuyvesant.

It was addressed to Stuyvesant, in a woman's writing.

Stuyvesant ripped open the flap, and slid out the contents.

A photograph of Sarah, trimmed to fit the cigarette case, and a letter.

Grey's absence from Hurleigh that day. Suspected, too, that the Cornish retreat was not to be a permanent state.

"Have you heard from his people? The Project?"

"Not yet."

"Will you go, if you're asked?"

"I said I would. It's still active, then?"

"So far as I know. Carstairs himself came out of it remarkably well, all things considered. Baldwin insisted that he be fired, but the Army decided they could use him again, and he's just moved bag and baggage over to them. He'll do well for them, in the next War."

With the menacing noises coming out of Germany recently, who really doubted another war would come, sooner or later? And couldn't a man who'd proved himself able to manufacture evidence efficiently, then commit murder to back it up, be a valuable commodity in certain circles?

Carstairs' methodical, meticulous work was both impressive and terrifying. More than once in recent weeks, Stuyvesant had been struck by the same shiver of relief that comes with a narrow escape from walking off a cliff on a moonless night.

The worst of it was, he did not think Carstairs was finished with him, either.

"Are you staying here the night?" Grey asked.

"I could find a tree to sleep under."

"I can do better than that. But I'd suggest you go back to the house now, before it gets any darker."

"Aren't you coming?"

"I can find my way in the dark, but if you wait much longer, I'll end up having to carry you."

Stuyvesant stood and extricated himself from the bramble-crowded rock. When he turned, Grey was standing at the very edge of the Beacon stone, hands at his sides, face raised to the western sky.

"Did—" He stopped. *Did you know, that Laura was going to blow herself up? Did you deliberately walk out of the chapel and allow her to choose death?* And the most terrible question of all, *Did you even begin to suspect that your sister would try to take herself along?*

Questions that could never be asked, and never answered.

The true nature of Laura Hurleigh's death had been kept out of a crazy fixation on Richard Bunsen comes over, locates a couple of Bunsen's associates, tortures them for information, and kills them, then aims himself at Bunsen. In the meantime, a bomb is sent to the Duke of Hurleigh, made to look like it came from Bunsen."

"But that's two ends of rope that don't connect."

"Yes, except, what if Bunsen had been killed by that bomb? What if at, say, one thirty-five that afternoon, Bunsen is sitting down to lunch when he's given a message on the Duke's stationery saying something like, 'Please come immediately to my study, and stand near the collection so as to explain your presence in case you are seen.' Bunsen would go, and at one forty-five, boom."

"Was there any such note?"

"None was delivered. But by that time, all plans were shot to hell."

"If Bunsen were dead—"

"—having been killed by his own treacherous bomb," Stuyvesant added.

"—there would have been no one to deny the act of the unbalanced American."

"Framing me would also have set up a nice high protective barrier against any interference from the U. S. of A. After all, what right would the U.S. have to protest a change in British politics after they'd been caught playing fast and loose outside their own borders? But then the bomb failed to go off as planned, and suddenly the whole elaborate edifice tumbles to the ground. Richard Bunsen is a hero, Harris Stuyvesant a misled but well-meaning American, and—" Stuyvesant stopped, and changed it to, "and the Truth Project is just a harmless piece of governmental research."

"And Bennett Grey," Grey added, supplying the missing detail, "instead of being thrust down Baldwin's throat as the missing linchpin—the man who could have prevented the terrible atrocity of a Duke's murder if only the Major had been given sufficient authority to repel that meddling Yank—instead, Bennett Grey is a minor curiosity permitted to slip back to his Cornish retreat."

Stuyvesant didn't deny Grey's suggestion, although he had begun to suspect that, in fact, Carstairs had gone to some lengths to ensure

"I understand the Duke wanted to raze the chapel down to the ground. The Duchess won't let him, but he refuses to repair it. He's going to have it deconsecrated."

"You heard this through Sarah?"

If Grey heard the effort it took Stuyvesant to say her name, he did not comment. "You know she's been living at Hurleigh, since getting out of hospital?"

"I keep track, even if she won't answer my letters. I shouldn't be surprised."

"Healing takes time."

"Some wounds don't heal." Broken bones knit, but time has little effect on loss of a hand, a ruptured ear-drum, or the memory of one's best friend coming to pieces in one's arms. Nor on the feeling that an American suitor has been responsible for it all.

"She's strong, Stuyvesant. Give her time."

There was little answer for that. After a while, Grey stirred.

"What was the Major after, do you know?"

"Not entirely. It's like . . . have you ever been in a glass-bottomed boat? You get glimpses of life, but mostly you get the sense that there's all kinds of currents and behaviors and obstacles just outside your little window. I have spent most of the last three months finding out about Major Carstairs, and it seems he had larger plans for the Strike than just preserving order. And I—I just fed right into it. I gave him Bunsen, I tied him back to you. I think he planned on using me in a more substantial manner, too."

"How do you mean?"

"There were several things he did that, looking back, seem odder and odder. And things he lied to me about—that an experimental explosive had gone missing from an Army munitions depot, showing me pictures of some of the people linking that explosive with Richard Bunsen. Two of those people are now dead. The man, a Communist by the name of Marcus Shiffley, was found floating in the Thames that weekend we were at Hurleigh. His female associate turned up a few days later. And a stray Russian Bolshevik disappeared and hasn't been seen since. The more I thought about it, the more I saw the signs of a good, clean set-up, with yours truly the one being framed. I think his story was going to be, this American with

Stuyvesant took it gratefully. "I was wondering if you'd come after me with your axe."

"I might yet."

"I'd deserve it."

"I think you've been hit enough. You want something to drink?"

"I'll have what you're having."

Grey handed him the glass, saying, "You won't like it."

He was right. "God. What is that?"

"This morning's cold tea, with water."

"Maybe I could just have the water?"

"Come inside."

Grey gave the American a glass of water. Then he gave him a bottle of beer, and a plate of sandwiches, and another bottle of beer, and later, some coffee. When the sun was low in the sky, the two men walked up the hill to the Beacon.

The stone was almost hot to the touch with the day's stored sun, but Grey stretched out on top as he had all those months before, when the sun was thin and the hills were bright green instead of the tired shades it wore now.

Back in May, the General Strike had collapsed after twelve short days. The half-hearted commitment of the conjoined Trades Unions had proven no match for their government's intensive countermeasures. The revolution failed to ignite, and although the miners themselves battled on still, no one expected them to prevail.

"You're not drinking," Stuyvesant said.

"No need to, here."

"I'm glad."

"Every so often, I am, too. And you? How are you?"

"Empty. Yes, I think *empty* describes it. I sent the Bureau a letter of resignation."

"I thought you might."

"The Major offered me a job."

Grey sat up to stare at the American's face, then relaxed. "You didn't take it."

"I'd rather clean toilets. Funny thing is, even before . . . well, I was thinking of quitting. Getting a job repairing cars. Working on the Hurleigh estate."

THE AUGUST SUN was surprisingly hot in this distant corner of England, on the afternoon when a tall figure in a rucksack, boots, and walking stick closed in on a white washed cottage in Cornwall.

The owner of the cottage had been working in the vegetable garden when he had seen the rambler on the distant road. He had stopped to watch. When the man slid behind the hedgerows, the gardener put down his spade and went inside the cottage.

Now, twenty-five minutes later, he sat on the chopping block, his collarless shirt rolled up above his elbows, a glass in one hand. He took a swallow from time to time, and once mopped his forehead with a handkerchief.

Harris Stuyvesant reached the point where walls surrounding the narrow lane fell away and the farm yard began. Two chickens scratched in the soil near the shed. The blond man sat on his chopping block.

"I think I'm lost," Stuyvesant called. "I was looking for Land's End."

All he could do then was wait. If Grey went inside, or did not answer, he would leave, and sail for America next week.

But Grey stood up and walked across the yard. When he was standing in front of Stuyvesant, he put out his hand.

About the Author

LAURIE R. KING is the *New York Times* bestselling author of eight Mary Russell mysteries, five contemporary novels featuring Kate Martinelli, and the bestselling novels *A Darker Place, Folly,* and *Keeping Watch.* She lives in California's central coast, where she is at work on the next Mary Russell novel.

Acknowledgments

A book like this is built on the shameless exploitation of many experts. Thanks to John Tiley for adding the right booms and bangs; to Dick Griffiths, who helped fix one car and sabotage another; to Laura Crum, who named the roses; to my niece Jane King and her husband, William King, for catching stray oddities; to David Pryer of Dalesrail, who kept my train passengers on the right tracks; and to Annie, Carlina, Corgimom, Dave, Kerry, and Phil the Badger, for their help pushing my Cornish dialect a little farther west.

And to my longer-suffering-than-usual editor, Kate Miciak: Thank you. Thank you.

Chapter Sixty-One

ALDOUS CARSTAIRS SAT IN GREY'S dark and empty room at the clinic. He had sent all the others away, so he could think, and he now could feel the absence of life in the building.

Yes, he had badly underestimated the American. Not just the gloves the man had worn to search Bunsen's motorcar, nor the slick way he had managed to ingratiate himself behind the wheel of that very motor: Those might be expected of any experienced agent.

And it wasn't just that he had managed to spirit Grey away. Carstairs had thought he might. In fact, he'd anticipated some considerably more daring rescue operation, appropriate to a penny-dreadful novel.

But to walk in here in broad daylight, then lay out Grey's rescue with the brutal subtlety of a chess master, that was unexpected.

Still, the deed was done. And because neither man could be certain that their agreement would hold, Stuyvesant would not take Grey to Hurleigh House. By tonight, Carstairs would know where they had secreted him, but it hardly mattered, just so it was not at Hurleigh. He had his own plans for Hurleigh.

All in all, Aldous Carstairs was satisfied with how things were going, as they moved towards the final hours of play. He felt the absence of Grey, but Stuyvesant had seen the problem: The amusement had gone out of handling Grey, once the man withdrew from competition. What fun was there in setting oneself against a man who had given up? And the very real benefits of Grey's willing cooperation—thank you, Mr. Stuyvesant!—went far to mitigate any personal disappointment. After all, one could always lay hands on the man again: kidnapping, threat, blackmail. Or something more comple, given the leisure to create.

Now, however, was time to concentrate on the larger affairs of Aldous Carstairs, and of his country. The Carstairs Proposal had made its rounds; it was on the minds of the powerful. It required but a single audacious—one might even say Machiavellian—demonstration for it to be seized and woven into the fabric of British law.

No more slips, no time for hesitation. The country needed an *uomo crudele ed espedito,* a cruel and efficient man.

Who had little more than twenty-four hours to get it right.

Snow was glad for the instructions Carstairs had been able to give him concerning the maps. He had been right, the American had hidden his motor in the back road; on a fast motor-cycle, there was no problem overtaking him.

He had a bad moment when he saw the driver was not the big American, but a small woman with hair the same color as Grey's. However, when he shot past the motor, he spotted a large object in the back, and knew it to be the man.

Changing his coat, turning it inside out, removing his goggles, adding a scarf, and keeping his distance along stretches of road where there could be no turning off let him follow the motor to the fringes of Hurleigh. He'd stopped at that last turning, which was just as well: a glance at the map had assured him that they could only be headed for one place, a tiny dot without so much as a name.

He settled his goggles, tucked away the maps, and circled his motor-cycle back in the direction he'd come from.

Chapter Sixty-Two

THIS TIME Stuyvesant managed to not shove a gun in the face of the person shaking him awake. Which was just as well, that person being Sarah Grey.

"We're here," she told him. "At the Dog and Pony?"

"You two go ahead."

It took him a while to extricate himself from the cramped bed, since one leg was asleep and his neck was frozen at an odd angle, but he made it to the ground without landing on his face. Once out, he stamped his feet and tried to crack the discomfort from his spine, which attracted the frank interest of two small barefooted children and a quizzical dog, who settled into a row to watch.

"Not a whole lot in the way of entertainment out here, huh?" he asked them. The kids giggled; the dog grinned.

Giving a final loud and satisfying crack to his neck, he left his audience to their bare stage, walked around the same bicycle propped against the wall, and ducked inside the Dog and Pony.

Grey and Sarah were just concluding business with the innkeeper's wife, who, it seemed, did have two nice, light, upstairs rooms, both with adjoining baths that could be considered private baths, since there were no other guests just at present, although the rooms weren't next to each other, she hoped the lady and gentleman didn't mind that? They were ever so nice, especially the one at the far end that had a view over the hills, although come to think of it, its most recent occupant had been a year before, or perhaps it was 1924, in any case it was the year the river flooded, but it hardly mattered because both rooms could be set to rights in just a shake, fresh sheets and all, if the gentleman and lady would like to sit in the garden for a while?

She bustled off. The wizened innkeeper and his three customers (who appeared the same trio who had been in residence when Stuyvesant had been here a week before, in the same seats, wearing the same clothes) gazed in silence at the foreigners. Sarah beamed at them and led her brother out. Stuyvesant asked if there might be a public telephone box in the village.

The gnome gave a jerk of the head, which turned out to be a remarkably efficient means of communication: The gesture indicated that yes, there was a phone box; the angle of the jerk said it lay to the north, and the slight simultaneous tip to the chin suggested that Stuyvesant should go out of the door before turning north. Stuyvesant thanked him, and found the box just where the man had indicated. Unfortunately, the gesture had failed to communicate that the instrument was not working. He went back into the inn.

"It doesn't seem to be working," he told the innkeeper.

"Goat chewed t'line. Two week back."

"I see. Is there another?"

"Hurleigh village."

"That's the closest public telephone?" The man just looked at him, which Stuyvesant took for a yes. "What about a private one I might use?"

"Hurleigh House."

Clearly, the twentieth century was not in huge demand in this part of the world.

Outside, he found the Greys sitting in the sun.

"I need to be getting back," he told them. "Will you be all right here, for a day or two?"

"A door that latches on the inside and a pub downstairs; what else could I ask for? I'll be fine."

Sarah laughed, taking his words as a jest.

Stuyvesant told him, "I'll come by first thing tomorrow, when they've settled to breakfast."

Grey scratched the hair on his chin, which was nearly enough to qualify as a beard. "You think the landlord would have a razor I could borrow?"

Sarah said, "Thank goodness, I wondered if you were growing a beaver. While you're doing that, let me motor Harris over to Hurleigh House."

"Oh no, that'd mean going clear into Hurleigh village and back. It would take you longer to drive than it would for me to walk it."

"Not much longer, and I need to see Laura for a minute. I'll stop in the village on the way back and pick up a few things. I hadn't planned on spending the night away, and Bennett's come away without his suitcase."

"But—" He caught himself, before he could introduce Laura's problems into the conversation, and changed it to, "In that case, I'm happy to save my shoe leather. If you need anything, Grey, maybe you could ask one of those urchins out front to bring a message to Hurleigh House."

Sarah stood up and kissed her brother's cheek. "I'll pick up a tooth-brush and a fresh shirt for you in Hurleigh. Anything else?"

"Cigarettes."

"Fine. Come, Harris."

"You go on, I'll be right there."

When she was out of earshot, he said to Grey, "Would you feel better about things if you had the gun?"

"I can't spend my life with a revolver in my pocket. And if I need to commit murder, I'm sure the innkeeper has a shotgun."

The touch of humor in the suggestion cheered Stuyvesant no end.

"Carstairs isn't finished, you know," Grey said. "He has his eyes on a larger prize. He felt as much relief as he did frustration, when you offered your compromise. As if he was glad to have an unexpectedly difficult problem taken off his hands."

"Any idea what the larger prize might be?"

"No."

Stuyvesant sighed. "Well, we're sure to hear eventually." He started to put out his hand, then hesitated, but Grey reached out and grasped it.

"Thank you," the small man said.

"You're welcome."

"And, Harris? In the absence of a father in my family, you have my permission to pay court to Sarah."

Stuyvesant laughed aloud.

As Bennett Grey watched the American stride off to Sarah's motor, he treasured the tiny pulse of bright optimism the man had given him.

As Stuyvesant had thought, the road circled well away from Hurleigh House before returning in the direction of Hurleigh village. On foot, he would have been passing the chapel about the same time they came in view of the village church spire.

"Look," he said. "You don't need to take me to Hurleigh House, just drop me here and do your shopping."

"Harris, I need to go there anyway, as I said, to have a word with Laura."

"But you told me you didn't want to distract her."

"That was when I didn't know where Bennett was. Now, if she doesn't hear from me, she might start to wonder, if I'd found him after I talked with her on Friday."

"I could just pass on the message, if you'd rather."

"Oh no, it'll just take a few minutes to motor you there, and walking it takes a half-hour."

Stuyvesant couldn't think of any reason to keep Sarah from delivering her reassurance in person. However, he did want to stop in the village for his own reasons.

"Okay, but can we stop here and you do your shopping first? I need to use the telephone, and that one in Hurleigh House is kind of public."

"Of course," she said, and pulled over in front of the village store.

"Oh," he added casually, "do you by any chance know the number of that clinic? I forgot to tell them to send your brother's suitcase to Cornwall, and I might as well do that, too."

She reached into the back for her handbag and took out an old, worn address book, copying down the number and exchange on a scrap of blue envelope.

They agreed to meet in twenty minutes, and went off in separate directions.

The secretary Lakely answered at the clinic number, but Carstairs was still there, and came on the line.

"That unfinished business," Stuyvesant said without preamble.

"Yes, Mr. Stuyvesant. I trust you have had a good trip, and all is well?"

"It's going fine, we just stopped for lunch. Have you done anything at all the past three days other than sitting on Grey?"

"Further information concerning our, hmm, mutual dilemma seems thin on the ground. It would appear that none of the . . . participants were informed concerning the ultimate purpose of the material, and without the missing man, we cannot be certain that . . . your friend was the purchaser." In other words, the man who'd stolen the explosive didn't know if Bunsen was the ultimate buyer or not.

"You can't find Shiffley?"

"Names, Mr. Stuyvesant." As if the exchange operator might be listening in for mention of a missing Communist.

"You've lost him?"

"He has thus far eluded us, yes."

"Lots of boats in an island country," Stuyvesant commented. "Has anyone thought to look for . . . peripheral materials . . . in 'our friend's places of business?" Snippets of wire, the odd detonator.

"Thus far, we have found nothing."

"Great."

"You will, however, remain vigilant?"

"Yeah, vigilant, that's me. If you mean am I going back to keep an eye on things at . . . at the meeting, then yeah, I'm headed there in a while."

"And you have found no indications there of . . ."

"Not a thing."

"That is probably for the best."

Was it Stuyvesant's imagination, or was there a trace of disappointment in Carstairs' voice, at the thought of no bomb at Hurleigh House?

"If it's there, we'll find it," he said, and told Carstairs he'd talk to him Monday in London.

He stood, looking unseeing at the village War memorial. *If it's there, we'll find it.*

One way or another...

He shook off the thought, and went to help Sarah carry her parcels to the car.

This time, the entrance to Hurleigh House was not blocked by a neatly fallen tree, but the Duke's man was there, swinging his heels over the pedestrian bridge. He recognized Stuyvesant and tugged his cap; Stuyvesant thought the guise would be more effective if the man had been given a fishing pole.

At the house, they separated, Stuyvesant going in the direction of the servants' hall to change his rumpled clothes, Sarah to the house for a word with Laura. They happened to return to the drive at the same time.

"Much better," she said, approving his unwrinkled shirt, shaved face, and fresh tie.

"Did you see Laura?"

"She's looking a little harried. I'm glad I came, that's one thing off her mind."

"I better get in there and see if there's anything I can do."

"I'll see you in the morning, Harris."

With servants looking on, she did not kiss him, but the touch of her hand made him smile.

What man needed sleep, when he had Sarah Grey?

Chapter Sixty-Three

STUYVESANT FOUND THE HOUSE FULL of wandering men, cups of tea and glasses of punch in their hands, so he took it that he'd hit the break between the afternoon sessions. He asked one of the mine owners' assistants if he knew where Lady Laura was, and the man told him he thought she'd been headed to her rooms.

On the stairs, he passed Herbert Smith and Stanley Baldwin coming down. Baldwin had a pipe in his hand, and was saying something about Utopian ideals in the poetry of Coleridge. If Stuyvesant hadn't known better, he would have thought the men were old school chums.

He hesitated in the corridor outside the private rooms, then tapped quietly on Laura's door. He heard footsteps, and she opened the door, looking so weary, he immediately regretted having disturbed her.

"Mr. Stuyvesant—Harris. Do come in."

"No, you should be resting."

"I'll rest tomorrow. Come."

"Are you sure I should—"

"We're grown-ups here, dear fellow, and during this week-end, this room is my office. Besides, I need to sit and I don't want to shout at you in the corridor." He stepped in, and she shut the door behind him.

"I'm sorry you didn't get more of a rest," she said, dropping into the chair before the fire. "Sit down, please. Sarah told me you helped her find Bennett. Silly man, what's he thinking, not to tell anyone that he'd gone to visit friends?"

"I don't suppose he was thinking too straight," Stuyvesant agreed, thinking that he'd have to kick Sarah for not warning him of their story. "The sooner he gets back to Cornwall, the better."

"Very true. He's all right at the Dog and Pony?"

"He seemed comfortable enough. But Miss Hur—"

"Laura, please."

"Laura, then. It might be a good idea not to mention where he is to anyone."

"Of course," she said, a touch stiff. She thought he meant, she shouldn't mention it to Bunsen, but he wasn't going to argue.

There was a knock at the door, and she excused herself. It was Gallagher, who needed clarification as to the evening's seating arrangements. While she was going over the details with the butler, Stuyvesant picked up the day's newspaper from the low table, accidentally knocking the envelope beneath it to the floor. He bent to retrieve the contents, half a dozen photographs, and was pushing them back inside when Laura returned.

"Sorry," he said. "I knocked these off the table. I wasn't snooping."

"Which—? Oh, those. I used them this morning when one of the mine owners lost his temper, just to remind him that we were talking about the livelihoods of two million men, their wives, and their children. I find that photographs help put a personal face on the issues. Take a look."

Stuyvesant pulled out the pictures. The first showed a weeping woman at a funeral. "That is Maisie Collins," she said, her voice taking on the rhythm of an oft-repeated liturgy. "Maisie is burying her eldest son following a cave-in at a pit in Yorkshire, a mine whose owner is known for his disregard for safety—Mr. Branning knows him, is aware of his reputation: I didn't have to tell him anything but the name of the mine. Maisie's husband died in the same mine, under similar circumstances, seven years ago. Two of her other sons currently work in the mine, with a third due to go down next month, when he comes of legal age."

The next photograph showed a family of six seated down to a meal. The bowl in the middle of the table was not much larger than a porridge bowl, and looked like potatoes and carrots swimming in a pale broth. "Sunday dinner, after the miner has been out of work for two months following an injury. What meat they have is given them by their neighbors."

The other photographs were similar: happy children playing barefooted in a muddy road; a near-naked child smeared with black and standing beside a cart of coal, which the boy had been pulling through a tunnel too small for a grown man; a man with pale eyes looking at the camera, cradling his truncated right arm.

"I asked him to bear in mind that Richard and Mr. Smith are here as the spokesmen for those men and their families, who take pride in their labor. I reminded him that we had less than forty-eight hours together, and that the health and security of the entire country depended on what we did here. He may not agree with them, he may even think them greedy and unreasonable, but we all owe them the dignity of respect."

Stuyvesant slid the photographs back into the envelope.

"Now, Harris Stuyvesant, what can I do for you?"

"Nothing. I just needed to let you know I was back, and see if there was anything I could do."

"Oh, no, thank you . . . well, actually, there is something." She sounded uncomfortable.

"Name it."

"Keep Richard occupied? It's just, he's rather used to being the center of everything, and is apt to become irritable if he feels pushed to one side. And unfortunately, the only way I could see to handle this was to, as it were, become the center myself. If you see what I mean?"

In other words, Bunsen's getting jealous and is apt to spoil everything with a tantrum. But not to say that to his loyal lady. "I'll be happy to let him chew on me for a while, although it may give him indigestion."

She laughed, her weariness lifting for a moment. Then there came another knock at the door. This time it was Julian Exeter, asking if they might arrange for another room in the servants' hall for his men.

Stuyvesant made his escape.

The afternoon session went well. Although no agreements were signed, no handshakes made, the air of cooperation, even friendliness, that came out with the delegates was marked, and it carried them through tea-time with the Canaletto, the Constable, and the eighth Duke's curry puffs.

Laura Hurleigh was the first in the room when the delegates reassembled, dressed for dinner. Any second thoughts that might have risen as they threaded their studs and wrestled with their bow ties had no chance to develop: Lady Laura Hurleigh believed that every man there was working towards the same goal, and they found that they agreed. When everyone was there and the orchestra of voices were being tuned to her satisfaction, Stuyvesant slipped away to the Great Hall, and peeped under the table-linen and in the flower arrangements for anything more explosive than words—just in case.

When he heard voices from the stairs, he left, and as soon as the first course was in front of the diners, he went upstairs for a closer look at Bunsen's room.

It took an hour, lifting every piece of furniture, checking under every carpet, opening every book, but at the end he was certain: There was no place in the room where Bunsen could have hidden anything more deadly than an exploding cigarette.

Of course, the man had the house at his disposal, and he could have tucked it on top of a toilet cistern, into one of the myriad vases, or behind any of a dozen life-sized sculptures that dotted the house and grounds.

Doing so would suggest that Bunsen thought someone was onto him, and he hadn't been acting that way.

Which in turn suggested that there wasn't any bomb to begin with.

Still... He went down the corridor to Laura Hurleigh's room and conducted a more cursory search. This room had been lived in for many years, and the accumulation of objects was considerable. He searched the more obvious places where a woman would be apt to hide a packet for her lover, and other than a decidedly non-working-class collection of undergarments, he found little of interest.

He walked down the corridor to the toilet (where by habit he looked on top of the cistern), checked his tie in the looking-glass, and went to join the others.

Again, Laura permitted the men very little time on their own before she returned. Stuyvesant watched her move through the room, noting how her beauty, after thirty hours of intensely delicate maneuvering among the sharks, had become ethereal with fatigue. Every man there was aware of the tall, slender body moving inside its blue-silver gown.

Including Richard Bunsen. Who was, as Laura had implied but not quite said, not well pleased with the increasingly obvious authority held by his mistress.

Up to now, Bunsen had kept his irritation under control, doing little more than shooting her the occasional glance when her laugh rang out, or scowling when her hand rested too long on another's wrist.

Alcohol, however, encouraged a man's control to slip. Twice, he made sharp remarks aimed in Laura's direction. The first time, Laura shot him a glance of apprehension; the second, her eyes sought out Stuyvesant.

He picked up his half-smoked cigar and moved over to where Bunsen stood, propped against the brass fender around the fireplace, his conversation with the Prime Minister temporarily forgotten as he watched Laura attend to something Lord Stalfield was saying about his daughter. Stuyvesant moved casually in front of Bunsen until he was blocking the man's view of Laura, and said, "So, Mr. Bunsen, what's your game?"

Bunsen was far from drunk, but he had taken enough to lend a slight exaggeration to his speech. "What do you mean, my game?"

"I mean to say, a man in your position, the Army and politics and all, I imagine you've done a bit of everything—billiards, snooker, darts, chess, checkers—no, you don't call it that here. Draughts, is it?"

"So?"

"So, what's the game you're best at? What's the one where you always have to be careful to lose a few points when you're playing with someone you don't want to humiliate too badly?"

"What makes you think there is one?"

"Because I've known you for a week now, long enough to be sure that you don't settle for second best, in anything. And I know also that you don't need to advertise, that you're happy enough keeping quiet about some things. It's enough to know you've got something, without having to shout about it."

Stuyvesant was very glad to see the light of awareness creep into Bunsen's eyes: He'd been afraid the man might be too far into his cups to read the hidden meaning behind his words. Instead, Bunsen studied the American's face, then shifted his cigar to the hand that held the glass, clapping Stuyvesant on the arm. "You're absolutely right, Stuyvesant. I don't advertise. And it's darts."

"Ha! I thought so. I don't suppose they'd have a dart board here?" Stuyvesant looked around at the walls, none of which held the tell-tale circle of punctures.

"Darts!" the cry rose, as Baldwin's assistant caught the word.

The long-suffering Gallagher was dispatched to the distant room where passions past were stored away, returning with a handful of beautifully shaped if somewhat tarnished darts, and a lesser servant carrying the heavy board. In sympathy for the four-hundred-year-old linenfold walls, Stuyvesant suggested that they tack a heavy throw-rug behind the board; the butler shot him a glance of gratitude.

As it happened, the enthusiastic civil servant fell out of competition early, leaving the field to Bunsen, Stuyvesant, and one of Mr. Branning's assistants. Stuyvesant was eliminated next, and Bunsen and the mine owner's man played with increasingly forced joviality. Competition was in their blood, after all, and Stuyvesant began to wonder if this had been a very good idea. Clearly, Laura thought it was not, as she stood with her hands wrapped white-knuckled around her glass, envisioning all her work coming undone in a childish contest.

Bunsen and the assistant were neck and neck, with Bunsen look-

ing to edge the other man out with his final throw, when Stuyvesant
sidled near Bunsen to murmur, "What was that we were saying about
advertising?"

The hand clenched down hard; Stuyvesant thought for an instant
that he was about to have the dart in his neck. But Bunsen stood still
for a count of three, then reached down for his glass, took a final
swallow, and readied the last throw. It hit just outside the bull's-eye,
leaving him one point down.

The game went to the mine owners, but with Bunsen's good-
natured congratulations, the tension leaked out of the room. The
evening broke up twenty minutes later, with expressions of goodwill
riding them up the stairs.

Tomorrow would be Sunday. They would go to the chapel, pray
together, then return to the house, filled with holy purpose, for a final
vote on the proposals made during Saturday's meetings.

Stuyvesant trotted to the servants' hall and threw off his formal
dress, donning clothes more suited for lounging on guard duty all
night, then hurried back to resume his chair in the corridor. He had
scarcely taken up his position when the door to Bunsen's room came
open. Bunsen saw Stuyvesant sitting there, and stopped.

"Can I get you something, sir?" Stuyvesant asked.

"I, um." Bunsen's eyes flicked briefly down the hallway, then
came back to Stuyvesant. Stuyvesant held his gaze evenly, thinking
the words he'd have liked to say aloud: *The poor woman is absolutely shattered with fatigue. If she wants you, she'll send for you;
if she doesn't, you'd be a real shit to inflict yourself on her, just to re-
assert your importance.*

Something of the non-verbal message must have gotten through.
Bunsen glanced down the hall in the other direction, where there was
absolutely nothing to see, and said to his watch-dog, "No, I was just
checking if you were here."

"All night," Stuyvesant answered implacably.

"Good," Bunsen said. "Well, good night, Stuyvesant."

He closed the door and locked it; Stuyvesant was amused at the
clear thread of hate beneath the joviality.

But to his disappointment, shortly after that the door to Laura

Hurleigh's room opened and she came out. Her hair had been combed, her make-up refreshed, and she was wearing a pair of walking shoes and her overcoat. Perhaps she'd forgotten to bring a dressing gown, Stuyvesant thought as he got to his feet. Or maybe she thought it too revealing a garment for a country house corridor peopled by guards, and she'd put on her coat over it.

In any case, she was loveliness in a cloth coat, pale but undaunted: She'd never looked more like her ancestress in the painting, the human equivalent of the husband's sword. His heart went out to her gallant self.

She closed the door without a sound and came over to where he stood, whispering, "Good evening, Mr. Stuyvesant."

"Evening, Miss Hurleigh."

"Perhaps you wouldn't mention to anyone that I'm not in my room," she said, meeting his gaze evenly.

"You're far too tired to be disturbed," he agreed.

"Either that or I couldn't sleep and went for a breath of fresh air."

"One or the other."

"Good night, Harris. Thank you for everything." She reached out and touched his arm, and turned to go.

But to his astonishment, instead of heading down the hallway to Bunsen's room, she turned towards the stairs. Make-up; walking shoes; overcoat: Good Lord.

"Miss—Lady—er, Laura?"

She stopped to look over her shoulder at him.

"Would you like me to distract the guard?" She smiled at him, and Harris Stuyvesant would have happily sliced open an artery and bled onto the guard's foot to distract him, if she'd asked.

They went through the silent house and past the kitchen to the back door. He touched her shoulder and breathed, "Wait here until he's gone. And I should warn you, there may be another guard up past the chapel."

"It won't be a problem," she said.

He slipped out, and nearly stepped on top of Gwilhem Jones, who cursed in surprise and asked what the hell he was up to. Stuyvesant said, "I thought I saw someone making off down the road out in front, and wondered if it might be one of the guards. But it's not you."

"Let's go see."

They went to see, and found what Stuyvesant expected, which was nothing. But when they got back to the door, there was no noble-woman standing behind it.

Chapter Sixty-Four

LAURA HURLEIGH CLIMBED THE HILL her feet had been climbing since she could walk. She stopped for a minute when she came to the viewing place above the servants' hall to sit on the wrought iron bench, looking across the roof-tops of her home by the light of the almost-full moon.

Two or three windows glowed with light, but the outside lamps had been shut down. Without their interference, she could see the white mass of Grandmamma's Madame Alfred Carriere roses along the wall, and behind them the faint sparkle of moon off moving water in the valley below.

She'd wandered these hills in moonlight since she was a child, letting herself out of the ancestral house and into the pale blue countryside, whose every lump and hollow she knew as well as the lumps and hollows of her own body. She had developed a reputation for dreaminess in those years of early adolescence; she thought it curious, then and now, how no one noticed that young Laura's dreaminess corresponded to times of full moons and clement weather.

But people didn't notice, generally speaking. They just created an image, and only if something happened to shatter the image completely did they see what lay behind it.

Even Richard. She was his helpmeet, a bright and dedicated combination of secretary and mistress who had brought with her a dowry comprising immense respectability and familial authority. She had felt his eyes on her this week-end, first approving, then increasingly astonished, and had no doubt that tonight he was lying in his bed picking over his grievances. By the time they assembled for church tomorrow morning, he would be cold and resentful.

Had she wanted to disarm the process, she would have had Harris Stuyvesant look away for a moment while she went to Richard's room.

Men were such simple creatures, easily handled.

But instead, here she was, taking her leave of Hurleigh, about to set out across Gloucestershire in the middle of the night.

She should turn around and go back to Richard.

She did not.

With a final look at the other-worldly view, she took a torch from her pocket and switched it on, pointing it at the ground. She did not need it, and it made the world vanish in its dazzle, but it served to warn the guard of her approach.

"Who goes there?" a startled voice demanded.

"Hullo!" she called. "Sorry to surprise you like this, I just wanted a few minutes alone to say my prayers. Oh, it's Laura Hurleigh," she added, turning the light on her face for his benefit.

"Yes, my Lady. I thought everyone at the house was asleep for the night."

She pointed the light back at the ground and continued moving towards the chapel. "The rest of them are, but it's been a long day, and I couldn't sleep. Do you mind awfully, if I just go in for a few minutes? You can come and watch, if you like. To make sure I don't plant a bomb or anything."

He chuckled along with her, and said, "I'm sure it will be all right."

No doubt he was thinking how charming it was, that even a Red like her had prayers to say. He let her in, lit one of the paraffin lamps mounted on the walls, and went to the door. Seeing her kneel onto the cushion in one of the front pews and bow her head over her hands, he went outside, letting the door swing shut.

The tossing flame settled; more slowly, Laura's thoughts did the same. She recited aloud the declarations of belief and her own pleas for help and guidance, ritual phrases that had not changed since childhood, words that ran through her lips with the familiarity of prayer beads through fingers. Empty, perhaps, but there were times when emptiness was to be desired.

At the end, she eased herself onto the smooth wood and pulled the oversized Hurleigh prayer book from its slot in the pew ahead. She let the pages fall open, let her eyes skip over the words she had recited a thousand times. Those words had not been empty to the men who shaped them: The words had burst like flame from their pens and their minds, shaping the hearts and souls of generations of Englishmen. On the other side of the globe, where the sun had already brought the Lord's Day, men and women were opening their copies of the *Book of Common Prayer,* fingering those worn gilt letters on the cover, and listening to the day's lessons and Gospel reading. Men in Nairobi and Delhi, women in Hong Kong and Sydney, reciting the liturgy of their grandparents, unaware as yet that the very heartbeat of their empire was about to falter and change irrevocably.

She'd heard that a heart could stop beating and then, under the impetus of a hard shock, start again. She'd also heard that, when a person dipped into the edges of death and was brought back to life, he was never the same.

Like Bennett.

That was what England was about to undergo, a transformative shock to its heart: shattering, heart-stopping, all-changing.

She closed the covers of the book and ran both thumbs across it, looking at the lettering.

St. Paul called it bearing witness; Emma Goldman called it propaganda by deed. In one week the miners' agreement would run out and, she had no doubt, despite their efforts here, a strike would be called that would place the worker at the fore in Britain. The parasitic owners' class, the class into which she had been born, was in its final days.

Testimony by deed.

The weight on her shoulders made her want to lie down before the altar and weep. She felt flattened by the consequence of all she had done that day; the fates of those sleeping men in the house below; the future of the sea of her countrymen with work-hardened hands and coal-blackened skins. She could not breathe for the awareness of what she owed family alone: her father the Duke, her mother the Duchess, her brothers and sisters, all the generations of a noble line. And that wasn't even thinking of the burden of friendship and loyalty, all those women and men who had devoted their time to build Look Forward and Women's Help.

And all the while, underlying it all, was the continual awareness of a blond man with emerald eyes, the only man she had truly loved, all her life: her responsibilities towards him were enormous.

As this endless day had worn on, she had felt more and more translucent, worn down by the effort of keeping the exquisite balance of forces. And she had done a good job—no, she had done the perfect job. For once, she was content with herself: No person on earth could have made more of this event than she had.

One more thing, yet to do.

Or rather, two: one for the world and the future, and one for herself alone.

Laura Hurleigh, in whose veins ran the blood of heroes, whose bones were the bones of warriors, sat in the quiet stone chapel amidst the looted artworks, feeling the prayers on her lips and thinking about tonight. It would be, she supposed, a betrayal of loyalty, but it could also be seen as a restoration of an earlier loyalty, set aright.

She sat in the Hurleigh chapel and searched her heart, and one by one, the objections fell away. When the last doubt had gone, she bowed her head, grateful for peace at last.

She put the prayer book into its slot, her thumb brushing a last time on the shiny lettering, and rose, holding to herself a comforting absence of thought. She let herself out of the chapel, thanked her father's man politely, and walked back to the pathway.

At the viewing place where the paths converged, Laura raised her face to the stars. Then, instead of turning downhill to the house, she went up to the ridge, away from Hurleigh House and Richard Bunsen, and towards an earlier loyalty.

Bennett Grey came instantly awake at the first brush of finger-tips on the door-handle. His room was lit only by moonlight through the wide-drawn curtains: the rich odor of the Gloucestershire countryside wafted through the open window. The handle was slightly loose, and shifted a fraction of an inch in its housing before the mechanism engaged; it was that faint rattle that had snatched him out of sleep; movement in the strip of dim light at the door's lower edge confirmed that someone stood there. The knob turned but the latch held. He heard a faint scratching sound at the wood.

His first thought was that Sarah needed something, and he started to call to her but it occurred to him that it could as easily be Stuyvesant. He lit the candle on the bedside table and walked softly over to the door, putting his mouth to the wood to say, "Who is that?"

The answer was a whisper. "Bennett?"

"*Laura?*" He shoved back the latch and opened the door.

"Shh!" she hissed, and stepped inside. He eased the door shut behind her, and stepped around so the candlelight shone on her face.

Whatever brought her here, it planted no turmoil in her. She radiated calm, and looked as sure as a Madonna, her eyes smiling as she reached for the buttons of her coat.

"Will your neighbors hear us?" she whispered.

"Sarah's at the far end," he said, "and the innkeeper and his wife sleep underneath her room, so if we keep our voices low they—"

She let the coat slump to the ground and stepped towards him. His voice strangled in his throat as she lifted her mouth to his.

Her body against him was like a live electrical wire. The kiss went on, broken only when her fingers made contact with the bare skin of his back and shot a current up his spine, jerking back his shoulders and head, breaking the connection. He gasped and took a dizzy step away, feeling as if the top of his skull had come loose; his fingers dug into her shoulders as much to keep himself from falling as to hold her away.

"I can't—God, Laura, you mustn't do that. It's, just...it's too much."

"No, Bennett my love, it's not."

His fingers tightened, pushing her, pulling her. "Laura, no, think about this. You and Bunsen—"

"Do you want me to go away?"

"Yes. No." *God,* he swore, or pleaded.

"I need you, Bennett. Tonight, I need you. Please."

He said nothing, as his excruciatingly sensitive nerve-endings listened to her heart beat, felt the night air uncurl from her hair, smelled the warm odor of silk from the blouse against her skin.

"Do you want me to go?" she repeated.

"I can't..."

"You can," she said, and the warm-honey intimacy of her tone made it hard to breathe. He knew that voice, had bathed in the sweetness of it during the weeks before he had gone away. Knowing and assured, it was the essence of the woman she had grown into, the woman he had helped to create, the woman who had matured in his arms and under his body. Now, the voice flooded into him, bringing him to a halt, the laboriously constructed machinery of his personality falling to pieces at her touch, all control ceded to her will.

All he could do was wait for her to put him back together again.

He didn't know what she was seeing in his face, but she suddenly laughed—not a sound of triumph, but of understanding, even sympathy.

"Bennett, my sweet. I have made many choices in my life, but the only one I deeply regret was letting you walk away without saying a proper good-bye. May I do that, tonight?"

So, she was not proposing to throw over Bunsen and all his works; rather, she was proposing a coda on their long-over affair, giving it a rightful finish after all these years. He knew he should object, that she was being unfaithful to the man she had bonded herself to, but he could not summon the righteous protest: In truth, Richard Bunsen had nothing to do with this.

Some slight change in the fingers on her shoulders gave her his answer, and her eyes crinkled, a tiny shift of facial muscles that made him want to fall at her feet. Her hands came back up to rest on his ribs, and in an instant he was again connected to the electrical mains.

Her smallest gesture set him afire; there was no hope that he could control his body's reaction to her. "I don't think—" he started, but she silenced him with a gentle brush of her lips, warming now with the room.

Her fingers were warm, too, as they came down his belly to the waist of his pajamas, and continued inexorably on. His breath caught, and he struggled for control, but when a small sound of deep content came from her throat and her body pressed against his, he cried out.

"God," he started to say, *I'm so sorry,* but her finger was on his lips, and she was looking at him with those dancing dark eyes. "Now," she said, "maybe you'll be able to keep your mind on me."

He laughed breathlessly, and reached for the top button of her silk blouse.

Laura left in the morning when the stars began to fade. He pushed back the bed-clothes and sat up to light the candle again, but she stopped him.

"I want to remember you this way, rumpled and with your head on the pillow."

"And unshaved."

She bent down to salute his bristle with lips that were swollen with the night's activities, then wrapped herself in his dressing gown and ducked next door to the bath-room. He got out of bed to retrieve the lower half of his pajamas and pulled them on, then obediently lay back and waited for her to return.

For the first time in eight years, ever since the essence of Bennett Grey had trickled into his new-born body on a battlefield in France, he felt at home.

The splashing noises ceased and after a minute she came back, rubbing her hair with his bath-towel. He watched her every move, the shift of her shoulder muscles as she bent to pull up her silk pants, the angle of her arm as she fastened the clasp on her brassiere, the smoothness of her leg stretched to receive the stockings.

Finally, she stood, brushed her skirt unnecessarily, and came to sit by him on the bed. They held each other until the dark threatened to leave from the sky, and she sat back, her hand cupping his face.

"Good-bye, my dear heart."

"Come to Cornwall with me," he said, although he knew what her answer would be.

"Maybe I will," she said. "I'll buy a pig and raise ten children with you, there at the end of the world." She did not intend him to believe her. It was her way of telling him that their paths were going separate ways.

He knew it, anyway.

He kissed her hand, feeling her strong, supple fingers tighten on his, then loose again as her will took hold. "I won't see you again, not for a long time."

"Actually," he said, "I thought I might come to the chapel this morning, for services."

She sat back sharply. "Please don't."

"Why not?"

"Please, Bennett, promise me you won't. I couldn't bear saying good-bye twice."

He studied her face, frowning slightly, listening to unspoken messages. But in the end he nodded, and she kissed him again.

"Besides, it would be too much of a shock to see a pagan like you with a prayer book in his hand two Sundays in a row. And who knows?" she said as she stood up. "You may look up one of these days in Cornwall and see me."

"And what if you find that I already have a wife raising her own pig and ten children?"

"Then I suppose we'll just have to talk about converting into Mormons or Moslems or something polygamous."

"Take care of yourself, Laura," he said. "Don't let Bunsen push you around."

"Never," she said with a grin.

And she was gone.

He blew out the candle and settled back against the pillows, smelling her, feeling the air against his face that had so recently lain against hers. The world was filled with her again, and paradoxically, her means of saying good-bye had guaranteed that she would be with him forever. He lay with his eyes on the ceiling and his inner vision on Laura's face, and wondered what it was that so alarmed her about seeing him in church. Before he could solve the problem, sleep claimed him.

He slept so deeply, he did not consciously hear the sound of the motorcar pulling up in front. Did not hear the pounding on the innkeeper's door or the raised voices from the far end of the building. It wasn't until the feet were outside and the fist was at his very door that Grey startled awake from a dream, paralyzed with horror and the sure knowledge that he had overlooked something: something frightening and immediate and terribly, terribly urgent.

Chapter Sixty-Five

THE CLOCK HAD JUST CHIMED seven on Sunday morning when Laura Hurleigh climbed the stairs in the family house, greeting the man who had spent the night napping lightly in the hallway.

"Good morning, Mr. Stuyvesant."

"Good morning, Miss Hurleigh," he replied.

"I fear you are not very rested," she said.

"Not very, no."

"Nor I," she said, "although I think for rather different reasons." She showed him an unexpected and demure dimple, then let herself into her room.

He stared at her closed door, and gave a startled bark of amusement.

When everyone was tucked into their breakfast ninety minutes later, Stuyvesant went to his quarters. He bathed and shaved and eyed his bed with longing, then looked at his watch: 8:55. If he hustled, he could just make it to the Dog and Pony and back to the chapel to meet the 10:00 service. He put on his coat again and climbed the hill past the chapel to the ridge path.

The morning, when Stuyvesant turned his mind to it, was perfectly glorious, with all the requisite birds, flowers and fluffy white gamboling lambs. His mind, however, was bouncing around rather like one of those lambs between that delicious and suggestive dimple, and the thought that although breaking into Bunsen's office was a priority, perhaps he didn't need to address the job tonight, ending up wondering if Sarah would find stage plays too bourgeois an entertainment.

Distracted by both the thoughts and his surroundings, Stuyvesant didn't register the car parked at an odd angle in front of the Dog and Pony until he was climbing the penultimate stile and the sun, reflecting off its wind-screen, momentarily blinded him.

He looked, and looked more closely, and then he was pounding across the field and hurdling the last stone wall in one leap. He diverted only to slap his hand on the car's hood—still hot—then swung around the permanent fixture of the leaning bicycle and through the door of the inn, bounding up the stairs, not needing to follow the sound of raised voices to know where he was going.

Grey's door was shut but fortunately not locked, or he'd have smashed it from its hinges when he went through it; as it was, the door crashed open so hard it bounced off the wall and slammed shut again.

Aldous Carstairs whirled at the interruption, cutting short his harangue and taking a step back from the object of his wrath. Grey was huddled on the edge of the bed, bent over his knees in a futile attempt to find shelter from Carstairs' words.

"Stuyvesant!" Carstairs snarled. "My God, you'd better hope nothing comes of this or you'll spend the rest of your life in a British prison, I'll see to it personally."

Stuyvesant shoved himself between the two men, then stepped forward onto Carstairs' toes, forcing him to retreat.

"Let's you and me go outside and you can tell me what the problem is," he said firmly, but before he could get Carstairs out the door, the man dumped everything across Grey's head.

"They found Bunsen's work-room, where he made the bombs, that's the problem. And Captain Grey here spent all last week-end in the company of your Mr. Bunsen, but didn't think to mention that the man made him the least bit suspicious."

"Did they find any sign of the missing explosive?"

"The missing—? No, nothing, just the equipment."

"*Bomb?*" said a voice. The big man glared furiously at Carstairs, then turned to see Grey, squinting as though into a bright light, his face screwed up with the pain.

"Yeah," Stuyvesant said. "Mr. Carstairs here got rumor that some of the Army's bomb-making materials walked off. Looks like more than a rumor." He looked back at Carstairs. "When did you come across this? Have they had a chance to look for fingerprints?"

"No, they haven't had a chance to look for fingerprints, bloody hell, man, Bunsen's made a bomb and I want to know why you didn't bother to ask Grey about—"

"For Christ sake, Grey spent maybe five minutes in conversation with Bunsen, all week-end."

"Then you should have arranged for them to talk further!" Carstairs shouted. On the heels of his shout, small sounds came from two directions: Outside the door, Sarah tentatively called her brother's name; from the bed, a thin sound of protest, obscuring a word.

"You're not helping matters any," Stuyvesant snapped at Carstairs, and squatted beside the small man. "Bennett, I'm sorry. Did you say something?"

"She..." Grey said, and gasped, pressing the heels of his hands into his temples. "Ah, God. Something."

The door creaked open, but Stuyvesant didn't look around.

"She? You mean Sarah? Or Laura? Laura was here, wasn't she?" One pained eyelid crept open, looking a question at him; Stuyvesant gave a shrug. "Somebody had to get her past the guards."

"You let Lady Laura out of the house? And you call yourself a bodyguard!" Carstairs sneered. "Sounds to me like you've got them wandering all over the bloody countryside. Do you even know where Bunsen is now?"

"Shut up!" Stuyvesant ordered over his shoulder, then calmly went on to Grey. "What did Laura tell you?"

Carstairs was bending over Stuyvesant, snarling at the back of Grey's neck. "Have you been up to something with the Hurleigh woman? Christ, Grey, maybe you're in on it, as well."

"Carstairs, back the fuck off!" Stuyvesant said warningly.

"Bennett, please, if you have something to say, now would be a really good time."

"Hard to think. There was . . . church."

"There's a church service about to begin, yes."

Carstairs' arm snaked past Stuyvesant and locked on Grey's hunched shoulder. "Is something going to happen at the service?"

Grey cried out at Carstairs' touch, and Stuyvesant snapped upright. In a convulsive twist of muscle and sinew, his left hand drove upwards with the strength of his entire body behind it, connecting with the point of Carstairs' chin. The Englishman's head cracked back and he fell, limp before he hit the floor. Sarah peered wide-eyed at the dark rag-doll at Stuyvesant's feet.

"Sorry," Stuyvesant told her, and stepped over Carstairs' legs to feel his throat for a pulse: alive. Sarah's voice came, asking what was happening, if that was—but he turned his back on her and returned to Grey, holding his hand over the hunched shoulder, not quite touching him.

"Bennett, tell me."

Grey tentatively raised one eye from his fetal crouch. "Did you kill him?" he croaked.

"Not yet. What is it about Laura?"

"She said. She was here, all night. I thought . . . It felt like the parting we never had, those years ago. Not unfaithfulness, you understand?"

"Bennett, for Christ sake. *What did she tell you?*"

"Sorry. There's something, I can feel it there, the Major got in the way." Stuyvesant forced a lid on his impatience, seeing at last that the man was trying to retrieve some stray piece of knowledge driven into hiding by Carstairs' arrival.

"It was deliberate," Grey said suddenly. "She did everything she could to keep me from paying attention to what she was thinking. Like that time in the crowded pub, with you. There was something you were hiding, I just couldn't hear it behind the noise. Was that about the bomb? And you didn't want me to know?"

"Yeah."

"You should have told me."

"Bennett—" Stuyvesant began, but the man waved his reminder away.

"She came here while I was asleep. Two minutes after she came in, her hand was on my cock, and two seconds after she left this morning, I fell sound asleep. She knew I would. Deliberately not giving me a chance to stand back and listen to her."

Stuyvesant made an impatient gesture. "You told me that, what's that got to do with—"

"I mean, good-bye. Final. She said she might see me again, but she made certain that I would not come to the church service, and the way she was holding herself—it was halfway to good-bye."

"Shit," Stuyvesant said as his mind opened to the knowledge.

Not Bunsen: certainly not Bunsen alone.

Laura. Lady Laura Hurleigh, the natural-born strategist.

The chapel, God damn it. He looked at his wrist-watch—quarter to ten, and no telephone in miles. Was that a church-bell?

He turned to the door, then stopped, and knelt to dig into Carstairs' pockets—keys in one pocket, gun in another.

"Get your brother out of here," he told Sarah. "Take him to London, take him to Cornwall, I don't care, just get him out of here."

Without waiting to answer her protests, he dove into the hallway and down the stairs, taking them three at a time, to explode out of the front door of the hotel. He dropped behind the wheel of the car, and shoved in the key.

(*Why was Carstairs so shit scared?* his mind nagged. *The idea of a bomb a week ago didn't make him turn a hair, but this morning it scared the hell out of him.*)

The city car bounced up the rutted lane to the wooden gate at its end. Stuyvesant drove straight through it, sending pieces of wood flying, one of them coming down hard on the wind-screen ahead of him. Past the spider-web of cracks he could see a stretch of bumps and stones and terrified sheep, and the car cracked and screamed as he forced it cruelly over the rough pasture, his mind chewing at the question.

(*Carstairs didn't believe in the bomb, until his men found the evidence.*)

(But he went ahead as if he did. Why?)
(Because it kept me happy while he worked on Grey?)
Another gate fell to the fenders, then another—
(He thinks the bomb is Bunsen's. Grey thinks it's Laura's. Are the two doing it together?)
—the last of which bent metal back into the tire, making steering almost impossible—
(But why the chapel this morning and not the dinner last night?)
—and sending a scream that put his teeth on edge until the rubber shredded and the car tried to dig itself into the field—
(The Duke wasn't at the dinner last night.)
—but there was the gate to the Hurleigh woods—
(two ounces could level a room)
—so he abandoned the crippled car—
(propaganda by act)
—at the top of the path and ran.
(The assassination of a Prime Minister? Or the murder of a Duke?)
(A human Zinoviev letter, a last-minute blow to swing the weight of public opinion.)
A martyr for the cause.
Stuyvesant ran.
Down the winding path he flew, crashing through the trees to cut past loops and nearly coming to grief a dozen times, until ahead he caught the gleam of the white gravel path.

Only when the chapel bell tower came into view did his steps falter.

He wouldn't trust Aldous Carstairs' claim that the sun was rising in the east, yet here he was, about to draw his gun on some of the most important people in England, based on Carstairs' evidence.

But if there was a bomb—he had no choice, did he? Christ, he wished Grey really was a mind-reader, it would make life a hell of a lot easier.

As he came near, he heard singing, a hymn accompanied by an organ. A man stood outside of the chapel's porch; he saw Stuyvesant coming and moved down the white path towards him: Gwilhem

Jones, he was glad to see, rather than Exeter or one of the other government men—long discussions would not be necessary.

When Jones was close enough to hear, Stuyvesant started to talk, but kept trotting towards the chapel. Jones fell in beside him.

"There may be a bomb, no details but with everyone gathered together like this, I think we need to clear the church. I need you to back me up, and be ready to shoot anyone who makes any sudden move. Can you do that?"

"The Prime Minister's in there. And the Duke and Duchess."

"I know. Try not to hit one of them."

The Welshman looked queasy, but he reached under his coat-tails to loosen his gun, which Stuyvesant took as answer enough.

He paused for an instant in the porch, hand on the latch, and looked at Jones. (*If Carstairs is shitting me around on this, I'll murder him.*) "We're particularly concerned about Bunsen's party. And Lady Laura."

Jones's eyebrows shot up, and he opened his mouth, but then he gave a sideways shrug as if to say, *It's your neck, Yank.* Stuyvesant opened the door.

Inside the chapel lay a Sunday image of men in suits punctuated by a very few ladies' hats. Candles burned, the windows glowed, and a boy in a white robe was settling a cross into a holder up near the altar. This hymn was the processional, and the service had not yet begun. The priest, who had been watching the boy for mistakes, turned away in satisfaction to face the congregation, only to have his gaze outraged by a wind-blown, red-faced individual dressed in rough, mud-spattered tweed, crashing down the center aisle. When his eyes traveled down to the revolver in the intruder's hand, he took a step back and his jaw dropped open.

The congregation did not notice at first, since the hymn had just ended and they were fussing to trade their hymnals for prayer books, but the priest gaped at Stuyvesant, clearly expecting to be shot dead by a madman.

Stuyvesant rounded the pews and came to a halt with his back to the priest and altar, directly in front of the family. The Hurleighs were in the front row, behind a solid wooden divider that held prayer books and needlework cushions for kneeling. Laura Hurleigh sat between her father and the Prime Minister. Richard Bunsen sat in the pew behind them, next to Herbert Smith; the Duchess was on the Duke's other side.

"What is the meaning of this?" The outraged voice belonged to the Duchess.

"Sorry, ma'am," Stuyvesant said. "We've got a bit of a problem. I need you, the Duke, and Mr. Baldwin to leave immediately. Everyone else keep very, very still, and by that I mean do not move except to breathe. We don't want any accidents here."

Jones was at the front of the other row of pews, his gun out and pointing over the heads of the congregation. Faces went slack with shock, but as far as Stuyvesant could tell, no faces showed more nervousness than others. Baldwin stood up, his only sign of uncertainty the prayer book he still clasped in his hand. Julian Exeter, seated in the back, rose, as well.

"Mr. Exeter, could you take everyone down to the view-spot, please?"

Neither Baldwin nor the Duke would go before the Duchess, and she stood her ground, ripe with indignation, until Stuyvesant snapped, "Now. Please, Your Grace."

He could feel the burn of her eyes, threatening the wrath of the Hurleighs, but in the end she turned and marched out of the chapel. Baldwin followed, and the Duke allowed himself to be removed, as well.

The moment Hurleigh had cleared the door, Stuyvesant said, "Now Mr. Branning and Lord Stalfield—just the two of you." The two mine owners scurried out, dignity cast to the winds. "Now, Jones, if you would be so good as to accompany Mr. Bunsen and Mr. Smith outside, we can begin to clear the decks here. And, Jones? Pat them all down before you let them go to the house. Every one of them except the first three."

Jones looked a bit ill at the idea of taking indignities with the men who had just walked out, but he summoned resolution and followed the miners' representatives outside. Stuyvesant drew what seemed to be his first breath since he'd entered the building.

"Now the rest of you can leave," Stuyvesant said. The others—

assistants, servants, and a couple of people who looked like farmers, shot up and jostled for the exit.

Not Laura Hurleigh. Stuyvesant's eyes held her in her place.

She looked up at him, and he knew.

"I think you lot should go now," Jones said over Stuyvesant's shoulder. The priest and the choirboys fluttered out, until the chapel was occupied by two men and a woman.

"Jones, you need to supervise out there. Make sure everyone is searched. Then take them down to the house and give them all a drink."

"Righto," he said.

God bless career soldiers, Stuyvesant thought. No questions, no arguments.

He and Laura Hurleigh were alone in the chapel.

Chapter Sixty-Six

STUYVESANT WALKED AROUND the low divider to the end of Laura's pew and settled onto it. On his knee was a gun; on hers, an oversized *Book of Common Prayer.*

"You and I have not been properly introduced," he told her. "You know my name, but the fact is, I don't actually work for the Ford company. I'm an agent with the Justice Department's Bureau of Investigation. At least, I was. I've botched this so badly, they'll probably fire me."

"I've been really stupid, haven't I? Under my nose the whole time, and all I saw was Bunsen. I looked at him and saw a bomber. I looked at you and saw..."

"Beauty?" she said, with just a touch of bitterness.

"Oh, honey, you're way more than beautiful. You're...extraordinary."

"Thank you. Although I honestly don't know what you're—"

"Margery Anne Wallingford," he said. "Killed jumping out of a Chicago fire, last July."

Her face shifted; for the first time, he could see a resemblance to her mother. "Margery Wallingford," she whispered. Her thumb traced the lettering on the book on her lap. "That poor child."

"And the riot afterwards?"

"People were hurt, yes, and property damaged. No one else died."

"My brother was hurt. Timothy Allen Stuyvesant. Frankly, death would have been a mercy."

Her dark eyes came up to his. "Oh, Harris," she said. "I'm so sorry."

The terrible thing was, he believed her. Even now, seeing the guilt in her eyes, he could hear her sorrow. His finger twitched on the trigger, but he caught himself.

"July in Chicago. November in Scranton. January in New York. Although that last one turned out to be a dud. It wouldn't have gone off even if the bottle was lifted."

"Yes, I know. The wire wasn't touching."

He stared at her. "That was deliberate?"

"My only mistake was Margery Wallingford."

She watched him calmly while he worked it out. "Terror without bloodshed?" he said at last. "Was that what you were after?"

"It started back in July, when Richard and I were in America and he was asked to talk to the Chicago group. They were losing their cohesiveness, their authority. His response was a series of tutorials. Mine was an act that would galvanize the city around them. I put on one of his suits and a fake moustache, and made a bomb. They are simple mechanisms, really."

"And put it in a box of groceries. But at least one of the Reds must have been in on it. Who?"

Her lips tightened, and she shook her head.

"And in November?"

"In November, Richard and I had had a bit of a falling-out. He and some friends snuck off to Monte Carlo, which annoyed me. So I packed a suitcase full of his clothing and went to America again, under his name. Booking a second-class cabin, and staying in it the whole time. I enjoyed it, truth to tell—one achieves a remarkable freedom, dressed in male clothing. And while I was there, I heard about this judge, and decided he should be my second demonstration."

"If he hadn't been driving hims—" He stopped. "You're saying you knew? That the driver would be out that day, and the back seat would be unoccupied?"

"I suggested to friends that the driver might be drawn into a night on the town, which went on rather longer than he had anticipated. I achieved my goal without resorting to murder."

"But he went on to decide his case against the Unions."

"The case would have been decided that way even if he had died. Perhaps especially if he died. Now, judges across America are looking over their shoulders."

"Terror, pure and simple."

"I don't know that I'd call it simple."

"And January?"

"January's materials I'd brought with me, instead of having to scrape things together there. And actually, I intended to set it in one of the houses to which we had received invitations—a Duke's daughter is a popular addition to parties, you know. There was even talk of the White House. But I heard of this meeting from one of the local Communists, something overheard by a sympathizer who worked as a maid in the hotel. I paid her fare home, to her own country, and she gave me her key. I set the defective device in place, and the very next day the entire town was talking about it. None of those men will ever go into a meeting without wondering what awaits them."

That much was sure as hell true.

"Why there? Why not here, on home ground?"

"Richard wouldn't let me. I almost think that if I'd proposed to kill people, he might have gone along with it, but the idea of creating terror from nothing more than mirrors and smoke was an innovation he couldn't approve, not on his own territory. I thought that two more incidents in America would do the job. The press would have the entire country seeing terrorists in every tree-limb, which would bring the serious issues of workers' rights back into debate."

"And once you'd proven it there?"

"Then perhaps it would be time to open negotiations here."

"And Bunsen agreed with this?"

"Richard knew nothing about it. I wasn't going to tell him until it was finished."

"He taught you how to build a bomb."

"There's nothing illegal in teaching."

"Laura, they found where the bombs were made," he told her. "If your prints are there, they'll know, very soon."

She smoothed her palm against the book in her lap, and Stuyvesant noticed that she was wearing a crude ring on her wedding finger, something a child might have made. After a minute, she gave a small nod.

"What was the point?" he asked, his voice nearly pleading. "In another three hours you'd have had an agreement, signed and approved. Now it's all gone to hell."

"I didn't want an agreement. An agreement would have indicated support for a system that is corrupt and wicked to its very core. A system that corrupts everyone it touches. Some structures are beyond mending. One can only knock them down and begin anew."

"By assassinating a Prime Minister? They'd have blamed the unions, the mine owners would have won, and Labour would never have a say in government, ever again."

"Not just by assassinating a Prime Minister. By a Hurleigh assassinating a Prime Minister."

"An *attentat*."

"A Hurleigh, bearing witness to the injustices of her age. What man here, knowing what I—I, Laura Hurleigh—have done these past two days, would be able to belittle my act, explain it away as the gesture of a madwoman? The Spartans giving their lives at Thermopylae paved the way for the victory at Salamis. A hundred hunger-strikes and trials brought women the vote. Sometimes all it takes is one. One act to catch the conscience of a king. Or to stop up the sand in the throat of an hour-glass."

"Your mother will never forgive you for this."

The smile she gave him would have bewitched a stone. "But my father will understand."

"Don't know about that. So," he began, but the door at the back of the chapel opened, and a Cockney voice said, "There's a chap here says he has to talk to you. Blond hair, green eyes."

For the first time, Laura's face showed fear.

"No," she said.

That was enough for Stuyvesant. "Send him in."

"He's got a girl with him," the man added. Before Stuyvesant could stop him, he'd opened the door and the two Greys swept into the chapel.

They'd clearly left on Stuyvesant's heels, for Bennett wore a suit coat over his pajama shirt with bare ankles peeping between trousers and shoes, and his sister had on a well-buttoned overcoat and bedroom slippers. Sarah darted down the aisle, her brother came more slowly behind.

Sarah slid into the pew behind the one where Laura and Stuyvesant were sitting, stopping directly behind Laura. She perched on the edge of the bench, one hand on Laura's shoulder. Laura had eyes only for Bennett. He followed his sister, sitting where Richard Bunsen had been.

"I hope you didn't wreck the car as badly as I did Carstairs'," Stuyvesant said.

"I hit a rock in that last field and there was a horrid crack and the steering went," Sarah rattled out, without so much as a glance at him. "Laura, dear, what is going on?"

The little chapel waited for Laura's answer, silence wrapping around the congregation of four. Laura sighed, but said nothing.

"Hell," Stuyvesant said—ignoring his mind's idiotic reproach for swearing in church—and told them. "Your friend here decided to assassinate a Prime Minister, as a demonstration of her solidarity with the oppressed classes."

Sarah stared. *"Laura?"*

The first born of the Hurleighs just looked into Grey's eyes, and said nothing.

"Okay," Stuyvesant said. "There'll be time to sort it all out later. Where is it?"

"Where is what?" Laura asked.

"Laura, you know who I mean by Aldous Carstairs?" She said nothing, but her face grew pinched. "About twenty minutes ago, I knocked Carstairs out, in Bennett's room at the Dog and Pony. He'll be coming around about now, and organizing himself some transportation. When he gets here, he'd love nothing better than to push me aside and take you to a small room and make you tell him absolutely every detail about your whole life. If you want me to keep you out of his hands, we need to move fast. And we need to start with where the bomb is."

She looked down at the ring on her finger then, and started to twist it back and forth. Her lovely Renaissance mouth stayed firmly shut, until Bennett Grey leaned forward to run one finger down the side of her face. Stuyvesant took his eyes off her long enough to glance at Grey's face, to see how he was taking it. To his astonishment, he saw a man who looked strong and whole, a Bennett Grey he'd only caught glimpses of up to now. The heaviness had left him, and his love for the woman in front of him filled the chapel like incense.

Touchstone had found his gold.

"Is there a bomb, Laura?" Grey asked.

She said nothing, but he nodded as though she had. "Where is it?"

Again, she said nothing, and only the faintest twitch of her eyes revealed that she had even heard his question. Grey frowned in concentration, studying the objects in the direction her eyes had gone: the wooden divider, the kneeling cushion worked with the Hurleigh coat of arms, the slot to hold the books.

"Was seating arranged beforehand?" he asked.

Stuyvesant answered him. "Every sitting arrangement was worked out in advance, for every meal, every discussion."

"Laura, did you put it in a prayer book?" Grey asked her gently.

She jerked her head to the side, but Stuyvesant was sitting bolt upright, hit by a vision: Prime Minister. *Prayer book.* "Jesus Christ," he burst out. Baldwin had held on to his prayer book as he walked out.

"Jones!" he bellowed, but to no response—the guards had already begun to escort their charges to safety.

"Bennett, I want you to swear to me, you won't let her escape."

The other man didn't take his green gaze from the woman. "I promise you, Harris, I won't let her walk out of here."

Stuyvesant fumbled to get his gun into his belt while running down the length of the church. He skidded on the polished stones but grabbed the end of the pew and swung through the circle, letting go to launch himself through the door.

Ten or twelve people remained at the viewing place, mostly

guards and servants, but with them stood Baldwin, the Duke, and the Duchess, lingering in some damned sense of captains and their ships. Stuyvesant hoped to God that Baldwin didn't decide in the next five seconds to say a prayer over the survivors.

The big American's panicky approach had them all standing back, the guards touching their weapons as Stuyvesant staggered to a halt before the startled Prime Minister.

"Mr. Baldwin, did you bring a prayer book from the chapel?"

"I don't—why, yes, I have it right here," he said, and started to pull something from the pocket of his overcoat.

Stuyvesant grabbed the great man's arm, ignoring the offenses of *lèse majesté,* and ruthlessly worked his other hand into the pocket until his fingers were grasping the book. The lettering on the cover glittered in the morning light as he drew it out:

BOOK OF COMMON PRAYER

"Everyone get back," he shouted. The guards closed in on their charges, hustling them back up the path.

Stuyvesant waited until they were well clear, then stepped to the railings, glancing below to make sure there wasn't a crowd down there. Checking that the book's spine was pointing out, he brought his arm across his body, then loosed a mighty back-handed pitch. His arm snapped out and his fingers let the book go, as he dropped to the ground and flung his arms around his head against the blast.

Chapter Sixty-Seven

THE CANDLE FLAMES WERE STILL LEAPING from the American's passing when Laura raised her eyes to Bennett Grey. "I need to talk to
Sarah," she told him. "We haven't much time."

"You're wearing the ring."

She looked down at her hand, resting on the prayer book.
"I am."

"I could give you another one. Something that doesn't tarnish
quite so much."

"That would be nice," she said.

For an instant, Bennett Grey's heart started to soar, then fell just
as swiftly as the world closed in again.

"Kiss me," she asked.

For an instant, her mouth tasted of brass. He nearly jerked away
in horror, but then he caught a sweetness, the taste of stream-cooled
wine on a summer's day. He could feel the fear in her skin, and the
hesitation and uncertainty that fought to seize her mind, and the
brassy cold despair that moved in the depths. But there was love
there, too: love for the Movement, love for the future, and above all
love for him.

He drew back to look into her Spanish eyes, and as he watched, the uncertainty faltered and the terror withdrew, until there was nothing but love.

The dark eyes held his, and a spark grew in their depths. The smile she gave him was like a flower, and she said, "If the road is made easy, it is the right one."

"And here I'd always thought the reverse," he replied. He gave her another brief kiss, then stood up and scuffled down the aisle in his ill-fitting shoes.

Harris Stuyvesant peered out from under his sheltering arm, braced for a bright light and explosion the moment the book came open.

Nothing happened. The book flew well out from the hill before the air caught it and opened the covers, and changed it from a solid maroon square to a fluttering, wind-blown book. It tumbled, open-paged, in a gentle path down out of sight.

Stuyvesant got to his knees and gaped over the railing, feeling like an utter idiot. The book lay sprawled in complete innocence on the slates of the servants' hall roof.

"Laura, please—"

"Sarah, we have maybe two minutes before Harris comes back, and I may never have another chance to talk to you with no one listening in. So just listen.

"Harris was wrong. Or partly wrong—oh please, Sarah, *please* let me talk, we don't have the time. It's important that you know this."

"Tell me why," Sarah begged.

"That . . . vision you had, five years ago—when the Margolin baby died in your arms? The endless stream of dead infants, pouring through an hour-glass. I've never been able to shake that image. It haunted me. Until I finally found something that might be big enough to stop the flow."

"Killing the Prime Minister?" Sarah sat back in horror, too shocked to protest.

"Listen, Sarah, listen to me. Sacrifice is such an old-fashioned idea, but it is powerful, nothing is more powerful. Sacrifice sticks in the throat, catches the mind, takes a person by the shoulders and shakes him to attention."

"But, taking the life of—"

"Not just him. Me."

"You mean...?"

"Think of it. A Hurleigh, offering herself for the cause. I thought maybe—just maybe—a Hurleigh's blood would be sufficient to stop the flow of dead infants."

"Sweet Jesus, Laura—"

"But now it's all come apart. Harris came and the Prime Minister is gone, and I don't...I don't know that I'd have had the resolution to carry it out, anyway, not after Bennett and I..."

Laura held out her left hand, looking at the ring with its misshapen brass heart; Sarah could see that she was fighting hard not to weep.

"Oh, it will all be so tawdry now, trial and prison and the family name dragged through the tabloids. It seemed so right, but I can't do it. I can't."

Sarah looked at Laura's face, but she was seeing the tumbling gray grains of dying children pouring unstoppered through the neck of the glass.

She looked at Laura, and she saw her friend's sixteen-year-old self, holding aloft Juliet's vial and declaiming, "*Come, vial. What if this mixture do not work at all?*"

Sarah saw the decades of women who had gone before them, the demonstrations and the brutal arrests and the hunger-strikes and the forced-feedings, all in the cause of winning the vote.

She saw Emily Davison, who threw herself in front of the King's horse in protest, and was trampled to death.

She saw a thirty-guinea shroud warming the neck of Molly Margolin, ten years old now and still not safe from poverty and oppression.

She saw Laura Hurleigh, proud daughter of a proud family, reduced by love to a joke and a failure in prison drab.

And against it all she saw an act, one bright, shining, decisive act, a bolt of lightning to ignite the people, once and for all. Some idea, some electrifying event that would not only galvanize the working classes, but would stick in the minds of the powerful like a stone in the neck of an hour-glass, cutting off the flow of poor.

"Where is it?" she heard herself ask.

"What, the Device?"

"You didn't give it to Baldwin, did you? Where is it, Laura?"

Laura's fingers tightened around the book she held. Sarah looked down, and like a bolt, knew that the means of their salvation was literally at hand.

Stuyvesant was running again, another lap in this nightmare traverse of the hillside, back past the Prime Minister and the inhabitants of Hurleigh, past the guards with expressions ranging from confusion to outrage, pounding up the white gravel path, lungs burning, hoping against hope that the stone chapel would continue to sit on the top of its hill, a beacon of faith and light as it had been since the days of St. Columbine.

The lych gate, the cemetery, and here was Grey, curled over his knees on the church porch. Stuyvesant shoved past, hand outstretched for the door.

And then he was falling, with two steely arms circling his legs.

Laura, too, was curled up, over the prayer book that she fought to keep away from Sarah's fingers. A great thud came from the door, and startled her into glancing up. In an instant, Sarah's hands thrust past her. Laura shouted at her not to do that, it was dangerous, what did she—

Stuyvesant crashed down on the porch floor, his fists cracking against the heavy wooden door. He squirmed around to pound at Grey's arms.

And the world exploded.

When the guards reached the chapel, they found Harris Stuyvesant, dazed and deaf and struggling to get out from under the remains of the door, but otherwise intact. A small blond man in peculiar cloth-ing was picking himself up from the ground outside, stumbling in a circle before he headed towards the chapel.

But the big man was upright and he stepped in front of the smaller man, folding his arms around him, keeping him from the smoking doorway as if it meant his life.

The chapel windows were gone, the ground a carpet of glittering glass shards. Inside, they found the front pews lying crooked as if kicked by a furious giant. A fine layer of dust and blood lay over everything.

Oddly enough, the small Tiepolo of the Madonna and Child and the time-blackened carving of the life of Christ were found in the lee of the altar, dusty but undamaged. Almost as if someone had taken them down from the wall before the service began, and placed them there, for protection.

Chapter Sixty-Eight

St. Columbine's chapel was destroyed shortly before ten-thirty that Sunday morning. Within ten minutes, neighboring farmers were beginning to arrive, to see if help was required. One of them was dispatched back home to fetch his farm lorry.

It was thought faster than waiting for an ambulance from the city.

It hadn't been the Army's experimental explosive, although its effect on Laura was devastating enough. But Sarah was still breathing when they brought her off the hill on the Hurleigh stretcher. She was still breathing when they got her settled on the feather bed laid in the back of the lorry, and when they tucked the blankets around her torn body. Grey got in on one side, with a farmer's wife who had trained as a nurse, and the lorry started off.

Stuyvesant watched the farm-lorry ease gingerly away. He wanted to grab his head and scream, he wanted to curl up and weep. Most of all, he wanted to climb up beside them and help Sarah take one breath, then another.

Then he was running, catching it opposite the stables. He pulled himself up, startling the nurse with his sudden appearance.

"Laura said Bunsen had nothing to do with this. Was she telling the truth?" Grey's eyes did not leave his sister.

"Grey, I have to know. *Was Bunsen involved?*"

The lorry lurched over a pothole, and Grey bent to hold Sarah steady. There was as much blood on him as there was on her, his tight grip supplementing the tourniquet on her arm.

"Bennett," he begged.

The lorry was nearly at the ford before Grey looked up. Stuyvesant didn't need his hearing to read the answer on the other man's face.

"No. Bunsen had nothing to do with it."

After a long minute, when accusations and self recriminations passed back and forth between them, Stuyvesant let go and stepped down to the drive. He watched until the vehicle was out of sight, then began the long uphill trudge to Hurleigh House.

He did not see the garden or the lodge, did not think where he was or what he was doing until he somehow found himself inside the house, with a familiar face talking at him.

"What?"

It was Alex, the Hurleigh footman. He repeated loudly, "Luncheon, sir. It was thought that people might need to eat, regardless. We've set it up in the breakfast room. However, if I may suggest, perhaps you might permit Mrs. Bleaks to treat your injuries first. May I take you to her?"

Stuyvesant looked down at his hands, then at the front of his shirt. Clothes and hands were stiff with dried blood, but it wasn't his it was Helen's. No, not Helen...

"No. Sorry. I'll take care of it."

As he passed through the house, he overheard pieces of conversation that came as through cotton-wool; for all their meaning, they might have been distant birdsong.

"Why did they send the fire teams? There's no fire."

"Oh, you know the village, they're always—"

Those voices drifted out of his hearing, replaced by, "Mrs. Bleaks wants to know if they've decided about the afternoon meeting, will it be—"

"I do not care to disturb the Duke." This was Gallagher. "Perhaps the Prime Minister would—"

"Mr. Gallagher, sir, there's a problem in the drive, I—"

Stuyvesant heard the words, if dimly, but could summon no more interest in the all-important afternoon session, when declarations were to be signed and loyalties declared, than he could for the problem in the drive.

He walked out of the house to the circle, where he paused, distracted by the change that had taken place in the past few minutes.

The circle was now clotted with vehicles, from a shiny fire-truck to a rustic cart whose horse was eating the white roses. Gallagher came out of the gate behind him, spotted the desecration, and set off at a unbutlerian sprint to pull the animal away. Stuyvesant watched the man as he might have watched a cat stalking a mouse or a bird flying through the sky, a simple creature going about its business. His inability to make out Gallagher's words made the ensuing event as compelling as any celluloid adventure on a big screen: faintly comic reaction, wild gestures, theatrical emotions of the butler's fury and the cart driver's disdain, two men facing off nose to nose. Stuyvesant wouldn't have been in the least surprised if captions had appeared before his bemused eyes.

He was dimly aware that his brain was not exactly functioning at peak sharpness, but there seemed no particular reason to worry. It was more comfortable this way.

But then the cinematic adventure playing out in front of him took a decidedly bizarre and ominous turn, when Aldous Carstairs walked on stage.

Carstairs was, as always, entirely in black from his shoes to his collar. In the clear light of a spring day, he looked like something brought from another world, winding through the frozen vehicles and their owners.

Then Carstairs saw him. Stuyvesant had never before had a dream in which a character looked at him, registered his presence, and turned towards him. He closed his eyes hard, then stretched them open again.

Carstairs was still coming. What's more, Gallagher appeared to have noticed the intruder as well, for the butler was breaking off his attack on the cart driver to perform his age-old task of greeting visitors.

This visitor ignored him. He was closing in on Stuyvesant.

Perhaps it wasn't a dream.

Carstairs' face said it wasn't. Carstairs' face was swollen, his mouth scabbed, as if someone had punched him. Someone *had* punched him, Stuyvesant recalled, his fist tingling with the memory. Was that what was making Carstairs so angry? Because he was furious, but he was frightened, as well—far more frightened than he had been in Grey's room at the Dog and Pony. He looked almost desperate as he rounded the alpine planting in the center of the circle.

Stuyvesant saw the man's full lips part and move, but the sounds refused to sort themselves out. He held up a hand to stop the man.

"You're going to have to talk loud and slow," he said. "I'm half deaf."

Carstairs glanced at his wrist-watch and pursed his mouth in irritation, but when he spoke, it was slowly enough for Stuyvesant to make it out. "What happened here? They said something about a bomb in the chapel?"

"Yeah. Laura Hurleigh blew herself up."

Suddenly, the dreaminess of the past couple of hours quivered, and took a step back. Stuyvesant became aware that his body was bruised and bashed and cold. He craved a bath, as he had never craved anything in his life.

"With what?"

"What do you mean, with what? A bomb. She wanted to assassinate the Prime Minister."

"Laura Hurleigh?"

"Yeah. Not Bunsen, after all. I haven't talked to him. Figured it wasn't my job."

Carstairs glanced again at his watch. "Where is everyone? The Prime Minister? The Duke?"

"In the house. They're serving lunch."

Carstairs' face went taut, his mouth tugged in on itself: being unable to hear his voice's subtleties, Stuyvesant had to go by the man's face, and what it looked like to him was sheer panic. "We've got to get them out," Carstairs blurted, and took a step towards the house.

Stuyvesant caught his arm. "Why?"

Carstairs jerked away.

"What's going on?" the American demanded. "Why do we have to get them out?"

"It's just, if there was one bomb, there could be another."

It had the desperation of a spur of the moment story, and Stuyvesant didn't believe it for an instant. He hung on to the man's arm, his thoughts whirling.

"Why are you here? And how the hell did you know where—"

He stopped. Carstairs knew where to find Grey because he'd had them followed the previous afternoon. And Carstairs was in a panic—actually sweating, this man of ice. Why? The bomb was over and done and everyone but Sarah was...

He saw Grey's face twisted with pain: *He's planning something.* The sense that Carstairs was working on two levels. His sudden interest in Bunsen, after dismissing him as without importance.

And now, the look of desperation, as if some plan was about to blow up in his face.

Blow up...

"You have to tell me," Stuyvesant said. Carstairs tore his gaze from the stones of Hurleigh House. He looked up into the American's hard eyes, then down, for the third time, at his watch.

"There's another bomb," he said.

"How do you know?"

"I..."

"You know because it's *yours*. You? Set a bomb in Hurleigh House?" Stuyvesant's hand must have clamped harder because Carstairs grabbed it and worked to pull it off. He let go, but felt it make a fist. He wasn't going to knock the man out again, much as he would love to: Carstairs couldn't be so sure.

"I didn't set it, but it's there. It's due to go off at a time when the D—when the delegates are elsewhere, in their afternoon session. It is just to frighten them. Who could have imagined that..." The man's words trailed away.

Who could have imagined that a real bomb would go off, rendering a planted one highly suspect? Stuyvesant had time for one stark self accusation—*Would Carstairs even have considered a bomb, if I hadn't laid a bomber in his lap?*—before his mind snapped to attention.

"When?"

"One forty-five."

Stuyvesant looked at his wrist, found his watch missing, and grabbed at Carstairs': One-oh-seven. Thirty-eight minutes. If the timer was accurate.

"Where is it?"

"I'm not—"

"You lie to me, I'll break your knee, right now. In the Great Hall? The solar? Where. Is. It."

Carstairs slumped. "It will probably be in the Duke's study."

"You're trying to murder the Duke of Hurleigh?" Stuyvesant said, appalled. Carstairs glanced around, but there was no one close enough to have heard.

"It's a fake," Carstairs said, or maybe, *It's a feint.*

"The bomb's a fake?"

"The bomb's real. The attempt is a fake. He's supposed— He *was* supposed to be with the others in the Great Hall."

All that meticulous planning, all those precise timetables and specific seating charts had flown out the window with Laura's *attentat* in the chapel. God only knew where the Duke would be, now.

Stuyvesant wondered vaguely who Carstairs' inside man was, but this was not the time. "Where is the bomb hidden?"

"The Duke collects Staffordshire dogs. Porcelain, you know? A parcel was delivered yesterday, with a thank-you gift for his collection. It's inside that."

"What does it look like?"

"I have no idea. Lakely bought it."

"Great," Stuyvesant said. There must be hundreds of the damned things in the house. "What about the device itself? What's the explosive? Does it have any detonator but the timer?"

Carstairs shook his head.

"I should just shoot you here," Stuyvesant told him, "but I need you to get everyone out. Nobody goes back to their rooms, everyone gets accounted for, family, servants, and delegates. I don't care what you tell them, *everyone* out in five minutes."

Without looking to see Carstairs go, Stuyvesant turned to shout, "Gallagher!"

His voice seemed to be loud, because the butler leapt as if a gun had gone off. His return speed through the cars and lorries in the circle wasn't quite as fast as his outward sprint had been, but it was fast enough.

"Yes, sir?"

"A parcel arrived for the Duke on Friday. One of his porcelain knickknacks."

"Yes, sir. An anonymous gift, although he knew it was from Mr. Bunsen."

Stuyvesant was distracted enough to ask how he'd known.

"It came from the same dealer as a smaller one that Mr. Bunsen gave him last year."

"Right. What was it?"

"Sir?"

"The thing. What did it look like?"

"I don't know, sir. I carried it into the Duke's study and he unpacked it there. He's very particular about his little treasures, sir."

"You didn't see it at all?"

"Not then. Although I did, of course, notice that he had put it into his cabinet."

"Of course you did. Where did he put it?"

"On the center shelf, towards the right. Which indicated that he was rather taken with it, sir."

"Thank you, Gallagher. Now, there's a problem in the house and I need you to help get everyone outside, fast. You'll find a fellow named Carstairs, starting the job. But," he said, and hesitated. To trust Grey, or not? If he'd been wrong, or distracted, or lying... Stuyvesant made up his mind. "Find Mr. Bunsen and send him to me. I'll be in the Duke's study. And we'll need tools—wire snips and screwdrivers, an assortment."

"Mr. Bunsen is... rather indisposed, sir."

"I hope that doesn't mean dead drunk."

"I wouldn't know, sir. Although I did leave him with a decanter."

"Shit. Well, bring him, anyway."

Most of the work Stuyvesant had done with bombs involved the result, not the object itself. When it came to defusing Carstairs' bomb, the best chance they had was a sapper's iron nerves and steady hands.

A drunk, Communist sapper whose lover had just deliberately blown herself to pieces.

Chapter Sixty-Nine

STUYVESANT FOUND THE OBJECT, as ugly a piece of art as he'd ever seen, but it did seem to be a prize to the Duke, since he had placed it in the middle of the right-hand glass door.

Once he'd found it, he left the little china dog alone. He took up a place at the back corner of the study, as if that might get him out of its range, and waited with twitching nerves.

He jumped when the door came open and Gallagher peeped in. He quickly crossed the room and led the butler back down the hallway.

"Mr. Bunsen will be right down, sir," Gallagher told him. "He is ... not quite as indisposed as you feared. Would you ... I should be happy to stand outside the door if you wish to cleanse your hands. There's a lavatory directly across the corridor."

Stuyvesant looked down at himself. "Good idea."

He tried not to notice the color of the water that ran across the white porcelain, but he briskly scrubbed his face and hands. When he came out, Gallagher was still there. "Thanks, Gallagher. You go on with the rest of them. I'll let you know when you can come back inside." I will, or a loud boom, he thought.

Back in the study, he glanced at the clock on the Duke's desk:

creeping away from one-twenty. Christ, he hoped the bomb-maker hadn't cut corners and bought a cheap clock.

Three minutes later the door opened again, and the part of Stuyvesant's heart that wasn't in his throat sank. Bunsen looked like the tail end of a bad month. His handsome face was drawn, his skin gray, his eyes dull.

"Gallagher said you needed me." The words came out as if each were being pulled, and the effort of speech nearly had him turning his back and leaving.

"There's a bomb."

The man studied him as if waiting for the end of a remarkably tasteless joke.

"*Another* bomb. Someone sent the Duke one of those damn porcelain dogs he loves, only it's filled with explosives. Set to go off in sixteen minutes. I need you to disarm it."

At last a flicker of emotion passed over Bunsen's face, but his slight frown was merely curiosity. "Who *are* you?"

"Honestly, does that matter at the moment?" Stuyvesant asked. "Bunsen, you need to disarm that bomb."

"Why?"

That rocked Stuyvesant back on his heels. The man was serious.

A major shock was required. "Because if you don't, Laura's sacrifice—her *attentat*—will be lost. Everything Laura was, all you worked for together, was aimed at what happened in that chapel. But if there are two bombs? And one of them is here, aimed at her father? Two bombs makes her a madwoman, not a martyr. Worse—an incompetent madwoman, whose death was an accident. They'll write her off. She gave her life for your cause, Bunsen. You can give her death meaning. Only you."

Fifteen minutes.

"And I should also mention, the dog—that one with the blue bow around its neck—will be traced to you."

Bunsen's hand came up and drew hard down the length of his face. He glanced at the cabinet. "Fifteen minutes?"

"That's what I'm told. Assuming the timer is accurate," Stuyvesant added, unable to help himself.

"There is always that question, with a timed device," Bunsen said. He sounded more in control.

"Can you defuse it?"

"Be more sensible to carry it out and drop it in the river."

Stuyvesant felt a flood of relief at the thought—why hadn't he thought of that?—then a cold question: *Who was going to carry the thing through the house?*

He started to force himself upright on unwilling legs, when Bunsen added, "Of course, it might have a backup trigger."

"Wouldn't that have gone off when it was shipped and unpacked?"

"It would depend on the sophistication of the device. Perhaps I should take a look."

Jesus. *Take a look.* Stuyvesant wanted to tip himself out of the window and take his chances with the ground below; instead, he went to the box of tools on the desk, aware with every step that, if the dog blew up, the left side of his body would be shredded.

"What tools do you want?" he asked Bunsen.

Bunsen came to paw through the tools, and Stuyvesant despaired: Bunsen stank of booze, and he wove slightly as he crossed over to the cabinet. "Uh, look, Bunsen. Your hands may not be quite steady enough for this."

The man held up his hand with a pair of jeweler's wire snips in them. Dispassionately, he watched them tremble. "You should leave."

Yes oh yes please. "I'll stay."

The look Bunsen gave Stuyvesant was as cool and amused as his expression that first evening they had met. Grief, shock, bewilderment, fury—everything was clamped down, leaving nothing above the surface but the iron-nerved sapper. "You're sure?"

"Can we get on with it?" Thirteen minutes.

"You want to help?"

I want to run. "What do you need?"

"Talk. If you take my mind off what I'm doing, it'll go just fine."

"Talk? About what?"

The odd amber eyes rose to look at him. "Why don't we begin with why my replacement driver has such an interest in explosive devices, Mr. Stuyvesant?"

Somewhere a clock ticked, a slow grandfather-clock kind of a tick. Stuyvesant felt the sweat down the side of his body, while Bunsen just stood and waited, wire cutters in his hand. He looked as if he could wait forever.

And Stuyvesant was fresh out of lies.

"I'm an American agent," Stuyvesant told him. "I came here hunting a bomber. I thought it was you."

Bunsen considered that for a moment, then said, "Go on," and turned to the object on the shelf.

Stuyvesant's own voice came dimly through the cotton-wool in his ears, but the stream of words seemed to buoy the sapper's movements. Bunsen's eyes remained focused, his hands controlled, so long as Stuyvesant's tale flowed: coming to London; meeting Aldous Carstairs; Carstairs' offer to help; forging the links between Bennett Grey and Sarah and Laura to Bunsen himself.

"But Carstairs has plans of his own, and when I came to his office with my story of a mad English bomber, he probably thought, Why not? Here's an English Communist, working with the Unions, who's already suspected of similar crimes in America. At a time when England is teetering on the brink of class war, when one outrageous act is all it will take to convince the great voting public that the Unions have to be crushed, absolutely and permanently. And then one of the country's most powerful and beloved individuals invites a group of men to his home for the purpose of forging peace: Wouldn't it solve a whole lot of problems if that English Red were to turn viciously on his host and try to murder him?

"So he arranged for a bomb of his own, and I have no doubt there will be a number of arrows pointing at you, and that those arrows will be ready for instant publication in the press. In the end, they will prove groundless, but by that time he will already have what he was after, and your career will be ruined.

"I should apologize, by the way. For what that's worth. I didn't mean to, but I set him on you."

"The rise of the Fascists." Stuyvesant was startled by Bunsen's voice, echoing from the storage cabinet.

"Could be. In fact, knowing Carstairs, it wouldn't surprise me a bit." For the first time since he'd launched into his story, Stuyvesant glanced at the clock and felt a cold rush of terror: He'd been talking for five minutes: 1:37. "Do you think—" he started to say, then broke off.

Bunsen stood away from the cabinet with the dog in his hand, a hole in the bottom of it showing a spray of wires. "This? I finished it yonks ago. I just wanted to hear what you had to say."

Stuyvesant lowered his forehead to the Duke of Hurleigh's desk, and left it there for a long time.

An explosion, he reflected, would have made everything a lot simpler.